ADVANCE PRAISE FOR *THE INNOCENT*

"Lynne Golding has opened a magical door to the past and ushered us into Edwardian Brampton to marvel at a simpler time... [*The Innocent*] will make you laugh and weep and wonder, and be fondly remembered long after the final pages are read."

—Cheryl Cooper, author of the *Seasons of War* series

"Lynne Golding knows how to tell a story. With yarns she gathered at her great-aunt's knee, she has woven a compelling story that harkens back to a time of pre-war innocence in a town I've always been proud to call my own."

—Former Premier the Honorable William G. Davis

"It's easy to forget that everything about the roads we drive, the hydro and water to our homes, the schools and health care we need, comes from the cradle of community. This book is a journey back in time to what was needed for building a future that cares for many thousands for decades to come. Through a fascinating family, Lynne Golding's novel leads us into the past in a whimsical way that can't help but connect to our own ambitions."

—Lorna Dueck, CEO, Crossroads

Beneath the Alders

THE INNOCENT

LYNNE GOLDING

BlueMoon
PUBLISHERS

CONTENTS

ACKNOWLEDGEMENTS

With thanks to my proofreaders, my mother-in-law Carol Clement and my late father-in-law John Clement, for their diligence and enthusiasm for every chapter dispensed; my good friend Candace Thompson for her marginal happy and sad faces, letting me know that the parts intended to be humorous or sad hit their mark; and my father, Douglas Golding, and his oldest friend, John McDermid, for their many helpful reflections about Brampton in years past.

With gratitude to the second-floor librarians at the Brampton Four Corners Library who helped me manage reels and reels of microfiche; to the thorough investigative work of Samantha Thompson of the Peel Archives; and to the fabulous team at Blue Moon Publishers: Allister Thompson, Talia Crockett, and Heidi Sander.

With heartfelt thanks to my husband, Tony Clement, who encouraged me year after year to continue the project, and to my children Alex, Maxine, and Elexa, who endured countless retellings of "interesting" tidbits I came across in my research.

Finally, with appreciation to my mother Barbara Golding, whose promise to read the book once it was complete spurred me to make it so.

We shall not cease from exploration
And the end of all our exploring
Will be to arrive where we started
And know the place for the first time
—T.S. Eliot, *Four Quartets*

Chapter 1

THE CARNEGIE LIBRARY

As far as first memories go, mine is extremely apt. For there, in one scene, are nearly all of the elements essential to my early years: politics, religion, morality, higher learning, municipal development, family, and friends. It is a panoramic view, this first memory, with many moving parts. There I am, four years old, perched on a white, straight-backed chair, a pink and white pinafore over my white short-sleeved dress, my white-socked, black-shoed feet dangling beneath me. My head, adorned with a high-set big bow, tilts back as I look up at Ina, my older sister, standing beside me. She commands me to stay put, to reserve the three chairs that are our joint responsibility to hold.

Sitting midway back near the centre aisle of the dozens of chairs, I am surrounded by neighbours, friends, and family. There are the butcher who sells our meat and the green grocer from whom we buy our vegetables. Ahead is the man who delivers our milk and cheese. Behind is Mr. Thauburn, who owns the general store. Just to my left are the people who sit behind us at church. Rows ahead, in his best Sunday suit, is my friend Archie McKechnie, sitting with his sisters and their mother and father. Over to another side is my friend Frances Hudson wedged between her parents. My family is too busy to sit with me.

Behind me, my brother Jim and his friends are delivering single Dale roses to the women assembled. To the side, my male cousins, John, Roy, and Bill and their friends are throwing pinecones over the red, white, and blue bunting that cordons off the area in which we are gathered. Up at the front, beside the concert band, are my mother, my father, and others from our church choir leading those interested in singing. At the podium organizing his notes is James Darling, my uncle, a former town mayor and the owner of the local bakery. To his right, separated by a long ribbon, scissors in hand, standing with other town dignitaries, is my Uncle William, the current town mayor, and next to him, my grandfather, Jesse Brady, the famous builder.

At last, the formalities begin. Ina and Jim scurry back to the seats I have successfully maintained. Father leads us in the singing of "God Save the King." At the end of the final stanza, he, the chairman of the high school board, joins his brother-in-law and others near the ribbon. My Uncle James, still at the podium, directs our attention to the large drawing behind him—the Beaux Arts style, red-bricked library to be built. Like twenty-five hundred other libraries in small communities around the world, it will be funded with a grant from the Andrew Carnegie Foundation.

The decision to build the Carnegie Library was not without controversy. Perhaps in a poor display of gloating, from the podium my uncle recounts some of the obstacles that had to be overcome. He refers to the arguments of those opposed to taking money from the steel magnate Andrew Carnegie, possibly the richest man in the world. Some predicted that money acquired as were the Carnegie fortunes would rot the books to be housed within the new library. Other obstacles included those created by the Carnegie Foundation itself, which refused to provide the funds until the plans for the building were altered to prevent its use as both a library and a concert hall.

Uncle James then calls upon a man in a brown suit, a representative of the Carnegie Foundation. With a strange, slow way of speaking, he thanks the crowd for its warm welcome. He points out the signature features of a Carnegie Library, including the lamppost in front, a beacon to enlightenment. The prominent wide doorway accessed from four steps outside the building and the five steps inside together symbolize how every man (or at least able-bodied man, for there were no elevators in the library in those days) is elevated by learning. He describes how this library will differ from the town's current library, known as the Mechanic's Institute; how it will be open to all; how it will no longer be necessary to execute a contract to borrow a book; and how patrons will be able browse the shelves themselves, without requiring books to be retrieved by the librarian from behind a counter.

Returning repeatedly to the podium, Uncle James invites other dignitaries to come forward. They speak on and on, generally repeating what has already been said. Finally, a cheque is presented to my Uncle William, the mayor, by the man in the brown suit, and a spade is plunged into the ground. The crowd erupts in applause.

Ending the ceremony, my Uncle James, invites everyone to walk to the Presbyterian Church for a short religious ceremony to consecrate the soon-to-be-built library. I watch as the masses stand and walk down Queen Street. Everyone goes: my friends, their parents, our doctor, our neighbours, my aunts and uncles, my cousins—everyone, except for me and my immediate family. As the throng departs down Queen Street, my mother, my father, my brother, my sister, my grandfather, and I walk along Chapel Street to our home two blocks away.

* * *

The year was 1907. The location was Brampton, a town in the County of Peel in the Province of Ontario, in the Dominion of Canada. Located on and around a part of the old Indian trail known as the Hurontario, the town was at that time home to nearly four thousand souls, predominantly Protestants of Anglo-Saxon heritage. It stood on rich farmland, making it an agricultural centre and home to local, national, and international industries. Inching into modernity, it was a town with a road system but no hard roads, with telephones but no telephone system. It had a department of public health but no hospital, a sewer system, some electricity, and sidewalks, although the latter were just being converted from wood to cement.

The town in 1907 suffered no shortage in the methods of transportation for its citizenry. The stagecoach ran down Hurontario Road, which connected Lake Ontario at the south to Lake Huron at the north. Cars were not unseen, but they were vastly outnumbered by horse-drawn carriages. The two rail lines that cut through the town's centre provided its inhabitants with a swift mode of travel. People and cargo could be transported all over North America from Brampton's centre. Significantly, one method of travel was not available to Bramptonians. Although the town possessed two minor water courses, allowing for swimming, skating, fishing, and in the case of one, annual flooding, neither had the width, depth, or regular volume of water to foster shipping of man or freight.

Once known as Buffy's Corners, the town was originally named after William Buffy, a shoemaker who in the 1820s sold both shoes and alcohol from his store on the main and likely only thoroughfare. Though Buffy kept only a few bottles of liquor on his premises to serve his good customers, he was held responsible for the early debauchery of that area. Historical records do not indicate whether his customers' need for such imbibement was due to the distance and conditions they had to endure to reach his premises or their shock at the prices or selection of his wares. Whatever the reason, years later, when leading Primitive Methodists settled in the area, the dens of licenced hotels and taverns were closed, and the name and reputation changed. Buffy's Corners became Brampton.

* * *

The party with whom I walked home that day was quiet and small. At the front of our pack was my father, Jethro Stephens, known to most as "Doc." My father was a local dentist and community activist. For twenty-five years he served as chairman of the high school board and chairman of the water commission, organizations responsible for bringing good education and clean water, respectively, to our town. Hardly ever given to laughter, Father ruled our household with an iron fist. A thin man with light brown hair parted to the side, he wore a pair of white patent leather shoes almost year round.

Beside Father walked my mother, Mary. A handsome, round-faced woman with a full but not large figure, she was the epitome of sweetness. I never heard her raise her voice. She doted on my father, who rarely returned the kindness. Her greatest pride was her three children, yet she was far from the smothering type of mother. Her time spent maintaining our large home and supporting her church and other social commitments kept her too busy to spend an inordinate amount of time with us.

Behind my parents walked my brother Jim and my sister, Ina. Ina had bestowed upon her the moon face of our mother (a matter about which she was indifferent) and the stocky frame of our grandfather (an inheritance that pleased her not at all). Perhaps because she felt her essentials could not change, she chose not to care for the minor matters that were within her control. As a result—despite constant hectoring from Father—she was frequently seen with the buttons on her dress misaligned, her hair unbrushed, her socks more down than up. Since she was eight years older than me, Ina's actions generally denied my existence as a sibling. Her filial allegiance rested entirely with our brother Jim, three years her senior, with whom she was quite close.

Jim was a wonderful boy blessed with the sweet nature of my mother, the athletic prowess of my father, and the artistic drawing skills of my grandfather. He was a hard worker and was well liked by his friends and their parents. His affection for each individual family member was well known and often exemplified by a unique nickname. By Jim alone, Grandpa was known as "Old Man." Grandpa reciprocated by calling Jim "My Boy," something Father never objected to (although Father objected to a great many things). I fared better I thought, being referred to most often by Jim as "Little One." While the pet name was usually accompanied by a tug on one of my ringlets, the minor discomfort was more than compensated by his term of endearment.

The final member of our party, and my walking companion, was my grandfather, Jesse Brady. My grandfather came to live with my parents for a short while in 1905 and stayed for over twenty-five years. In 1907, at the age of seventy-two, he was still a fit, sturdy man with a large head fully covered in thick, short grey hair. It matched the colour of his moustache and the neat beard that was cut squarely and hung an inch below his chin. His days, which were formerly filled building the town, were by that time spent tending his gardens as an amateur grower and supporting his townsmen as a member of the International Order of Foresters and the Odd Fellows Club. In between those pursuits, he found time for curling, lawn bowling, choir singing, and talking to me, his favourite—or so I thought—granddaughter.

This was the family that resided in the Stephens house located on the corner of Chapel and Wellington Streets in Brampton. But that house was home to more than those who technically lived there. It was home as well to Father's two sisters, Rose Darling and Charlotte Turner, and their husbands and children. Likewise, their homes were ours. All residing within easy walking distance to each other, we moved from one home to another like sheep changing pastures, depending on whose family had the largest roast to serve, whose family was celebrating a birthday, or whose turn it was to host the dinner of a special occasion. Each dining room table could accommodate all fourteen of us, and we children were equally at home at an aunt's table as we were at our mother's.

We came and went through each other's doors without regard to the time of day, never considering knocking. I suppose because our aunts and uncles so often fed us, they believed that they bore other parental responsibilities as well. We cousins were, therefore, as likely to be praised by our aunts and uncles for good grades, admonished for poor ones, encouraged in future pursuits, and reprimanded for bad conduct as we were by our own parents. My cousins, however, could expect far less criticism from my parents than I could from theirs. At least in the early years of my childhood, my father reserved his wrath for his own children, and my mother was throughout her life far less judgmental than were her sisters-in-law. In short, our family of five was really a family of fourteen. We shared our resources, our hopes, and dreams, and our experiences, which made the fact that Darlings and Turners went to the consecration ceremony at the Presbyterian Church when we Stephenses did not all the more strange.

We walked those two short blocks home in silence. We were, I assumed, all wondering what we were missing at the Presbyterian Church, and, in my case at least, wondering why we were missing it. Certainly it was no surprise that we were. When Father declared at breakfast that morning that our family would not attend that portion of the ceremony, Mother, Ina, and Jim knowingly nodded in concurrence. Only my grandfather and I opened our mouths to reply, but no words—which in my case would have formed a question—escaped. Father's edicts were always obeyed.

One never asked for an explanation. That is, one never asked *him* for an explanation.

The home we walked to was new, having been recently built by my grandfather. To my mind it was perfectly situated, being just three blocks away from the main "four corners" intersection that formed the commercial centre of the town, two blocks away from Gage Park that formed the outdoor leisure centre of the town and only a little farther from Rosalea Park, which formed the outdoor athletic centre of the town. Clad in red brick, our house possessed a round tower topped with a graceful spherical dome and a small black spire. Tall windows below stained glass panes were surrounded by large green shutters. The attic, which formed the third floor, had two finely sculpted gabled windows below dark green roofs, which rose at various levels. Grandpa's signature white-painted wooden verandah wrapped around its two street-facing sides. Together, we ascended the wide steps leading to the verandah. Father pulled back the wooden screen door and allowed us entry to our home.

On the other side of the front door was our foyer, a large room about two hundred feet square, from which one could enter the parlour to the left, the kitchen through a passageway straight ahead, or the second floor via a grand staircase to the right. We called that staircase the "front stairs" to distinguish it from the narrow, steep, poorly lit staircase accessed from the pantry behind the kitchen. Those stairs also led to the second floor, but as they opened onto that floor next to the maid's room, they were referred to interchangeably as the "maid's stairs" or the "back stairs."

We rarely used those stairs. Our reticence to do so sprang not from any fear of interference with the maid, for although we had a maid's staircase and we had a maid's room, we had in fact no maid. Father's confidence that one day we would have the means to retain such an employee meant that the maid's room never became anyone else's room, even though its vacant position required me to share a room and bed with Ina. That room across from the three-piece washroom was centrally located on the second floor. Grandpa's large bedroom was to one side and Mother and Father's to the other, with Jim's across the hall and in between.

As I changed from my good dress, I considered who could enlighten me about the strange episode relating to the Presbyterian Church. Ina, the person to whom I had the greatest access, was the last person I would ask. I reached back to remove my white hair bow from the knot on the top of my head. Finding it stuck, I clasped another elastic and a simpler blue bow and walked down the hall to my parents' room. I took the stuck bow to be a good omen. Mother's delight in brushing my long, curly brown ringlets usually allowed me to obtain information she might not otherwise wish to impart.

"Mother, why were we not allowed to go to the church for the last part of the ceremony?" I asked, trying not to wince as she removed the elastic that held my earlier hair arrangement. I was perched on the little chair in front of her dressing table situated in the tower that formed a part of my parents' room. Mother, who was extremely deferential to Father, would never countermand his orders. But when we were alone, she would often elaborate on them or at least repeat them nicely. On this occasion, however, she would do neither. My hair brushing ended almost before it began. The elastic to be wrapped around my newly arranged hair was quickly snapped into place. The blue bow I had carried to her was jabbed into the new knot.

"You heard your father," she said curtly. "We do not go to THAT church." Clearly dismissed, I slowly walked out of her room.

At four years of age, I was not well versed in the differences between Brampton's many places of worship. I knew that there were two Methodist churches: our church, Grace, which was originally Wesleyan Methodist, and St. Paul's, which was originally Primitive Methodist. Presbyterianism was obviously a different type of religion. Were Methodists not allowed to go to Presbyterian churches? Certainly many other people from our Methodist church were among those walking to the Presbyterian Church. Father was a stickler for rules. Maybe this was a rule that he observed but others did not. I was certain that Grandpa would know and went in search of him.

My quest was brief, as I heard his voice immediately upon descending the front stairs. The big oak front door with its etched-glass top was open.

Only the screen door separated the foyer from the verandah on which Father and Grandpa were speaking. Hoping that theirs would not be a long conversation, I silently joined them. My heart leapt each time it appeared that their discourse was complete, and then fell when after a few moments of silence either Father or Grandpa made a new observation, speculation, or pontification. It eventually became clear to me that neither had any intention of ending their exchange. While Grandpa was with Father, there was no chance my curiosity would be satisfied. I went inside in search of my brother.

I found Jim alone in the sitting room, a room between our parlour at the front of the house and the dining room at the back. Sitting next to him on the couch under the big window, I rushed to put to him the same question previously posed to Mother. Jim usually tried to ease compliance with Father's often inane dictates.

"Jim, do you know anything about the Presbyterian Church?" I asked plaintively.

"I know it was built by Grandpa," he replied.

"Built by Grandpa?" I had not expected that.

"Yes, that is, he did the masonry work and the plastering work." This made the mystery all the greater.

"If Grandpa built it, why can we not go in it?"

"That I cannot tell you, Little One," he said while tugging at one of the brown curls that had escaped the elastic on the top of my head. "You are far too young to understand the answer to that question. Just know this: our family is never to enter that church. I never have, and you will not either."

Having exhausted all other sources of elucidation, I had no choice but to ask the question of Ina. My sister was generally disinclined to do anything that would bring me relief or pleasure, unless of course, doing so would provide her with an even greater measure of it. Nonetheless, few things brought Ina more pleasure in her dealings with me than displaying (though not necessarily imparting) her superior knowledge.

Returning upstairs to our room, I found her sprawled on her large stomach on our bed, her head facing its foot, her knees on her pillow, her feet crossed at the ankles in the air, a book in her hands, still wearing her fancy dress. "Ina," I ventured, "do you know why we can't go into that church?"

"Of course I know," she replied confidently. "I am not a child."

Father's bellowing voice interrupted our exchange. "Ina, have you changed yet? Why aren't you attending to your piano practice? Jessie, get down here! Why are you not helping your mother?"

Jumping off the bed, Ina shouted that she was just about ready and quickly began to change. I asked her another question. "How old were you when you found out?"

"I was three … or … four … or five," she spewed, quite unconvincingly. I noticed as she said this that the colour in her face rose. Then, attempting to regain the upper hand, she added defiantly, "But I was much more mature than you are."

"Which?" I asked. "Three, four, or five?"

"I don't remember!" she shouted as she pulled on her day dress.

"I don't think you know, either," I said quietly. "Maybe you are too young to know too."

"They might think I am too young," she sneered. "But I do know! I do know. It has to do with Grandpa. It has to do with his work. 'Self-made. Others-destroyed.' I've heard them talk about it. It's all about him." With that she ran out of the room, the buttons on the back of her day dress mostly unfastened.

All about Grandpa. In that case, I was sure to find out. I just had to be patient.

Chapter 2

JESSE BRADY ARRIVES IN BRAMPTON

Mother always said that Ina was a scientist at heart, a meteorologist from her earliest days. As a mere babe in arms, she was fascinated with the sun as it caused green and red beams to shine through stained glass windows. Mirror in hand, Ina as a young infant eschewed her rag doll and bright building blocks in favour of further refracting the sun's beams. As a toddler, she ran through the room attempting to grasp hold of each intangible colourful prism.

As a young schoolgirl, she devoted any opportunity to paint to the portrayal of clouds—a practice Ina's teachers believed displayed an extreme lack of imagination. Lost to them were the intricate details Ina brought to the pictures, painstakingly evoking the light grey fog-like stratus or the big cauliflower-shaped cumulus.

As a teenager, Ina regularly transformed our verandah into a laboratory. Oversized thermometers and barometers accompanied hand-made contrivances designed to measure wind direction and speed and snow and rain accumulation. Once the instruments had amassed to a certain point, Father would banish them from our outdoor living area, but over time, one by one, they would return.

Like many children in those days, Ina kept a journal. But hers recorded none of life's pleasures or disappointments. From the age at which she could read and write, Ina recorded the day's weather. By the time she was ten years of age, she was analyzing past records and identifying weekly, monthly, and annual trends. As a teenager, she was forecasting the weather, although she did not do so every day. Ina was judicious in her predictions, preferring to make them less often but with greater accuracy.

As it happened, it was Ina's fascination with the weather that allowed me to begin to unravel the secret as to why we Stephenses were not permitted to enter the Presbyterian Church. Certainly my own carefully considered and determined efforts had met with no real success.

Thinking that the best time to engage my grandfather on the subject was while he was in his gardens, I once offered to help him weed his beloved rose and blackberry bushes. Grandpa loved best those plants with thorns. An hour after extending the offer, Grandpa's gardens were banished of stubborn weeds both at the front of the beds, where he could easily clear them himself, and under and behind the bushes, where he gratefully acknowledged the contribution of my smaller hands, legs, and torso. For my part, I received two bruised kneecaps, one red and swollen palm, thoroughly scratched fingers, arms, and cheeks, and the meagre insight that he did indeed know why we were forbidden to go into that church.

Focusing next on Grandpa's healthy appetite, on another occasion, I convinced Mother that we should bake an array of his favourite cookies. Her concurrence was obtained only when I agreed to help her complete the household tasks she had already scheduled for that day, walk to the store to purchase the necessary currants, and participate in the baking and cleanup. Taking advantage of the thirty minutes that afternoon when Grandpa and I were alone in the house, I plied him with a plate of the baked delicacies, only to hear from him too that I was not yet old enough to know the reason we could not enter that church.

Turning my attention instead to the first part of the clue Ina had provided, "self-made, others-destroyed," on a walk home from our family bakery some days later, a loaf of warm bread in one hand and one of Grandpa's big hands in the other, I learned only the meaning of "self-made" but received no confirmation that he was of that ilk.

Just as I was beginning to lose hope that I would gain any further insight into the mystery until I was much older, a storm settled upon us. It arrived one hot and humid summer night. I lay on my side of the bed

I shared with Ina, the length of which ran four feet away from our room's only window, a tall but narrow break in the thick walls. The shutters, which had been closed over it earlier in the day, had been open since dusk. The window's blind and sash were fully lifted and its curtains tied well back as we sought to permit whatever hot air could be ejected from the room to depart and to welcome in whatever cool air could be enticed. With a breeze just beginning to form, the room was only slightly cooler than it had been in the hottest moments of the afternoon.

I lay on my back in my lightest cotton nightgown, my hair piled loosely on the pillow above my head, the top sheet and usual covers pushed down to my feet. Seeking only sleep to relieve my discomfort, I was irritated by Ina's constant movement. She was in a miserable mood, but not because of the weather conditions, at least not because of the discomfort they produced. Her annoyance arose from a forecast she made earlier that day— one of her first—to which no one in the family attached much credence. It was impossible to know what caused her greater irritation: the skepticism of Mother and Grandpa toward her newly forming abilities or the fact that her forecasted storm had not materialized.

Just as I was about to implore her to be still and quiet, a large gust of wind burst through the screen of our window, billowing the drawn-back curtains. As though in answer to its call, Ina leapt from her side of the bed and ran to mine. Squatting down, her elbows on the low window sill, she looked due north and uttered, "It's coming." Springing back to her side of the bed, she hastily donned the dress she had worn earlier in the day and which she had since strewn on the floor. After pulling it over her cotton nightgown, she opened the door to our room and hurried out without another word.

It would have been better if I had followed her or called out to her or otherwise alerted the others in the house to her strange conduct. I confess that in my confusion as to her behaviour, I took none of those actions. Only when I heard the back door close minutes later and realized who had likely crossed its threshold did I react. Shortly, Mother, Father, and Grandpa were roused, the house searched, and those still within its walls assembled in the kitchen. It was 11:00 p.m. Of little concern to any of the adults was the fact that my fifteen-year-old brother Jim, who had been out with his friend Eddie earlier that night, had not yet returned. Of singular concern to all was the fact that twelve-year-old Ina appeared to have left the house, half-dressed at a late hour, with no one knowing her actual or intended whereabouts. Both on the original questioning and on the numerous examinations that followed, I imparted all that I could: she looked out the window, she said, "It's coming," she hurriedly dressed, and she left.

"What's coming?" Father asked as we heard rain begin to fall. Mother and Grandpa looked meaningfully at each other as they rushed to close the kitchen windows.

"The storm," Mother and Grandpa said in unison.

"She's gone to see the storm," Mother declared.

"See the storm?" Father cried. "Why the deuce would she do that? What does she need to see? And why can't she see it here?"

"She's been talking about wanting to see one at a high vantage point for some time," Mother said. "You yourself offered her the attic view."

"I did," Father conceded. "But we've checked the attic, and she's not there."

Mother and Father rushed to dress. As they returned to the kitchen to pull on their old shoes and jackets, I heard them listing the tallest buildings in the town: the Dominion Building, the fire hall, the bell towers of nearly every church, the top floor of the Queen's Hotel, the upper floors of some of the larger Brampton residences. My anxiety rose. I was worried for Ina being out alone in the dark rainy night, but I was petrified at the thought of Mother going into it as well. My lone pleas for her to stay behind, my declared confidence that Father alone could find Ina, my efforts to physically hold her back, were all in vain. Mother and Father told Grandpa where they would start and where they would end if every site in between required investigation and stepped out of the house, Father muttering all the while that Ina was too much like his mad sister.

From the parlour, I watched them run down the street toward their first destination: the bell tower of the fire hall on Chapel Street, next to the site of the new library. The two human images, barely perceptible in the gas-lit streets through the tears in my eyes and the rain around them, soon faded from view. I cried out of fear for the safety of my mother, my sister, and my father, and when I remembered that my brother Jim was also out there, I cried even harder. Grandpa's big, warm arms and his repeated mutterings of "it's just rain" had begun to stem the tide of tears when we heard the first groans of thunder off in the distance. My wailings reached a new crescendo.

Seeing the futility of theory on the subject ("thunder never hurt anyone"), Grandpa chose physical proof. He wrapped me in a quilt and carried me onto the big swing chair on the verandah. Under the verandah's large roof, we were sheltered from the rain and the mounting wind. We sat there a long time, gliding gently as branches blew and rain pelted everything around us. Just when my tears stopped, when my breathing returned to an almost even rhythm, the thunder that had rumbled closer and closer was joined by a bright display of lightning.

As I began to quake again, the storm raging around us, Grandpa decided to pursue a different tack to calm my fears: diversion. "Jessie," he said, his big arms and the soft quilt wrapped around me, "is there anything you'd like to talk about?"

Despite my extreme anxiety for the safety of my family and notwithstanding the concern I felt for my well-being, I was able to recall the one thing I wanted to discuss with Grandpa. My throat sore from sobbing, my words barely comprehensible for the little gasps that followed each syllable uttered, I managed to ask, "Grandpa, are you self-made?"

"Yes, Jessie, I guess I am." He began to tell me how that came about.

* * *

My grandfather, like so many immigrants to the New World, came to this land with only the clothes on his back, the skills of his trade, and a driving ambition to succeed. He was born on Christmas Day, 1835, in Wiltshire, England, the third of three children born to Joseph and May Brady, a working class couple. He had no formal education, but with the assistance of an older sister and the family Bible, he learned to read and write. All the arithmetic he needed to know he garnered in the course of his training to join his father in the masonry and building trades. As a child, he learned to count the nails and the pieces of brick, slate, and stone that had to be obtained at the beginning of a day and that which was left at the end. Later, as his father's assistant, calculating the number of six-foot scaffolds required to build a one-hundred-foot-high belfry, he learned multiplication and division. Later still as his father's partner, he learned the most important mathematical lessons of all, calculating the amount to charge a customer for a project, considering the cost of materials and labour and including a generous amount for profit. Jesse learned these lessons, and he learned them well, for unlike other students whose mistakes might cost them a mark on a test or even a grade at the end of term, Jesse Brady knew that his mistakes might cost his family members their meals for a time or his father his reputation more indefinitely.

As Jesse grew older, the late-night hours that he formerly spent learning to read were spent sketching designs for large projects he and his father would one day undertake. He dreamed of futuristic building styles and revolutionary methods they would bring to their craft. He imagined the zeal with which he and his father would convince customers of the advantage of their designs and the effort they would take preparing drawings, assembling different tradesmen, ordering supplies, and executing their plans.

The dreams rarely involved Jesse's older brother Jack, who, though also trained as a mason and builder, shared none of Jesse's enthusiasm for the trade, Jack preferred to spend his daylight hours being specifically directed in the next stone to chisel, brick to point, or lath to plaster, never taking the initiative in any such matter.

Jack's evenings, on the other hand, were devoid of any direction save that which polite society demanded, as he spent nearly all of them in the parlours of Wiltshire families with eligible daughters. Eventually, when Jack was twenty-four years of age and Jesse twenty-two, the many parlours Jack formerly frequented were reduced to a single one, and after three months of near-nightly visits to that specific parlour, an invitation was proffered to its owners and their family to take dinner with the Bradys after church the following Sunday.

Knowing how important the first meeting of the two families would be to Jack, the Bradys spared no expense in preparing for the occasion. Jack and Jesse's mother selected the best loin of pork, catch of trout, head of cauliflower, and round of cheese the local market could provide. The finest linen cloth was retrieved from the old trunk, what silver the family had was polished, the best china, though old and chipped, was pulled from its felt wrappings and set on the table. The Davises arrived. Warm greetings were exchanged. Convivial conversation ensued. Dinner was enjoyed. Impressions were made. By the late afternoon, when the party dispersed, Mr. and Mrs. Davis were entirely admiring of Mr. and Mrs. Brady; Mr. and Mrs. Brady were entirely admiring of Mr. and Mrs. Davis; Jack and Jesse Brady were each in love with Louisa Davis, and Louisa Davis, after three months of knowing Jack and only just having met Jesse, was smitten with them both.

Two months later, when formal declarations of love to Louisa had been made confidently by Jack and regretfully by Jesse, when it was clear that Louisa could not decide which Mrs. J. Brady she preferred to be, and when it was equally obvious that Jesse and Jack could no longer work under the same merely framed roof, let alone live under another fully constructed one, Jesse left for the ports of Liverpool and thence for America. For six long weeks he lay in the bowels of the steerage compartment as his vessel was blown off course down to the Bay of Biscay before righting its course and crossing the Atlantic to its intended destination in Nova Scotia. Jesse Brady, just twenty-two years of age, contemplated all he left behind: a loving mother and sister, each of whom begged him to stay; an aging father and business partner, clearly resentful of his decision to leave; an aggrieved brother who considered Jesse's feelings for Louisa to be a conscious attempt to usurp him; a woman whose eyes he could not stop his own from seeing, whose laughter he could not banish from his ears, whose scent he could not rid from his memory. What lay ahead of him? He did not know.

Jesse spent a night in Nova Scotia before devoting nearly all of his remaining funds to the purchase of a ticket on a schooner that would take him east to the City of Toronto. The trip was providential, as on the first day of the short passage, Jesse befriended a successful builder named Nelson, returning to Brampton, a small 1,500-person village northwest of Toronto. On the second day, Nelson hired Jesse as one of his builders and convinced a middle-aged couple to follow them to Brampton. As the foursome completed their journey, the middle-aged couple hired Nelson to build their new homestead.

It was a testament to Nelson's marketing skills that he was able to convince not just one person but three people to follow him back to Brampton. But Nelson understood the promise of the small village that had recently been connected to Toronto and markets all over the world by the Grand Trunk Railway. The railway was revolutionizing the village that only ten years earlier had a population of just over five hundred, roads that were nothing more than mud tracks, no post office to its name, no local government, and few industries.

For the next two years, Jesse worked tirelessly with Nelson as they built custom houses for the new settlers or for farmers just outside of the village who were ready to replace the log cabin homes, built when their land was first cleared. Nelson's instincts about young Jesse's talents were confirmed within a day of seeing him work. Nelson was impressed by the boy's knowledge not just of masonry and carpentry but all trades involved in the construction of a house. His work ethic was obvious from the start, but Nelson could quickly see that Jesse was also conscientious about the quality of his work. Over the course of those two years, Jesse rose from being one of Nelson's crew of regular or occasional labourers to his second-in-command.

Nelson's credo was to build to his customer's specifications. As most of his customers were English immigrants, most wanted Georgian English country-style homes, albeit on a smaller scale. Though his customers were well off enough to pay for a home a British squire may have occupied, they were generally not affluent enough to have a home such as that of a British lord. Accordingly, Jesse and Nelson built one or one-and-a-half-storey mini-Georgian-style homes, each covered in a plaster-like mixture called "roughcast," with a front door centred below a peaked roof and two large first-floor windows, one on each side and each equidistant from the door.

Though he worked hard by day, Jesse spent most of his evenings in his small room above the local tannery. He had only two pastimes aside from attending and singing in the choir of the Wesleyan Methodist Church: writing and drawing.

On Jesse's arrival in Brampton in 1857, he sent two letters to England. The first was to his mother, letting her know where he was settled. That letter was easy to write. The second letter was to Louisa, apologizing for the way in which he left (he hadn't even said goodbye) and wishing her well in her life with Jack. That letter was hard to write, and though he knew he should not do so, he added in a hastily written postscript: if she ever wanted to see him again, she need only write, and he would come for her.

Within two months he had a reply from his mother, advising him that a wedding date had been set for Jack and Louisa and that the two had decided to immigrate to Australia following their marriage. His mother begged Jesse to return to England to resume business with his father, the cause of his dissociation soon to be removed. Jesse's reply was immediate and firm: he would not return to England, and he begged his mother never again to mention to him either Jack or Louisa. With that behind them, mother and son engaged in monthly exchange of letters that would carry on until her dying days.

When not writing to his mother once a month, Jesse spent most of his evenings drawing pictures of the homes he dreamed of building. He had a strong hand and could make a piece of lead flow like ink. A blank page could be brought to life with his swift strokes, hard lines, and soft shading. Within minutes the intricate ideas in his mind became a picture, with every detail clear for those who might look on. Unfortunately, at least initially, few did. His drawings stacked up one on top of the other in various piles in the room he rented above the tannery.

The homes Jesse drew were not mansion homes, like that of George Wright, the successful flour miller and retailer whose palatial home known as the Castle was near the village's centre. No, Jesse dreamed of building homes for families of more modest means. Each had three bedrooms, a kitchen at the back, numerous large windows to let in the sun's warming rays, and various roof lines, abandoning the confining design limitations of the symmetrical houses he and Nelson built. Each had a front door a full four feet off the ground, far above the snow in all but the worst winters. Most importantly, each front door was accessed from a wide verandah, which ran all the way across the front of the house. Jesse envisaged a Brampton where families would have leisure time they could spend in these outdoor parlours, watching their children play and socializing with their neighbours. He envisaged houses of brick with distinguishing characteristics, turrets, and small towers.

Jesse knew that his dream could only become a reality if these houses were affordable. To accomplish that, he proposed to build his houses fairly close together and to build them in unison so that efficiencies could be realized in the purchase of supplies and in the construction process. He also proposed that each house have similar, though not identical elements.

Nelson suggested that Jesse's time would be better spent looking for a woman with whom to share a house of his own than dreaming of houses for others. But since he could not convince Jesse to abandon his dreams, Nelson listened cheerfully as Jesse shared his development ideas. Nelson promised that one day, when they had met the demand of all of those who had money to purchase custom-built houses, they would look at building in the less conventional way that Jesse suggested. But Nelson chuckled as he said this. The way the little village was growing, he didn't think that Jesse would be building the houses of his designs anytime soon. Only the death of Nelson in 1859 by a massive heart attack meant that he did.

Nearly immobilized with grief over the loss of his closest friend and mentor, Jesse took stock of his situation. In the two years he had been in Brampton, he had developed a name for himself as an excellent builder. He was known and liked by the local tradesmen and suppliers. He had a vision of what he sought to build. Though he was just twenty-four years of age, he resolved to turn down all offers to work for other builders and to forge his own path. With the small amount of funds he had accumulated, he could afford to spend a few months seeking the land and the capital to build the homes of which he dreamed.

His first task was to buy a piece of property. The property had to be within easy walking distance of the centre of the village. It had to be on an existing road with at least two hundred feet of frontage. In short order, he found a perfect lot just beyond the developed area of the village, the southernmost end of a larger farm property. The one-acre fallow lot was being promoted as an ideal mansion property. Jesse walked back and forth along the road fronting the property, picturing the eight homes he could build on it when he collided with another man similarly absorbed. Their collision, mild physically, was cataclysmic from a business and community perspective.

The Duke—as the other distracted walker was known—was a native of Wales, about twenty years Jesse's senior. He had come to Brampton in the hope of assisting in the development of a sustainable, productive, prosperous community that would be home to his children (of which he then had seven), grandchildren, and great-grandchildren. Though entirely unpretentious in his bearing, his genteel background quickly garnered him his nickname, and he eventually stopped objecting to the regal mantle he would wear for the rest of his life.

Soon the Duke knew of Jesse's plans and vision. It was a vision for a developed community that the Duke shared. The men quickly formed a partnership. There were only two matters on which the men disagreed. The Duke thought no man—even a man of modest means—having travelled to the North America would ever agree to live on a piece of land with less than fifty feet of frontage. Further, he dismissed the notion that a working man would ever have the leisure time to sit on a verandah. Thus, on the condition that Jesse reduce the number of houses to be built from eight to four and on the further condition that he eliminate the verandahs and for a fee equal to thirty percent of Jesse's profits, the Duke agreed to act as Jesse's financier.

As part of the arrangement, it was determined that the Duke would buy the land from the selling farmer. After it had been acquired, it would be subdivided into five lots. Four of the lots would be equally sized and front onto the road on which the Duke and Jesse had collided. The fifth lot would be the remainder of the land acquired behind the first four lots, backing onto a less travelled road. That fifth lot would either be developed later or sold. The Duke approached the farmer and offered him an amount twenty-five percent less than he was willing to pay. The farmer feigned great shock over the offer.

Over a month that Jesse could only describe as agonizing, the Duke and the farmer negotiated a price that in the end was ten percent more than what the Duke had originally offered. They resolved to complete the transaction in a further month's time. The Duke was delighted at the low price he had negotiated, since it would make Jesse's homes even more affordable to the intended purchasers. The farmer too was overjoyed at the price, boasting to all who would listen how much more he had realized selling his land for use as a mansion than in using it himself for farming.

Having arranged the financing and the acquisition of the land, Jesse's next task was to organize the labour. To develop the first four lots, he required a workforce that could build four houses at once. It was as Jesse began to enlist that workforce that he and the Duke encountered their first real obstacle. For in recruiting the work force, word spread about the project.

It was at that time, in 1859, that Jesse and the Duke learned what many Brampton developers would later discover, namely, a farmer is willing to sell a man a piece of land for one price if he thinks the man is going to use it for his own pleasure, but he will only sell it for a much higher price if he knows the man is going to develop it for use by others. Upon learning that the land he had committed to sell was to be further severed and resold, the indolent farmer became incensed. He railed at the Duke and Jesse about the history of the land: how it had been provisionally acquired by his parents from the Crown; how they had cleared the primeval forests from it within the mandatory period, thereby earning full title to it; how it had been plowed, seeded, and harvested every year since then, with back-breaking effort; how he could not part with it for less than its full worth; how embarrassing it would be to do so.

He threatened to walk away from his agreement to sell the land. Jesse and the Duke tried to reason with him. The farmer's parents had not paid anything for the land, and neither had he. Over most of the past three decades, the land, when combined with the other lots acquired by his parents, had been highly productive and had garnered a good income for his family. He and the Duke had previously agreed on the price; surely that represented its worth. The Duke would sell it for more than the cost of the land and its improvement, but that was to compensate him and Jesse for the risk in undertaking those improvements.

No amount of reasoning on the part of Jesse and the Duke could convince the obstinate farmer. In the end, Jesse and the Duke agreed to pay him five percent of the profits from the resold houses rather than sue him to enforce the original bargain. Jesse revised his budget. Another five percent would have to be added to the ultimate sale price for the finished lots—for this "anti-embarrassment" tax, like many other taxes that would apply in the future, was certainly not going to be borne by the developer.

With the land acquired, the labourers assembled, and the supplies being delivered, the next challenge for Jesse was to actually sell the houses, which he was building entirely on speculation. He wanted the houses to be purchased long before the construction was complete; early enough in the process to reduce the financial risk but late enough to prevent demands for customization of the houses. He knew from his work with Nelson and his father before him that customization drove up the costs and slowed down completion. He had no competition for the sale of houses of this nature, and so he did not need to meet that kind of customer demand.

Jesse need not have been concerned that the houses would be purchased too early in the process. Though many people expressed interest in the houses while they were being built, people were not willing to complete a purchase at that early stage, despite Jesse's detailed drawings. It was only as the houses were nearly framed on the outside that Jesse received his first offer. He thought the offer marked the turning point in the project. That was not the case, however, as the buyer's wife took one look at the closely situated homes and decided then and there to return to England. Reluctantly, the man reneged on the contract, and leaving Jesse with the deposit, he returned to England with his wife and family. The experience behind him, Jesse put the lot back on the market with the others and mentally jacked up the price of each by a further five percent. More than ever, Jesse realized the risk for which he needed to be compensated.

A third setback occurred just as the lath on the inside walls was about to be applied. This was a setback of a different sort. It was a personal circumstance that necessitated a two-month leave of absence. Each day the Duke walked to the building site to view Jesse's progress. One day, while the Duke was conducting his daily inspection, Jesse's landlady, the tanner's wife, came to the site bearing an envelope. Jesse did not demand or expect any such personal delivery, but his landlady was a curious woman who took any opportunity she could to see if the project of her favourite tenant really was as outlandish as her husband's customers said it was.

Even if she had not been in the habit of regularly visiting the site on the pretence of delivering correspondence, she would have done so on this occasion, for though the letter she was carrying had been mailed from England and was written in a feminine script, it was not written by the hand that wrote monthly to Jesse. She feared that this letter, which was light in weight, was written by Jesse's sister, because their mother had been rendered unable to write it herself. Indeed, Jesse's thoughts were likewise when he took the flimsy correspondence from her. Turning away from the Duke and the tanner's wife, Jesse opened the letter and silently read the ten words written on it.

He took a deep breath before turning back to the Duke and the landlady. With tears in his eyes, he slowly explained the situation. Although Jesse thought he should defer the trip until the project was complete, the Duke and the tanner's wife—both staunch family people— felt he needed to leave immediately. In a short time, their view prevailed. Jesse searched the four houses, found Cowan, his best man on the site, deputized him to oversee the completion of the houses, apologized to the Duke, and left.

When Jesse returned to Brampton two months later, he was delighted to see all four houses complete. Covered in roughcast, they were a long way from the brick Gothic Revival homes he dreamed of building, but architecturally they were an improvement over what was previously available to all but the wealthiest in Brampton. While none of the houses had a verandah, each had a covered porch. Each had a second storey, adding to the front of the house two windows immediately above those below. Small, peaked roofs had been added to each house, as had windows and gables. The upper roof line of each house was trimmed with gingerbread.

As Jesse stood on the street, admiring the houses, the Duke approached him with news he was sure would dampen Jesse's spirits. The first related to Cowan, the man appointed by Jesse to oversee the construction in Jesse's absence. He had so enjoyed the responsibility that once the project was complete, he formed a partnership with another businessman. Cowan was about to build six houses on a lot, all in the same method and style as those built by Jesse. The Duke was infuriated that Cowan would so unabashedly steal Jesse's concepts. Jesse, however, took the opposite view, and soon the Duke, who was equally confident in the future of their little village, agreed that there could not be too many houses being built.

In any event, Jesse was about to embark on a number of new projects. His innovative work on the four houses had captured the attention of a number of people wishing to build new homes. They were custom homes— but they were homes that Jesse designed. Though few customers were yet willing to incorporate the towers, turrets, and verandahs he longed to include, they were willing to incorporate new architectural detail. He could build for them houses with less symmetrical features and with multi-roofed lines, with bay windows and jutting doorways. He could move away from roughcast plaster and wood siding. Finally, he would be working again with brick. He hoped that these projects would grant him the prestige and reputation needed to build the churches and other institutions required to support the growing village. With sufficient capital in hand, he could then construct the larger developments of which he dreamed.

The second piece of bad news related to one of the four houses in their nearly complete subdivision. Cowan, the Duke reported, had performed well as a supervisor, but one of the other workers, Billy Judge, resentful at not having been selected for the overseer's responsibility himself, created a great deal of trouble. To keep Judge from poisoning the working environment for all of the other workers, Cowan and the Duke relegated him to a single house. They both regretted not sacking him from the project altogether, because the work inside that one house was not complete, and what was finished was not up to the standards that either Cowan or the Duke found acceptable. Jesse was similarly calm upon receiving this news. He told the Duke he would take that house and finish or refinish it himself over time. The Duke embraced his young friend. They agreed it was time for Jesse to have a family home of his own.

* * *

Over the course of Grandpa's story, the storm ended. The wind dissipated, and the deluge of rain was reduced to a fine mist. Looking down the street, I could see four wet and bedraggled figures approaching us. Father and Ina were in front, he on the side closest to the street, his hand firmly on her arm. Mother was behind them and Jim behind her. They must have come across him somewhere in their search for Ina. Grandpa gave me a little squeeze. "You see. There they are and they are all fine—wet but fine. Let's get you up to bed before they get in the house."

He carried me upstairs to my by then much cooler room, laid me on my bed, still swathed in the quilt retrieved earlier, said goodnight, and slipped downstairs to greet the returning drenched family members. I lay there for a long time considering what I had learned. Grandpa had suffered many setbacks: there was Nelson's death, the requirement to give so much of his profits to the Duke, not being able to build the houses he really dreamed of and then having to give more of his profits to the farmer, losing his first sale, having his friend Cowan go into competition with him, and having Billy Judge ruin one of his houses.

I wondered whether any of these incidents was the act that constituted "others-destroyed." They represented setbacks created by others. But Grandpa seemed to have overcome all of them. Furthermore, at any of those points, had he yet been "made"? No, there was more to his story. The storm that I had only wanted to end two hours earlier, was, I then realized, too short. I would have to wait for another opportunity to hear more of Grandpa's story.

My father was downstairs, hollering at Ina. One by one, others escaped the uncomfortable though clearly justified outburst. I could hear Jim come up the front stairs and slip into his room, just at the top of the staircase. Grandpa followed Jim but turned right at the top of the stairs to walk to his room, just past mine. As he did so, I called out to him. He came and sat beside me on the bed.

"Grandpa, I have just one question," I said.

"Just one?" he replied.

"Just one, for now," I amended. "What did the letter say? What were the eight words your sister wrote you?"

"There weren't eight words," he said. "There were ten words, and it turned out they weren't written by my sister. They were written by your grandmother." I looked confused. "Not your great-grandmother—not my mother," he clarified, "but your grandmother—my wife. The ten words were: 'If you still love me, come and get me. Loui.'"

"Louisa? She was your wife?" I asked.

"Well, she wasn't my wife when I left to get her, but she was by the time I came back. She had broken her engagement to my brother two years prior to that—almost immediately after she entered into it. Since that time she had tried to forget me, as I had tried to forget her, but neither of us was able to. We married in 1860 and had forty-five lovely years together. She was a wonderful woman. You were only two years old when she died. I wish you had truly known her."

"I do too," I mumbled. "One day will you tell me the rest of your story?"

"One day," he said. He kissed me on my forehead and left the room.

Chapter 3

THE SNEEZE

Fortunately, we as children are not limited in the number of our desires. At the age of four, I held two most fervently. The first was a new desire: to understand my grandfather's history and hence why my family was not allowed to enter the Presbyterian Church. I knew that this desire would require patience in its satisfaction. Thus, while it was always with me, it was not always top of mind. The second desire was much longer in standing: to gain a younger sibling who would be my true and faithful companion. That desire, I knew, could be satisfied more immediately. It required only the cooperation of my mother and our family's physician, for every child in Brampton knew that babies were delivered to married ill women by Dr. Heggie from within his big black bag.

Whenever my mother had the slightest headache or cough, sniffle, or sore muscle, I would implore her to call Dr. Heggie to our house for treatment. "Of course not, Jessie," she would say. "If you'll just run down to Stork's and get me some Shiloh's Cure, I'll be as good as new by tomorrow morning." Or, in response to the same appeal on other occasions, "Goodness, child. Why would I sacrifice a jar of my best mustard relish to have him tell me I have a head cold?" Mother was referring to the additional amount Dr. Heggie would charge to see his patients in their homes: three fresh eggs or a quart of milk or a bottle of Canadian whisky or, in our home, where none of the foregoing was likely to be available, a jar of whatever preserves he liked best from our cellar. Even when Mother was truly ill and needed to see Dr. Heggie, she would usually insist on walking to his office on Main Street South rather than calling him to our house.

It is a delicate matter to pray that one's dearest family member would become ill enough to necessitate a doctor being called into one's house but not so ill that she would succumb to the cause for the summons. The creation of such a condition of poor health for my mother and greater wisdom regarding my grandfather were the subjects of my prayers throughout the summer of 1907. That July, both prayers were answered, though in neither case did I obtain what I actually sought.

It started with a sneeze. It was a Thursday afternoon, Mother's at-home day. Ina, Frances Hudson (my dearest friend), and I sat in my family's sitting room while Mother entertained her last remaining guest—Frances's mother—in the parlour beside us. Ina sat on the sofa under the window reading a book. Frances and I sat on the floor, dolls in hand. Frances's doll beckoned my doll to look at the bird beyond the window, and so I happened to be looking at Ina when we heard a sneeze from the parlour. I saw Ina's instant recognition of the sound and her immediate reaction as she slammed her book shut and jerked her face toward the parlour. The big pocket-sliding solid elm doors between the two rooms were nearly fully drawn, so although we could hear the sneeze, we could not instantly discern from whom it issued.

On hearing Mother utter the customary "God bless you," Ina breathed a sigh of relief. Then she turned on Frances. In a tone a crown attorney might reserve for the examination of one accused of a capital offence, Ina demanded to know the nature of the illness from which Frances's mother was suffering; the primary and secondary symptoms; the hour her mother had first detected them; the extent to which Frances was experiencing any of the same conditions; and why Frances and her mother had knowingly entered our home and contaminated our family. Frances denied any knowledge of ill health on her mother's part. While she timidly confessed to sneezing herself just that morning at breakfast, she assumed it resulted from the pepper her father had liberally applied to his eggs. Her sheepish acknowledgement that she had given no thought as to whether she might on this day infect others brought both girls to tears. Frances flew to the parlour and into her mother's arms. Ina, wrapping her baggy sweater tightly around her, ran to our bedroom, where she stayed for three days.

They were a long three days. Though they began with Father's reprimands uttered through the door regarding Ina's treatment of Frances, they ended with entreaties for her to vacate the room. But whether those entreaties were expressed as a hopeful wish by Jim (who promised her an outing with his friends), a demand for access to my own room and belongings (resulting in an unceremonious dumping into the hallway of many of my worldly goods), a bribe by Mother of Ina's favourite foods, or a demand by Father, Ina would not end her confinement.

To be fair, the self-imposed internment might have ended earlier if the contagion that Ina so feared had not actually materialized. While Mother was, on the first day of Ina's confinement, able to assure Ina that she felt perfectly fine, the next day, at the very moment that Ina took one of her three daily trips to the bathroom across the hall from our room, Mother had the misfortune to sneeze. The following day she woke with a sore throat and a congested chest. By that afternoon she had an earache as well. A fever set in that night, and the next day it was so high that Dr. Heggie had to be summoned.

Dr. Heggie prescribed cold compresses, a special elixir, and plenty of bed rest for Mother. Having been apprised of Ina's state, Dr. Heggie also prescribed treatment for Ina: a trip to Toronto for her and me, the duration of which was to last until Mother was well. He examined my throat and ears, ran a stethoscope over my back and chest, and repeated the procedure for Father, Grandpa, and Jim. Through the door to our bedroom, Dr. Heggie proclaimed us to be in perfect health. He then left our house with a jar of strawberry preserves in one hand and the famous black bag in the other. To my great dismay, the black bag was the same size and apparent weight when it left our house as it had been when it entered it.

On the condition that we would immediately leave for Toronto, Ina agreed with the proposed arrangement. Father cabled his sister, Lillian, the only member of our family who resided outside of Brampton, and a few hours later walked Ina and me to the train station. As we walked, he reviewed the arrangements he had made. If Lulu—or Aunt Lillian, he corrected himself—was not at Union Station to meet us when our train arrived in Toronto, we were to walk to Spadina Avenue and take the horseless streetcar to her home just south of Bloor Street. He handed Ina some money just in case his sister forgot to feed us and promised to see us in a week, by which time he was confident Mother would be restored to good health.

My worry for Mother's health was profound, and my disappointment regarding the contents of Dr. Heggie's black bag great, but as the train neared Toronto, thoughts of those matters were replaced by the prospect of spending a week with our beloved Aunt Lillian. This was an adventure that Ina, Jim, and my cousins had each enjoyed every summer since they turned eight years of age. The annual excursion was particularly enjoyable for Ina, who, for one week a year, was able to live like an only daughter again. I am sure my presence on this sojourn would have resulted in her defection from it but for her great relief at being removed from our infected house.

Aunt Lillian was the eldest of my father's three sisters. She was without a doubt the least conforming member of our family. As a child she chose pants instead of skirts, sports instead of dolls, the company of her father and brother over that of her mother and sisters. As an adult, she rejected religion, politics and, eventually, the epitome of the two—in our family at least—Brampton itself. At twenty-four years of age, she moved to Toronto and purchased a house in a heavily leveraged transaction funded in small part by her savings of the previous five years but completed largely on the guarantee of payment made by her brother and by the promise of the income to be generated from the use of her house by boarders. She lived a happy life as a single woman running a boarding house for male university students and teaching history at the nearby Toronto Central Technical Institute. Her high school students routinely judged her their favourite teacher for the way in which she brought historical figures to life.

Aunt Lil's looks were, naturally, unconventional. Her lips were slightly fuller than the fashion. Her flawless cream-coloured complexion accentuated her eyes, which sparkled beneath lids slightly too heavy. In an era when a woman's hair was always pinned back to her scalp, she wore a red, curly mane down her back. When it was covered, which was infrequent, it was rather adorned, generally by an ostentatious, oversized, brightly coloured headpiece. Her favourite colour, green, was almost the only colour she wore. Father said she looked like an upside down carrot. Tall and thin, he remarked that if someone picked her up by the toes of her green-coloured stockings and let her loose red hair fall below her head, she would be a perfect imitation of that root vegetable. Green was the colour of her eyes, the colour of the ink with which she wrote, the colour of the walls in her home. Her choice of the colour whenever an opportunity for a choice presented itself marked almost the only predictable element of Aunt Lil's life.

Our extended family visited Aunt Lil twice a year, once in late August, when we went to Toronto to attend the Canadian National Exhibition and to buy clothes for school at the Eaton's department store, and once in the spring at Easter, when most of her borders were with their own families for the holidays. We children took bets as we rode the train from Brampton as to whether on this occasion Aunt Lil's house would be so cluttered as to prevent any of us from finding a place to sit or so bare as to lead us to wonder whether anyone at all lived in the home; or whether it would be so hot so as to have each of us shedding our clothes, although it was cold outside, or so cold that each of us would seek blankets from the boarders' beds.

One Easter Sunday, fourteen of us appeared on her doorstep. The table had not been set; there was no food on the sideboards; the kitchen was cool and the cupboards bare. No one had the heart to ask where dinner was, and we all left ravenous three hours later. The next year we went laden with hams, potatoes, pies, and peas, but detecting the aromas of beef, fish, and yams wafting out her front screen door, we quickly hid our provisions under the front porch and carried them all back home at the end of the day. Our parents reprimanded us children for engaging in wagers regarding Aunt Lil's likely conduct, a practice they deemed unchristian on multiple accounts, but I could tell that Father at least was placing his own silent bets.

Aunt Lil had no regard for conventional rules. She had her own rules. She was habitually late and incredibly disorganized. Though a single woman, she saw no impropriety in operating a male boarding house or any arrangement that involved her inviting multiple men into her home for cards or a discussion of an important matter. In the rules according to Aunt Lil, only the invitation of a lone man to her home was taboo. "Bedtime" was not in her lexicon. When at Aunt Lil's, children went to bed when they were tired. Given how entertaining she was, children were rarely tired before midnight. She did not require children to eat the entirety of their main course before they were served dessert; some meals were comprised only of dessert.

But the thing we children loved the best about Aunt Lil was that she never lied to us. She was incapable of it. She treated children like adults—never sugar-coating or avoiding a subject that others might consider inappropriate for young ears; she never spared feelings to avoid telling exactly what she thought of our dress, actions, or temperament.

Some people would have been put out at having two nieces arrive on their doorstep with less than six hours' notice, but those would have been ordinary people displaying an ordinary reaction. Aunt Lil, being anything but ordinary, had no such reaction. As Father feared, she did not meet us at the train station, but thanks to some directions provided by good-natured Torontonians and Ina's vague recollections, Ina and I were, within a few hours of leaving our home, in that of Aunt Lil. Our bags were thrown to the side of the door as she quickly had us in a circle, holding hands and singing as we skipped around an imaginary maypole. The evening proceeded in a similar spirit as we sang, danced, ate cake, reviewed magazines, and gazed at late-night stars. At last we all retired, me into a little second-floor room beside Aunt Lil's and Ina quite far away on the third floor.

Sleep did not come easily to me that night. As I lay in the little bed in the little room, listening to Aunt Lil pad about between her room and the bathroom, I reflected on the merry things we had done since arriving at Aunt Lil's. Eventually, when I ran through our activities three or four times, and when I no longer heard Aunt Lil moving about, my thoughts cast further back. I thought of my ill mother back home and of my brother, grandfather, and father. As I did so, imperceptibly, melancholy replaced elation, trepidation superseded anticipation, and ultimately, guilt ran rampant. For as I contemplated the past days, it came to me that the whole time Ina had shut herself in our room, I had only half-heartedly begged her to come out. The most earnest of all my pleas was for my belongings, but once they were provided, I found myself somewhat indifferent to her situation.

Since I had no access to my own quarters, I was happily ensconced in Jim's room while he was relegated to sleeping with Grandpa. I confess I delighted in having a bed to myself. I found it an absolute delight to take a meal with my parents, my grandfather, and brother without receiving a single snide look from my sister.

But it was not my attitude toward Ina's confinement that particularly struck me. It was my conduct towards my dear mother. Just as I heard Mrs. Hudson's sneeze, I also heard Mother's first sneeze. I admit it did not cause me concern. It gave me hope. "The Lord helps those who help themselves," Father often said. As I lay in the border's bed at Aunt Lil's house, I became ashamed of how I had tried to help myself—at Mother's expense. We had two apples in the house when Mother first sneezed. I confess that in order to deprive Mother of their preventative powers, I ate them both.

Over the next two days, I never once suggested she consume chicken soup. I never once mixed honey and lemon for her cough. I never brought her a blanket to avoid a chill. I never suggested a mustard plaster for her chest. While I did not pray for her condition to deteriorate, I did not pray for it to improve. I had brought on Mother's ill health, and my only contribution to her improvement was in running to get Dr. Heggie when I was finally permitted to do so. While I did that with alacrity, it was not for Mother's sake but for my own. I was willing to jeopardize Mother's health in order that I could obtain a younger sibling. The more I reflected on my conduct and on the ill health of my poor mother, the more my mood sank. I concluded that I was a bad person—quite possibly as bad as Ina always said I was.

That realization brought tears, quiet at first and then louder and louder. The noisy tears brought my aunt, who came to me clad in a billowy flannel nightgown, her red hair stacked high on her head in cotton ties, her face covered in white cream. Had I not already been awash in tears of pity, the sight of her would surely have brought tears of fright. Aunt Lil immediately assumed my tears sprang from worry, and, too ashamed to declare their real cause, I did not disabuse her.

"Oh Curly Top," she cooed—a term of endearment reserved for me, her lone niece with hair the texture if not the colour of her own. "Your mother is going to be perfectly well."

Taking a deep breath, I managed to ask why, if Mother's health was so certain to be fully restored, it was necessary for Ina and me to leave our house?

"As I understand it," she replied, "that prescription had less to do with your mother's health and more to do with Ina's. Dr. Heggie determined that the best way to treat your sister was to remove both of you on the pretense of your mother's poor health. And you don't mind, do you? We'll have lots of fun together while your mother rests."

Because the explanation was provided by Aunt Lil, I knew it to be true. But as I continued to rue my part in the events of the past three days, my tears did not abate. Finally, Aunt Lil grew tired of trying to reassure me, and, possibly because she had so little experience dealing with children in this state, she asked me how my tears could be overcome. No one had asked me that question before. I thought about it and between more shallow sobs suggested what I knew my mother or father would suggest: "Should I pray?"

"You can do that if you like," she said, with little conviction as to its utility. "But for myself, when I get into that state, I look for a diversion."

"A diversion?" I inquired, not understanding her meaning.

"Yes. Something to get your mind off your worries." As she said that, I recalled my last crying jag. It wasn't that long ago, and I realized diversion was the method ultimately employed by Grandpa on the verandah swing as we waited for my parents, Ina, and Jim to return in the storm. She was right. Diversion worked perfectly well—at least it did when I didn't know that someone was attempting to divert me. But I was willing to try it when consciously applied. I had not heard the whole of Grandpa's story. Aunt Lil was a history teacher. Maybe she could tell me more.

"Aunt Lil, do you know the story of Grandpa and Grandma?" I asked.

"Their story?" she replied. "Do you mean their story about how they met and how they settled in Canada?" Seeing me nod, she went on. "I know that story. It is a very romantic one. Do you know any of it?"

"Not really," I said. "I only started to hear about it recently."

"Then I shall tell you it all—but I warn you it is a long story, and I won't be able to recite all of it tonight. We will make it your bedtime story this week!" She was quite enthusiastic. "But tonight we can get started."

"Wait," I said. "Before you do, do you have a picture of Grandma? I would like to see what she looked like. I heard she was very pretty." Aunt Lil left the room and returned a few minutes later holding two framed photographs.

"This was taken about ten years before she died," she said, holding out one of the two photographs. "It doesn't do justice to the beauty she possessed in her youth—but her eyes and her mouth are little changed from their younger days." I stared at the sepia portrait of my grandmother. She had a well-lined forehead atop a square-shaped face. Her wide cheeks and solid chin allowed ample space for her well-defined nose. Her thinning grey hair was parted in the middle and pulled severely to the back of her head. Of her neck nothing could be known, for it was covered to the top of her throat with the long bodice that extended over her upper frame. Her mouth, like all mouths portrayed in photographs of the time, was unsmiling. Her lips were full. In her large, piercing eyes, there was only steel. I was mesmerized by the photograph as I tried to determine the character of this obviously strong woman, but before I had an opportunity to do so, the picture was taken from my hands and replaced by another.

"Here," Aunt Lil said. "Don't you want to see what your grandfather looked like at that time?"

"I already know what he—" I began as my eyes moved disinterestedly toward the frame being extended to me. But as the picture came more fully into view, I realized it was not of a man I recognized. "This isn't Grandpa," I said as I took the picture. I had no idea who this thin-faced man was. He had light hair pulled straight back from his high forehead. He had mutton chop sideburns and a moustache, which dropped down on both sides of his mouth, giving his lips at rest the image of a frown.

His chin was small. His skin was smooth—barely wrinkled, except for the little crows' feet at the corners of his eyes, which, extending upward as they did, made his eyes, visible under heavy lids, appear to smile. I could see that he had once been a very handsome man.

"Of course it is your grandpa," Aunt Lil replied. "It was taken when he was very late in life and does not show his very handsome face. But it is him."

I was still not convinced. "That's Grandpa?" I asked. "Grandpa Brady?"

"No. Of course it is not your Grandpa Brady!" Aunt Lil replied, clearly disgusted with my lack of intelligence. "Grandpa Brady is your mother's father. This is a picture of Grandpa Stephens: my father; your father's father."

"Oh," I said, realization dawning. "Then this Grandma," I said, pointing to the first photograph I studied, "this is not Grandma Brady?"

"Jessie, why ever would I have picture of your Grandma Brady? This is my mother, your father's mother, Grandma Stephens. Are you interested in your Stephens heritage?" If I were more like Aunt Lil, I would have replied in the negative. But I was able to fib to avoid hurting someone's feelings, and so I quickly proclaimed my heartfelt interest in that side of my family. Over the next week, Aunt Lil made an honest girl of me.

※ ※ ※

Jas and Selina Stephens' emigration to the new world was entirely different from that of Jesse Brady. Jesse and his few worldly possessions travelled to North America in the cramped, vermin-infested, squalid quarters available to those crossing the Atlantic in a ship's steerage section. Selina and Jas Stephens travelled on a similar ship but resided in an airy upper compartment surrounded by all of the comforts of home—at least all of those comforts that could be accommodated within the three large trunks with which they travelled. Their vast remaining possessions were packed in crates shipped ahead of them under the stewardship of her maid and his man servant.

Jesse spent his many days crossing the ocean longing for fresh air, decent food, and relief from those moaning, groaning, and retching near him. Jas spent most of his journey happily gazing at the cloud formations in the skies above the ship and befriending the captain and the ship's other officers.

My grandfather Brady arrived in the new world with no particular destination in mind, settling in Brampton at the urge of a fellow traveller. My Stephens grandparents arrived in the new world determined to settle in Springfield, an area west of Toronto on the banks of the Credit River known for producing the Clinton grape. Jas Stephens, a man who enjoyed the finer things in life, was confident that an area that could cultivate European bound vintner-quality grapes was worthy of his domain. Upon their arrival in Upper Canada, Jas was disappointed to learn of the absence of any available land in Springfield or its surrounds. Although Selina urged Jas to take his time in considering other options, Jas quickly purchased a large farm property considerably north of Springfield in a township called Chinguacousy, just north of the village of Brampton.

While Jesse Brady came to the new world to forget the love, the desired spouse, and the family he knew he could not have, Selina Stephens came to the new world to embrace her love, her spouse, and to create a family. Though she and Jas had been married for five years, they had not been successful in producing children. Selina, a devout Protestant, attributed the deficiency to an insufficiency in their humility and worship and to the oversufficiency in their idleness and pleasure. She was determined to gain the necessary contrition in their new homeland, chiefly through personal toil and sacrifice. She resolved that they should grow their own vegetables, cook their own meals, bake their own bread, and launder their own linens. She would attend to all of these matters without the assistance of Jas, who thought the good Lord would supply them with the desired family without such sacrifices. She would have, though, the help of her maid.

Whereas Jesse Brady easily fell into his profession as a carpenter in Brampton, Jas fared not so well in the pursuit of his. Happily adopting the profession of a gentleman farmer (the first profession of his life), it soon became clear that he had too few of the qualities necessary to be a successful farmer and that farm life offered him too few of the opportunities necessary to enjoy the life of a gentleman. Within five years of being on the farm, with three children safely born and a fourth on the way, Selina Stephens, by then an able cook, baker, and laundress, agreed they could leave the farm and take up an easier life in the village of Brampton.

The circumstances that led to her capitulation on this point derived from the one thing that Jesse Brady and Jas and Selina Stephens had in common: their love of music. For a short time, all three sang in the choir of the Wesleyan Methodist Church. The Sunday services and Thursday evening rehearsals were effortlessly arrived at by Jesse Brady, who lived less than a five-minute walk from the church. The same could not be said for the Stephenses, whose ability to traverse the ten-mile journey from their farm to the village depended considerably on the weather, generally, and the state of the roads, in particular. While Jas and Selina were prompt and regular attenders of the church when the weather was extremely cold (and the roads ice or snow-packed) and when the weather was extremely hot (and the roads dried hard), their attendance was less reliable at other times.

Nonetheless, Selina cherished the Wesleyan Methodist Church and looked forward to every occasion on which she could worship within it. She esteemed the pastor as a fine and insightful orator; she admired the building in which they congregated; she cherished the many good and loyal congregants who had befriended her and Jas. It was only the chance to give it all up: to join the Primitive Methodist Church, a church that worshipped in a dark building above a butchery; whose adherents sat in square, hard-backed pews; that was led by an odious pastor with an irritating voice; that was populated by congregants who interjected shouts of "Hallelujah" and "Amen" into prayers and sermons; that allowed Selina to agree to their relocation.

The opportunity was brought to Jas and Selina in the form of a typhus outbreak that claimed the lives of a local couple. The earthly departure of the man and wife was quite personal to Mr. Lawson, the odious pastor of the Primitive Methodist Church, since the deceased were not only members of his flock but leaders within it. She played the piano and he led the choir. Rather than dwell on the loss, which he was certain was in keeping with the Lord's divine intentions, Mr. Lawson took it as a means to save a soul—in this case that of Jas Stephens. For years Mr. Lawson had heard two things about Selina Stephens that interested him, namely, her great devotion and her strong musical abilities. His interest in Jas Stephens ran along similar but not identical lines, namely, his idleness (and hence insufficient devotion) and his deep baritone, which the pastor had come to appreciate in monthly Masonic lodge meetings.

The day after Mr. Lawson received the sad news regarding his parishioners, he drove to the Stephenses' farm, and after a short amount of idle banter (the most that Mr. Lawson could possibly summon), he offered Selina the position of organist and Jas the position of choir leader within the Primitive Methodist Church. As Selina began to refuse the offer, Mr. Lawson interrupted. There was one detail he had neglected to mention. The offer was conditional on one thing: to accept it, the Stephenses would have to move into the village. His congregation could not be at the mercy of the ten-mile dirt road connecting the farm and the Queen Street Church. Noting the smile on her husband's face, Selina readily accepted the joint offer. In short, she exchanged her sacrificial life of toil on the farm for a bigger sacrificial life in the village. Jas, whose face always bore a smile, was content with the arrangement as well.

At that time, three branches of Methodism worshipped in Brampton: Wesleyan Methodists, Primitive Methodists, and Episcopal Methodists. What they all had in common was their belief that life's truths were all to be found within the bible, that all humans were born of sin, and that salvation could only come from faith. Primitive Methodists were considered the most fervent of the three branches, promoting the participation of trained laymen and decision-making by the adherents, evangelism, and a strict lifestyle.

Their image was typified by one of their earliest local leaders, William Lawson, who in the early 1820s, when he was not evangelizing in the streets of Toronto, could be found preaching in the undeveloped areas outside of it. It was while he was preaching "in the bush"—as Brampton and the area around it were then called—that he came upon his old friend from Cumberland, England, and fellow Primitive Methodist, John Elliott. Lawson saw so much potential in the area and its people that he sold his business in Toronto and moved near Elliott. In no time, Lawson and Elliott had many adherents to their bible-based view of the world. They shut down the taverns and distillery, changed the name of the area from Buffy's Corners to Brampton, and set about making the area a more pious place. By the time Jesse Perry and Jas and Selina Stephens settled in Brampton, it had long been the heart of Primitive Methodism in what was to become Canada.

Sitting in front of the organ of the Primitive Methodists, Selina Stephens cringed every time she heard the irritating voice of her odious new pastor, the nephew of William Lawson. In addition to preaching loudly, Pastor Lawson sang loudly. Selina flinched every time someone in the congregation extemporaneously shouted "Amen" or "Hallelujah." She became awash in grief each time she looked at the crude second-storey room above the Queen Street butcher shops in which the Primitive Methodists congregated. With each cringe, flinch, and suppressed sob, she smiled feeling the full measure of her sacrifice.

From a building Jas purchased in the four corners area, the Stephenses realized an income that supported Jas and his many gentlemanly pursuits. From their stately home on Union Street they raised their growing family, soon comprised of four children.

* * *

Ina, Aunt Lil, and I received two telegrams over the days that followed, both informing us that Mother was on the mend. Six days after our arrival, we were summoned to return to Brampton. As I sat on the train listening to the iron wheels transport us along the now well-worn tracks, I thought of all that I had learned over the past week. I didn't know anything more about Grandpa Brady (who would always be just plain Grandpa to me) or how he became self-made or others-destroyed. I knew the identities of the four children of Jas and Selina Stephens. My father was the boy—the first-born. Aunt Lil was the second-born. My Aunt Charlotte was the third-born and Aunt Rose the fourth. I comprehended how each of our Brampton families fit together; how all of my cousins shared the same grandparents. I was completely unaware that the family whose connections I now so well understood was about to be put asunder.

Chapter 4
THE TURNERS LEAVE

As a child, I never heard my mother cry; I only heard her play her music more mournfully. I never heard my mother's voice raised in anger; I only heard her bang the piano keys with more fervour. When she was sad, she played cheerless pieces, as if in a trance, never stopping to gather new sheet music or to turn a page of notes. Agony articulated itself through her fingers on the ivory; through her feet on the brass. Her eyes closed, her chest, neck, and head heaved as she reached for distant keys. Her fingertips wrung out notes as her fine hands made their way to and from each other. I knew better than to interrupt Mother as she expressed herself in this way. Eventually, she would play herself out. At a certain point, she would stop, look at her hands, then stand and carry on with the routine tasks of her life, the matter that gave rise to the outburst either expelled or stifled until it could be dealt with later.

Mother's delight at seeing Ina and me on our return from Aunt Lil's house was heartfelt but short-lived. We had barely exchanged greetings and unpacked our valises before we heard her at the melodic keys. At first I did not recognize the exercise for what it was. A day did not pass during which Mother did not play the instrument—a stolen fifteen minutes here or possibly a half hour there—whenever she was not required to engage in more productive pursuits. Most of the music she played consisted of hymns and constituted her practice for the weekend's demands at the church. My mother, like her mother-in-law before her, was a church's pianist and organist. Depending on the hymn, one could be forgiven for confusing it with an outpouring of grief. But throughout the week following our return, my ears rang with one woeful sonata after another. I soon realized their deeper meaning.

Mother's sorrowful state was noteworthy not just for its duration but also for its sharp contrast to Father's disposition at the time. Throughout the week, I only heard him raise his voice once at Mother. Coming upon her at the piano one evening, after the completion of her nightly chores, he interrupted a morose piece. "Enough of this misery and gloom! It isn't as if someone has died!" The rest of the time, his intercourse with her was actually ... kind. On one occasion, he told her she would need a new dress. This was only partially unusual. He frequently criticized her plain wardrobe, although being without the means to replace it, he rarely suggested she do so. But at this time, the observation sounded somewhat hopeful. "This will be an occasion worthy of a new dress, don't you think, dear Mary?"

Often dejected, Father was, throughout this period ... buoyant. His walk, which was sometimes slow and crestfallen, was then ... tall and proud. Often laconic, Father was at this time ... animated. While we ate, he waxed on about our small town and how one day, if led by the right people, it would be a large town—possibly even a city. He was almost giddy as he explained to the five of us how this transformation could occur. On nights like those, I was grateful for our strict table rules that prevented children from speaking unless invited to do so. I had no idea how to respond to his grand vision, nor, it seems, did anyone else. It mattered not. He appeared to be rehearsing a speech more than seeking the input of Grandpa, Mother, Jim, Ina, or me.

The extended family meal on the Sunday after I returned from Toronto was held in the evening at the home of my aunt and uncle, Charlotte and William Turner. Their Church Street home was situated between the Wesleyan Grace Methodist Church, which we always attended, and the Presbyterian Church, which we never attended. Our walk to their home that afternoon was quick and purposeful. Father set the pace. Twice he told Mother to quicken her step and to "brighten up." As for me, I could not have walked faster nor been brighter. The house to which we were going had once belonged to Aunt Charlotte's parents, Jas and Selina Stephens.

Although I had been there countless times in my short life, this was the first time I would enter it with the perspective I had gained from my time with Aunt Lil. I longed to see the house as Jas and Selina would have seen it. As if that wasn't enough to make me smile, Father told us as that we would not on this day be returning to church in the evening, as was our custom on Sunday nights.

The odd nature of the week continued through that late afternoon. As we entered the Turners' main door, Dr. Heggie exited it. In their large sitting room, we found the home's occupants. The boys were sitting quietly (which was queer) and motionless (queerer still) on a little sofa staring at one of Bill's fingers, then freshly bandaged. Aunt Charlotte and her sister, Aunt Rose, were locked in an embrace on a long sofa across from them. Uncle William and Uncle James stood silently in front of the fireplace. No one rose to greet us. No one invited us to sit down. Our entrances to church were not carried off with the level of silence that pierced this room. In a true testament to the singular nature of the scene, Ina and I *shared* an unknowing glance. Neither of us knew what had befallen our family, and neither, it seemed as we looked at them, did any of our cousins.

Within minutes, we all found places, Father joining the men near fireplace; Mother, the women on the long sofa. In the silence, I contemplated the despair within the room. Dr. Heggie's bag seemed heavy as he left the house. His right arm was fully extended above the hand that gripped its handle. That recollection, and the morose countenances of the adults within the room, confirmed to me that no baby had been left behind.

Eventually, Uncle William turned his soft grey eyes from the mirror atop the mantel and looked at each of us. He was a handsome man, tall, with a near full head of brown hair parted to one side and swept across his high forehead well above his clean-shaven face. "Children," he began, addressing his remarks primarily to his two sons on the little couch to his left and four of their cousins on the couch in front of him, "some of you were cautioned that I had sad news to impart. It is time that I disclosed to you something that the adults in our family have known for a little more than a week." He spoke slowly. "I have made a decision that is going to change all of your lives—particularly, of course, those of you, Roy and Bill.

But I am not insensible of the affect my decision will have on your young cousins," he turned to us, "or indeed, on their parents."

He looked around the room and then back at Roy and Bill. "I know that my decision will deprive them of something very valuable—your society and that of your mother." He looked at Aunt Charlotte as he said so. "I have not made this decision lightly or without thought to your future," he said, turning back to his sons. "Indeed, I pray that you will one day understand that this difficult decision I have made, I have made primarily for your future."

He stopped, looked toward the window in front of him, and then went on. "In short, I have taken a position as Western Manager of the Maple Leaf Milling Company. We will leave for Winnipeg soon—possibly even within the next two weeks, assuming," he said, even more quietly and yet quite seriously, "that we are not driven out before then. I am sorry that we were not able to tell you earlier. My current position, of course, made it necessary that the matter be kept in confidence until all of the arrangements could be made and the appropriate notices given. I have reason to believe," he said, looking knowingly at Father, "that the last of the arrangements will be made this evening and that my relocation will be announced tomorrow. I will require each of you to keep the matter within our family until that time—but it is not such a long way off. Can I depend on you for that?" We all nodded in assent, no one saying a word, although I felt well qualified to vouch for the dependability of secret keepers within our family.

The stillness that had enveloped the room prior to our entrance returned, and we sat not knowing quite what to say or do, until a little squeak emanated from the couch on which Roy and Bill sat. Seeing all heads turn to him, Bill held up his bandaged finger, being more able, it seemed, to admit the current pain of a gash than the anticipated pain of longing. But that little sob was enough to break the silence. Hannah, John, and Ina rushed to the little couch, gathering around Roy and Bill. The sisters on the long couch renewed their embraces and began to sputter. Father and Uncle James, who were both in front of the fireplace, stepped even closer to Uncle William, who was between them. I stayed where I was, observing the three scenes.

Roy, it appeared, was taking the news somewhat better than his younger brother Bill, and being the more jovial of the two by nature, he sought to lighten the mood. "Bill, don't let that little bang get to you. Just imagine—yours is the first accident we have had with the new car. It will be remembered for all time." It was revealed that Bill had caught his finger in the heavy door of the Turners' new car earlier that afternoon. "At least Dr. Heggie didn't require the car to be destroyed. Remember when Ed Jones' dog bit my leg when I was riding my bicycle home from school last year? Dr. Heggie gave me ten stitches." He pulled up his pant leg to show us the scar above his ankle. "And then he had the dog shot. Poor King. He was only trying to have some fun." Looking at the faces turned up to him in wonder, Roy took on a new approach. "Come to think of it, if we aren't going to be here to guide you young cousins…" he said, turning now to look at the three of them on the floor in front of him.

"Ahem," Ina interjected, pushing an errant strand of hair from her face. "I am the same age as Bill."

"But you are younger than me, cousin," Roy replied. "As I was saying, if we are not going to be here to guide you, I think there are a few lessons about Brampton that we had better go over before we leave. Let's get started. You know the big oak down at the Flats? Come on, we'll show you what you can do within it." The group started for the door, Aunt Charlotte calling after them, "Mind you are wearing your Sunday clothes. And be back in an hour."

I chose not to join them, and it seemed I was not missed—neither by the gaggle of cousins and siblings walking out nor the cluster of aunts and uncles staying in. Instead I moved to the little rocker nestled in the corner of the room. The little rocking chair had for a time belonged to each of Jas and Selina's children and grandchildren—always by the youngest of them who was able to sit independently. Unless Dr. Heggie obliged me with the delivery of a younger sibling, I knew I would be its longest occupant of my generation. The chair was conveniently placed, being in the room in which the adults generally congregated but tucked in a corner between a big couch and the small couch perpendicular to it.

Just as the ladies' view of me from their long couch was obscured, so was mine of them, but as I rocked, I listened to their words. "Oh, Charlotte," Aunt Rose cried. "How will we bear it? In all these years, we've never been apart."

"I agree, Rose!" Aunt Charlotte replied. "Though somehow I am sure we will manage."

"It will not be the same," Mother added. "It will never be the same again."

"You are right, my dear sister-in-law," Aunt Charlotte replied. "You are so right."

The ladies went on, repeating in a variety of ways that Aunt Charlotte would be missed and that she would miss Mother and Aunt Rose.

"Your brother, Charlotte," Mother added. "You will be heartily missed by him."

"And I shall miss him in turn, but you know, Mary," Aunt Charlotte said to Mother, "this move may not be all bad for Jethro. William's resignation may provide Jethro with the opportunity he has long sought."

"I know, dear Charlotte. And who is more deserving?" Mother asked with true sincerity. "But at what cost?"

While I tried to discern the opportunities that would be presented to Father, Uncle William reminded his wife of her desire to show the other two ladies the peonies in the back yard. The three ladies rose and left the room.

My attention turned to the men, still standing by the fireplace, which, since it was July, emitted no heat. Their preoccupation was principally the politics of the move. This was an appropriate topic for discussion, for at that time my Uncle William was the mayor of the Town of Brampton. The move to Winnipeg would necessitate his resignation from office five and a half months before his term would otherwise have expired.

"When do you expect to hear from Handle?" Uncle James asked as soon as the ladies left the room.

"Any moment," Uncle William replied. "He has been consulting with the town fathers all day. I was sorry to ask him to do this on a Sunday—he's a good church man himself, but he loves backroom politics, and he told me last week that I just had to give him the word and he'd start the process. As soon as I entered our church this morning and saw the peculiar way that Treadgold looked at me, I knew that he knew, and I knew, of course, that it would not be long before the rest of the town fathers knew. That would be a grave outcome for you, Doc," he said, referring to Father. For over four decades Mr. Treadgold had been the proprietor of the local piano shop. Over those years, when not selling musical instruments, he had been an active member of the local town council.

"I fear your chances will be materially jeopardized if the town fathers are so angry with me that they refuse to consider my brother-in-law as my ideal successor," Uncle William continued, "so before sitting in our pew, I feigned a headache and left the church. I practically ran up the street to retrieve Handle from your church. Fortunately, he had not yet entered."

"Damn that John Cooney," Uncle William cursed, his profanity confirming to me that he was unaware of my proximity. Then, turning to my other uncle, he went on. "You were right, James, I should not have spoken to that real estate agent until after the announcement was made. He has likely already lined up a buyer, and while he had no notion of why I was intending to sell, the fact that I had not also asked him to secure a new location for us likely led him to a conclusion that was in fact the truth— that we are leaving town. But I felt I could not wait longer to speak with him. I truly fear we will be driven out. We need to be able to move quickly."

The men continued their exchange. Uncle William made it clear that he hoped that Father would succeed him as the mayor of the town. Uncle James agreed, suggesting that Father's experience as chair of the high school board and chair of the water commission would allow Father to continue Uncle William's reform agenda. "What this town needs, we all know, is industry, and industry will only come if we have the electricity, sewers, and roads to support it and an educated workforce. Some of us, of course," he said, looking somewhat critically at Uncle William, "are more optimistic about obtaining that industry than others."

Uncle William confessed to feeling less optimistic about the town's future. He considered the late 1870s and early 1880s to be Brampton's heyday.

"Brampton has made great headway over the past ten years," Uncle James argued. "You saw the Dominion's report released last month. Not many towns in all of Canada have seen such growth. And yes, it took you quite a bit of effort to convince Whitewear to start their business here, but look at the other industries that have done so. The Williams Shoe Company now employs nearly a hundred. Add the Dale Estate and Copeland Chatterson," he said, referring to two large local employers, "and you have another three hundred."

They went on, exchanging figures and company names but with numbers so large and names so complicated and with the constant rocking of my little chair, I began to drift off to sleep.

I was awakened some time later by a voice confirming the state I had just left. "That's my daughter, Jessie," Father said. "We hadn't even noticed her there. But she's asleep, Handle. No need to worry about her presence." I continued in my head-drooped pose. I did not know who Handle was, but I knew my father and my two uncles. I found all of them gruff and somewhat terrifying at the best of times. I did not relish the thought of being discovered eavesdropping—something I was most assuredly doing. Daring not to look up, I watched the legs and feet of the men as their discussion ensued.

This was not a conversation to be had sitting down, apparently, as the men did not move significantly from the fireplace, although there were seats in the room for thrice their number. I knew that Uncle William was closest to the fireplace, toward its centre. I could easily identify his pinstriped black pants and expensive-looking polished black shoes. Uncle James stood to his left. He was a bigger man, and his black pants, while obviously well made, displayed a greater amount of fabric. Possibly to support his additional weight, his black shoes were somewhat heavier-looking. Father wore his signature white patent leather shoes below his brown well-worn slim-cut slacks and stood to the right of Uncle William. The new man—Roger Handle was his name—stood in front of Uncle William, his back toward me. His legs were like tree stumps, wide and tall, covered in volumes of grey fabric. I could only imagine his height. Mr. Handle wore big black shoes, only the heels of which I could see.

His toes pointed toward Uncle William in front of him, and they never moved once the entire time I watched them.

"What did you find, Roger? Who did you speak to?" Uncle William began.

"Well, it's not pretty, my good fellows," Handle answered. "Not a pretty sight. They're mad. And they're disappointed. But they're mostly mad. You made a good decision, Billy-boy, in calling on me to act as your intermediary."

"Billy-boy." I wondered whether my young cousin had re-entered the room. Stealing a glance upward, I realized that Mr. Handle must have been referring to my Uncle William by the abbreviated name that the rest of us applied to his son.

"Yes, it is a good thing you called me. Otherwise I'm afraid they'd be just mad. But I worked on the sympathy angle for you, Billy-boy. Said you had bills to pay and big expenses coming your way. Said that you lived beyond your means and that you had to take that fancy job in Winnipeg to get out of your problems. I said, though, that you weren't going to leave the town high and dry—that your brother-in-law had agreed at your particular request to fill the breach, and given your brother-in-law's civic commitment and experience, that you actually thought the town was better in his hands than in yours." An awkward silence filled the air.

"I confess, Roger," Uncle James replied slowly, "I hadn't thought of you taking a tack like that."

"Well, of course you didn't, Jimmy-boy," Handle replied. I quickly determined he was referring to Uncle James. "That's why Billy-boy called me. I know how these people think. Know them all like they were my own family. I know as sure as I know the sun will rise tomorrow that if those good men discover that your brother-in-law has so little hope for the future of our fair town that he sought out opportunities for himself and his family elsewhere, they'd run him out of town and possibly the rest of your family too. That would not have aided the cause. Besides, I saw that new Russell outside this house today. You can't tell me, Billy-boy, it is easy to afford an automobile like that."

After a time, Uncle William broke the silence. He took a step closer to Mr. Handle. "So what is the upshot of it all, Roger? With whom did you speak? What will they support?"

"Let me tell you first the town fathers I spoke with. Not that it was easy to do this on the Lord's Day but because they all know me so well and because they trust my political instincts, I was able to pry them from their pews and family dinners long enough to impart what I had to impart and extract what I had to extract."

"Yes," Father said somewhat impatiently, "with whom did you speak?"

"Don't be so impatient, young man," he replied. I realized that Mr. Handle had not the wherewithal to further abbreviate either Jethro or Doc and add the word "boy" to the appellation. Of course, the term "young man," which consisted of more syllables than "Doc," was no abbreviation at all. I concluded that Mr. Handle must be a very old man if Uncle William and Uncle James were boys to him, and Father was a young man. "I know what you want out of this. And it's likely to be a long road, so you'd better be patient."

"In summary," Mr. Handle said, speaking principally to Uncle William, "of the twelve, two will gladly now see the back of you, three are considering discrediting you, and two are sad you are leaving. Two may support Doc as your immediate successor. The others are on the fence. They, gentlemen, hold the balance of power. I will leave you and return in an hour or two's time with their final resolution."

Within minutes, I was found and dispatched by my mother to retrieve my siblings and cousins. Though the mission would have required me to walk but two blocks, I got no further than the Turners' driveway. There, I found my brother Jim sitting behind the wheel of the Turners' new motor vehicle. Automobiles had begun to appear in Brampton in the early 1900s. The first made its entrance under the power of Lord Minto, the Governor General of Canada who drove to Brampton and his wife Lady Minto to inspect its famous greenhouses. But in 1907 there were still very few cars in Brampton. The Turner family was among the small group of automobile owners. Uncle William had promised to take us all for a ride in his newest vehicle later that day.

Like all new technologies, the public was divided in its support for the new means of conveyance. Most members of my family were cautiously optimistic about their future acceptance. They believed that once motorized vehicles were built more reliably and once they were priced more affordably, they might become the predominant mode of transportation. Those in that group were certain that such conditions would never be met in their lifetime. But that group did not include my brother Jim. He was confident that the automobile would replace the horse and buggy within ten years. That group also did not include Aunt Lil who, naturally, took a different view. Though she was rarely a defender of tradition, Aunt Lil took a strong stand against the new means of transportation. She considered automobiles to be noisy, smelly, unsociable, and dangerous. She predicted that it would only be a few years before the contraptions were banned.

The car in which Jim sat was not running, and after being assured that it would not actually go anywhere, I allowed him to pull me into it.

"Wouldn't it be exciting to own one of these, Jessie?" my brother mused.

"I don't know," I replied. I didn't like to take a position contrary to Jim, who I idolized, but I secretly fell into my Aunt Lil's camp. Cars scared me. "I miss Daisy and Petunia." Daisy and Petunia were the Turners' two horses, both of whom had been moved out of the barn at the back of their house and sold to make way for the automobile.

"The car eats a lot less hay than Daisy and Petunia do," Jim said. "And we don't have any horses that we would have to get rid of to make way for a car. Of course, it costs a lot of money, and I expect we will have to wait for the price to come down before Father can buy one. I saw this car, this Russell F, advertised in the *Conservator* last week. It cost $3,750. It's the top of the line model made by the Canada Cycle and Motor Co. It has a forty horsepower engine and can sit seven people in these two bench seats." He rubbed his hand over the dashboard. "The frame is pressed chrome steel. Isn't it beautiful?" He didn't seem to notice my lack of response as he went on.

"Mark my words, Little One, in another ten years no one in Brampton will be riding in horse-drawn carriages. They'll all be riding in automobiles. And they won't look like this either." I shuddered at his premonition regarding their full-scale adoption but nonetheless asked for an explanation regarding their future look.

"Look at this car, Jessie," he explained. "It is shaped to look exactly like a buggy. Two long, curved benches in the back with a long motor in front, very much resembling a carriage pulled by a horse. This," he said, waving at the area in which we sat, "is not a carriage and that," he added, pointing to the engine at the front, "is not a horse. There is no reason for the automobile to look this way except to make us all feel comfortable with the familiar shape. But the vehicle may look better and run more efficiently if it were shaped differently. Who knows," he said wistfully, "maybe someday I will discover that better form."

"Do you know how to build an automobile?" I asked.

"Well, I don't know now but I could learn. There are hundreds of people across the world trying to build them. Some have figured it out."

I sat there running my hand along the various parts of the interior, enjoying my brother's animated description of every component and instrument. It was only the hollering of my cousins from the street in front of the house that reminded me of the errand I was supposed to have run. Clearly, I wasn't needed for that purpose.

Ninety minutes later, our meal ended with a knock at the door. Uncle William, announcing that it was likely Mr. Handle, rose to retrieve him, and the children were excused. Aunt Charlotte, praising my civility, accepted my proposal to clear the table. It was an inaugural offer made for the true motive of hearing the outcome of Mr. Handle's engagement—an offer I nearly recanted when I first took in the countenance of the man then being admitted to the dining room. It seemed impossible to me that the stranger with the young, child-like face was the man who had referred to my two uncles as boys and my father as a young man. However, upon viewing his tree-like legs and heavy shoes and hearing his greeting to those assembled, I slowly began to lift the empty plates.

Neither the men nor the women made any attempt to move to the sitting room, and so Mr. Handle was invited to address the entire group seated at the dining room table. Whether this surprised him or not,

I could not tell, but as political conversations in our family so often took place around such tables and hence involved the women as well as the men, it was not surprising from my perspective. Indeed, the discussion over the prior hour had primarily centred on the very matter at hand— Mother expressing her abject disbelief that anyone would consider Father unsuitable for the vacancy about to be created. She even suggested that the views of the town fathers be ignored, if necessary, in favour of a direct appeal to the electors. This notion received short shrift by Father, who declared that if the town fathers did not want him for the position, he did not want it.

After declining Aunt Charlotte's offer of dessert, Mr. Handle began, first apologizing for the delay in returning. "It took longer than I thought it would. The town fathers, while united on some matters," he said, looking at that moment toward Father, "were quite divided on others."

Mr. Handle turned to Uncle William. "The upshot is that the group requires you to leave Brampton right away—before you change your mind. I think that some within the group see great opportunities for themselves if you exit politics quickly."

Turning toward Father, he said, "The group requires that there be a race for the mayoralty, even though there are only five months left in the term. They will not support the appointment of an acting mayor."

"Who else do they propose be on the ballot?" Father asked.

"They are going to run Treadgold."

"Treadgold," Father said, relief evident in his tone. "That old coot?" I suppose Father thought he could easily beat the elderly gentleman.

"Yes, Treadgold," Mr. Handle confirmed. "But not just him." Father had hoped for this addendum, but not the next. "Charters is going to run too, but on the understanding that he will serve the five-month term only. He plans to run as the Conservative candidate in the next provincial election, which he believes will be called in the spring of '08. While that will create an opening early in the New Year, I am sorry to say, young man," his remarks continued to be directed to Father, "that they want that vacancy filled by Billy-boy's other brother-in-law—you, Jimmy-boy," he said, turning to Uncle James.

Uncle James said nothing, but Mr. Handle assumed, I suppose, that he would ultimately agree. Father was equally quiet and bowed his head. Mother, who had moved beside him, turned her attention fully to her husband and put one of her hands on one of his. Father yanked his away, crossed his arms over his chest, and turned his head up toward the ceiling. Everyone else remained focused on Mr. Handle, who continued.

"If this is agreeable, Billy-boy, then your resignation will be tendered at tomorrow night's regular town council meeting. Nominations will be open for a week, and the election will be held the week after that. In that regard, it is a condition that all the usual nomination formalities and niceties occur. To that end, in true Brampton fashion, you, Jimmy-boy," he said, looking at Uncle James, "and each of Charters and three others will nominate each other to stand for mayor. Each of you will decline the nomination except Treadgold and Charters. If asked, Billy-boy, you will say that your motivation for leaving the town springs from Mrs. Turner's declining health and her need for the drier air of the West."

"My wife has never been sick a day in her life," Uncle William interjected. "Who would believe that explanation?"

"The men would. They never notice things like that, and it is chiefly their opinion we are concerned with. The notion that you were impecunious was found to be incredulous.

"Give me your word as a gentleman that you will go along with all of this, and you will get a proper send-off with ceremonies in your honour hosted by the town, and the local Liberals—of which you are a great supporter—will give you a grandfather clock."

"You do make it difficult for me to leave," Uncle William said sarcastically.

With that Mr. Handle left the house and I moved the last of the napkin rings to the sideboard.

We Stephenses were a sorry lot as we walked home that night—though Ina, who was particularly close to our cousins Roy and Bill, was especially forlorn. Jim was dejected as well because the promised ride in the Russell had not transpired. Mother was sad because Father was sad. Father was the saddest of all. No one suggested that he pick up his step or brighten up.

Chapter 5

NEW YEAR'S DAY

The mortification experienced by my father that tumultuous day in the summer of 1907 appeared to have entirely dissipated by early January six months later. Time had whiled away the humiliation he experienced at the town fathers' rejection of him and the betrayal he felt at his brother-in-law's rejection of the town. For most of his adult life, Father gained his self-esteem from his profession, and in those months he sought and received particular solace in it. One of Brampton's three or fewer dentists for much of his career, Father was a well-known and—for the most part—well respected member of the Brampton community. The nickname "Doc" by which he was referred by nearly all Bramptonians is evidence of the dominant effect his career had on his entire life.

It was a career for which he was well prepared. After graduating from high school with honours, Father worked for two years before pursuing a degree in dental science from the College of Dental Surgeons in Toronto. After taking the gold medal for the best practical work, he travelled to Philadelphia, where he obtained a second degree, this one in dental surgery. Once again he distinguished himself, graduating within the top five members of the 119-person class. Fortune then struck, as his return to Brampton coincided with the death of one of Brampton's two dentists. Acquiring the long-established business, Father closed down the "dental parlour" of the late Dr. D. MacFarlane and moved the acquired patients and such of the equipment he desired to keep to the second floor of his father's Queen Street building.

To mark their son's accomplishments, Jas and Selina presented him with a black-and-white twelve-by-eight-inch sign engraved "J.G. Stephens, D.D.S., R.C.D.S." The sign was installed next to the small street-level door of their Queen Street building. When Father's office was open for business, a small wooden sign hung just below it so indicating. Over the years, Father added a third sign. Owing to its intended temporary nature, this sign, usually somewhat askew, read "Please push firmly to open," and then in smaller letters below, "and close tightly behind you." The fact that there was never an occasion to remove this temporary sign was a clear indication of my father's inability to use a planer on the swollen door and his failure to hire someone else to do so.

Once the door was firmly pushed open and then tightly closed, Father's patients were met by a dark, narrow staircase illuminated by two small wall sconces and whatever natural light penetrated the frosted glass in the transom above the street level door. Here the patients were also introduced to the mint-green walls that would surround them within the staircase and throughout Father's offices. In all the years he occupied them, the colour of the walls never changed—only the extent to which they were marred by fingerprints of sticky-handed children, gashes and gouges made by the belongings moved up to and down from the second floor, and the general dirt and grime of the town caused in large part by the iron mills located behind the building.

At the top of the stairs, the door to the right led to a small apartment. Straight ahead, the door bore a sign, identical to the black-and-white sign at street level. A bell announced the admission of people walking through that door and into Father's windowless, multi-doored waiting room. Four chairs and a small sofa were arranged against the walls, two end tables and two coffee tables among them.

No receptionist was there to greet patients. Instead, a framed rectangular sign affixed to the far wall directed patients to take a seat and wait until the dentist was available to see them. There were no prearranged appointments. Patients came to see the dentist when they had the need and the time, and the dentist saw them as he had the availability.

In addition to the waiting room, Father's offices were comprised of a treatment room, a lab, and a business office. The four rooms were laid out in a square with doors connecting each room near their confluence. Once, while Father stood on the street talking to a departing patient, I ran eight circuits through those connecting rooms. Eventually, Father's roar ended my frolic. By that time my stomach was nauseous and my head reeling.

After Father escorted a patient out of his treatment room, through the waiting room and to the door to the landing and stairway, he turned, greeted all assembled, inquired as to who was next, and based on that honour system, escorted that patient into the treatment room. I firmly believe that this was the part of his practice that Father enjoyed the most: standing in that room, surveying all who sat waiting to see him, all who believed that obtaining his services was worth the wait, the time required to be away from their own businesses, the time it took to travel from their farm into town, the time away from their schools or hearths or any other things that they might have liked or needed to do.

An exception to the "first come, first served" rule was made in the case of children. Children were always seen at the first available opportunity. This custom led Father's patients to believe he had a special fondness for children, but his motivation in seeing them early sprang from an entirely different direction. Father desired to have all children treated and removed from his offices before their cries distracted him or his patients and before their fidgeting caused havoc among the newspapers and other adornments in the waiting room.

No matter the motivation, the practice made Father a favourite among the parents of young children, although, I can vouchsafe, no favourite of the children. One of the competing dentists in town was a man we affectionately referred to as "Old" Dr. French—although he was no older than Father. Old Dr. French was a jolly man carrying a few too many pounds around the middle. He had a full allocation of white hair, which he wore on the top of his head like a mop and on his face in the form of friendly mutton chops. Enjoying the company of children as he did, he had no qualms keeping them in his waiting room for as long as it took for him to see them in the ordinary course. Erupting cries from that room were usually silenced by a lollipop. At the end of the visit, all minor patients were issued a coupon redeemable for one ice cream cone at the nearby dairy.

These practices, as Father critically pointed out, by inducing further tooth decay, created many more opportunities for the children to see Old Dr. French. This mattered not to the children, who adored him. Sometimes, on becoming newly acquainted with me and learning that my father was one of the town's dentists, a child's face would light up. My negative response to their next question as to whether my father was Old Dr. French sometimes produced an equal amount of disappointment on both our parts.

Amounts payable for Father's professional services were calculated prior to any procedure being performed, based on a schedule of fees also posted on a wall in the waiting room. Payment was due on provision of services, in cash or in kind. No statements of services rendered were prepared, as there were no insurers or any other third parties that required any such report. Father did maintain a ledger of patients indebted to him, given that, despite the signage, many did not pay on provision of his services.

The status Father attached to his profession compensated for what was often a deficiency in cash. Like Dr. Heggie, my father was often paid for his services in kind. In that respect, our family was very fortunate for the prodigiously soft teeth and poor oral hygiene of some of Brampton's best merchants and farmers. Generally, their accounts were settled over time with deliveries to our back door of farm-fresh eggs and fine cuts of meat. True, Mother did not have the luxury as some wives did of being able to plan the next day's main course meal, but we tried to make spontaneity a virtue.

We all knew when the Robertson family visited Father. It was generally a half-day affair with the parents, the elderly grandparents, and their growing brood of children. The decreasing number of teeth in the older generation was compensated for by the increasing number in the younger. Their signature form of payment was carrots. In the weeks following their visits, Mother served fresh-cut carrots for snacks, sliced, boiled carrots at dinner (as we called our midday meal), creamed carrots at tea (as we called our evening meal), and carrot soup and cake at both of those meals. Mother knew that the goods delivered to us were as good as money if they were used properly, and she never let them go to waste.

One of the many desirable aspects of the profession, according to Father, was the ability to expound upon one's political views without a contrary argument being waged. He delighted in telling us how he waited until a man's mouth was fully pried open, with one or more devices inside it, to "discuss" the latest issues before the town council, the elementary or high school board, the provincial legislature or the Dominion parliament. His greatest pleasure arose when the mouth so engaged was that of a Liberal or some other person who took a position opposite to Father's.

From the earliest days of his childhood, it was made clear to my brother Jim that he would enter the profession of dentistry and join Father's practice. My cousin John was spared the early presumption in this respect, but whenever the subject of John's future was raised in the absence of his father, my Uncle James, Father always encouraged John to join Jim in this pursuit. Father had great visions for expanding his practice to include both Jim and John, and as my Aunt Rose, John's mother, never dissuaded her brother from making these overtures, it was understood that she shared my father's vision.

Father relished every opportunity he had to expound that view. Thus, the arrival at our door of Uncle James's upstairs tenant while we enjoyed our 1908 New Year's Day dinner was not unwelcome to Father. Uncle James was barely out the door to attend to the burst pipes in his building when Father began. "It is a profession, boys. That is what sets it apart from nearly every other endeavour. No offence to your husband, Rose," Father added for the benefit of his sister, whose demeanour at the table made it clear that none was taken, "but anyone with a little capital can be a merchant. He might even be a successful merchant—until the next man with a little capital comes along and sets up shop right next to him, and having a newer, cleaner shop with slightly newer goods takes away the business from the first shop owner. Then the second shop owner thrives and the first suffers. Again, I say this meaning no offence to your father, John."

John, who was then eight years of age, took this insult to his father's occupation as would any young boy hearing it from his own uncle in the presence of his seemingly complicit mother—with silence rather than rebuttal, with a slight extension of that part of his body already under the table and a contraction of that above it.

"But isn't the same true of dentistry?" Aunt Lil chimed in. New Year's Day was one of the two days a year she "graced us with her presence," as Father would say. "Couldn't you open a dental clinic and have someone else open one near you? Isn't that just what Doc Al faced when you set up your clinic down the road from his? And did you not encounter the same experience after Doc Al retired with Doctors Peaker and French, who came to town after your practice was established?"

"But that is my point entirely," Father replied. "In the years since Doc French and I started practicing dentistry in 1891 until this year, there have been not been more than three other dentists in the entire town. Now how many merchants are there in Brampton, boys? Too many to count, obviously. And who knows how many there will be tomorrow? Because all you need to be a merchant is a little money and a modest amount of intelligence, no offence to your father of course, John. To be a dentist you need that same quantity of funds and more, because in addition to the premises you must acquire and equip as any merchant does, you must qualify yourself with years of schooling and you must be blessed with a very steady hand. This would elude most people. But as a result of the efforts of your fathers and your own intellectual and physical gifts, you boys will have the means to be so qualified."

"You concede, brother," Aunt Lil replied, "that should young John wish to follow you in this pursuit, it will have been his father's efforts as a successful merchant that gave him the financial means to do so?"

Father would have had to concede the point, but at that moment Mother was clearing the table and asked him to pass her the turkey platter. He was unusually solicitous in his efforts to assist her that day, gathering for her as well the cranberries, salt, and pepper. With those matters attended to, he resumed.

"Furthermore, and this too cannot be ignored, everyone who has actual teeth or wishes to have fabricated teeth is in need of the services of a dentist. But does everyone require the wares that merchants sell? Pumpkin, please, Mary, and only a bit of cream." Father didn't miss dessert, no matter how engrossed he was in a conversation or diatribe. "Of course not. Many a farmer's wife will make the bread that others will purchase from your father, John and, no offence intended, that wife would likely make it better and at less expense than that made in your father's bakery."

With every suggestion to which John was to take no offence, he sank a bit lower in his chair, being very careful all the while not to slouch. While Father was able to make these cutting observations of family and perfect strangers alike over the dinner table, we children were never permitted to slouch.

Aunt Lil interjected again. "That's true, brother. Everyone should see a dentist, but I recently read that quite a small percentage of Ontarians regularly sees a dentist, and of those that do, some may see a dentist as seldom as once every three or four years. Bread, on the other hand," Aunt Lil said, being sure to use an example that would raise her nephew up a few inches at the table, "is consumed by everyone every day, and statistics indicate that fewer and fewer Canadians actually bake it themselves. And so the person who may require a tooth to be filled once every two years will have purchased, assuming he consumes a quarter of a loaf of bread a day, over 180 loaves of bread between those two dental visits…"

"That, my dear, sister," Father replied, beginning to get cross, "is why I charge what I do to fill a tooth. It is more than fifty times the price of a loaf of bread.

"The scientific endeavours are not to be discounted either, boys," Father went on, swallowing his first piece of pie before doing so. He was directing his advocacy, as always, at John. It was well settled in our home that no convincing of my brother Jim was necessary. "Your father, John, might get some satisfaction in making yeast rise or in making pastry light and flaky. No offence to him, of course, but it cannot be anything to working with the dozens of chemicals and compounds I employ on a daily basis to make ever improving pastes, fillings, false teeth, pain relievers, and breath sanitizers." I glanced at Mother, who had made the pies in front of us. The pastry was light and flaky. Was she to have been spared the offence as well? From the placid look on her face, I concluded that she either took none or that her attention was entirely diverted.

"Finally," Father said, moving his empty plate forward on the table, "there is a question of lifestyle. Most merchants are required to work from dawn until dusk. Their stores must be open during all business hours and often, such as the case with a bakery," he said, looking directly at his still shrinking nephew, "he must work, or supervise others working, long before that time so that his wares are ready when his shop opens. A dentist, on the other hand, sets his own hours. I never arrive at the office before nine in the morning, and I rarely stay after five in the evening, Saturdays excepted, when I work in the morning only. I come home for dinner at noon every day, and on many occasions I will close the office at other hours so that I can meet with concerned citizens and do the good works every gentleman seeks to do. In this way, I am much more my own man than any merchant, no offence to your father, of course."

This roused Aunt Rose, who was finally about to speak, but before she could Aunt Lil took the floor again. "Really, Jethro. You can't possibly be suggesting that a successful merchant, who has ample staff to mind his store, couldn't contribute as much to society. James, of course, is a fine example, being at this time alone, merchant, mayor, and chief of the fire department."

Sensing that his aunt's rejoinder was as much for his benefit as that of his Mother, John spoke before Father could reply. "It doesn't matter, Aunt Lil. I don't want to be a merchant."

The look of satisfaction on Father's face could barely be contained. While I believe my father truly liked and admired his brother-in-law, James Darling, he most surely also bore him a certain amount of envy. It clearly gave Father a great amount of pleasure to see his nephew deciding to follow in his footsteps rather than those of his father. But his satisfaction was short-lived.

"I want to be a conductor," John declared.

"A conductor, Johnny?" his mother replied, askance. "I know you love your piano, and one day you may be a great pianist, but I am not certain one can earn a living conducting an orchestra."

"No!" John said, breaking the tension he had caused with a quick laugh. "Not an orchestra conductor. I want to be a train conductor. There aren't very many of them: only one per train. Every train needs one. I won't need any capital to be a conductor. I will see all kinds of people at each train station and bring smiles to the children as I wave my red kerchief at the boys and girls along the way. When the train breaks down, I will fix it. I'm good at fixing things. You've said so many times, Mother, haven't you?" By this point John was perfectly serious. He had stopped laughing, but once he asked this question, the laughter was resumed by the five adults in the room.

As they shared what they concluded was a great joke, I looked at the children around the table. John, red with embarrassment, sank so low in his chair at this point that he would surely have been reprimanded for slouching if even one of the adults could find their way out of the fit of hilarity in which they were engaged. Ina's face contorted with pity for her young cousin, mirroring what I expected was the look on my face. My brother Jim gazed down on his young cousin with a look I recognized. It took me a moment to place it. But then it came to me. It was a look I had mostly seen in the reverse; it was a look often applied by John to my brother, Jim. It was a look of complete and utter admiration.

When the adults finally finished their convulsing, rubbing their rib cages to massage away the pain caused by the great joke, Aunt Rose ended the conversation. "John," she said, "I am not certain that you will be a dentist one day, but I will tell you quite certainly what you will not be. You will not be a train conductor. No son of mine is going to take up a trade involving his hands." Then, realizing that to be a good part of what a dentist does, she elaborated, "Being immersed in wet filth." To that there was no reply. We did not then know what a cesspool of germs was the human mouth.

* * *

That night after changing into my nightgown, I slipped downstairs for a glass of milk. As I padded down the maid's stairs at the end of the hall, proposing to enter the kitchen from the pantry at the back, I was stopped by voices on the other side of the wall. I was certain that I heard Grandpa utter the word "destroyed."

Self-made; others-destroyed, I thought. I had been seeking to learn how these words applied to Grandpa, and suspecting I might soon attain that knowledge, I proceeded to the closed door that connected the pantry to the kitchen.

"It's been over four years," Grandpa said. "He was good enough to take me in when he did, but I never dreamed that I'd stay so long. I only planned to stay long enough to bring some order to what is left of my meagre savings."

"That's right," Mother replied. "But Father, I suspect you have little more the means to live independently now than you did four years ago. I am sorry to pry into your personal affairs, but you must see this. You did a good thing for our community twenty-six years ago. It nearly destroyed you. But you did what a decent person would do; now let us continue doing a decent thing for you."

"But it isn't your responsibility to pay for my mistakes. You are not the cause of the Scottish Fiasco. Why should you and your family have to suffer the consequences?"

"Father, we are hardly suffering. Jethro, the children, and I love having you here. And you know," she said slowly, "I know I shouldn't. I am a grown woman. But I need you here. You provide ballast to this sometimes tumultuous ship. We needn't speak of it, but I know that you can see that too. Please stay; if not for yourself, then for me."

"For a while longer then," he eventually said. "For a while longer."

I returned to my room by the stairs I had just descended, my thirst forgotten. I contemplated all that I had seen and heard that day. We were not in the habit of enunciating annual resolutions, but as I lay in my bed that night, I came to two. Firstly, I would learn the meaning of the phrase "Scottish Fiasco." The way it was uttered, I could tell that it was something undesirable. Surely it related to the "others-destroyed" phrase. Secondly, when I grew up, I would become a dentist. Reasonable hours, the ability to make potions out of chemical compounds and liquids, the captive audiences formed by one's clientele: it all seemed quite compelling to me.

Chapter 6

THE GOVERNOR'S STORY

As a child living in Brampton in the early twentieth century, I was afraid of many things: the smell of gas emitted by light fixtures; the tongues of fire that spewed from the furnace in our cellar; the sound of my father's voice when raised against my mother; the sound of my father's voice when raised against me. One thing I was not afraid of, though, was the institution designed to deprive people of their very liberty, to restrain those who had committed treacheries against their fellow man, to hold lunatics who would otherwise be a threat to themselves and others: the local jail. I was not frightened by its massive three-storey size, its foot-deep stone walls, its barred windows, its massive solid door, the small, isolated cells in which the prisoners lived or the gallows from which they were hanged. I was not afraid of the jail, even though the edifice stood on Wellington Street just two doors down from our house.

I once heard my cousin Bill ask Aunt Rose if she was afraid of the jail and its inmates. The question was particularly relevant, since her family, the Darlings, lived right across from the jail. Their house, the mirror image of ours, was also built by Grandpa. Wouldn't it be to her home an escaped convict would first go? Bill asked. My aunt assured him that if ever an inmate fled the jail, the last place in which he would seek refuge would be a house so readily available for search by the authorities. Her house, she confidently declared, was the safest house in the town.

He words provided me with great solace. I quickly concluded that if her house—the one directly across the road from the jail—was the last place to which a felon would escape, our house, just two doors east, was surely the third last place. In fact, I began to feel sorry for those in houses on the perimeter of the town, for surely their homes stood the greatest risk of such an intrusion.

Of course, my Aunt Rose also knew that most of the inmates of the local jail were not people of whom one needed to be particularly frightened. Few within it would actually desire to escape the relative warmth of its walls or the three square meals it provided (if you could call oatmeal for breakfast, soup and bread for lunch, and cornmeal for supper three square meals). Though the jail was regularly declared ill equipped to act as a place for the infirm or destitute, and though, as a result of the efforts of the Women's Christian Temperance Union, a house of refuge for the destitute had been built, the jail continued to house such misfortunates. Indeed, on a cold winter night many a poor God-fearing man would steal a loaf of bread or some other small trifle simply to have the privilege of being locked up in the jail until dawn restored the sun's warm rays.

When I was a child, there were at all times at least five people in the jail that you would be pleased to have to your home for Sunday dinner. They were the jail's superintendent, his wife, and their three children, all of whom lived in an apartment within its thick stone walls. The superintendent was actually known as a governor—a strange title, I always thought, for one with a principality of twelve thousand square feet and a population of between thirty and sixty souls. But as that was his official title, that was how he was always known.

Commensurate with the small size of his regime, the governor, it seemed, was not particularly well paid. Bob Parker, the governor I first remember, made many good-natured petitions to the more influential of the local ratepayers for an annual salary more befitting his position. His appeals were met with equally good-natured rejections. Governor Parker took the response in stride, but he never relinquished this quest. Since he could not persuade adult Bramptonians of the real perils from which his office protected them, he sought instead to convince their teenage children. Accordingly, once or twice a year, when the mood struck him and the teenagers were available, he would provide them with stirring accounts of some the jail's most perfidious inhabitants. The teenagers were delighted to be the vessels of this aspect of his campaign and dutifully relayed the told tales to their tax-paying parents. My parents' only criteria regarding the retelling by Ina and Jim was that it be done in my absence. Father declared my ears far too young to hear such accounts.

So it was that one day in late August 1909, less than a month before I began school, my friend Archie McKechnie and I came upon a gaggle of teenagers including my brother Jim and sister Ina, swarming the governor in front of the jail.

"You know what they're doing, don't you?" I asked Archie. "The governor is going to tell them a scary story about one of the jail's inmates."

"I know," said Archie. "Let's listen."

"Oh! I can't," I protested. "Father says that I am too young to hear such stories."

We were silent for a few minutes, but Archie, a year and a half older than me, the son of one of the town's leading lawyers and destined, his parents said, to follow in his father's footsteps, was always thinking of loopholes. He also had the advantage of knowing well the man about whom he would be directing his advantage. Before moving into our house when I was a toddler, the McKechnies were our neighbours. Our two families were well acquainted.

"Did your father ever tell you that you could not play around the jail?" Archie asked.

"No. He's never said that."

"Has your Father ever forbidden you from sitting on the steps of the jail and taking in the sun?"

"No," I replied, quite confidently. "He likes it when I take in the sun."

"Has he ever said you cannot sit in the sun and play ball while other people are having a conversation somewhere else?"

"No, he's never done that either."

"Wouldn't it be fair to say, then," he concluded, "that you are allowed to sit on the jail steps, take in the sun, and roll a ball back and forth between us while other people are having a conversation under the tree on the jail's front lawn?"

It was not the best deductive reasoning, but it was sufficient for a curious six-year-old. We scurried onto the big, concrete steps at the front of the jail where, hidden from the view of the governor and teenagers by the high concrete risers, we silently rolled a ball back and forth as the governor, surrounded by a dozen teenagers, told his scary tale.

"The inmate on whom this tale dwells was no ordinary man. He was a vile, wicked creature who committed heinous crimes. He arrived in these thick walls in 1892, about the same year many of you were born. He arrived at the conclusion of an exhaustive manhunt involving nearly all of the men of this town. When he finally arrived, I placed him in the smallest cell I had, for he deserved no more space that what would hold his hard cot and his small pot. The situation in which he had been caught provided the direct evidence that the courts would require to keep him behind bars for eternity, but there was only circumstantial evidence of the larger crime. The magistrates required a confession to that offense in order to see him hang.

"'Governor,' the magistrates said to me, 'you are a social man. You can make a mute talk. Our plan is to tell the rogue that we have the evidence that will lead to him swinging in the gallows. If he thinks he has nothing to lose, he may just tell you everything. If he does, an extra month's wages will be credited to your account.'

"The fiend was not initially inclined to discuss anything with me, though I tried on a number of occasions to get him to do so. Finally, after about a week, on a night when I proposed to make only a short visit to the cells before joining my wife and others for cards, he called out as I passed his cell.

"'Governor, I am not a stupid man. I know that you want my story. Tarry here. I am in a loquacious mood, and I know not when I will be again.'

"I thought briefly of my wife waiting for me in our rooms, but I knew I had to take this opportunity while I could. 'May I retrieve a chair?' I asked.

"'Not if you want to hear my account tonight,' he replied contemptuously. It was clear that he wanted me to suffer somewhat in the telling. I thought about the extra month's wages I would earn in the endeavour and prepared to withstand some amount of discomfort.

"'Oh, and Governor,' he said, 'not a word from you. This is my testimony, and I will tolerate no interruptions. If you are patient, you will have all the details you require.' And so I prepared to stand and hear his avowal.

* * *

My father arrived in Canada in 1873, a dark-haired thirty-year-old Irishman with no wife, trade, or education. He came to Brampton with a view to becoming a farm hand, but when he arrived his plans were diverted by a recruiter who thought Father's kind manner could be put to use as a groundskeeper within the domestic staff of one of the town's leading gentlemen: Kenneth Gilchrist, Esq., then a member of the local town council and a successful grain merchant and stone quarry owner.

The Gilchrist family resided in a newly constructed Italianate Villa mansion located on the top of a hill on the west side of Main Street, just south of the town centre. Palatial by local standards, the yellow-brick home was known as Alderlea for the stand of alder trees located on the enormous lawn that separated the house from the street below. In addition to the two full floors for the family, the home boasted two large attic spaces for the staff and a square glass cupola above it all, from which all of the town and its surrounds could be viewed. Guests arriving from Main Street drove their carriages around a lengthy circular drive before being deposited at the foot of a myriad of stairs leading to the terrace that surrounded Alderlea above.

Father moved to Alderlea, where he was settled in one of three small rooms reserved for male employees in its north attic. He took up the post of groundskeeper, tending anything outdoors on the estate. A few weeks after arriving, Father was dispatched to the train station to collect the Gilchrists' newest employee, a Scottish seamstress who had been retained to sew new draperies and linens for all the rooms within Alderlea. She was to replace those purchased and installed haphazardly when the house was first constructed. Father was pleased to learn that the object of his quest was the small, pretty seventeen-year-old girl with long brown curly hair who stood silently waiting for someone to collect her.

Carrying her bags, Father entered the south attic female-servant rooms of Alderlea. He returned two weeks later to rearrange the rooms. The seamstress had been assigned two rooms—a large room accessed from the third floor hallway and a smaller room comprised of a dormer accessed from the first room. It was assumed that the smaller room would be used for sleeping and the larger room for sewing, but the light was better in the smaller room, and by having Father arrange the sewing machine at the front under the window and by having him install two narrow cutting tables along the sides of the small front room, she was able to accommodate all of the furniture she required and to obtain good light most of the day. When he next returned to the south attic two months later, it was to make them his home. The Gilchrists were delighted with the marriage of their reliable, gentle groundsperson to their capable, sweet seamstress. Having determined that their septuagenarian butler posed little physical or moral risk to their aging female staff, the female cook and housekeeper were moved to rooms in the north attic with the butler. Father and Mother were permitted the sole occupancy of the south attic.

Within a month, Mother was expectant, and three months later talk turned to whether in her condition she would be able to finish the task for which she had been hired or whether it would be necessary for the Gilchrists to replace her. By that point, Mother had completed all of the window coverings, bedclothes, and other linens for the second floor rooms. She still had before her the massive first floor rooms. Mother would hear nothing of the Gilchrists replacing her. As Mrs. Gilchrist saw the exemplary quality of Mother's work and noticed how much Mother could accomplish even while pregnant, she stopped speaking of replacing her.

Mrs. Gilchrist quite liked Mother and over the course of her pregnancy bought her bolts of cloth from which Mother could sew baby clothes in her free time. Of course there was no free time for Mother, and eventually, seeing this Mrs. Gilchrist made her a proposition. If Mother could complete all of the sewing for which she had been hired two months ahead of schedule—just before the baby came—then Mrs. Gilchrist would pay her the entire contract price at that time. Mother would then have two months to sew for and look after the baby before having to look for another position. This was an attractive offer that Mother readily accepted.

Mother's arms frequently hurt from lifting the heavy velvets and brocades used to make the twelve-foot floor-to-ceiling full-pleated draperies that covered and surrounded the many large first-floor windows. Her right leg throbbed from the repetitive pushing of the treadle. Her back ached from constantly hunching over her growing stomach as she worked at the cutting tables and the sewing machine. Nonetheless, Mother revelled in the days she spent sewing and singing in her sunny room overlooking the bustle of the town below.

As time went on, the beneficiary of all of these endeavours, Mrs. Gilchrist, became concerned. She could see that these efforts were having a detrimental effect on Mother's physical condition, and she worried about the health of the baby. She regretted making the early completion offer and on several occasions tried to vary it. Mother dismissed all such attempts. Her discomforts were minor, she argued, and to be expected during a pregnancy. As for the baby's wellbeing, she offered as evidence the large size of her stomach.

Mother finished the last of the draperies on the ten-month anniversary of her wedding date, and as if on cue, the baby began to make its way from the warm protective cocoon of her womb to our cold, heartless world. Cook, who had relieved many a woman of the burden of her labours, took charge of the delivery. At first everything proceeded normally. Mother was calm in the long minutes between her contractions. She held Father's hand and spoke soothingly to the still *in utero* baby about the wonderful life it would have in this new land, in this beautiful home surrounded by such good people.

With her sweet, soft Scottish lilt, she practically sang out the details of Alderlea and its inhabitants, everything she knew about the town, the county, the province, and the country she and Father had made their own. In an operatic manner, she described the school the child would attend, the church in which it would sing, the streets on which it would play. Father, so besotted with love for her and the baby about to join them, was mesmerized.

Cook, who had at first found the communication charming, realized by the end of the second hour that the labour might be a long one. She urged Mother to preserve her strength and to try to rest between contractions. But Mother would not be swayed. She herself had been brought into the world by the sing-song voice of her mother, and she sought to have her baby similarly welcomed.

Having the time to impart all the things she had not been able to while sewing so feverishly, she described to the baby every detail of its forbearers in Scotland and Ireland. Father sat in the chair beside her bed, holding her hand and listening to her every word as if attending a concert. Her voice stopped only once every five minutes or so while a birthing pain shot through her.

When she had exhausted all of this—and the amount was not inconsiderable, as Mother had a good head for details—and with the pains four minutes a part, Mother moved on to her occupation. Continuing in her sing-song voice, she told the baby everything she knew about the proper way to prepare fabric before laying it out to be cut; the direction in which the nap should run when folded; the difference in sizing of the lining; the size of scissors best for delicate lacy fabrics versus coarser wools; the proper way to thread a sewing machine; and the amount of pressure that should be applied to the treadle by the right leg. Though this surely would have bored any other man, Father was in rapture listening to it, knowing that it helped Mother pass the time as the pains, eventually three minutes apart, dragged on and on.

As the contractions finally moved to a two-minute frequency, Mother sang out biblical passages, psalms, prayers, and then finally hymns. Her voice, as cracked and weak as it was at this point, was still music to Father's ears. Finally, after eighteen hours she stopped, never having succumbed to the earlier entreaties of Cook to rest herself. She stopped because there was, at last, nothing more to be sung and in reality no voice left with which to sing it.

Perhaps realizing that the baby had received all the wisdom it could gain from its mother in this state, it finally took the last part of its voyage, in the end not drawn to her voice, as Mother had desired and predicted, but perhaps in search of it. When the baby's small head finally began to descend, Cook prepared to receive it, but then everything stopped. The baby was stuck. Cook tried to pull out the baby, but the usual methods were to no avail. It was as if the baby's foot was caught on something deeper within Mother. The physician, who had been summoned hours earlier, finally arrived. He checked the position of the baby, Mother's eyes, her pulse, her breathing, and took Father outside the room. Father stood in the hallway until he heard the baby's borning cry. Then he left the house. Having cut Mother open, the doctor found the baby—its foot in an odd direction, stuck just as Cook had said it was.

Mother was buried in the little cemetery next to the Guardian Angels Catholic Church. After the committal, Father closeted himself in my parents' rooms for four days. He spent the entire time in the dormer constituting Mother's little sewing room, seeing and hearing the town as Mother would have: the acres of alder trees spreading out in front of and beside the house, the roofs of the new county courthouse across the road, the Etobicoke Creek running along Main Street, and the stage coach clattering by on its way to far off Orangeville.

Around the room he saw the small bolts of fabric purchased by Mrs. Gilchrist for clothes and linens for the baby: four bolts perfectly stacked on top of one of the cutting tables. On the shelf below that cutting table he could see Mother's sewing accessories all neatly organized: the thread, bobbins, extra needles, scissors and shears, the brass thimble that protected her finger while she did dainty hand sewing, straight pins and cushions and boxes to hold them, ribbon, elastic, and buttons. Nothing lay on top of the other cutting table, but in the two shelves below it were neatly folded piles of fabric echoing the draperies and linens that adorned the house. Mother could not let anything go to waste. Every length of fabric was cut with care to avoid it. Any remnant longer than a foot was saved to be put to some unknown future use. Father did a quick count. There were easily sixty pieces of cloth on the shelves below.

On the fourth day of his reclusion, Father, tired, hungry, and possibly delirious, determined that since Mother would never again enjoy the view from the sewing room, no one else would either. Leaving their rooms for the first time in days, he went to the basement workshop before returning to Mother's sewing room, a hammer and nails in hand. Recalling her instructions to their baby on curtain-making, he gathered a large piece of heavy white lining fabric and a piece of dark velvet. He folded both to produce, once cut, three pieces of each to precisely match the shape of the three windows within the dormer and nailed both layers around the window openings. Before shutting the door for the last time, he dismantled the two gas light bulbs in the fixtures on the back wall of the little room. It was completely dark. The door once shut was nailed to its frame. As long as he occupied these rooms, no one would ever again cross the threshold of Mother's sewing room.

Cook and Mrs. Gilchrist were in the kitchen while Father was attending to these last rites to the memory of his dead wife. They had no idea what he was doing but were heartened to hear his feet on the stairs as he went to and from the basement. They could not hear the hammering noises a full two storeys above them, but the results of his foray into the basement were made evident to all of the inhabitants of the house the next day when they drove up the long driveway to the mansion and saw the solid white blind now covering the gabled windows of the south attic. Investigating further, Mr. and Mrs. Gilchrist soon found the door to the sewing room nailed shut. While they had every right to demand the door be opened and the blinds removed, out of respect to their faithful groundsman and his beloved wife, they did not.

Father knew it was time to see his child. A week had passed since its birth. He did not even know whether it was a boy or a girl. He had no idea where it was. He had not heard it cry since that first lusty bellow shook the hallway while his wife died. He sought out Mr. and Mrs. Gilchrist, who confirmed that the baby was being cared for by a wet nurse. They had identified a couple in the country that was willing to take and raise the baby. Father was shocked by the suggestion. A lengthy exchange of apologies and assurances followed. Father made it clear he would leave the Gilchrists' employ so as not to inconvenience them, if that was their preference. The Gilchrists confirmed their fidelity to their employee and whatever family he desired to maintain. Before finalizing the matter, though, they begged Father to hear all the details.

It was only then that Father learned that he was the father of not one child but two—both boys. The baby that Mother thought was a good size would have been so if the weight she was carrying had been stored in one fetus, but split between two—the babies were in fact quite small. Father considered this briefly. It did not change his decision, although he conceded that perhaps the babies would have to stay longer with the wet nurse than otherwise.

The Gilchrists went on; there was more to be told. The leg of the first-born had indeed been caught on something in the birth canal—the armpit of his younger brother, and the reason it could not be pulled out was due to its long irregular shape. He was club-footed. The feet of the second baby were fine. The divergences did not stop there, although it was some years before they all became known. Cook later summed it up by saying that when the good Lord was handing out body parts, he really only had enough for one full boy—so what he had available had to be split between the two.

My feet, as you can see, Governor, are perfectly well formed, and I can run like the wind. My brother drags his one club foot behind him in his slow and laboured walk. My eyesight is very poor. To put things in focus, I need to be in close proximity. My brother can see perfectly clearly both near and far—at least we think he can. He has never been able to tell us, since in his entire life he has never spoken a word. We discern his meanings through his grunts and hand gestures. My face, as you can see, is of ordinary shape and size. My brother's face is rather square and flat. People who do not know him are often frightened by him.

Of course, not all of this was known to Mr. and Mrs. Gilchrist as they explained to Father the state of the legacy left to him by his dead wife, but enough was known to make most men refuse the offering; to make most men see the wisdom in leaving the boys to someone else's care. But not Father. He agreed that we boys should stay with the wet nurse until we were weaned but no longer.

At the age of fifteen months, we were united with our Father and came to live in Alderlea. The big room in the south attic was fit with two beds. The double bed that had formerly been Mother's and Father's became our bed, and a smaller bed next to it was his. The beds were moved off to the corner so that the main part of the room could be available for my brother and me to play, or later, to read or attend to our schoolwork. Father had not wanted the other inhabitants of Alderlea to be bothered with the sounds of crying children, so in his spare hours waiting for our arrival, he double-lined the already thick walls and floor of our room.

At six years of age it was determined that we would go to school, but after a short stint there, the teachers concluded that my brother would not benefit from public education and should stay at home. After a week of my attendance at school without him, the antics I displayed led the teachers to conclude that they were wrong in their original assessment. They determined that I would not benefit from a public education either. Eventually we developed a routine where Father would teach me lessons in the evening, and my brother and I would repeat them during the day while Father worked. Once I was able to read, we procured books from the Mechanic's Institute library. I spent a good part of the day with my eyes fixed on the pages, reading them aloud to my brother, never knowing whether he was able to glean anything from what I said.

From our youngest days, Father recited to us at bedtime everything Mother had spoken of in the hours of her labour. Night after night, we heard about his family's history and hers, the nursery rhymes, biblical passages, and the hymns that she sang and about how to make draperies. We knew from our earliest days the window coverings and other linens in Alderlea that were made with Mother's hands, and although we were taught to keep our hands off the walls and finery of Alderlea, we regularly rubbed up against, touched, or stuck our face within the lengths of the draperies, taking great joy in touching what she had touched; seeing the fabrics the way she would have seen them. Because she had draped each room, we could feel Mother everywhere in Alderlea. Although there was no picture of her in our quarters, in our minds we never had difficult conjuring the petite, pretty woman with fine features and long, brown curly hair who was our Mother.

Over the years, Father's responsibilities at Alderlea expanded. In addition to tending the grounds, Father also became the unofficial right-hand man to the tradespeople brought into Alderlea to fix the increasing amounts of mechanical equipment, motors, pipes, and wiring within the mansion, the stables, and throughout the property. Father had an uncanny ability to look at a motor or a piece of equipment and immediately know how to touch, prod, push, bind, or oil it to bring from it the utility it was to provide. That ability, however so gained by him, was bestowed on me as well.

By the time we were ten years of age, Father ruled that we boys had had enough book learning and our education should become practical. I accompanied Father on all his mechanical workings, and my brother accompanied him on all his more menial grounds tasks such as shovelling snow, cutting grass, and weeding gardens.

As a result, shortly after we began our vocation, the Gilchrists determined that Father could hold two positions: groundskeeper and household mechanic. I became the under-fixer, as we described Father's second-in-command on the mechanical side, and my brother became the under-gardener. We were not paid a wage for our work, but Father's wages were doubled.

We attended church on a weekly basis, where we sat in the last row, arriving one minute into the service and leaving one minute prior to its end. Father never went to confession. I assumed it was because Father had nothing to confess. He was a God-fearing man who never so much as took the Lord's name in vain. Just after Orangeman's Day in July 1878, when my brother and I were four years old, the little Guardian Angel's Church in which we Catholics worshipped was burned to the ground. Shortly afterward, the congregation purchased from the Presbyterians a building on John Street and began to renovate it to suit our worship style. My father had little to contribute financially to that endeavour, but for the next year he spent two afternoons a week assisting with the construction, making it ready for a proper Catholic Mass, while working three evenings for the Gilchrists in lieu thereof.

Occasionally we would attend one of the many fairs or circuses in Brampton, but the curious glances directed toward my brother made me uncomfortable and sometimes angry. Children would point and stare and in barely concealed whispers urge their siblings or parents to look on at the strange sight of him. Those accompanied by parents would quickly be admonished for pointing, but not until the parents took long, dragging looks at my brother. My anger in those instances seethed, but I contained it within myself. The situation was different, though, when gawking children were not accompanied by their parents. Those children who had forgotten their manners then forgot their decency. They would taunt my brother. That was more than I could tolerate. My anger turned to rage, and on more than one occasion, I attacked the provokers. Eventually my father would pull me off the unsuspecting youth. Father left these scenes apologizing to the villainous young people and chastising me. After four or five similar incidents occurred, it was determined that we should avoid such outings.

We preferred being in Alderlea. We were not without social outlets there. Our meals were taken with the staff. Cook loved to prepare food for us, as, unlike the Gilchrist family who were the prime recipients of her labours, neither my brother nor I were particular eaters. We devoured everything she made, although in her opinion we ate too little. We had no interaction with other children, it is true, but we did not think that we were any worse for it. The five Gilchrist children gave us a wide berth. They were respectful to us when our paths crossed, but except when we were working on the gardens, that was quite rare.

Our interactions with Mr. Gilchrist were also quite infrequent. His life changed considerably in 1875 when my brother and I were just over a year old. At that time, John Coyne, the Conservative Member of Provincial Parliament for the area, died and Mr. Gilchrist was elected to fill the vacancy. From that time on he spent much of his time in Toronto at the legislature. When in Brampton, he was busy attending to his charitable pursuits. Though born to a Catholic mother and originally raised as such, he came to embrace Primitive Methodism, to which he converted before his marriage to the daughter of John Elliott. He also supported other Christian sects and was highly regarded for providing the lands on which the Baptists built their church, for donating the lands on which the Primitive Methodists built theirs and for donating the stone for the new cathedral-like Presbyterian Church. Some say that he did these things just to advance his political career, in order to reassure the Protestant majority of his constituents, but my father never believed that formed any part of his motivations.

Mrs. Gilchrist, on the other hand, always had time for us. She didn't treat us as though we were her children—she had enough of those—but she always treated us as though we were her responsibility, as she considered all of her staff. Clothes, books, and toys that the family no longer required were freely given to us.

Thus, life continued relatively happily for us until our fourteenth year. The event that changed it all was the forthcoming marriage of Mrs. Gilchrist's niece. One Sunday morning, as the staff ate breakfast before church, Mrs. Gilchrist advised us that the wedding service and reception were to be held at Alderlea six months hence. Over a hundred people were expected to be in attendance, and Mrs. Gilchrist determined that the entire house should be redecorated for the occasion. It had been a number of years since the walls had been painted, and they were looking tired and dated. She avoided saying exactly how many years it had been, but we all knew that the number of years corresponded to the age of my brother and me and that the exact date on which the last of the rooms was made over was the day before Mother's demise. It was expected, Mrs. Gilchrist said, that Father and my brother and I would attend to the painting. A local upholstering firm had been retained to recover all of the furniture, which would be attended to on a room-by-room basis over a five-month period.

Similarly, she added, her eyes cast at the floor as she said so, a number of local seamstresses had been hired to replace all of the draperies and linens. The seamstresses would not live in Alderlea as Mother had. Brampton was a much bigger town in 1888 than it had been fourteen years earlier. Several good seamstresses resided in Brampton and conducted their businesses from their own homes. As they would be working concurrently, the work that Mother accomplished through Herculean efforts in twelve months would this time be completed in five. Work would begin in a month's time after the fabrics had been ordered and delivered. We were silent after Mrs. Gilchrist left. Father asked Cook if she would get us boys to church. Without waiting for an answer, he walked to the door and left the house. My brother rose to follow him, but Cook held him back.

Father did not return to Alderlea for three days. In an effort to conceal his absence from Mrs. Gilchrist, my brother and I worked doubly hard during that period, doing all of the work that Father would have done.

The other staff knew how much the draperies meant to us, and for the first day of Father's absence we spoke about nothing other than how we could preserve our only vestiges of Mother. The staff humoured us as we contemplated taking all of the draperies and linens up to our south attic room and keeping them there with us. They gently reminded us that the fabrics were far too voluminous to fit in our little room if we were also to sleep and reside there.

By the second day of Father's absence, my brother and I had settled into the reality that we were—once and for all—to lose our mother, and we began to worry that we were also to lose our father. When he returned the next day, he told us he could not participate in the removal of Mother's draperies. We had to leave Alderlea while the draperies were still hung. Over the next month he would be leaving Alderlea fairly regularly as he looked for a different placement for us. He notified Mrs. Gilchrist of his decision that night.

It did not take Father long to find an alternative situation for us, although it was vastly different from our circumstances at Alderlea. Father had not been able to save any of his wages in the first five years of our lives—every cent had been used to pay for our nurses. But in the subsequent nine years, he had saved considerable amounts. As a result, Father was able to buy a small two-storey building not far from Alderlea. In the first floor of that building it was proposed that we would operate an iron works repair shop in which he would fix stoves, tractors, anything made of iron and, to the extent demanded, motors. We would reside on the second floor. We would be out of Alderlea before the first drapery was parted from its rod, just as Father had desired.

While the thought of leaving Alderlea before that day provided a great deal of relief to my father, I discovered, to my surprise, that it created in me an equal amount of anxiety. The day that Father announced his purchase of the shop, as we called it, I dreamed not of our own business, which truly excited my father, but of the soon to be abandoned drapes. At night

I dreamed of Mother, childlike, labouring over those drapes, her swelling stomach requiring her to bend over it to see the work in the machine. In those dreams she insisted that I stand and watch her work, explaining exactly what she was sewing and why. She said that if I could see this, I wouldn't possibly let her draperies be disposed of like pieces of common trash. "Watch me," she said as she worked away. "Watch me."

The same dream returned a number of nights. I asked Father whether he ever dreamed of Mother. He told me that in the early years after her death he dreamed of her nearly every time he slept. But over time, the dreams came with less frequency. He seemed embarrassed to admit that his mind no longer returned to her in its unconscious state.

It became clear to me that Mother had chosen me as her instrument of communication. Had she entrusted Father to this task, surely she would have found a way into his slumber. I resolved to keep her nocturnal sojourns a secret. As the nights went on, the dreams increased in intensity. I began to awake with a start. Once awake, I could not return to sleep. I became tired through the day, anxiously awaiting the night's relief, only to be deprived of it again as the dream returned more vividly than before. Eventually the dreams took on a nightmarish aspect, and I would wake covered in sweat. It became clear to me that I needed to stay at Alderlea, at least until the draperies had been replaced. Mother clearly was depending on me to ensure that the results of her great efforts were tenderly removed.

Near the end of the third week following Father's announcement of our departure, as he began to pack our few belongings, I sought out Mrs. Gilchrist and learned that while she had filled the groundsman position, she had not filled the fixer position. She would be willing to keep me on for the position if I felt I was up to it. Would I be able to take down Mother's draperies? I said I would, for I had devised a way to meet the desires of both of these women. Mrs. Gilchrist would no longer be burdened by the sight of the old draperies, but in removing them myself, Mother would see that they were carefully handled. I found a space in the back cellars of Alderlea that was dry, dark, and unused. The Gilchrists themselves never descended to those parts of the mansion. Mother's curtains could safely be stowed there for years.

Father was dumbstruck that I was staying behind—even for a short time. He did not know about my dreams, and he concluded that my attachment to those draperies was not as great as his. But at fourteen years of age, I was nearly a man. He knew he could not force me to join him. My brother, once he heard that we were to be parted for the first time in our lives, tried to drag me out of Alderlea. When he realized that I could not be pried, he clung to me as if he wished to stay. Only the combined strength of Father and me was enough to force him out while I stayed behind—in our south attic room with a single bed and my few possessions.

The day after Father and my brother left Alderlea, the redecorating work began. The children's bedrooms were first. Each curtain, blind, and topping flounce was carefully removed and shaken. I ran my hands over each length before folding it in upon itself, repeating the process over and over until a large pile of fabric was assembled in each room: brown-and-orange plaid in one room, pink gingham in another, blue-and-gold stripe in another. Once the stacks were assembled, I carried them down the two flights of stairs at the back of the house, gave each stack a parting embrace, and lodged them carefully in a dark empty corner of the cellar. On my return, the absence of Mother from the rooms was palpable, but I inhaled deeply, stood straight, and began to ready the room to apply the paint. The process repeated itself for the next five months as we moved from area to area within the mansion. The only rooms untouched by the process were the attic rooms.

For a time, my dreams of Mother sewing abated. I took this to mean that she was satisfied with the care I was taking with her work. But at times, particularly when the rooms on which I had been working were complete and I was waiting to begin the next rooms, she returned. I no longer needed to be quiet when she woke me in the night, and I sometimes raised my conscious voice against her. "Mother, I am doing what you asked. Now let me sleep," I would cry. But she would not let me sleep, and by the time we were on to the last of the main floor rooms with its high windows, the dreams returned every night. Like in the earlier dreams, Mother was hunched over the sewing machine, the treadle pulsing up and down, faster and faster and faster. "Watch me," she said. "Watch me."

"I have watched," I cried. Hadn't I done everything I could to preserve her work? What more was there to be done?

"Watch me," she said. "Watch me," as the sewing machine's needle raced at a feverish pace.

One night, a few days after the walls of the parlour had been repainted but the new drapes were not yet installed, I was near delirious from lack of sleep. I sat in my small room trying to think of what else Mother could want from me. "Watch me," she said. "Watch me."

I paced the small room, trying to determine what she wanted. Back and forth, I walked the length of the south attic room, the door to the hallway on one side and the permanently shut door to Mother's sewing room on the other, and then I stopped. The shut door to the sewing room. Permanently shut. I walked to the door and felt its edges. Father had never permitted us to enter the room beyond it. He said that it contained everything the way Mother had left it, and it should never be disturbed. But perhaps Mother wanted it disturbed. My fingers grazed the nails along the frame of the door. With great alacrity, I sped down the back staircases to the basement to retrieve my hammer and a crowbar.

The room was exactly as Father described it. The two cutting tables still stood on each side of the room. The fabrics on the shelves underneath were dusty, but having been sheltered from the sun, I recognized all of the remnants as bolder, sturdier versions of everything I had removed over the past five months. The baby fabrics on top of the one cutting board were lined up neatly on their cardboard bolts. The sewing machine, covered in cobwebs, sat underneath the window. As soon as I saw it, I realized how wrong Father had been to lock up this room. This room was not meant to be a museum. It was meant to be in use. The fabrics were meant to be sewn. The machine was meant to sew. *Watch me. Watch me.* I knew what Mother wanted—she wanted others to use this machine in the way that she had. I set out to find someone.

It took a few days. Then one Sunday afternoon when I was believed to be in my south attic room reading, I snuck out of Alderlea and made my way to Queen Street, where I stood next to a stand of bushes across from the Anglican Christ Church. I watched as families came and went from its doors and continued watching as youngsters returned and then left again without their families. Finally, around four in the afternoon, I saw one girl leave the church unattended. She was just what I required: a young girl, around eight years of age, small-boned with long brown curly hair, just as Father had always described Mother. In one quick motion, I reached out from the bushes, covered her mouth, and grabbed her by the waist. I pulled her into the bush and kept her there until dark. Around 7:30 p.m., people started to file back into the church. A children's concert was to be held. Once the parishioners were inside and singing aloud, I carried the little girl back to Alderlea, took her up the back stairs to the south attic, and deposited her in Mother's sewing room. I placed her wrists and feet in the shackles I had previously soldered to the heavy iron sewing machine and left her with some food, water, and a bucket for her personal needs before I hammered the door shut.

The first week or so was nerve-wracking. Large search parties were organized to find the girl, whose absence only became known when she failed to appear in the Sunday evening children's concert. Her parents had not been concerned when she had not come home for tea between the Sunday afternoon rehearsal and the evening performance, as they assumed the rehearsal had taken longer than expected. Only when the entire concert was complete and she did not once appear in it did they realize something was awry. The girl had been secured in Mother's sewing room for two hours at that point. A feeble effort at locating her was made that evening with the townsmen, but only the next morning at dawn's light did a full search begin. Every able-bodied man in Brampton was called to the task, I among them. On the first day we checked all public spaces including the ravines, parklands and the spaces between buildings.

By the second day, it was determined that the spaces inside the buildings had to be searched as well, first, the business premises and then, though the officials were loath to do it, the local homes. It was a long process. They did not get to Alderlea until the fourth day. Mr. and Mrs. Gilchrist welcomed them to check every room and directed me to escort them. I considered "accidentally" leaving out the two attics, but I feared that could lead to a negative inference, and so they were the last rooms to which we went.

Our inspector was a heavy, older volunteer fire fighter, well known to the Gilchrists. I took him first up the two flights of stairs to the north attic, where of course nothing was amiss, before escorting him back down to the main floor across the house and up the stairs to the south attic. Huffing and puffing, slightly stooped over and tired, he took no notice of the renailed shut door to the sewing room. After one quick look around my small, dark room, he heaved himself down the stairs and went on to the next home on his list. No one ever returned to Alderlea looking for the girl.

Once the investigator had departed Alderlea, I pried open the door again. The girl was in the room, in a lifeless state. The meagre food and water I had left a few days earlier were long gone. I obtained more and by slowly pouring water into her mouth was able to revive her. When I had her back to a reasonable level of strength, I put her to the task for which she was intended: sewing.

At first she claimed a lack of knowledge of the skill. She claimed in fact never to have used a sewing machine. But I knew all about its operations and about the preparations required in order to sew. Mother had told it all the night she died, and Father had repeated it to my brother and me as youngsters as though it was a nursery rhyme. The curly-haired girl was a quick, though unenthusiastic learner, and in a short time, she could sew adequately. And sew she did—every morning and every afternoon. There was no natural light in the room, and so she sewed by gaslight during the day, but I could not have the room lit at night, for fear of it being noticed by a Main Street passerby. So at night she did not toil. On those few days she did not sew, she did not eat. So you see there were very few days that she did not sew. Mostly she sewed drapes, but from time to time I required other things. There were after all several bolts of cloth to be used to make clothes for infants, and so she made those as well. They were not of very good quality—particularly the first renditions, but as I told her, practice would make perfect.

Once all of the fabric had been sewn into one thing or another, I had her unstitch all of it. Then she began again. I occasionally let her fashion a dress for herself out of one of the formerly made curtains. Sometimes she would cry out, but no one but me heard the cries, as the rooms had been thoroughly sound proofed by my father years before. I did not like the sound of her cries, though, and so on the days that she cried, she again did not eat. She soon stopped crying.

From time to time, parties would be formed to search for the girl—or to search for her remains, as it was eventually assumed that she had met her demise in the Etobicoke Creek, but no searches of houses were ever again conducted in her pursuit, and I was never suspected of anything untoward. Cook stopped complaining that I ate too little. As the fixer, rather than the under-fixer, it appeared that I had developed a fuller appetite and was frequently hungry between meals. Cook was only too happy to prepare plates of leftover food from each meal for me to take to my room.

Although I missed her to a certain extent, it was mostly a relief that Mother stopped visiting me at night. I continued to be an excellent employee of the Gilchrists. I saw Father and my brother occasionally—not as much as they would have liked, but I felt I could not leave Alderlea very long, and Father refused to enter it again. He bore the Gilchrists no ill will, but he felt that aspect of his life was behind him.

My situation would have happily continued if I had not made three mistakes. Yes, I made three mistakes, and unfortunately for me, I made them in such quick succession that together they led to my downfall.

Of all the tools of Mother's trade, only two were not made available to the brown-haired girl. The first was the little brass thimble that was to be worn on the index finger to prevent it from being pierced when it pushed a needle through thick fabric. In attempting to show her how to use it one day, I accidentally dropped it. It rolled behind the heavy iron sewing machine and became wedged in a crevice between the wall and the floor. It was difficult to reach and impossible to dislodge. Its loss was of little consequence in my estimation. The second item I consciously removed from the room was the set of large cutting shears. The smaller scissors used to cut thread and remove stitches I left with her, but the large shears were only to be used under my supervision. As a result, she did most of her cutting while I had my afternoon breaks and on Sunday afternoons.

But I got careless, and one afternoon, I forgot to remove the large shears she had been using to recut a set of baby clothes. The scene that greeted me when I opened the door to Mother's room at the end of the day was horrific. I shall never forgive her for so defiling the pretty chamber. The room that had provided Mother with hours of happiness became stained with the blood of that deceitful girl's wrists. I knew I had to remove her before the blood began to seep through to the floor below and before the body began to decompose. I rummaged through the cloth in the little room seeking a piece large enough in which to wrap her, but the fabric in that room had been sewn and cut so many times that none was adequate. Finding the large accumulation of old curtains in the cellar, I retrieved a green-and-gold brocade panel that had framed one of the high parlour windows. After unlocking the girl's shackles, I wrapped her in the drape, and waited for full darkness to fall. It was a cloudy, moonless night and I was confident that no one saw me carry her out of Alderlea, down Main Street, and to the bushes that ran along the Etobicoke Creek. I deliberated removing her from the old curtain, but I knew I would have to dispose of that blood-soaked cover as well, so I left her in it. That was my second mistake. I then spent hours covering her wrapped body with loose sticks, old leaves, and dirt before I washed my hands in the creek and returned to Alderlea.

When I finally lay on my bed, I slept the sleep of the dead. But that was the last night I did so, for the very next night my old nightmares returned. There was Mother again at the sewing machine, slumped over it, her forehead creased in concentration, her right foot pushing the treadle up and down, up and down, faster and faster. Her leg was a piston, and she cried, "Watch me. Watch me." She returned night after night. I was again delirious from sleep deprivation, making terrible mistakes in my work and being generally unpleasant to Cook and the other staff. I knew I had to do something, and I knew what I had to do.

I began to look for another small girl with fine features and long, brown, curly hair. It did not take long to find one near the creek late one afternoon. She was there with friends, but they were a good deal away from her. I held her in the bushes twenty minutes before they realized that she was no longer with them. They assumed that she had gone home, and shortly thereafter, they left. She was feisty, this one, and in my quest to keep her mouth covered, I nearly lost control of the rest of her. Yanking her back to me at one point, her head fell back against a rock. Her unconscious state aided my efforts to keep her silently in those bushes. When darkness descended, I carried her back to Alderlea, staying in the shadows of the big trees and houses that lined Main Street. But that was my third mistake. I took her too soon, you see, for once again a full search was commenced, just as it had been four years earlier, and the next day one of the local men came upon the mound I had made myself only two weeks before.

The events that next took place were well known, long before they were published in the local paper. A dimwitted constable was called to the scene of the uncovered mound, and word quickly spread that the young girl, missing for only a day, had been found dead. Her father was summoned to identify her. Sobbing and shaking, he made his way to the scene only to discover, to his intense shock and incredible relief, that the body which the constable should have known was far too decomposed to be that of the newly missing girl was not his daughter at all. Other townsmen were called upon, and the body was soon identified as the girl who disappeared four years earlier. Dr. Heggie conducted an immediate autopsy. It was learned that the girl had only recently bled to death from injuries inflicted to her left wrist; that her right index finger was completely callused; that the muscle tone on her right leg was like that of an athlete, but her left leg was almost completely atrophied; that her forehead and the skin around her eyes was permanent marked with squint lines. They could not imagine what could have caused these anomalies. But as a result of their discovery of the first missing girl, the constabulary began to consider whether these two disappearances were related.

Searches were again conducted both indoors and out. While the men of the town engaged in that exercise, one clever woman considered the mystery from another angle. For Dr. Heggie, it seems, frequently took his work home—his wife long having realized that if she did not invite him to do so, he would never come home at all. He had cut a swatch of the green-and-gold brocade fabric that covered the dead girl's body. He thought the pattern looked familiar, but he could not place it. It was out of context and such a small sample that it took Mrs. Heggie herself a few hours, but before long she recognized the unique imported French fabric that had hung in the Gilchrists' parlour for fourteen years. Every established family in Brampton had congregated in that parlour two or more times a year. The full-length curtains that bordered each side of the high windows of the room made quite a striking impression.

Soon the Gilchrists were spoken to. Of course they recognized their old fabric but had no idea to where it had been disposed once it had been removed from their parlour years prior. I was called upon to provide an account, but unprepared for such a question, my response was feeble and could not be corroborated by witnesses or by fact, as a three-day forage in the town dump determined. My suggestion that someone may have retrieved the old curtains from the dump before they had had time to be covered was determined to be possible but improbable. A fuller search of Alderlea was conducted. The stack of old drapes in the basement was found first. The girl in the sewing room was found second. She was reunited with her parents, and I was relocated to this cell.

So there you have it, Governor. That is my story. The courts will sentence me to death, and I am willing to take that sentence. It will at least reunite me with Mother, for she is surely in that dark and fiery place to which I will go. Why else would she have haunted me the way she did? Hers was not the work of an angel. How she deceived Father concerning her true nature, I do not know, but I will not disabuse him of his fond memory.

Now I have told you my story, Governor—I have satisfied your curiosity and given you the means of some financial improvement. There is only one thing I would ask of you. I wish to go to the noose with some dignity, to be reunited with Mother in properly sewn clothes. You can see that the entire length of this pant leg is torn at the seam. Could you indulge me with a length of thread, a needle, and a dozen pins?

* * *

"I told him I would consider his request and left him in his small cell. My wife was none too pleased by my late night emergence from the cells, but we made our way to our friend's home, as I knew the crown attorney was to be among the guests. Happy to be removed from the whist table,

I recounted to him as best I could the tale just now visited upon your ears, including the one request he made at the end, to which the Crown Attorney felt I should accede. Without fanfare or ceremony, the requested paraphernalia was delivered to the inmate the next morning. I left him with the morning light steaming into his cell through the thick steel bars of his window far above the head of his straw mattress.

"Returning at noon, I expected to see him shirted, the needle, and thread in his right hand, his torn trousers in his left, both of them held an inch or so from his beady eyes. What I saw was entirely different. His torn pants continued to drape his long legs, but his shirt was removed. He was not sitting on the slim cot but lying on it, his head turned to the side and down, his myopic eyes fixed on the door. Blood streamed from a dozen minor pinpricks to the heart. He had fashioned a new pincushion. A note was left on the wall drawn from the blood of the vile creature. *With this I cease to be the vessel of my mother's evil wishes, but there is another whose bidding she can still command.*"

With that the governor stopped. He had spoken with little interruption for nearly two hours. Only with the tale complete did Archie and I acknowledge the agony within our backs and legs from having sat so long and in such a contorted position on the concrete steps. As the teenagers drew out of their attentive stupor and began to rise and talk, Archie and I quickly snuck to the back of the jail.

Archie and I never spoke with each other about that tale. Indeed, I never spoke about it with anyone. To my talented mother's utter dismay, I refused to learn to sew.

Chapter 7
OFF TO SCHOOL

My first day of school was filled with the feelings experienced by nearly all children on this singular occasion. I glowed in the pride of wearing a new dress made for me by Mother and carrying my first school supplies gathered for me by Grandpa. My emotions soared in the anticipation of meeting my first teacher and plunged with the anxiety of knowing so few of the people with whom I would share her pedagogy. The physical security provided by my father as he accompanied me to the place where I would commence my formal education barely overcame my concern that I had insufficient intelligence to succeed there. In that first fifteen-minute walk to school, I felt all of those sensations common to primary school freshmen and one sensation less common: utter terror. But let me begin with the usual experiences.

We left our house far earlier than required, Father perhaps thinking that I would on this day adopt the tarrying ways of my sister that resulted in their late arrival at the Queen Street Primary School on her first day eight years earlier. As we walked, Father told me what to expect and how I was to behave both in school and on my way to and from it.

We began by walking along Chapel Street toward Queen, passing in the first short block the large homes of our neighbours, nearly all like ours, finished in brick. As I looked anxiously at their front doors for evidence of other departing school children, Father told me that the path we were then on was the course to which I must adhere every time I went to and came home from school. The instruction was particularly important given that I would walk this route four times a day, every school day for the next four years, and I would never again be accompanied by one of my parents as I did so.

There were a number of routes one could take to arrive at my school, which was approximately six blocks and nearly half a mile away from our home. But years earlier, Father determined that the one we were on was the safest in that it did not involve walking over or beside open areas of the creek that ran through the downtown area. As this was Father's edict, in the four years that I attended my little primary school, it never occurred to me to take another route.

We passed the fire station, its morning bells having rung at 7:00 a.m., an hour earlier and then the new Carnegie Library. Father assured me, as we turned the corner onto Queen Street, that my seat in the classroom, located near the front, would be nearby Frances'. In this my father was perfectly correct.

The early morning bustle of the town became more apparent as we moved down Queen Street toward Main. Horses passed us pulling their rattling delivery wagons, their hooves making a familiar clip-clop on the hard dirt street. Awnings over merchants' windows were being unfurled. The sidewalk in front of the Queen's Hotel was being swept. As we walked by the hotel, Father described to me the blackboards on which my teacher would apply her chalk and the notebooks in which I would employ my pencils. Each "scribbler," as the notebooks were known, would be monogrammed with a picture of the world-famous Dale Rose, an export of the renowned Dale Estate, Brampton's pre-eminent horticulturalists. In this too my father was perfectly correct.

As we walked closer to Main Street at the bottom of the hill, passing the Dominion Building and the post office within it on our right, Father advised me of what I would learn in the first term of school: there would be my letters and how to read; there would be numbers and how to count. I would do this not only with children of my own age but also those in forms more senior to mine. I would do so not only with children who lived in Brampton proper but also those who lived outside it and who were brought to Brampton by carriage each day. In this too Father was quite correct. Our twin peaked, red-brick schoolhouse was considered massive for a primary school in that it had not one but two large rooms. The one room housed those in junior and senior first form; the other, those in junior and senior second form. The country children considered this to be quite superior to the one-room country schoolhouses that accommodated children spanning eight or more years.

We crossed Main Street, passing the new Mercantile Bank on the southwest corner, and then the Queen Street Bakery, a place nearly as familiar to me as my own home. Its big glass window stood between us and my Uncle James, its proprietor, just inside and behind the counter. Across the street and down the road a bit stood a building equally familiar, housing on the second floor Father's dental office. Father then told me about Miss Wilson, my soon-to-be teacher, how long she had practiced her profession and how well she was regarded by her students and their parents. He told me that I would come to like her, but in that prediction he was wrong. I immediately adored her.

We walked a further half block and prepared to cross George Street to commence our ascent to the school at the top of the hill two blocks away. At this point, I found myself on somewhat less familiar terrain. The many errands to Queen Street I had made independently or with others to that time had all terminated at Uncle James's bakery or Father's dental office. While I had previously travelled farther along Queen Street, I had done so infrequently and always in the company of others. I had, as a consequence, little regard to my actual surroundings. I knew that the Kelly Iron Works Repair Shop stood beyond the bakery—its state was one that made quite an impression—but until that day I had not considered what was done there and who might toil and reside within its walls.

The shop, on the southwest corner of Queen Street and George Street, was the precursor of the modern garage, its owner the forerunner of the modern mechanic. In the first floor of the two-storey building, farm equipment, carriages, and even lately, automobiles were mended, restored to life or in some cases, dismantled. The building in which these procedures were undertaken was set back from the street, creating the opportunity for a nice lawn or garden to surround both of its street-facing sides. To the chagrin of many Bramptonians, including Father, the spare area facing

George Street was instead devoted to outdoor storage of bent, banged, and rusted versions of the equipment, vehicles, and contrivances being repaired inside the building.

"Travesty," Father said, changing the conversation from Miss Wilson's many attributes. "An abomination. A blight on our streets. How the town fathers can let that man stay in business here I have no idea. A little more time on local planning and a little less time on train schedules—that's what this town needs."

I often failed to understand the politics of which Father spoke, but in this case, it was clear even to me. Between the picked-over engine carcasses and the oil seeping from them onto the street, the George Street-facing side of the Kelly lot was like a vehicle abattoir. It didn't accord with the other enterprises on and around Queen Street.

The Queen Street-facing side of the lot was clear but spare, adorned only with a large wooden stoop. "And that," Father said, looking just beyond the mound of iron and steel still across the road from us and to the stoop at its right, "is the worst abomination of all. That boy should live in an attic, not in the second-floor family quarters of this building!" I was oblivious to the subject of Father's outburst, not being able to see the person of whom he spoke and being distracted at that moment by a red-faced Jim running towards us.

"What in the deuce are you doing here, Jim?" Father asked. The high school attended by my brother was in a different part of town. Jim had left home particularly early that morning to help a teacher erect a sign. The sign was already installed by the time Jim arrived, he said, and so he thought he would join Father and me on my first walk to school. He tugged at one of my long brown ringlets. We recommenced our walk. I felt warm in the company of not only my admired father but also my cherished brother.

The blissful feeling was only briefly enjoyed since within a dozen footsteps we found ourselves directly in front of the wooden stoop that provided customer access to the Kelly Iron Works Repair Shop. In the one corner of the stoop, sitting in an iron chair, sat an odd-looking male of indeterminate age, with a flat, square face, unusually protruding ears, and wispy fair hair. He wore plain black slacks and a plaid shirt. On seeing us, he rose, exposing short, stubby legs, one of which jutted from his hips at an odd, crooked angle. Excited grunts, clearly designed to catch our attention, erupted from his throat. In support of that effort, one of his short thick arms waved wildly in the air above him, and the other waved excitedly at us, his index finger pointing in our direction. It struck me that I was the finger's particular object.

We stopped for just a second, but in that short space of time, all of the words of the governor rushed back to me: the twin brother. How had the governor said he communicated? Through grunts and gesticulations. For what did the father and the second son leave Alderlea? A shop from which to fix things, situated within an easy walking distance from that mansion, conveniently equipped with an apartment on top. Hadn't Father just said that this odd little person lived here, in the building in front of us, and were those not the roofs of Alderlea just to the south? Why would this odd person seek my attention? I looked down at the pretty brown dress Mother had made for me. The white pinafore on top of it formed a contrasting background to the dress below and my long dark brown ringlets atop. Terror seized me. I was glad that Father had imparted so much to me during the prior four blocks of the walk, as I heard not a word either he or Jim uttered as we walked uphill the remaining two.

My first morning as a student proceeded, as Father predicted, with the usual introductory matters. At noon, we town children were excused to return home for our noontime meal. The thought of descending the hill and walking in front of the Kelly Iron Works Repair Shop paralyzed me. I envied the country children as they stayed in their seats, reaching into their bags and pulling out the sandwiches and other victuals their mothers had prepared for them. I briefly considered testing the generosity of my new country acquaintances when I was relieved of the dilemma by Frances. Seeing my failure to join those lining to leave, she took me by the arm and led me toward the door.

"Aren't you afraid to walk in front of the Kelly Iron Works Repair Shop and that scary person on its stoop?" I asked when Frances and I met Archie outside the school. As a junior second former, Archie received his lessons in the room next to ours. I looked particularly meaningfully at Archie.

It took him and Frances a few seconds to realize of whom I was speaking, since, in their view, the character was not scary at all. Apparently he had merely waved to them as they crossed his path that morning. I took no comfort from that, considering Frances's obviously red hair and taking into account Archie's sex. On hearing my experience, they conjectured that he was just excited to see me because I had been the first student to pass him that morning. With several students walking past him, there would be no reason for him to display such enthusiasm. Without any real choice in the matter, the three of us joined the throngs then walking down the hill, with me positioned deliberately between Frances and Archie.

At least ten children walked ahead of us as singles, doubles, or in one case a quartet. As they passed the Kelly Iron Works Repair Shop in front of us, I noticed that none crossed the road to the other side, none ran quickly by that stretch, none tried to hide themselves by walking on the outer edge of the sidewalk next to a bigger student—all actions that I was considering. Some even turned to wave toward the stoop on which I presumed the scary person sat.

I was relieved as we neared the shop that only the usual sounds of the street could be heard. I imagined myself walking normally by the shop, my eyes forward, my elbows locked in those of my two best friends. Indeed, that is how I did walk until the very moment I was in front of the stoop. At that point, the scary man-boy rose, and the grunting and gesticulating of the morning recommenced. Without hesitation, I broke away from Archie and Frances and sprinted along Queen Street, running between and around classmates, bumping no less than two and creating a number of shrieks at least as loud in volume as the sounds emanating from the stoop. I stopped only once I crossed George Street and ran a full half block further to the front window of the Queen Street Bakery.

"You're right!" Frances said when she and Archie finally joined me. "He hates you!"

"Or likes you," Archie said in a knowing way.

"We can't really tell," they agreed in unison, an exchange they uttered frequently thereafter, since Scary Scott, as he came to be known to us, gestured and gesticulated on each occasion when we walked by him.

It was not long before my entire extended family became acquainted with my fear of Scary Scott—though not my underlying reasons for it. At first, I was not believed when I described his antics toward me. Eventually, though, most family members witnessed his behaviour or heard about it from others. His conduct only confirmed Father's opinion that the boy should be locked up in an attic, an opinion I quite frankly shared.

One day at a large family tea, Father declared that he would go to the repair shop and have a stern talk with Mr. Kelly (a spectacle, again I wholeheartedly supported). However, the rest of the family urged calm as they considered the matter. The problem, Mother said, was that we didn't know these people, the Kellys. They did not socialize with our family or any of our acquaintances, and as they were Catholic, we did not church with them either.

Jim offered, somewhat authoritatively, that Mr. Kelly was a widower and that his son was really quite harmless. I turned to Jim with a look of incredulity. How could he say such things? He and Ina had both heard the governor's report. They knew the truth! I expected no sympathy or understanding from Ina. My expectations of Jim were otherwise.

Uncle James, whose bakery was in some proximity to the Kellys' shop, corroborated Jim's report. He noted that the young man seemed only to be outside while the children came and went from school. Watching us clearly gave him pleasure, given the absence of any other useful purpose or occupation. Of course, I knew why he only came out then. He was tracking his prey! His brother, that vile criminal, had, before his death, warned the governor that the source of his evil deeds—the haunting mother—was still at large, and his brother was another vessel for her machinations. My straight-haired cousin Hannah, in response to a question from her mother, reported that in her four years attending my primary school, she had never had any trouble from the boy. Uncle James suggested that I ignore him, and the subject changed.

Thus began the principal challenge of my first year of school. It was not my letters, although I was not initially a very good reader. It was not my penmanship, although at first mine was very poor. It was not spelling or my recollection of history or geography, all of which were reinforced at our dining room table. My chief challenge, four times a day, every single school day, no matter the time of year, no matter the weather, was getting to and from school in such a way that I was never alone while walking along that quarter-of-a-block stretch in front of the Kelly Iron Works Repair Shop.

Each school day morning, I rose early and ate my oatmeal and toast quickly in order that I could be outside my house before either Archie or Frances exited theirs. My noon meal was eaten, to the extent permitted by Father, with similar rapidity. As a result, I rarely found myself alone as I walked to school, even if Archie or Frances was ill or had left for school unusually early. On those occasions, when neither was available to accompany me, I tried to follow close behind another child or group of children whose destination was my primary school. But sometimes even that was not possible. No amount of beseeching or tears would move Father to accompany me to school, and he forbade anyone else in our household to do so. On those days, I walked alone as far as the Queen Street Bakery and then waited outside its glass windows for someone—anyone—walking west on Queen Street, whom I could follow on the last leg of the course.

One late autumn day, after waiting outside the bakery for a length of time that was sure to expose me to the school's tardiness strap, I noticed my Uncle James leave his position behind the counter and begin walking toward the bakery door. Expecting him to shoo me away, I slowly began my solitary walk toward the corner, fearing the loss of my liberty with every step. I had not walked far when I heard the door of the bakery open and close. I assumed that someone had entered it.

A moment later, I realized my mistake. The door had opened to allow for a delivery from the bakery. Uncle James, a loaf of bread under one arm, quickly overtook me. Walking along Queen Street, he crossed George Street and then proceeded up the hill in the direction of the school. Not a word was said or a gesture made as I quickened my step and tagged along behind his big frame. At the top of the hill, Uncle James turned left on Mill Street, and I slipped into the school's door. From that day on, I never had to wait long in front of his bakery before he coincidentally walked out of it with a crusty loaf under one arm to a destination beyond the school, ignoring as he did the grunts and gesticulations directed at his shadow.

Chapter 8
JIM AND EDDIE'S FOLLY

In the year 1910, our small town was populated by 3,200 souls and occupied by over a dozen churches. The places of worship were of various denominations: Presbyterian, Methodist, Catholic, Anglican, Baptist, and Salvation Army. On any given Sunday, each was filled multiple times. One would have thought that with so many devout people all praying for the common good, their reasonable requests would have been met. But alas, when the Lord heard the prayers of the good people of Brampton in the Spring of 1910 (and in every spring since the mid-1850s) He was surely quite confused; for as all of the adults prayed for salvation from a spring flood, their children prayed for just the opposite.

Brampton, like most newly founded settlements in Canada, was located around a waterway. In this regard, Brampton appeared to be particularly blessed, for it had not one but two watercourses within its boundaries: Fletcher's Creek, a tributary of the Credit River, to the one side and the Etobicoke Creek on the other. Neither of these creeks proved to be as resourceful as the Credit River further to the west, but Fletcher's Creek could at least be counted on to maintain a steady and predictable velocity and to keep to a reasonably straight path. The same could not be said for the Etobicoke.

Named for the Mississauguan Wah-do-be-kaung—the place where the alders grow—the thirty-eight-mile Etobicoke Creek was a tributary of no great force. It entered the world somewhat hesitantly through eight or more spider-like streams from a flat plain on the southern edge of Caledon. Possibly because it saw nothing of interest in the first fourteen miles of its southerly procession, the Etobicoke maintained a fairly true course to that point. But once it reached Brampton, it began to meander, narrowly jigging and jogging back and forth across Main Street.

For the most part, the Etobicoke flowed through Brampton as a mere trickle or slow-moving stream. It was a mark of shame to some Bramptonians that one of the few mills the Etobicoke ever powered within the town was the grain processing mill for John Scott's distillery. It did not even constitute a source of food, its habitat proving welcoming for no fleshy fish, the occasional pan fish and trout excepted.

Had the Etobicoke been merely a lazy watercourse, that could have been tolerated, but unfortunately when the creek was not being merely slothful, it was downright destructive. Each spring, ice dams broke north of the town, and water rushed through its banks, flooding the downtown area.

The devastation caused by the Etobicoke was not all the fault of the creek. The pioneers who settled the area must take some responsibility for its conduct. The Brampton they came to was a marshy area full of bog and trees atop a foundation of impermeable Peel plain clay. It was the mission of those early settlers to clear and drain the land, not only eliminating from the creek's banks the very alders for which it was named but also eliminating the marshes capable of absorbing great amounts of water.

The result was that by 1857 there was nothing to store the water that filled the Etobicoke Creek's basin during the spring runoffs or any other time of the year during relentless rains. That year, Brampton experienced its first severe flood when a day and a half of torrential August rains left the town under five feet of water, the planks of its roads and sidewalks upturned, a house tossed on its side, and numerous bridges torn from their foundations.

The resourceful Brampton townspeople coped with the creek's challenges in many ways. Footbridges were built to cross it where necessary, and when they proved insufficient, larger bridges were constructed, broad and sturdy enough to hold both pedestrians and horse-drawn carriages, rising at times five feet or more over the creek's bed. When this proved impractical to maintain, roads were elevated—eventually standing eight feet higher than their first construction.

In the early 1870s, tall conduits were built under the roads and sidewalks, permitting the creek to flow through them. By the time I traversed the streets of Brampton, the creek was entirely buried in the four corners area so that except when flooding, the creek was invisible from the point where it met the east side of Main, just south of the railway tracks, until it re-emerged aboveground across from St. Paul's, the Primitive Methodist Church.

For all its less fortunate features, the Etobicoke was able to provide Bramptonians with some pleasures and uses. In the warmer months, it was a place to swim and sail small hand-made paper or stick boats. In the wintertime its frozen form provided a lengthy skating rink. One time, our family went to a party at a farm outside the town, travelling the entire distance on skates.

Beyond the downtown area, the flood plains around the creek also had their uses. The Northern Flats, as we called the flood plains across from the high school and near the home formerly owned by the Turners, and the Southern Flats, as we called the flood plains just south of our home across from Gage Park, provided places to throw balls and climb trees.

In 1910, none of the children of the town had ever experienced a flood of the magnitude we so eagerly sought. But we had seen pictures of prior floods, and there were always adults willing to expound upon their depth and might. In addition to the August 1857 flood, we heard about the sever flood in September 1873 that left one foot of water in the stores along Main Street and caused $200,000 of damage. We heard about Christmas Day, 1893, when Bramptonians were required to convey themselves and their presents to their holiday dinners by raft as an early break-up of ice sent huge blocks of it hurtling down the waterway, jamming the bridge at Main and Wellington and flooding the downtown with five feet of water. We were all familiar with the story of the local merchants who in a previous flood had floated a flat-bottomed boat down the main street. Complete with a mast, it was named *Admiral Nelson's Flag Ship* after a local politician of the same name.

We wanted to witness a natural disaster that would be talked about for years to come, just as we talked about those that had preceded us. The prospect of missing a few days of school had its attractions as well! We went to school each spring day ever vigilant for the signs of drastically rising water, ever watchful for the signs of oncoming plunder.

As in every other spring, in the spring of 1910, business owners along Main Street inspected the floors of their premises to be sure that all inventory was stored on racks at least one foot off the ground. (None were so foolish as to have a basement.) Town officials filled the sand boxes set up about the downtown area, issued sandbags, and ensured that spades for filling the bags were kept at the ready. Local tradesmen touched up the caulking on store front windows, although it was recognized by all that if the water rose high enough to reach the lower sills of those windows, it would have already breached the gaps beneath and around the front doors.

* * *

On Sunday, April 17, 1910, the day before Jim's eighteenth birthday, it appeared that the prayers of the children were to be answered. The conditions were ripe for it. That year we experienced a greater than average snowfall, a late thaw, and a sudden warming. These factors, combined with the abundance of rain of the preceding day and a half, elevated the creek's watershed by four feet. An ice dam had formed north of the town. When it broke, millions of gallons of water would fill the remaining banks of the creek and spill onto Brampton's streets. From the pulpit that morning, pastors cancelled afternoon and evening services. The men of the congregations were asked to assist with the placing of sandbags around the churches as they departed, and the single young men who were not needed at home were asked to mind the bags over the succeeding twenty-four hours. Jim and his friend Eddie were among the first to volunteer their services at our church. The rest of the congregation was encouraged to proceed directly home and to take what steps were necessary to protect their houses and businesses. Parents were urged to keep young children at home or at least within their sight. Children were commanded to stay away from the creek. Congregants were advised to stay indoors unless sound reason required them to be out.

While in 1910 the priests, pastors, ministers, and other communicators of the Word were generally held in high regard in the town of Brampton, the disparity in the people's treatment of the Lord's commands versus the commands of their earthly spiritual leaders was on that particular day all too evident. Despite their commands, pleas, and implorations, dozens of adults and children milled up and down the banks of the creek waiting for the barrage of melted snow to arrive.

I first witnessed this near irreverent conduct as we left church. Ordinarily our family would have walked home along Main Street. That day, however, Father would not permit us to walk along that street or any other street near the open or above the buried Etobicoke. But as we walked along, always looking for firmer higher ground, we continually passed others walking toward the areas we were avoiding. Noting the stools, umbrellas, and blankets carried by the adults and the toy boats carried by the children, Father scorned the poor judgement of the parents who saw the oncoming cataclysm as a sport. No one, he said loud enough for those passing us to hear, in his family would so callously flout the havoc the flooding creek could wreak.

Finally arriving on Chapel Street, we crossed paths with our cousins, the Darlings, who similarly were taking a less direct route home from their service at St. Paul's. Father complimented his brother-in-law on his wise decision to have his family members exit by the church's side door and thus keep them away from the dangers posed by the front of their church. Father was referring to the fact that the two main sets of doors of that church, accessed by a high, wide stone staircase, fronted on Main Street directly across from the open creek.

"Certainly," Uncle James replied. "Those front steps are a source of danger right now. Rose and the children would have surely tripped and fallen over the dozens of men, women, and children gathered on them to watch the anticipated calamity.

"What time do you expect it to break street level?" Uncle James eventually asked Father.

Father, Grandpa, and Ina had been speculating on that very matter. Earlier that week, Ina had affixed a number of yardsticks along the struts supporting the Wellington Street Bridge. Six times a day she ventured to the creek side of the bridge to record the rising water levels. Based on the rate at which the water had risen over the past thirty hours, and taking into account the warm weather, the rain of the previous day and a half, the additional precipitation she expected, and the amount of water reported to be flooding the fields north of the town, Ina conjectured that the water would reach street level within two hours. Grandpa supported her in that forecast. Father and Uncle James both thought that timing too aggressive but agreed the point would be arrived at before nightfall.

As the meteorological matters were discussed by Ina and the men, the two sisters-in-law rearranged their plans for the remainder of the day. It was quickly determined that the birthday celebration that had been scheduled to take place at our home that evening should be rescheduled, given that the guest of honour would not be in attendance. The extended family would instead congregate throughout the afternoon and evening at the Darlings'. Uncle James needed to be readily accessible to those who might need him, whether in his capacity as mayor or as the chief of the fire department. There was no need to protect our home from the expected flood. Located at the highest point on Wellington Street, there was no real concern for a breach of its walls or floors.

The rest of my afternoon was marked by reports of the rising water levels and the state of readiness of the downtown merchants, and exchanges with the dozens of people who walked by us on their way to watch the coming onslaught. My cousins and I were desperate to go with them—any of them—to see first-hand the swelling waters about which we had heard so much over the years. Unfortunately, our expressed desire to obtain enhanced scientific enlightenment by accompanying Father and Ina as she measured the swelling creek was deemed too dubious, our desire to check the sandbags around my father's and uncle's business establishments too insincere, and the swimming prowess we had demonstrated the prior summer too irrelevant.

Hannah, John, and I were relegated to sitting on three wooden verandah chairs with a set of binoculars between us, taking in what little view could be obtained of the big bridge at the foot of Wellington Street between the

Baptist Church on the north side of the street and the courthouse on the south side. When not parroting the castigating comments of our parents regarding the activities of those foolhardy people so close to the water, we lamented the admonishments that prevented us from joining them. The feeling of great deprivation we shared was assuaged somewhat when Frances and her father joined us on the Darlings' verandah.

Mr. Hudson shared the view of my father that creek-side viewing of the rising water level was not an activity appropriate for children or their parents. But that feeling—where misery loves company—was fleeting as Frances had not long joined me in my chair when Archie and his father approached us. The toy boat in Archie's hand was more than sufficient to convey their proposed destination. Waving enthusiastically, they seemed to know better than to invite us to join them.

The departure from the verandah of Uncle James shortly afterward gave my father and Mr. Hudson an opportunity to take up the age-old Brampton debate. We knew it would come. Whether the annual flood was large or small, the debate always came. The arguments never changed; the proponents and opponents never changed. Fortunately, the friendships did not change either. For as long as the creek had been flooding, the townspeople and their newspaper editors had sought ways to dam or redirect the annual runoff. No shortage of effort had been spared to obtain political support to reroute the creek—or divert it—from the downtown core, but no progress was ever made toward its realization. In 1873, the Legislative Assembly passed an enactment that authorized the village council to change the course of the creek. But the amply supported policy of the provincial legislature was not matched by any similarly supported outlay of provincial funds. The significant cost to complete the diversion would have to be met through local taxes alone.

Thus arose the crux of the debate, replayed undoubtedly hundreds of times that day and over the days that followed. Father was not shy in stating his position that the expenditure and corresponding tax increases were too much to be borne by the local citizenry and likely far in excess of the amounts expended even on a year-over-year basis to address the damage the floods caused. His good friend, Mr. Hudson, who supported the expenditure for the savings Bramptonians would ultimately enjoy, was equally committed to his opinion.

An hour or so later, as the voices of the two men rose above the level of polite conversation, Uncle James reappeared. He had completed his inspection of the fire station and then conducted a similar inspection of the downtown area. He reported that Main Street was clear. As Ina had predicted, the water level was just at the street level. There were no horses or people on Main Street; only an old green carriage sat on the street next to the Dominion Bank. Children were no longer playing near the water. Nearly everyone had moved to higher ground. He guessed that there were a hundred people on the upper lawns of Gage Park, thirty on the higher ground in front of the courthouse, and an equal number on the steps of St. Paul's and in front of the Baptist Church. We could see that there were easily another ten people on the Wellington Street Bridge.

"Oh. And there is one other thing I saw that was a little curious," he said. "On my way to the fire station an hour ago, I saw Jim."

"Jim?" Father asked. "Where did you see him? You didn't go as far as the church, did you?"

"Goodness, no," my uncle replied. Uncle James was a large man. It would have been hard to imagine him being able to do all he had done and also walk as far as Grace Church and back in the hour he had been gone. "No. I saw him on Chapel Street. He was leaving your house carrying a sheet. He seemed to be in quite a rush. I am not sure that he saw me."

Mother and Father had no explanation. We concluded that the clergy had sent all the young men home to retrieve bedding for the night.

"It's likely to be a long night for those poor boys," offered Aunt Rose, who had joined Mother on the verandah. She suggested that a plate of meat and vegetables be delivered to our church after tea that night, if it could safely be conveyed through back wet streets. Jim was not to be deprived of his meal, particularly when he was engaged in such a selfless pursuit.

"What a way to celebrate a birthday," Mother said by way of agreement, "stuck inside a church trying to prevent water damage. They could be shovelling sand all afternoon and evening and bailing the basement. He'll never forget this day, will he?"

Just then a wild roar erupted from Main Street. Minutes later, Father and Ina confirmed that the creek had broken street level. From that point on, they reduced the intervals between measurements. The ice dam north of the town had been breached. Water was pouring into Brampton. The road, the caverns under it, the parks, and likely a good many of the shops along Main Street were being flooded with cold water. The water level, which had risen slowly by inches over the last day and a half, began to rise quickly by feet. Within another hour, the creek was a full foot above street level; within two hours the street was three feet under water.

Most of the pedestrian traffic on Wellington Street had come to an end by that point. People who wanted to see the flood arrive had long since been in position. Some people had started to retreat to their homes, but most, it seemed, wanted to stay to see the water level off. It was surprising, therefore, late in the afternoon to see two young girls walking past us toward the bridge. They were mirror images of each other, being exactly the same height, precisely the same width, and each with the same creamy complexion. Both had big eyes and a wide smile. They wore their hair identically, although the blonde hair of one was tied with a blue ribbon and the brown hair of the other was tied in yellow. There was laughter in their talk and skips in their walk. They were clearly excited about what they were about to see. I knew them both to be good friends of Jim and his friend Eddie.

"Hello, Millie! Hello, Sarah!" I called out as Ina leaned over and swatted my arm. I turned and grimaced at her but looked back toward the road in time for the girls to recognize me and acknowledge my friendly greeting. "We're just on our way to see the big show," one of them said in a voice that cracked as she spoke. "Aren't you going to come?"

I was on the verge of saying that we were not allowed to do so when Ina saved me the mortification. "I've been watching it all afternoon," she said nonchalantly, smoothing her ruffled collar as she spoke. "Just taking a break now. I'll be going back down to see more of it in another fifteen minutes. You go on without me."

Millie and Sarah looked quizzically at Ina and then at each other before resuming their excited progress to what could no longer be called a street.

"Ignoramuses," Ina muttered. "Imagine calling a flood a show. Honestly, I don't see what Jim and Eddie see in those two. And did you hear Sarah's voice? How can they even listen to that?"

Twenty minutes later, though, when Father brought Ina back to us from her monitoring, we learned that the show Millie and Sarah had been referring to was not likely the swelling creek itself but an article starting to float down it. The men concluded that this was something appropriate for us all to see. Father led us to the front of the Baptist Church on the hill above the gushing creek. Approaching the bridge in front of us, bobbing down the water-filled road, was the big green carriage abandoned earlier in the day outside the Dominion Bank. The water was deep enough for the carriage to roll one way and then another without settling on the street below. Father was certain it would get caught on the bridge rather than proceed under it, but Ina expected the force of the water to push it under the bridge and through to the other side. The crowd burst into applause when the carriage performed as Ina predicted before it progressed through to the Southern Flats quicker than if it had travelled behind a team of horses. We wondered if it would make it all the way to Lake Ontario or whether it would get caught on something before that.

To the delight of Ina and myself, our cousins, and Frances, following the disappearance of the green carriage in the Southern Flats no suggestion was made that we return to our positions on the Darling verandah. Main Street was by then a two-lane river lapping the steps of St. Paul's on the east side and spilling into the vacant park land across from the church on the other. In the business section, it ran from the merchants' stores on one side of the street to the merchants' stores on the other. We were finally witnessing a flood like those we had heard so much about.

As the water continued to rise, its velocity also increased. Soon, roaring water was all that could be seen from the Grand Trunk Railway tracks that rose above the street north of the business section—all that could be seen, that is, except for one thing. I peered through the binoculars still looped around my neck to make it out. It was something one wouldn't ordinarily see on a street. I was not the only one who noticed it. Soon everyone was looking north. We assumed the pose we took as we viewed our summer-time parades, which always started from the north and progressed south down Main Street. This was no exception—but for the fact that this parade's float was truly buoyant.

"They'd better not be my students!" Mr. Hudson, the principal of the local high school, repeated over and over.

I might never have suspected them to be students but for the fact that Millie and Sarah appeared to be expecting them. As we stood on the terra firma of the hill's crest looking at the strange spectacle, I noticed Millie and Sarah moving toward the bridge. They gently pushed their way through the crowds, stopping at a midway point, facing north at the centre of the balustrade. Their efforts were too deliberate to be those of mere spectators. Mother had the same premonition and nudged Father, pointing to the girls on the bridge.

"They are all imbeciles, Mary," Father said, "every last one of them, including those two friends of Jim's. Can you imagine standing on that bridge as the waters swirl past its foundations? We'll be fortunate if the bridge lasts the day and doesn't sweep two dozen people away with it."

"I'm sure you are right, Jethro," Mother replied. "What I was referring to, though, was the conduct of Millie and Sarah. They appear to be urging on the boat. I fear that they may be well acquainted with its occupants."

"Don't be ridiculous, Mary," Father began, fully understanding her meaning, but then, not wanting to be wrong, he yanked the binoculars from my neck and lifted them to his face. His look through the device was too long to constitute an absolute denial of the possibility. As the boat came closer, he groaned.

"Is that my sheet serving as a mast?" Mother asked.

"I believe it may be," replied Father with some agitation as he muttered that his eldest child, about to turn eighteen, was not too old for a walloping.

As the vessel approached, its true nature could be discerned. It was not an actual sailboat with a keel but an old rowboat. The mast was more a banner, tied at the top and the bottom of each side to two posts rising from a horizontal bar at the stern. Embossed with the words "Jim and Eddie's Folly," it was clearly for decorative purposes only. There was no wind, and the velocity of the water was all that was required to propel the boat downstream. The two sailors in white shirts and dark pants stood gloriously side-by-side in front of the banner, each with a foot on the gunnel of the boat. They waved to the crowds, which reciprocated with cries urging them on. "Go Eddie! Go Jim!" they called.

Aunt Rose turned innocently to Mother. "I thought they were minding the church?"

"Perhaps the church should have been minding them," Mother offered.

"We did say it was a birthday he would remember," Aunt Rose replied.

"Let's just hope he lives to remember it," Uncle James added seemingly in jest, but shortly I feared it might have been otherwise.

My growing apprehension for their safety was soon caught by the crowds around us. As the boat came closer, it became clear that there was insufficient space to allow the banner and the erect boys to pass underneath the bridge. I envisaged the heads of Jim and Eddie colliding with the concrete base before they were thrown into the cold, fast-moving waters, the posts holding the banner splayed around their unconscious bodies as they were propelled through the swirling waters to Lake Ontario.

My heart leapt to my throat. But as I turned to look more closely at Jim and Eddie, my fears abated. Their eyes were trained on Millie and Sarah, who had by that point cleared the middle portion of the bridge of all other observers. Mother, seeing this too, turned to Father and Mr. Hudson.

"Jethro! Bill!" she cried. "They are going to clasp onto the bridge as the boat goes under it. Go out there and help them!" Mr. Hudson began to run toward the bridge, and Father, after thanking Mother not to tell him something that was so very obvious, followed him. As they rushed to the bridge, the attention of the crowd changed. Their voices, which they had lost when they realized Jim and Eddie's precarious position, were regained. As Father and Mr. Hudson ran, the crowd again started to shout.

"Save him! Save him!" they called.

Him, I wondered. Him? Not them? How could they select which one required saving? Jim and Eddie were both still in the boat. I turned to look at the crowds around me and realized that they were no longer speaking of our boys. They were looking beyond Jim and Eddie. As my eyes followed theirs, I could see why. William Whittaker, a young boy who had been watching the rising flood from the park across from the church left the safety of his family in pursuit of his dog. The dog was swept away in the creek's expanded course, taking him not under the bridge but around it. Within seconds the waters the dog was in would be united with those going under the bridge, after which he would be swept along on the fast course into the Southern Flats and beyond. Little William was right behind him. No one knew what to do for them.

In the seconds my eyes were cast the other way, Father and Mr. Hudson had reached the middle of the bridge, their arms extended over its parapets. Jim and Eddie readied themselves to grasp the north side balustrade.

"Only teenage boys," I heard my Aunt Rose mutter at that moment. "Only teenage boys." Years later I knew what those words meant. Only teenage boys with their incredible upper body strength matched by their equally large sense of infallibility would think they could throw themselves into a situation of such danger and survive. Whether they actually could have accomplished the intended feat we never found out, for a second before they were to grab hold of the bridge, Father, seeing what had just occurred with the dog and the boy, hollered at the boys to lie down and go under the bridge. Being obedient, if not somewhat reckless, they obeyed.

In a matter of seconds, Jim and Eddie went from standing in the boat to lying across its gunnels. The banner snapped off the boat as it collided with the bridge. Using their hands in the icy water to steer them, they quickly caught up to the struggling William and pulled him into the *Folly*. Within seconds the creek's torrents whisked the boat and its three passengers through the Southern Flats and out of our sight.

The day that had been spent largely on our own waiting for the creek to rise ended with Eddie's family, the Whittaker family, and hundreds of onlookers waiting to see whether our three boys would return home. Ninety long minutes later, we had our answer as they were all delivered to us, though one was inconsolable due to the loss of his dog. The upper body strength that Jim and Eddie had intended to use to propel themselves onto the Wellington Street Bridge was applied instead to a low tree branch they took hold of during the *Folly*'s fast course through the Southern Flats. Met by volunteer firefighters, they were wrapped in blankets and through a circuitous route taken home.

It was a spring; was a birthday; it was a flood that none of us would ever forget. For years, I prayed for a reprise.

Chapter 9

JIM'S DIVERSIONS

My brother Jim had many diversions: hockey, lacrosse, cycling, botany, debating, trains, and cars, to name a handful. His interests changed as he aged and matured and as he was exposed to new opportunities and experiences. But whatever his passion at any particular time, it could always be discerned if not from his conversation (and it could *not* always be discerned from his conversation), then from his sketchpad. Jim, like Grandpa, was an avid drawer. His hand as a young man commanded a pencil the same way Grandpa's had at a similar age, using dark outlines and soft shadings to draw not houses and buildings but pucks being shot, balls being captured, trains in motion, cars parked.

When Jim was younger, he was not shy about his drawings. He wore his passions on his sleeves and on the pages of his sketchpad. After an afternoon playing hockey on the frozen creek, one could depend on Jim to recreate the game later that day on manila pages. His adventures climbing trees at the Southern Flats were shown to us in images of large trees and small boys. The fruit or vegetables Mother would turn into his favourite meals were often drawn before they were cut. Whatever interested Jim was fit to be drawn. It was also fit to be displayed. The walls of Jim's room were strewn with his sketches tacked up wherever space could be found. When the space on his walls was insufficient (or when Father required Jim to clear those walls), the drawings were stacked in piles throughout his room.

In his younger days, Jim drew while we gathered in the sitting room before tea or at the dining room table after tea. In the summer, while we sat on the verandah drinking lemonade and reading, Jim sat with us drawing. Unselfconscious, we were welcome to watch him take his first cautious strokes and the definitive corroborating strokes that filled out the page. But as Jim grew older and his passions and interests became more personal, we were no longer welcome to watch him draw. He stopped displaying all of his final works. Some were not produced to us, even at our specific request.

Although I stopped asking to view Jim's drawings, I never stopped actually seeing them. Every few months or so, when Jim was out of the house and no one else was upstairs, I would slip into his bedroom and engage in a private viewing. Jim's room was the smallest bedroom in the house next to the maid's room, but as he had it to himself and as he spent far less time in his single room than Grandpa (the only other single occupant of a bedroom in our house) spent in his, this seemed justifiable.

Jim's room was furnished with a small bed that stood on the far wall across from the door and a single chest of drawers three feet from its foot. His dressing table lined the wall to the right of the door. To the left of the door in a little alcove stood a tall secretary's desk with a large writing table that could be pulled down when the bedroom door was closed. It was on that large writing table that the older Jim came to draw his images. It was on the long shelf across the top that he came to stack his work product.

Through these surreptitious viewings, I saw Jim's passions evolve. I saw his waning interest in hockey and his emerging interest in lacrosse; the decline of his interest in trains and the rise of his interest in cars; the extinction of his curiosity in flora and fauna and the advent of his fascination with faces—not just any faces: female faces. At least I assumed they were female faces. Their early formations were so bereft of features I could not be sure, but a certain amount of hair or hair-like shapes around oval forms lent themselves to a female characterization. The drawings were never complete. For months, the oval drawings were adorned only with eye parts—well-formed brows; long lashes; large pupils. Later, the drawings would include lips and noses. Ears and chins were eventually evident, although rarely on a drawing that included other features.

Eventually, though, the many different facial features began to be combined. More regularly a drawing might include hair, eyebrows, and a chin or hair, a mouth, and a chin. I sensed that the drawings were of a single person, but I could not make out the subject. My curiosity to divine her identity drove me to increasingly illicit viewings of Jim's work. I became more reckless in my incursions. Desperate to see the full face that was emerging, I sometimes went into Jim's room when Grandpa was upstairs in his; I sometimes went into Jim's room when Jim was actually in the house.

One time, I crept into Jim's room while he was in the washroom down the hall. My success in completing such sorties while others were in such close proximity emboldened me to do so more often and to be less careful in the process. Once, in a period where more and more facial features were being combined on Jim's pages, I stole into his room having merely confirmed that Jim was not in Grandpa's room or in Mother and Father's room. Pulling back his door, I reached for the pile of drawings on the top of his desk.

"Hello, Jessie," Jim said, emerging from his shallow closet on the other side of the room. "What are you doing in my room? I don't recall inviting you in here. And what are you reaching for?" I turned toward him, speechless.

"You weren't going to look at my drawings, were you?" he asked, not particularly kindly. When silence continued to be my only reply, he continued. "You know that looking at someone's drawings when not invited to do so is like—like, reading someone's diary or like eavesdropping on a conversation. You know how Father feels about that." I did know, and I flushed with embarrassment about my frequent forays in that area. I backed out of his room nodding, relieved he could not see the heat rising from the back of my neck. It was the first time Jim had ever been cross with me.

I would have remained entirely ignorant of the identity of the female subject of Jim's drawings but for a trip our family took later that summer. No summer in our family was complete without enjoying at least one day at the Forks of the Credit, a large nature conservatory fifteen miles north of Brampton. There, on the Bruce Trail, hills and dales and grasses and trees surround a deep gorge into which the Credit River plunges over the rock faces created by glaciers many millennia ago. As children we never tired of watching the fast-moving water rush over the falls, or swimming in the little lakes nearby, or biking along the many surrounding trails. Our parents preferred the more sedentary activities offered by the park: leisurely walks, sitting in meadows overlooking vistas, and in the case of the men, fly fishing. The adults and children alike enjoyed the big picnic meals that accompanied every such outing.

We travelled to the Forks of the Credit by train along a spur of the Canada Pacific Railway, a second rail line that ran through Brampton, accessed from a station a few blocks away from that of the Grand Trunk. Whereas the Grand Trunk ran through Brampton more or less on an east-west axis, the CPR ran from Meadowvale in the south to Orangeville in the north. Throughout the summer months, the train was filled with people seeking an excursion in the country to the north. On no day was the train more full than on July 1, the Dominion Day celebration of Canada's formation. In 1910, our family party there included not just Grandpa but also Jim's friend Eddie, to whom Mother had extended an invitation the day before.

As we stood on the platform waiting for the train to arrive at the station, we were surrounded by dozens of friends and neighbours. I spotted the entire McKechnie clan not far from us, the Hudsons beyond them, and beyond them still, the Lawsons, including Jim's friend, Sarah Lawson. Millie Dale, her best friend, stood beside her. As the large locomotive came into sight, Jim asked Mother if he and Eddie could sit on the train with Sarah's family. Mother's assent triggered a loud harrumph from Ina, who left us but then returned momentarily to ask if she could sit with the McKechnies. As Ina again walked away, it occurred to me that there was something different about her that day. It took me a moment or two, but then it came to me. Ina's hair was perfectly coiffed. Not one piece of it was out of place. The outfit she wore was pressed and clean.

Later that day, after our sumptuous picnic, the family members dispersed. The men, with their fishing poles, walked to the stream. The women, with their heads well covered, set off to view the wild flowers. The older teenagers went in several directions. After Jim announced that he and Eddie were going in search of Sarah and Mille, Ina, again with a harrumph, moved to join the older McKechnies. Archie McKechnie and his sister Marion came to me, as did Frances. Together with my cousins Hannah and John, we commenced a game of hide-and-seek.

There was no shortage of trees, rocks, dugouts, or other structures in or behind which to hide. The game was highly amusing until after several rounds I became "it," an unenviable position I was determined to hold for only one round. Everyone knew that the fun of the game was in the hiding and the racing to home base before the person who was "it" saw you and beat you to that spot. No one liked the seeking part of the game, least of all me.

The trick, I knew, was to stray no farther from home base—the big oak tree—than was necessary to confirm the sighting of one of the other competitors. As the youngest and the smallest of the players, I had no chance of returning first to home base if I sighted my quarry from a position further from home base than was that person. After leaning my head against the oak's trunk and counting to fifty, I turned my back to the tree and shouted as loudly as I could, "Ready or not, here I come!" But I didn't come. I didn't move very much at all. The strategy I had devised in the many rounds I spent hiding was to use the big oak as the centre point in a clock. I would move ten steps away from it to the twelve o'clock position, look for unusual shapes to tree trunks, movements behind a picnic basket, a raising head above a rock outcropping, the jostling of bushes, or the sound of giggling. If I saw or heard none, I would move to the three o'clock position and repeat the exercise. Only after making my way all around the clock would I move to a twelve o'clock position and take twenty steps from the big oak, where I would again circle the clock and begin the exercise again.

It was at the beginning of my third circumnavigation of the big oak that I caught a flash of blue within the branches of an old willow tree fifty feet ahead of me. Archie was wearing a blue shirt. I starred at the tree, deliberating my next move. The dilemma was the location of the tree. Going to it would require a significant departure from my strategy. The tree was a good seventy feet from the old oak. Moving toward it would leave home base wildly unprotected. If they moved quietly enough, anyone could run into home base from the three, six, or nine o'clock position while I was so far out toward twelve.

I looked around. With no other clues, I had no choice but to pursue the blue shirt in the old willow. The large tree could hold multiple players within its branches. If it held more than Archie, if it held John, Frances, and Archie or Hannah, John and Archie, or if it held all of them and if they were high enough in the tree and if I didn't get too far underneath its canopy, I was confident I could identify at least one of them before they all climbed down. Even with my smaller legs, I could run back to the big oak before the last of them.

But as I walked slowly toward the yellow-green tree, I questioned my judgement. Starring at it, I saw no further patches of blue or any other colour of fabric. The only sound emanating from the tree was a gentle wind-induced swish. I began to wonder if I really had seen anything blue in its foliage. Ten feet away from the first of its drape-like vines, a bloodcurdling sound destroyed the silence. "Home!" my cousin Hannah shouted. I turned and saw her running toward the tree from the nine o'clock position. Frances was within feet of her, coming at it from four o'clock. Archie's sister Marion was running in from three o'clock. She was still a good distance away—as far from the big oak as I was—but she was the tallest among us and had the longest legs. There was no point in racing to the tree to call her out. I was too far away.

My only hope of avoiding a reprise of the "it" role was within the branches of the old willow. If it held both Archie and my cousin John, I stood a decent chance. John was six years older than me, but he was quite short. I turned back to the tree and took two more tentative steps toward it, ready to pivot and run on the first indication of anyone scurrying out of its branches. I quietly took my last few steps, hoping that the canopy that prevented me from seeing Archie within it would provide the same obstacle to his sight of me. Once under the tree's umbrella, I snapped my head back, looked up into the willow's canopy, and hollered, "I see you!" But the blue-shirted Archie I expected to see was not there. The red-shirted John was not there. Looking up into the tree's inner branches, I saw not Archie. I saw not John. But I did see people. Four of them.

It was the blue-shirted Jim who spoke. "I don't think we are who you are looking for, Little One." The truth of that statement was too obvious for words. Backing out of the area, I uttered none. In viewing Jim, Eddie, Millie, and Sarah standing on various branches within the tree, none touching any other, I felt as though I had intruded on the most intimate and private acts. Being caught with my hands on Jim's drawings had not brought me the amount of embarrassment I felt at that moment. Staggering backward, I lost all contemplation of where I was, of who I was with, of the game I was playing, and of the people I sought.

"Home!" Archie and John hollered in unison somewhere beyond me. It all came back. I turned and walked slowly to the old oak. There was no reason to rush. I was once more in the reviled role of "it."

* * *

It was Frances who told me why I felt so awkward; why what I witnessed that day in that tree seemed so forbidden. "They are lovers!" Frances declared at her house the next day.

"Lovers?" I repeated in utter ignorance. "What do you mean?"

"You saw two boys and two girls in a tree, didn't you? That's what teenagers in love do! They climb trees." She was quite authoritative. I marvelled at how worldly Frances was.

"Who was with who?" she demanded. I stared at her blankly, still trying to comprehend why people in love would climb trees. "Which two were on the same branch? Jim and Millie or Jim and Sarah? Eddie and Millie or Eddie and Sarah?"

"I don't know," I confessed in reply. "I am not sure that any of them were on the same branch."

"Well then," she said, somewhat disgusted by my lack of observation, "we have no idea who Jim loves or who Eddie loves."

But on this matter, Frances was not quite correct. I had some idea. Jim loved Millie or Sarah. That was more than I knew before.

* * *

Jim's passions also extended to matters that could not so easily be drawn. One of them was debating. Upon becoming seniors in high school, Jim and Eddie were invited to join the Young Men's Debating Society. The organization held evening suppers and debates on a monthly basis, rotating them through Brampton's many church basements. That July, both the topic and the location caused Father a great deal of consternation, all of which was expressed to Mother, Ina, Grandpa, and me at tea one night, not long after our trip to the Forks of the Credit.

The location of that evening's debate was the newly constructed St. Mary's Catholic Church on John Street, just east of St. Paul's Methodist Church. Father bemoaned any occasion that required the boys to meet in a Catholic place of worship—particularly one with such a small basement. Surely, he conjectured, the basements of any of the Protestant churches would have been more commodious. I wondered if Father really intended to suggest that the club should have met in any Protestant church, even, for example, a certain Protestant church of the Presbyterian persuasion. Before I could dwell further on it, Grandpa diplomatically suggested that given the small size of the debating society, its dozen or so members could likely fit as well in the basement of the Catholic church as any other.

The topic of that evening's debate was temperance—a subject with which we, as good Methodists, were quite familiar. While our church's disapproval of card playing and dancing had eased over the years since Pastor Lawson evangelized on the streets of Toronto, its condemnation of the consumption of alcohol had never waned. For over thirty years, the Methodist church had been pressuring federal and provincial governments to prohibit the sale and manufacture of alcohol. The Methodists were joined in those efforts by many other churches and groups, including prominent business associations that valued a sober and responsible workforce. Although their efforts for legislated change had not yet met success, the consumption of alcohol was clearly on the decline.

The timing of the debate was quite auspicious, as earlier that day, Mother had hosted the monthly meeting of the local Women's Christian Temperance Union. Mother was a dutiful, if fairly passive member of that society. Though she would no more think of holding a bullhorn to her lips to decry the evils of alcohol than she would think of wearing a pair of trousers, she would provide a meeting place for both the subdued and strident members of the local WCTU. She would not make deputations to the mayor, the local Member of Parliament or the local Member of the Legislature on the benefits of temperance, but she would address and seal envelopes enclosing letters written by others on that subject. She would not hold an elected position within the local union, but she would bake goods for their occasional fundraising efforts. Her restrained nature would not permit her to do more, but her devotion to her community propelled her to do at least that much.

That day, fifteen women had gathered at our house to discuss local temperance activities. Voluntary temperance measures had been well adopted in Brampton at that time. It was clearly understood that no good Methodist family would serve alcohol within its home. But as Frances and I cleared away the tea things toward the end of the meeting, it was revealed that some WCTU members suspected that some of our good Brampton men were imbibing alcohol elsewhere.

"And what I have noticed, ladies," I heard Mother's guest Mrs. Handle say, "is a growing number of curlers in our community. Now, far be it from me to suggest that our menfolk are not sportsmen at heart, but I have never previously seen such athleticism in so many of them. The curling club now boasts a full membership and a waiting list of thirty more. It is opened earlier each fall and remains open later each spring, even, as I understand it, when there are no rinks of ice available. I don't like to besmirch the reputations of our husbands, fathers, brothers, and sons, who would not step foot in a tavern, but I fear that their interest in this pasttime is designed to provide them with a location in which they can secretly consume alcohol." As Frances and I cleared away the cups, a chorus of "no" and "oh my" sprang from the parlour.

* * *

"Why the deuce would anyone need to debate whether 'prohibition is a necessary condition for a good Christian life'?" Father asked, somewhat rhetorically, as we continued consuming our evening meal. He didn't expect anyone to provide a meaningful reply. "The case is so settled. What good Christian would possibly take the other side?"

"I certainly expect that Jim will not!" Mother said, clearly in agreement with Father.

"He may well," Grandpa said, "and it will be all the better for him to do so." Mother looked at him askance. "It isn't what you think, Mary." I suspected that Grandpa's decision to address his remarks to Mother rather than Father was quite deliberate. "These debating societies are designed to teach young men good reasoning and public speaking skills. One becomes most proficient in these areas by arguing a view contrary to one's own. What a wonderful experience it is."

Not waiting for Mother to reply, Father conceded that doing so would require quick wit, and Jim in his estimation was well endowed in that department. "Now that Eddie," Father went on, referring to Jim's best friend, "I can't see how he'd be able to argue a side opposite to his own. He's just not intelligent enough. He's a nice boy, but I wasn't surprised he did not receive an offer to attend the university with Jim." We all knew that Eddie had decided to join his family's business in the utilities sector and had not even applied to attend university. "In fact," Father said, "I think that Jim has rather outgrown Eddie's friendship. It will be highly beneficial to Jim when he moves to Toronto in September and makes new friends there."

With that remark, Ina declared the onset of a headache. She immediately retired. When I entered our room three hours later, I was glad to see her sound asleep, a state in which I soon joined her. In it I would have stayed until morning but for the sounds well after midnight of loud knocking, a door being pushed open, and a man's call for help. Bolting upright in bed, my heart racing, I asked aloud whose voice was calling for help.

"I think its Eddie's," Ina said. Throwing off the covers, she raised herself, reached for her robe on the floor, and made to run into the hall, but before doing so she stopped, turned on the gas light, looked in the mirror beside the door, and pushed back her hair. Then, leaving the gas burning, she ran out the room and down the stairs.

Within minutes we were all in the kitchen, Father and Grandpa lifting a bloodied, unconscious Jim onto a chair. Mother was riffling through a drawer looking for smelling salts. Ina was running cloths under the tap. I looked at the clock. It was 2:00 a.m. I stood in horror as I watched and listened to Eddie's explanation.

"The debate ended around one thirty. Jim and I were among the last to leave St. Mary's. We stayed to get more details about the next debate from Mr. Nicol and Mr. Griffin, the organizers. Little Charles Kennedy— you know, he's so small, he hardly looks like he graduated from primary school, let alone high school—he left just a few minutes before us. At about a quarter to two, Jim and I left the building by the back stairs. It seems that some drunken thugs were looking for someone to pick on—which as I think of it is a bit ironic given the subject of the debate—"

Father gave Eddie a fierce stare, and he returned to his explanation. "Well, seeing Charles leave alone, they chose him. Started calling him a cat licker, I guess—which of course he isn't—I mean he isn't a cat licker or a Catholic. When Jim and I came out, they had Charles on the ground and were kicking him. We yelled at them to stop—we didn't even know who they were going after at that point, but they wouldn't stop. So we went up to start pulling them off and saw that it was Charles. I took the two smaller louts on the left and Jim went after the one big one at the other side."

I don't think any of us were surprised to hear that Eddie took on two people at once. Over six feet tall, Eddie was a few inches taller than Jim and about half a foot thicker. He had a full head of thick dark brown hair on a large head around his square face. "Between the two of us, we got rid of all of them but one. That last one, before he ran off with his mates, turned and slugged Jim so hard, it knocked him over. When he fell he banged his head. That was when Mr. Griffin and Mr. Nicol came out of the church. Mr. Griffin stayed with Charles, while Mr. Nicol went to get help. I brought Jim back here." Our house was a block and a half from the Catholic church.

The smelling salts had the desired effect, and Jim was starting to rouse. Only as he did so did I get a full look at him and Eddie. Eddie was bleeding too, but not as badly as Jim. Eddie's hands were swollen, and his shirt was torn. There was a long scratch along his neck. I could see blood on Jim's hands and arms. His jaw was already starting to swell, and I could see a deep gash on his earlobe. A quick discussion occurred as to whether Dr. Heggie's presence was required. Jim was fully conscious by then, and after everyone else's views were expressed, he weighed in with his own. There was no need to wake Dr. Heggie. Jim was sore, but he would see the doctor the next day, if required. Eddie helped Jim upstairs to his room and onto his bed.

Mother offered Eddie the use of the long-vacant maid's room for the remainder of the night, but Eddie feared his absence would alarm his parents. He was sure the constables would be out, and the hoodlums would either be occupying a cell at the jail down the street or long out of town. Father and Mother concurred but insisted on walking him home. The sight of the large, sturdy Eddie accompanied by my much shorter parents did not cause great confidence in the protection they could afford, but I appeared to be the only one concerned about the risk. Taking Mother aside, I begged her to stay at home and let Father alone accompany Eddie. I had no more success with that request than with a similar request made years earlier when my parents walked into a storm to find Ina. Mother left with Father and Eddie, admonishing me to follow Ina and Grandpa and return upstairs to my bed.

As I reached the top of the staircase, I realized that Grandpa had not returned directly to his own room at the end of the hall but had gone into Jim's. He and Grandpa were in conversation. I stood on the second highest step and listened.

"You had to intervene, did you?" Grandpa asked in a way that was kind and caring as well as slightly critical. "You couldn't just have gone and gotten help?"

"No more than you could have, old man," Jim replied weakly, referring to Grandpa in the pet name he alone used when speaking to his beloved grandfather. "I learned my lessons from the master."

"You don't need to follow all of my examples, my boy," Grandpa said, calling Jim by the pet name he alone used when speaking to his beloved grandson. I was puzzled. What lesson had Jim learned from Grandpa?

In what fight had Grandpa intervened? Focussing on those questions, I failed to hear Grandpa's footsteps as they padded across Jim's wooden floor toward the doorway and the hallway beyond. I nearly fell down the stairs in my effort to avoid his collision into me.

"Jessie!" he said, clearly startled as he reached for my arm to steady me. "I'm so sorry. I didn't see you coming up the stairs." My lack of reply apparently revealed my true prior position. "Or were you standing here. Jessie, you weren't eavesdropping, were you?"

"No, Grandpa!" I declared. Having committed that offence so many times, I was used to lying about it. "I was just coming to see if Jim needed any help."

"Jim just needs some sleep. You can leave him be. But here, if you'd like to do something, take this shirt downstairs and put it in the sink. It will need to soak overnight if that bloodstain is to come out."

In the kitchen, I filled the basin with water and was about to plunge Jim's shirt into it when I noticed a large piece of paper in its pocket. It was the program for the evening's debate. Looking at it, I could see that Jim had not paid quite as much attention to the debate as Father may have thought. It was covered in drawings—many drawings. One appeared to be a liquor bottle. That at least was on topic. Quite a number were of cars. But one, just one, was of a face; a familiar female face. This face differed, though, from the dozens of others I had seen. This face had all of its parts. The eyes, the ears, the chin, the cheeks, the lips, and the hair. This face was perfectly discernable.

Settling into my bed a few minutes later, I took stock of what I knew and didn't know. I didn't know why my family could not enter the Presbyterian Church. I didn't know how Grandpa became self-made and others-destroyed. I didn't know the meaning of the Scottish Fiasco. But I knew that Jim loved Millie Dale. I didn't know if she reciprocated those feelings. I had solved one mystery and added another to my list.

Ina's mind was active at that time, too, though not, it seemed, in the contemplation of family mysteries. "I guess Father won't think that Eddie is such a bad friend to Jim now, will he?" She rolled over, and we both went to sleep.

Chapter 10

THE PHOTOGRAPH

My childhood was significantly affected by two promises made by my two uncles, though the impact was mostly in the keeping of one and the breaking of the other. One of Uncle William's promises to his wife as they prepared to leave the town in which they were born and raised and in which their sons had been born and nearly raised was that the family would return to Brampton for a month-long visit each summer. My Uncle William made the covenant, and each summer, my aunt and uncle and my cousins Roy and Bill made the 1,300-mile trip from Winnipeg to Brampton.

Eventually, once Roy and Bill became more settled in Winnipeg and with the onset of that Great War that changed our lives in so many ways, my aunt released her husband from that undertaking, and their visits to Brampton became less regular. For the formative years of my childhood, however, the arrival of summer holidays almost always coincided with the arrival in Brampton of the Turners. The tall, handsome, stylish family driving up Wellington Street in the latest automobile heralded upcoming picnics at the Forks of the Credit, swimming at Snell's Lake, Dominion Day fireworks at Thauburn's, tennis and croquet matches on the Darlings' lawn, Orange Day parades, and lengthy visits with neighbours near and far who sought to share a portion of the time we had each year with our family from the West.

The Turners always arrived by car, having made their way from Winnipeg on a combination of railways and roadways. Arriving in Brampton, they would drive directly to the Darlings', where the fashionable automobile would be parked on the Darlings' long driveway or in their new "garage." Our aunt, uncle, and cousins were barely greeted before Jim and John were in the driveway marvelling at the automobile, asking my uncle about its every feature and pleading for turns to ride in or drive it.

The luggage, of which there was always plenty, was then sorted and deposited in part at the Darlings' house and in part at our house. Each family received the boys for two weeks and the parents for two weeks. Breakfasts were taken by the Turners with the family then hosting them, but all other meals were taken by all of us together at our home or the Darlings', unless the Turners had made other arrangements for the day. I was wild about having my older cousins with us, enjoyed having my aunt at our house, and was indifferent to my uncle's presence. You learn a lot about people when you live with them for a month a year. I can confidently say that I grew up knowing my cousins, Roy and Bill, and their parents almost as well as if they had continued to live in the old Stephens house near the Presbyterian Church.

The summer of 1910 was the only year in which the beginning of my summer holidays did not coincide with the arrival of the Turners. Their delay by one month, announced just a week before July 1, threw Aunt Rose into a genuine state. Ever since the day that Uncle William announced the move of his family to Winnipeg, Aunt Rose had sought a commemoration to our extended family in the form of a photograph. The speed with which the Turners initially vacated Brampton denied them the time to pose for it and Aunt Rose the time to organize it.

With no similar excuses to prevent the pursuit during the Turners' first month-long visit in July 1908, the photography session was booked, but heavy grey water-filled clouds and intermittent expulsions from them prevented the taking of the picture on the appointed date at the appointed outdoor location. While the photographer and his assistant were willing to return the next day if the weather improved, my Aunt Lil was not. Some pressing matter of business, which she could not summon to mind, required her to quit Brampton that night and prohibited her return the next day. The same objective scheduled in July 1909 was cancelled when the photographer became ill.

By the summer of 1910, Aunt Rose was more committed to the photograph than ever. In mid-January she called A.E. McCollum, the local photographer, and arranged for his services for the second Saturday of July. Not wanting to take any chances with her sister Lil—or wanting to take the least chances possible with her sister Lil—Aunt Rose provided the full six months' notice to her as well. With more reasonable notice, she arranged for the attendance of the remaining members of the family. At the same time, Aunt Rose dispensed edicts concerning conduct and attire.

Mr. McCollum advised her in January that the sepia-coloured photograph would look best if everyone dressed in solid colours—preferably white, tan, or black. Aunt Rose wanted the family to look natural. Also, she did not want people perspiring as the photograph was being taken. They might have to stand for up to an hour in the hot summer sun. Accordingly, the wardrobe edict issued by letter in early June called for everyone to wear white shirts or dresses with tan or black slacks, skirts, or jackets; none too formal.

The timing edict was equally precise. Children and mothers were to be at her house by twelve thirty at the latest, fed and properly attired. Aunt Lil was to take the 11:53 train into Brampton. Even accounting for its frequent delays, she would easily arrive at the house by one o'clock, the same time the fathers were expected to appear. Everyone would be at the right location, in the right wear, a full hour before the picture was to be taken. If the weather did not cooperate, this would also provide ample time to move furniture in the parlour. The picture could be taken there, if necessary.

By the third Saturday in June, when Aunt Rose was confident nothing could go awry, she received a telegram that reminded her of the famous saying about the best-laid plans. The short communication advised her that the Turners' annual visit had to be postponed. Uncle William's work schedule would not allow him to leave Winnipeg until the end of July. That year, the family would be spending the month of August, rather than the month of July, in Brampton. Charlotte asked her sister Rose to reschedule the many arrangements and appointments that had been made for the month of July, the list of which was on its way to her by mail. Before alerting her husband to the change in plans, before alerting her brother to the change, or even Uncle William's brother, Aunt Rose called upon two people. The first was Mr. McCollum in his Main Street North offices. The second was Mother in our kitchen. I was with Mother when Aunt Rose arrived. I heard her explain the changed itinerary. I heard her report on her conversation with Mr. McCollum. I heard her pronounce the impossibility of his attendance at any time in the month of August.

"Impossible?" Mother asked. "There is not a single hour on a single day in the entire month that he can make himself available? No one in Brampton is in that much demand—not even Mr. McCollum, as good a photographer as he is."

"I agree," Aunt Rose said. "I don't think he is that busy. I think he just doesn't want people to know that he could be available on such short notice. He was quite put out with me, angry even. He didn't even look at his schedule. He just declared the amount of notice to be too short and waved me out with the back of his hand. I've never been treated so badly."

"Might there be another photographer we could use?" Mother asked. "Given the way he treated you, I'd really rather not patronize his business."

"I thought of that and even asked Mr. McCollum about it. He told me that there won't be a photographer worth his salt that is available in the month of August at this late date. And besides, he really is the best. I would like to use him."

"Let's put it off until next year then," Mother suggested. "You've waited this long."

"No!" Aunt Rose cried. "It can't wait until next year. It can't!" My normally calm, cool, collected aunt was nearly hysterical.

"Well, we'll have to think about how it can be done," Mother said quite practically. "In the meantime, do you not think we should let Jethro and James know about the delay? If you've told Mr. McCollum, the news is likely to get around town. It would be best if the men didn't hear about it from their customers and patients."

"Of course. You are right," Aunt Rose acknowledged, rising and pulling a handkerchief from her sleeve before dabbing it to her eyes. I had never seen moisture emitted from those steely eyes. I sensed it was a new sight for Mother too.

"Oh dear, Rose. Sit back down. Let's have a cup of tea. We will find a way to make this work." Mother moved to the nearby desk and extracted two pieces of paper and a pencil from the top drawer. Hastily jotting a note on each, she turned to me. "Jessie, please deliver these right away, one to your uncle at the bakery, the other to your father at his office." She was reaching for the kettle as she shooed me on my way.

I walked the route I took to school, along Chapel and then west on Queen, comfortable in the streets that were so well known to me, relieved that my errands would not require me to pass the Kelly Iron Works Repair Shop. I resolved to go first to my father's office. There was a good chance that my uncle would give me a loaf of bread. It would be better if I proceeded directly home while carrying it. By force of habit, I walked down Queen Street on the south side of the road—the side on which the bakery and my school were located. Father's office was on the north side across from the bakery.

Arriving at the bakery, I was about to cross the road when a loud bang stopped me in my tracks. My heart leapt to my throat. Something big had fallen. It sounded as though it had come from behind the bakery. I waited for the echoing sound of pain: a scream, a cry, a moan. I knew that a small pain could lead to the immediate emission of a cuss word, an epithet or simply the cry "ouch." I was not likely to hear any of those responses from my position in front of the bakery. The response to serious pain took moments to gather before being loudly expelled. I might hear that. My worry was short-lived, however, as moments after hearing the crashing sound, it was loud gales of laughter that emanated from behind the bakery.

I turned into the alley between the Darling Block, in which the bakery was situated, and the building block to the west of it. Behind the bakery, before the chasm that allowed the Etobicoke to flow out from under the four corners' businesses and into the street level park, was the Queen Street Bakery's flour house, the little house in which supplies were stored and the days' bread, pies, and cakes were baked. On that particular day, just outside the flour house I saw two things I had never before seen. The first was a big roly-poly snowman, which in a moment I recognized to be my Uncle James, covered from head to foot in flour. The second was the source of the laughter. There was no one else with him in the flour house. The person whose laughter was so loud that I heard it on the other side of the bakery was my uncle. In my seven years, I had barely seen the man smile. I was sure I had never before seen him laugh.

"Uncle James," I said, running toward him, "are you alright?"

"Jessie," he said, seeing me, still laughing, bursts of flour falling off his head and face with each convulsion. A glue-like substance was forming below his eyes. "Can you believe this? I was lifting a sack of flour down from the rafters just inside the flour house. I lost my grip. The bag fell, hit another rafter on the way down broke open, and well … you can see what happened." I think he would have continued laughing, but in providing the explanation he inhaled some of the powder and began to cough.

I ran to pat him on the back. The effort was not particularly helpful. My extended hand barely reached the mid-point of his large back. My uncle continued to cough while a flood of flour cascaded on me. Soon we were both laughing and covered in the white particles. After a long while, our levity subsided, and I helped him sweep up the fallen flour. Being closer to the ground, he suggested that I hold the dustpan as he swept into it the mounds we had constructed.

We passed a happy thirty minutes cleaning up the spilled flour. Covered in it, I somehow ceased to be the shy seven-year-old I was when with him, and he ceased to be the dour uncle he was with me. He expressed some real interest in my schoolwork and other pursuits, and I expressed some real interest in his bakery. Only once the last of the flour was swept off the flour and we'd each taken a suit brush to our clothes did our conversation tend to where it would have if the flour bag had not broken open on the rafters. I extracted from my pocket one of the notes that Mother had written, particles of flour seeping out of its folds, and then went on to deliver a similar note to Father. It was nearly noon. With the notes in hand, the two men were apprised of the delay just a bit earlier than they would have been had they simply been informed during their noon-time meal.

It was my father who got the photography session rearranged, via an exchange of which Father frequently regaled us. Mr. McCollum was a patient of Father's. He appeared in Father's office the first week of July in excruciating pain with an infection in the root of one of his molars. He required immediate attention, which Father explained he was unable to provide. "Perhaps next month," he offered. "No dentist worth his salt would be available to take a patient with so little notice."

"But you always see people when they need your services!" Mr. McCollum cried.

"So I do," Father replied. Mr. McCollum's tooth was pulled that afternoon. The appointment for the family photograph was booked immediately thereafter.

The actual day of the photograph was not without incident either. While my cousins and our mothers were assembled at Aunt Rose's home in their proper attire more than two hours before Mr. McCollum arrived, the intervening period was anything but idle.

My brother Jim, who, though the second oldest cousin of the generation, was considered to be the most responsible, was found in his picture-taking clothes on the Darlings' driveway under the hood of Uncle William's new car, a can of oil in his hands. When Mother discovered him there, she so startled him, he dropped the can. He managed to catch it before it landed, but in doing so, he caused the contents to spill all over his hands, shirt, and slacks. He was able to find another set of clothes to wear, but they were not as picture-perfect as the first, and though he scrubbed his hands thoroughly, to Mother's disgust he could not entirely remove from them the oil stains.

While Mother was in the driveway with Jim, my Aunt Charlotte was breaking up an impromptu wrestling match among my cousins Roy, Bill, and John in the middle of Aunt Rose's sitting room. After they had been physically restrained, Roy continued the spar with his brother on an oral level. "Maybe we should put this photograph off another year," Roy said as at his mother's command he began to unroll his white sleeves. "Maybe by then Bill will be old enough to wear long pants for the picture."

"Wear pants! What do you think I'm wearing?" Bill, who was two years younger than Roy, shouted in reply. He moved his hands from his head, where he was trying to straighten his hair, and pointed to the grey full-length trousers hanging from his hips.

"Calm down, Bill," Aunt Charlotte said, rebuking him. "Roy's just trying to get your goat. And you are serving it to him on a platter."

Aunt Rose appeared not to see the humour either. "No" she said, "we've put this off long enough! I'm afraid that if we wait any longer—" I thought she was going to say something dire. Instead, after a moment's hesitation, she joined in the fun. "I'm afraid that if we wait any longer, even my John will be out of short pants."

"Mother," her thirteen-year-old son exclaimed. "Look at me! I'm wearing long pants too!"

The jibes about the attire did not end with the length of the boys' pants. My cousin Hannah was most upset about the back hair bow her mother insisted she wear. It was attached to a knot at the back of her head, from which it stretched halfway to her shoulders. Hannah claimed she resembled a bat.

Aunt Charlotte tried to reassure her. "Honestly Hannah," she said, "big bows like that are all the style in Winnipeg."

Hannah muttered that she had never heard of Winnipeg as being a fashion capital. When Ina reproved her for her impertinence to Aunt Charlotte, Hannah countered by telling Ina that with the big piece of white taffeta wrapped around the knot on the top of her head, she looked like an angel. For good measure, she spat that the big white bow similarly placed in my hair gave me the appearance of a rabbit. Neither observation was meant as a compliment.

Aunt Rose considered sending the eleven-year-old Hannah to her room, but thinking that that could lead to tear-induced bloodshot eyes, Hannah was instead banished to the side yard, where she was instructed to take down and put away the tennis net and rackets in order to make room for the family pose. Hannah left us willingly, but not happily. As a means of sharing her ill humour, she asked loudly and to no one in particular where on earth Aunt Lil was.

It was a good question and one sure to get her mother's ire. Unpredictability was perhaps the strongest suit in Aunt Lil's deck of eccentricities. From her long-time employment with the Toronto District School Board, one can assume that she reported to her classroom as a teacher on a regular and punctual basis. The same cannot be said for any other occasion. A reply to an invitation issued to my Aunt Lil—no matter how formal, no matter from whom it had been extended or for what type of occasion—could never be relied on. She was as likely not to appear at a function she committed to attend as to actually appear at a function she had declined.

The result was that Aunt Lil's appearance at any affair always aroused expressions of surprised delight and warm embraces. Generally being the last to arrive, I am not sure she was aware that other guests were not similarly welcomed. She was oblivious to the consternation and disapproving head-shaking of the adults or the sighs of disappointment of the children at those functions to which she had said she would attend, but did not. That Saturday in August was no exception. We were all hopeful but not confident she would arrive.

Aunt Rose, Mother, and Charlotte looked at their watches. It was 12:20. Aunt Lil was to have arrived in Brampton on the 11:53 train. It was a nearly fifteen-minute walk from the Grand Trunk station to the Darling house. The fact that she was not then with us was no any indication that she would not eventually be. The promptness of the Toronto train was only slightly more reliable than Aunt Lil.

"Did anyone hear the 11:53 come through?" Aunt Rose asked. The Grand Trunk Railway tracks ran through Brampton on a northwesterly course, passing two blocks away from my house and only a slightly greater distance from the Darlings' house. We all heard the trains on those tracks as they went through town. The only question was whether we took notice of it. On that day, none of us could say we had heard the 11:53.

Ordinarily, one of the boys would have been dispatched to the train station to meet Aunt Lil—or to confirm that she had not detrained at the station. Based on the events of the last half hour, it was quickly determined by their mothers that they could not be counted on to walk to the train and back without somehow ruining or soiling their outfits. I volunteered to make the foray in their stead. I was happy to go. I had a question to ask Aunt Lil, the historian within our family. I could only ask it while we were alone.

The Brampton Grand Trunk Railway station, like dozens of others in small communities on tracks that joined Canada from sea to sea, was about 1,400 square feet in area. It was a single-storey building of no great height. A small tower and wide arches were the only concessions to architectural grandeur for an otherwise quite functional yellow-bricked box. Inside the station, there was an office from which the local train master surveyed his realm and a small wicket from which tickets were sold. On a cold day, twenty or thirty people could be accommodated within its walls, as long as all were prepared to stand and none was accompanied by luggage. On a hot August day, the air inside the station was stifling.

On that particular day, after Mr. Porter, the train master, confirmed that the 11:53 had not yet arrived, I took a position on a bench in the small amount of shade offered by the functional building in the hour surrounding high noon. Waiting for my aunt to arrive, I wondered whether she would have observed Aunt Rose's call for white, black, or tan casual attire. Behind the backs of our mothers, we children and our fathers had placed two wagers concerning Aunt Lil for that day. The odds were narrowly against her arriving at all, but if she did, the odds were overwhelmingly in favour of her wearing green. When I wasn't considering the likely betting acumen of my family, I considered how I would broach the subject I most wanted to raise with Aunt Lil. It had been a long time since I had advanced my efforts to solve the mysteries about the Presbyterian Church, Grandpa's position as a self-made and others-destroyed man, and the meaning of the phrase "the Scottish Fiasco." The members of my family who knew what those words meant refused to discuss them with me.

The one exception, I had always thought, might be Aunt Lil. She was the self-proclaimed and generally acknowledged historian of the family. Her head was full of historical facts, and she was unable to tell a lie. I had asked her once before about these matters, but I had not been specific enough. In asking about "Grandpa"—meaning my mother's father, Grandpa Brady—I instead received a lengthy discourse about my father's father—her father, my Grandpa Stephens. I realized I needed to be more direct.

"Hello, Curly Top," my aunt said, greeting me fondly at one o'clock. "Aren't you good to meet me here? Where is everyone else? It's a good thing I don't have a large trunk to transport, isn't it? My, you've grown since I last saw you, but I don't think that even your improved height could support the size of this bag." She pointed to her green-patterned carpet bag.

It was quite large. "Will you be staying overnight?" I asked her excitedly.

"Gracious, no," she replied, hoisting the bag's straps onto her shoulder. "I have a number of important matters to attend to in the city tomorrow. My, that was a pleasant ride, though. I so enjoy the train."

"You didn't mind that it was late?" Several passengers muttered about that as they disembarked before her.

"Was it delayed? I didn't notice."

As we walked along Church Street toward Main, Aunt Lil told me how happy she was to be back in Brampton, how much she enjoyed visiting Brampton, and how she so looked forward to leaving Brampton at the end of the day. It all made for a nice summer day, she said. As she looked about her and began to comment on her surroundings, I interjected.

"Aunt Lil," I ventured, "would you like to walk along Church Street, in front of your old house, before we go to Aunt Rose's house?" I knew that our time was limited, but the diversion would not take more than ten minutes. I hoped that if we walked to her old house, I could easily convince her to walk just the additional half block to the Presbyterian Church.

I did my best to present this option as more of a *fait accompli* than as an actual question, and so for that, and for other reasons, I was surprised by her response. "Why would I want to look at that old house, Curly Top? I don't live there and haven't lived there for years. No. I am quite content to walk directly to the home of my sister. Now tell me about everyone. I want to hear all the news," she said as we began to walk south.

Tell her about everyone? There were twelve of us, not including her and me. I didn't want to spend those precious minutes alone together telling her about Jim's summer job, Ina's latest weather experiment, or Hannah's latest tennis accomplishment.

"They are all fine, Aunt Lil," I said, hoping that would suffice before I changed the subject. I decided to be direct. "Aunt Lil, do you know why our family cannot go into the Presbyterian Church?"

"Yes, of course I do. I have a good head for historical details."

Thrilled, I prepared myself for what I expected would be a long, history-laden explanation. However, Aunt Lil's next words were not a narrative but were rather a question in return: "Do you know why you are not allowed to enter that church?"

"No," I admitted. "Will you tell me?"

"Have you asked your parents?"

"Yes. They won't tell me. No one will tell me."

"Ah, in that case, Curly Top, I won't tell you either."

As we walked the remaining steps, Aunt Lil prattled on about her summer. It gave me plenty of time to reconsider her designation as my favourite aunt.

We approached the Darling house from Main Street, walking over the big Wellington Street Bridge. We hadn't walked very far up Wellington Street when we were joined by Ina and all of my cousins, who encircled Aunt Lil as we walked the rest of the way. They all laughed and skipped, talking at once as they bobbed away from her and then back, in front of her and then behind, taking turns questioning her about the treats she had in her big bag, the news of her exciting city life, and the events of the train ride. As our mass approached the adults and the children peeled away, Aunt Lil was met by her sisters, all of whom greeted her warmly. Only as they reassembled and left Aunt Lil speaking momentarily to my mother did I hear my Aunt Rose say quietly to Aunt Charlotte, "Oh dear. What is she wearing?"

"At least she's here," Aunt Charlotte replied, "at least she's here."

Mr. McCollum took over from there, the lawn side wall of the big house that Grandpa built for the Darlings serving as the backdrop. In the front row, sitting on the grass, he placed six of the children, the girls all in white dresses, the boys in white cotton shirts, their sleeves rolled up to just below their elbows, two in dark slacks, one in light. My cousins John and Bill were still wearing their light-coloured ties. Roy's tie had been discarded, but his braces provided the panache a tie might have otherwise. Three of us were on our knees, three sitting cross-legged. Each of the boys and Hannah were holding tennis rackets. The net Hannah had been instructed to remove was still standing. Immediately behind us in that front row, just above the shoulders of the girls, could clearly be seen a bat, a rabbit, and a halo: Hannah's description of our hair accessories, unfortunately, was quite accurate.

In the row behind, standing, were the seven adults and my brother Jim. The couples were grouped together, the distance between them speaking volumes about their respective relationships. The closest and likely the most compatible of the couples, Aunt Charlotte and Uncle William, were standing so close together that her right arm was flat against his left. Their hands were touching, though neither was held. Next, each standing tall and staring straight into the camera, perhaps six inches from each other, were Aunt Rose and Uncle James, the independent nature of their personalities clearly displayed. Finally, my parents stood at least a foot apart, my mother closer to my brother and my father closer to his sister Lil than either of my parents stood to each other. Nothing could be seen of the palms of my brother's oil-stained clenched hands.

Everyone was wearing the white shirts my Aunt Rose requested, the collars on each of the women's blouses stretched up to their chins and the sleeve lengths extended down to their wrists. All but one was bare-headed, although my Aunt Rose held a dark hat in her hand. As for fashion, Aunt Rose looked striking in her solid white, fully fitted, floor-length linen dress. The V-neck shell Aunt Charlotte wore over her white dress, purchased in Winnipeg, was not as likely to stand the fashion test of time. To give Winnipeg its due, Uncle William, in a new high-buttoned black suit, also bought there, was clearly the most stylish of the men in attendance. My father's white shoes made a rather poor fashion statement—but on that occasion at least he could blame his sister's dress code for their appearance.

What of Aunt Lil? How did she, the woman who only wore green, fare with the instructions of her younger sister on that hot summer day? She did wear the requested white blouse, but not much of it was visible below the full-length herringbone green tweed suit, the jacket of which dropped straight from her shoulders to her knees. Below the jacket, rows of buttons ran from the waistband to the hem line of her skirt, just below her ankles, accentuating the skirt's long, undulating lines. Dark green velvet trimmed the collar and formed two eight-inch-long widely protruding French cuffs.

A fairly conservative hat, made of ribbon of the same green velvet with a small rim around it, covered her swept-up red hair. She looked like she just walked out of a fashion magazine—a winter issue, mind you, but a fashion magazine nonetheless.

We were all happy, I think, or at least content. Hannah, having been relieved by her father of the requirement to remove the tennis net and having somehow reconciled herself to the big black bat-like bow on her head, was no longer scowling. Having banished the Presbyterian Church from mine, my visage no longer displayed consternation. Consistent with the practice of the time, only one of us smiled for the picture. John assured Mr. McCollum that he could hold his smile for the time it would take for the camera to capture the still image. On the threat of pain from his mother, who was standing right above him, he did.

There we were: all fourteen of us. All white. All Protestant. All, but one, church-going. All English-speaking. All second or third generation Canadians. Every adult having completed high school, one with a university degree, and another two soon to seek one. A merchant, a dentist, and an executive; a spinster-teacher and three at-home mothers. All adults homeowners. For 1910, a fairly typical Brampton family.

* * *

Aunt Rose was right to insist that the photograph be taken that summer. Two months after we posed on the Darlings' side lawn, my Uncle James, the mayor of the town and also the fire chief, died. The cause of his death was not a surprise to anyone who knew him. The 280 pounds or more he carried on his sixty-nine-year-old frame made him an ideal candidate for the heart attack he suffered one October night while walking home from the curling club located just six blocks east of the four corners area. He had spent the evening throwing and sweeping forty-four-pound stones.

The news of his passing was broken to my Aunt Rose by my father, who was among the first summoned by Mr. Higgins of Higgins & Large, into whose pharmacy my uncle had stopped as he walked home that night. He feared he was suffering from indigestion. Father, who spent the night in the spare room at Aunt Rose's, came home early in the morning to tell

Jim, Ina, and me the sad news before going back to Aunt Rose's to be with her when John and Hannah awoke. Father asked us to join him at the Darlings' house in an hour. He wanted all of us there to comfort Aunt Rose, John, and Hannah, for as long as they required it. Before he left us, he did something quite remarkable. He walked around the table where we were sitting and kissed Ina, Mother, and me each on the forehead. To the shoulders of Jim and Grandpa he applied a gentle squeeze.

When we arrived at the Darlings' house we found John holding on to Father. He would not let go. Hannah, stoic as always, shed not a tear. Aunt Rose, in a state of shock, neither cried nor spoke. Mother sat beside her and held her hand. Father extricated himself from John. Aunt Rose nodded her assent, and he left to send telegrams, order flowers, meet with the mortician, speak with Uncle James's two full-time bakery employees, and summon Mr. Hudson, who would officiate the Masonic portion of the funeral. Before leaving he again bestowed a kiss on the foreheads of each of the females and patted the shoulders of the men. He reached the door and said he would be back before the body arrived.

We ruminated on those words. Ina was the first to speak. "Mother," she said slowly, "whose body will be arriving, and where will it be arriving from?" On hearing that Uncle James's body would come to rest in the dining room of his house and that his house would be the location of three days' worth of visitation and a funeral, Ina declared her aunt and cousins to be coping quite well and stood to leave. No one tried to stop her.

Jim and I were not so lucky. Having been charged with the responsibility of tending our cousins, we barely left the Darling house over the next four days, except to retrieve a change of clothes and other necessities from our house. Aside from that first night when Father stayed in the house, Aunt Rose required (or desired) no further adult company. In a somewhat catatonic state, she repeated over and over as each night approached and the last of the visitors left that she just wanted time alone with her husband. Hannah, who was my charge, was quite desperate to avoid time alone, and I was glad to keep her company at a distance from the coffin.

The night before the funeral, Hannah was asleep and I nearly was too when my repose was interrupted by a great wail. I sprang from the bed

I was sharing with Hannah and ran down the staircase, stopping at its base. The dam that had been holding back the tears of Aunt Rose finally broke. She spent the prior night, and intended to spend that night too, sleeping on a sofa pulled up near the coffin containing the body of her departed husband. From the sound of the cries, I could tell she was still there.

"You promised me, James!" she wailed. "Twenty-five years! You promised me twenty-five! Not fourteen! You promised!"

The anguished refrain was repeated over and over, broken only by punctuated sobs and the occasional bang. By the bruises on the side of her right hand, I realized the next day she had repeatedly hit the side of my uncle's large oak coffin with the side of her fist. Rose Stephens was twenty-nine years of age when she married James Darling, then a childless fifty-five-year-old widower. One of his inducements to her must have been a promise regarding his mortality.

I knew that I should go to her. But I had not yet been close to the coffin, and though I tried, I could not force my legs to move beyond the base of the staircase in the foyer. I could not will them to take me where they must go to comfort my dear aunt. As I stood there wondering how else I could help, Jim shot past me. He only looked at me for a moment, but in that moment I took in the full measure of his reproof. Reflecting on Jim's disappointment, I continued to contemplate how I could help. Eventually it occurred to me. I ran upstairs for my robe, shut the door to Hannah's room behind me, and fled back down the stairs. It was not yet midnight. I ran through the foyer, out the front door, across the verandah, down the steps, up the street to our house, up the steps and across our verandah, through our always unlocked front door and up the stairs to my parents' bedroom, where I entreated them to come to our aid.

Following the funeral, it was determined that Jim and I should spend two more nights at the home of our then much sadder and emotional aunt. With the removal of Uncle James's body to the local cemetery, I was less reticent to stay and willingly did so, forgetting on the Sunday night one other thing that would cause pain the next day: school. It had been decided by my father that with the funeral behind us, all of us children should return to our respective places of education the next morning. Such a message had not been conveyed to Archie and Frances, neither of whom waited for me to join them in their walk to school that day. Furthermore, as no one woke us on time, we all went to school later than any of the other children in the neighbourhood. I had no one to walk with me past the Kelly Iron Work Repair Shop.

There was a chance, I knew, that Scary Scott would not be on his stoop at the later time that I went by. The entertainment he normally sought in a morning would be complete, to his knowledge. Nonetheless, thinking I could take no chances, I rooted through the hat bin at the back door of Aunt Rose's house before finding a floppy green cap that had once warmed Hannah's head. It was too big for me, but it covered my forehead and all of my hair, which I drew up into it. I began my solitary walk, stopping out of fear and respect in front of the Queen Street Bakery. A sign stuck to the door announced that it was closed until Wednesday. The shop was dark; the shelves were bare. Bowing my head, I walked steadily to George Street. Seeing no passing horses or cars, I ran across the street. I ran in front of the Kellys' steel-strewn lot. Was Scary Scott on the stoop? I refused to look. Just as I passed it, the wind came up. It caught the floppy rim of the too-big hat and blew it clear off my head. My brown ringlets fell streaming down behind me, and yet I did not stop. I did not turn. I kept running, and as I did so I heard the familiar grunting. I realized again just how much I was going to miss my Uncle James.

I hoped Hannah would not miss her hat. I had no intention of going back for it.

Chapter 11

THE FLOWER TOWN OF CANADA

There are times when two desired objectives pursued apart bring nothing but pleasure, but when pursued together bring only frustration. Certainly that was my experience in the summer of 1911 and in the summers before and after, whenever I joined a much-desired call upon the Dale Estate with a much-sought-out visit with my dear brother. To be fair to the characterization, perhaps the distress arose not from the fact that the two events were combined but from the fact that although they were intended to be, they rarely were.

The business of the Dale Estate began in 1863 with the arrival in Brampton of a garden vegetable grower named Edward Dale. From his initially small parcel of land at the village's northern extreme, Edward grew a variety of vegetables in the few months the Canadian climate permitted it. Noting the additional amount and types of vegetables that could be sown in a longer growing season and a more temperate climate, Edward set about to contrive those very conditions. Initially, he did so in a twelve-foot by twenty-foot dugout covered in clay and sod and kept warm by a flue furnace that burned throughout the day and night. By the late 1860s, Edward had created a thriving year-round business selling his potatoes, cabbages, cauliflower, asparagus, celery, radishes, and lettuce to eager buyers in Brampton and beyond.

Edward's aptitude for growing ran in his blood. Before long, his eldest son Henry (known to most as Harry) left school and joined his father's business. Harry's contribution to the partnership of Edward Dale and Son was unique. His passion was not vegetable propagation but floral cultivation—particularly the cultivation of roses. For each delivery of vegetables father Edward made to a lady's house, son Harry ensured a single rose accompanied the order. By 1869, Harry had convinced his father to add flowers to his greenhouse production. Before long, the quantity and profitability of grown flowers exceeded those of vegetables.

A horticulturalist at heart, though not by education, Harry sought to grow the world's sturdiest, longest lasting roses with the richest colours, the most uniform size, and the softest petals. From an old outdoor rose bush, Harry, after repeated experiments, created a variety of rose that could be grown inside a hothouse.

Before long, Dale roses were shipped throughout North America, England, and Europe. As the years went on, the family acquired further property around Edward's original homestead, and the single sod- and mud-covered dugout was replaced by a modern aboveground glass-sided structure. By the time Edward retired in 1882, the business had two stand-alone greenhouses; by the time I was born in 1903, it had twenty-one. By the summer of 1911, it had twenty acres under glass, producing ten million blooms a year, making it the third largest greenhouse operation in the world.

While Harry's brothers Tom, Ned, and Will were involved in the family business, on their father's retirement it was Harry whose name the business took and who continued as its directing mind. The business might have continued well into the twentieth century under the name Henry Dale Florist had it not been for the extraction of a troublesome tooth in 1901. The blood poisoning that followed felled the King of Canadian Florists. The business of Harry Dale—its assets and its liabilities—and the lands Harry had acquired to conduct that business fell into his estate, and for two decades, they never left it. The management that Harry Dale had so successfully provided to the Brampton business was assumed by his executors, including his exceptional business manager, T.W. (Tommy) Duggan.

Though the vast majority of Bramptonians celebrated the worldwide renown of its home-grown business, for the longest time my father did not. Driven in part by his contrarian nature, and likely in equal part by his envy for the Dale family's success, Father never lost an opportunity to belittle the famous enterprise.

"Sakes alive," he complained one night regarding his duties as chair of the High School Board of Education. "Roger Handle suggested that I order a Dale Dozen to present to Miss Keulman on her retirement. You'd think there was no other grower in this town. What about Edwin Calvert? He's got a good five acres here in Brampton and a mammoth greenhouse. He and his sons are surely deserving of the business. Or Jennings. His flowers are perfectly acceptable. We could have bought flowers from the Fendleys, too if the Dales hadn't swallowed up their operations." He was referring to the sale of a small plot of land by James Fendley, another grower, to Harry Dale. The sale preceded Fendley's son's marriage to Harry's sister.

Father's aversion to Dale flowers began to wane with the formation of two new Dale-Stephens associations. The first connection came about in the summer of 1908 when Jim took a part-time job with the Dales. The Dale Estate, with over two hundred employees, was the largest employer in Brampton, providing jobs not only to full-time permanent employees but also to students who were prepared to work part-time after school, on weekends, and throughout the summer. While students were principally required to till the soil, weed the beds, and tie up stems of roses, part-time relief was also required in the administration of the business, and it was to this area that Jim was formally assigned at the age of sixteen. Father often recounted how Jim's intelligence and his willingness to work in any capacity made him a great asset to the accounting staff as he matched invoices and payments, to the packing staff as he boxed the flowers in ice and newspaper, and to the shipping staff as he loaded the boxed flowers on horse-drawn carts for their short conveyance to the CPR station a few blocks away.

With each compliment Mother and Father received from one of the many Dale family members about their hard-working and respectful son, Father's disdain for the Dale Estate diminished. Any lingering apathy was utterly and completely extinguished with the blooming friendship between Jim and Millie Dale. One could not esteem Edward's great-granddaughter, as our entire family did, without admiring her roots, and so, by 1910 when Jim had been a two-year part-time employee of the Dale Estate and Millie a friend for one year, there was no question that the flowers Father would order for his brother-in-law's funeral would be from the Dale Estate. He was astounded by Mother's whispered suggestion that it might be otherwise.

As a youngster, I was always aware of the Dale Estate. One could not miss its massive acres of greenhouses at the north end of the town or the beautiful large homes of the Dale family members around them. The Dale rose printed on our school scribblers was a constant reminder of the local industry, as were the regular headlines in the Brampton *Conservator* declaring international tributes awarded to the flowers of the Dale Estate. Even when outside of Brampton, our connection to this undertaking was often top of mind. A reference to our hometown often elicited the response, "Oh, the Flower Town of Canada," a term all of the Brampton florists cherished.

Brampton children knew Dale flowers by more than mere reputation. The Dale Estate had high standards for the flowers it sold. Each flower was inspected to insure uniformity in size and colour; stems were checked for straightness and the leaves for a leather-like quality. Flowers that did not measure up were discarded—but not forgotten. Mother never thought to entertain a guest without a small arrangement of posies to adorn her table. When Grandpa's flowers were not in bloom or when they had been too much thinned as a result of prior dinners and visits, I was dispatched to the Dale Estate's dump pile to retrieve one or two handfuls of discarded flowers.

On any given day, Bramptonians of every age could be seen rummaging their way through the Dale cast-offs looking to form a near perfect bouquet. The exercise was in no way discouraged by the Dales. The Bramptonians who scavenged the refuse pile were perfectly civil—except the day of a high school dance, when the number of young men seeking a suitable arrangement for a corsage outnumbered the Dale rejects available. The practice only came to an end years later when the Dales learned that some enterprising Bramptonians were earning a living selling the Dale rejects.

In his day, Harry Dale conducted tours of his greenhouses, and his brothers and their families continued the practice after his death. While the Dales would not organize a tour for a handful of local children, if a tour was about to be conducted for more worthy visitors, on the condition that we kept up and kept quiet and of course that we absolutely did NOT touch the flowers, we were welcome to join the touring party. Frances and I joined such tours once a summer. Some summers we had to walk the half hour it took us to reach the estate six or more times to be there on a day and at a time at which a formal tour was being conducted. It was well worth it. Entering the sun-filled, warm, sweetly scented houses with row upon row of beautiful flowers, we believed we were obtaining a preview of heaven.

Thus my heart soared one day in July 1911 when Mother told me, around mid-afternoon, that an unexpected guest would be joining us for tea that night, that Grandpa's roses were not yet ready to be cut, and that it would be necessary for me to go to the Dale Estate's refuse pile to retrieve a suitable selection. Moments later my heart fell when she told me it would also be necessary for me to drop by the Dale Estate's office and deliver a message to Jim.

In response to a standing invitation, Mother had just learned that Dean Willmott of the University of Toronto's Dental College would be joining us for our evening meal.

"It's very important that your brother be here," she said to me, "given all that the dean has done for him and the important role he can play in Jim's future. Thank heavens I was in the process of cooking a chicken. Jim will need to cancel his plans to be with the McMurchys. They have him to tea once a week. They can do without his company this one night. It is just three o'clock. I am sure you can easily catch Jim before he is done work at four." Seeing me hesitate, she continued, "Go on. Dean Willmott will likely be here by five."

I breathed a great sigh and slowly walked out the front door, awash in self-pity as I began the half-hour trek to one of my favourite places to see one of my favourite people. This was not the first time I was being sent on such an errand. I had been dispatched to meet Jim at the Dale Estate on a number of occasions. Unfortunately, it was never easy to do. The problem was not the location of the administrative offices where Jim purportedly worked. Situated on Main Street, they were easy to find. The problem was not the staff in the administrative offices. The men who worked there were all warm and welcoming. The problem was that when I arrived in those offices and spoke to those men, no one ever knew where Jim was, and when he was finally found, he was never particularly happy to see me.

As I walked along the streets that day, kicking each lose pebble I crossed, I reflected on similar missions and their less than satisfactory results. There was a time three summers earlier when Jim forgot his sandwich and apple at home. Knowing how hard he was working, Mother packed a hot meal for me to deliver to him after our meal was consumed. I arrived at the administrative offices expecting to see Jim ravenous behind a desk or a counter. He was not behind any desk or counter that I could see. The staff in the office had no idea where he was, a fact that did not seem to concern any of them. One of the kind men suggested I sit and wait for Jim to "come by" the office. When he finally did, forty-five minutes later, it was difficult to know who was more surprised, Jim by my presence or me by his appearance.

"Jim, what is that odd outfit you are wearing?" I asked, looking up and down at the one-piece long-pant-and-sleeved garment covering him.

Jim whispered that they had some odd dress codes there, thanked me for the meal that was then stone cold, and sent me on my way. It was clear he couldn't have me leave him fast enough, but before I was completely out of his sight, he called me back. "Jessie," he said, quietly again, tugging at one of my ringlets. "Please don't mention what I am wearing to Mother and Father. They wouldn't understand." I agreed that they wouldn't, particularly since nearly every other man working at the Dale Estate wore a shirt and tie—even the men who tended the flowerbeds.

The next summer, Mother sent me on a similar errand. She had just finished making a tray of lemon biscuits and suggested I take a portion of them up to the estate so that they could be enjoyed by Jim and the office employees with whom he worked. The employees had no trouble eating nearly all of the baked goods—their hands reaching into the tin time and again—but they had a great deal of trouble finding Jim. They urged me to indulge in the lemon biscuits while I waited. When Jim finally ambled into the office, again seemingly by accident, Mother's treats were gone and Jim was again wearing the strange outfit I had seen the year before. This time his hands were nearly black with grease, unlike the hands of any of the office workers. I asked him how his hands got to be so filthy working in the office. He begged me be quiet and then led me outside, where he thanked me for the biscuits and motioned me toward the exit, saying that sometimes he was required to work outside the office.

The next year I arrived in the early evening. Jim had agreed to work until 9:00 p.m. one night a week that summer. The first such night, Mother sent me up to the estate around 6:30 p.m. with a plate of food. When I arrived at the office, it was empty and the lights were low. I could see people moving in the greenhouses beyond, and so I went into the closest one, not knowing who I would see there. To my great relief, the first person I came upon was Jim's friend Millie speaking with her grandfather, who, interestingly, was wearing an outfit just like the one in which I had seen Jim. Millie was surprised to see me and even more surprised it appeared by my inquiry as to Jim's whereabouts. But then before I had a chance to explain where I understood Jim would be, she spoke again over the halting voice of her grandfather.

"Oh my goodness, Jessie, I completely forgot. It's Wednesday, isn't it? I think he may have made a delivery to the train station. Why don't you leave the food in the office? I'll be sure he gets it." Then she took her grandfather by the arm, and they left the greenhouse. Shortly afterward, I watched Millie running along Main Street in the direction of the four corners. I wanted to do as she suggested and simply leave the plate in the office for Jim, but after the biscuit debacle of the year before, Mother had instructed me not to leave Jim's food where it could be eaten by someone else. It was a long forty-five minute wait in that dimly lit office before Jim arrived, out of breath, once again to a cold meal.

* * *

As I approached the Dale Estate offices that day in July 1911, I wondered how much time I would have to spend waiting for Jim. I hoped it would not be long, although I consoled myself knowing that at least on this occasion I had flowers to gather as I waited. That consolation was of little value, it transpired, since when I arrived at the office, I was told that Jim had already completed his work that day. To the knowledge of the staff, he was no longer on the Dale grounds. Assuming he was already at Eddie's house, I retrieved a half dozen barely wilted roses from the refuse pile, wrapped their thorny stems in the kerchief I pulled off my head, reversed half of my earlier steps, and walked to the distinctive McMurchy home a block south of the Grand Trunk station.

The closer I got to the house with the prickly cloth-wrapped bouquet swinging in my hand, the happier I felt. I passed the Castle across from the Grand Trunk station and the Copeland-Chatterson manufacturing building, between the station and the McMurchy home. With each step I became increasingly relieved that I would not have to wait long to convey Mother's message to Jim. When I reached Eddie's house, I positively smiled.

The red-bricked two-storey McMurchy house was unique not just for its time but for all time. The first of its two very distinct features was a filigreed gingerbread that dripped from each of its many A-framed rooflines. This lovely ornamentation would have been much admired if it were not so overpowered by the second unique feature of the house: the extremely unusual blue stones which formed its foundations and the pillars that supported its verandah. The masonry, all imported especially for the McMurchys from their native Scotland, was to the mind of Father and many other Bramptonians ridiculously out of place. As an unsophisticated child with obviously less taste than my father and his peers, those blue stones brought me nothing but pleasure.

On my arrival, Mrs. McMurchy, who had invited me into her foyer, predicted the purpose of my attendance. "I suppose you are looking for Jim," she began. "He isn't here now, and I am not sure—"

Before she had an opportunity to tell me of what she was not sure, Eddie bounded into the house. "Hello, Jessie," he said as he came between his mother and me. "I guess you're looking for Jim. I expect he'll be here any minute. It's rather warm inside, isn't it? Why don't you wait on the verandah, and I'll go get him." He ushered me out the door and onto a wooden chair before dashing down the street, too quickly to hear my objections to the plan. Since he was running in the direction of my house, I wondered why he could not just tell me where Jim was. I could have met him myself.

As I watched Eddie's long legs stride down the street, I reconciled myself to the fact that I was once again sitting and waiting for Jim in the course of running an errand to the Dale Estate. Making myself comfortable and letting my mind wander, I thought of how close Eddie and Jim were. They had actually gotten closer in the previous year, not more distant, as Father had hoped. While Jim had attended the University of Toronto in September of 1910 and Eddie had not, Jim's stay there was not long. A serious illness sent Jim home to the care of our mother just three weeks into his studies. Though his recovery was full, it was so long in coming that it was determined he should wait and resume his studies the following September. Jim spent the balance of the year assisting Father with the administrative aspects of his practice and working at the Dale Estate. A strange turn of events involving Eddie meant that both boys would be attending the university in September of 1911. The family business it was assumed Eddie would join would soon cease to be a family business. Eddie needed to chart a different course.

The McMurchys operated a successful utility business almost as old as the Dale Estate. The electrical company operated by John McMurchy, Eddie's uncle, had been created by another man, John Hutton, who resided west of Brampton on the Credit River. From the surges of that river, Hutton created and transmitted the new utility to places around him, including Brampton. By the late 1880s, Hutton had successfully lit a number of Brampton streets, including the area on Queen Street outside of the Queen's Hotel.

Looking to expand his power-generating business to indoor locations, Hutton sought an initial customer that by its very nature would expose his product to numerous potential residential customers. What better indoor location, he thought, than a church, with its hundreds of weekly worshippers. Eventually he negotiated an arrangement with the Anglican Christ Church on Queen Street, just up the road from the Kelly Iron Work Repair Shop. In 1890 the church elders proceeded with the conversion, replacing their gas-powered lighting system with an electrical one. Unfortunately, the church found the continual sputterings that emitted from the early electrical light fixtures not conducive to quiet moments of prayer. Indeed, while the local priest appreciated the burst of attentiveness the irregular loud knocks created among the adult congregants, their effect on the otherwise sleeping babies resulted on the whole in less attention being paid to his sermons. Within weeks, the trial was deemed a failure and the electrical lights were removed.

Hutton changed his marketing strategy. He looked for another indoor customer—a customer for whom noise was no obstacle, a customer that was used to and even desired noise. He chose a factory floor, and after a number of years of experimentation and further development, he had key customers in the Brampton Knitting Mills, located down the street from our house, across from the new library, and W.B. McCulloch's Planing Mills, not far from the Grand Trunk station.

It was that business with forty-three customers that Eddie's uncle bought in 1897. Over time, McMurchy expanded the power plant. With the advent of the incandescent light bulb in 1903, a quieter source of light supply emerged, allowing his customer list to grow from forty-three to five hundred. By 1910, McMurchy's generated electricity was being supplied to Brampton over five hundred poles and nearly twelve miles of electrical line. Bramptonians became hungry for more electrical power. The town council sensed that the town's needs could not be met by McMurchy alone, yet many councillors were of the view that the encouragement of competition would be "needless." A consensus began to emerge that Brampton should be connected to the province's continuous source of electricity and that McMurchy's operations should be purchased by the newly formed provincial Hydro Electric Power Corporation. The inevitability of that outcome seemed even more certain in the summer of 1911.

Indeed, the matter had been the subject of discussion at tea at our house earlier that week as Father criticized the town council for even considering paying Mr. McMurchy an astounding $15,000 for his utility company. "The drain on the ratepayer's purse would be a debacle no less than that created when the town chose to bring in the railway," he lamented.

"A debacle, not at all," Uncle William retorted. It was July, and the Turners were in town for their annual sojourn. "Doc, you know full well that that the expenditure on the railway made by farsighted Bramptonians forty years ago brought Brampton the commercial success denied to countless towns and villages that have since stagnated or disappeared without direct access to rail. Besides, the taxpayers will have their say on this matter. I hear that the council is going to hold a referendum on the matter next year."

The recent decision of the McMurchys to steer their son Eddie toward another career path seemed quite astute to my young mind.

Fifteen minutes after Eddie set out, Jim arrived at the McMurchys' verandah, once again out of breath. "Jessie," he huffed, "what is it? Have the Turners returned early from Snelgrove? Are they now expected for tea? I didn't think they were to be back until eight this evening."

"No they haven't returned. It is someone else who is coming and—where have you been and why are your hands so dirty?"

"I had to do a few extra things today after work," he explained, looking at his fingers, "and, in fact, I am not quite done. Are you saying I should go home?"

"Yes. Mother said so. She said the person coming has been very good to you, and you need to make a good impression."

"A good impression," he said derisively, and then, softening and tugging at one of my ringlets with his greasy fingers, he went on. "Don't I always make a good impression, Little One?"

"Most of the time," I said, turning up my nose at his dirty hands.

"Except when I am working," he volunteered.

"Yes, except when you are working *in the office*," I replied with emphasis.

He flushed a bit. "Someone I need to impress? Who is it then?" He looked quite intrigued, almost hopeful.

"I can't remember his name. Someone from the university."

Enthusiasm drained from his face. "Maybe one of my professors. What does he teach?" Jim appeared resigned.

I didn't recall but then his name came back to me. "I think his name is Dean."

"Ah, yes. Dean Willmott. Well, I can see why Mother wants me home. Alright, why don't you run ahead? I need to make my apologies to Mrs. McMurchy and get cleaned up a bit. I'll see you back at home shortly."

Shortly, I thought. I expected it would take Jim some time to clean up.

The cast-off roses were arranged in the vase and set in the middle of the table just before Father arrived from the train station. Dean Willmott, who accompanied him, had a commanding presence in every sense of the phrase. In his early seventies, he had an impressive amount of thick white hair, which covered his large head and half the skin on his face. Big, bushy white eyebrows topped his large, deep-set eyes. Thick, pronounced lines connected his large nose to his handlebar moustache. His forceful, booming voice matched his physical attributes. I was greatly relieved when Father directed him to a large wooden chair on the verandah across from the smaller chairs usually occupied by Ina and Grandpa. I did not think the smaller ones could possibly contain him.

Dean Willmott and Father were twenty minutes into discussion before Jim joined us. "Well, if it isn't the next dentist in the family," the dean said, lifting his large frame from the wooden chair and extending his big white hand to Jim's nearly rubbed-raw red one. "It is good to see you looking so hale." He went on without giving Jim an opportunity to reply, "If you become half the dentist your father is, you'll be a great addition to the profession. Your classmates were sorry you were not able to return to the college last year. They'll be happy to see you back among the freshman in the fall."

Over the next three hours on the verandah, at the dining room table, and then in the parlour, Dean Willmott and Father discussed dentistry: the practice of dentistry in a small community; how it compared to practicing in a city; the latest developments in dentistry in Europe; politics inside the Royal College of Dentistry; new initiatives in research; collaborations with physicians; new compounds; and troublesome patients. Realizing how much they had monopolized the conversation, after Dean Willmott had been returned to the train station, Father, somewhat sensitively, thanked us for feigning such interest in the conversation. He was visibly surprised to see which one among the five of us denied the existence of any pretence.

* * *

Aunt Charlotte and Uncle William arrived back at our house shortly after Dean Willmott's departure. With their evening's cigars in hand, Father and Uncle William left for the bowling green. Mother and Ina went upstairs to open the windows and draw back the curtains. The house was hot and stuffy.

Aunt Charlotte came into the sitting room, where she found me cross-legged on the floor in the middle of the room in front of a pile of coloured sticks. After some entreaties, she joined me in the game of pick-up sticks, sitting on the floor beside me, her legs crossed at the knees and folded to the left under her long skirts. Eventually, her enthusiasm began to match mine. She was ahead of me two games to one when we were joined by Mother and Ina.

"It will be cooled down in no time," Mother announced before asking, with a little chuckle in her voice, how Aunt Charlotte was faring.

"We have quite the match going, Mary," Aunt Charlotte reported. "I can tell you that Jessie is much better at lifting these sticks than her cousins were at her age. Ina, would you like to play? I'd be willing to forfeit my position to you as long as you assure me that you'll maintain the slight edge I have over this talented player."

"No, thank you," Ina replied. "That game is for babies." I did not know how to respond. The game was clearly not for babies, but a very convincing argument to that effect might bring about an undesirable change in players. Fortunately, Ina quickly announced her intention to read the latest library book on condensation and precipitation and settled into the chair next to the cold fireplace.

Jim entered the room shortly afterward. "Aunt Charlotte, when you are finished playing with Jessie, would you like to join me on the verandah?" he inquired. "It's nice and cool out there." It was cooling down in the sitting room too, I noticed, and so I was somewhat hurt when she told me that she had previously agreed to a late-night meeting with Jim to discuss a private matter. She promised to play again with me another time, but as the Turners were leaving in two days' time, I took little comfort in the promise.

"Can I come with you onto the verandah, Jim?" I asked as I put the coloured sticks back in their shiny blue canister.

"No. Not this time, Little One," he replied kindly. "I have to talk to Aunt Charlotte alone." They walked out of the sitting room, through the parlour, and the foyer to the verandah. My curiosity increased with each step they took.

"Jessie," Mother said, coming up behind me, "it's time you went upstairs to bed." I might have resisted were it not for the opportunity that obedience would provide. Walking at half my usual pace through the parlour and the foyer and stepping precariously close to the verandah's screen door, I could just make out Jim's voice.

"He's your brother, and you know him so well. I thought you could give me some advice about the best way to make him understand that what he asks is not appropriate for me."

"Jim, dear," I heard my aunt reply. "I'm very flattered that you sought my advice on this delicate matter. But he is your father, and his word must carry the day. Furthermore, I must agree with him, as I am sure you in your heart must as well. What he has proposed is absolutely the best course both for you and your family. I think you must reconcile yourself to it."

As I prepared for bed, snippets of the conversation, small as they were, danced in my head. What was Father asking Jim to do that Jim thought inappropriate? Why was Aunt Charlotte agreeing with Father? If I had tarried longer, would I have learned more?

Curiosity propelled me back down the stairs and into the foyer. Quietly I moved toward the verandah's door. Beyond it, all was silent. Had Jim and Aunt Charlotte left the verandah, or were they merely in silent contemplation? They had been sitting to the left of the door. I pressed my right cheek to the screen to obtain the best possible view of the area. The pose did not provide the vantage I desired, but in so positioning myself, I did at least hear one of them. It was Jim. However, his voice came not from the verandah ahead of me but from the foyer behind me. "Jessie," he whispered, tugging at my hair as I took in the empty verandah chairs, "what are you doing? You aren't trying to eavesdrop, are you?"

Overcoming the fright he gave me, I stood ramrod-straight and then turned to him, backing into the door slightly in order to avoid standing on his feet. "No. I am not eavesdropping. No." A true enough statement, since one could hardly eavesdrop on a conversation that was not occurring. "I couldn't sleep, and I came down to see if Mother would make me some hot milk." Again a true, if not complete statement.

"Mother isn't on the veranda," I heard him say as I looked straight into his chest. "She's still in the sitting room—where you left her."

"Right," I said, pushing past him and walking directly to the stairs.

"Jessie, don't you want to ask Mother for the milk?"

"No, thank you," I said, mustering as much dignity as I could. "The walk downstairs exhausted me. I'm feeling quite tired now." Looking straight ahead, I walked as far as the mid-stair case landing, but hearing the screen door open at that point, I turned and watched Jim walk through it into that still dark night, his head hung low.

Whether Father required Jim to give up his beloved lacrosse in favour of another sport; to cease his endless sketching in favour of more serious pursuits; or to forego his future summer positions at the Dale Estate in favour of working with Father in his dental office, or any other similar or entirely different activity, I had no idea. I added this question to the list of the many things about my family that I did not know.

Chapter 12

THE VERANDAH

My grandfather Jesse Brady dreamed of building a community, not just houses. He sought to build neighbourhoods, not fortresses. He was convinced that a house with a balcony—no matter how high— would draw its inhabitants out to enjoy the view, and that a house with a verandah—no matter how small—would draw its occupants out to enjoy the society of others. Jesse Brady pursued his vision notwithstanding the dissuasion of Nelson, who believed that practical homeowners would never desire more than a simple cottage. He pursued it in spite of the compromises the Duke had insisted upon when he agreed to provide Jesse the capital he first required.

By 1911, my grandfather's vision for the town was being realized with the residential streets lined with one brick house after another. No two houses were the same, but nearly all were fronted by verandahs, and many were adorned with an upper-floor balcony, often with no practical use.

For the most part, the verandahs were warmly embraced. On a summer's day, a family might take a meal on this outdoor dining space. So long as it was not too warm, ladies with large verandahs would use them to serve lemonade on a summer at-home day, their roofs providing sufficient shade from the sun's hot rays. A husband and wife might meet there before tea and discuss the day's events. In the evening in the late spring through to the early fall, families would congregate on or around them, moving from one neighbour's to another's, making predictions for the day to come. Their conversations were occasionally interrupted by a holler to the children playing on the road beyond them to make way for an oncoming horse and buggy or even a car.

A white, wooden-railed verandah wrapped around our home's north and west walls. Mother's sensitivity to the heat meant that this space was rarely required by adults during a summer's day. That fact, together with our verandah's great size, made it an ideal place for Ina to house her scientific laboratory and for me—once my chores, piano practices, and compulsory readings were complete—to play. One late August day in 1911, after Dean Willmott's visit and the return of the Turners to their home out west, our verandah was used as a forum for climatic experiments, a site for make-believe adventure, a place of courtship, a lecture hall, and a venue for public announcements.

Earlier that week, Ina had begun to re-equip her outdoor laboratory on the verandah's west side. Wind catchers streamed from the soffits, rain catchers were suspended from the balustrade, a thermostat leaned against the brick wall, pans of varying amounts of evaporating water lined the floor, and tin cans, lids, and other pieces of metal strung on stings hung from the rafters. Throughout the week, Ina ran from one instrument to another, jotting down her findings, monitoring all the while the types of clouds that loomed above us.

Over the same week, Archie, Frances, and I built a ship on the other side of the verandah. We devised masts from old sheets we strung from the pillars. From our stern we hung another sheet with a round porthole cut out at eye level. A homemade flag with a red rose on a white background tied to the lower railing indicated that our ship hailed from nearly landlocked Brampton. Our *Rose* was not to be confused with the *Excelsior,* which sailed within the verandah across the road from us. Its flag bore a hand-drawn picture of a lacrosse stick, another Brampton icon, and was crewed by our friends Willy Core and Morley Burrows and Collin Heggie, the son of the local physician.

Having completed a year-long expedition to China, the *Rose* was at that time in a fierce competition to be the first ship to return to our home port without being wrecked by storms or overtaken by pirates and before Father ordered the ship disbanded and the verandah tidied, an inevitable and veritable terminating event. We had been locked in pursuit with the *Excelsior* for three days, with Archie as our captain at the helm, me on the lookout step stool, and Frances drawing up the marketing plan for the sale of the silks and spices in our cargo hold. We had survived high winds and driving rains, a small bout of scurvy, a leak in our stern, and one attack from another ship that mistook the rose on our flag for a bloody chicken thighbone. The *Excelsior* was on our wake but beset with its own problems. From the lookout tower I could see that our friend Collin had been thrown to sea by a lose boom and that Willie, a mutinous sailor, had been made to walk the plank. The ship's crew was compassionate it seemed, though, as in both cases they sent a dingy to bring the scared and cowed sailors back to their ship.

We had just rounded the Horn of Africa on our return leg when Captain Archie, having momentarily assumed my lookout post, announced the approach of a familiar figure. "Ahoy, mates," he called, peering through the spyglass we had fashioned from rolled cardboard. "I spy Commodore McMurchy ahead."

"Commodore McMurchy?" I questioned. "Now?" It was not quite noon.

"Commodore—I mean Eddie—McMurchy?" Ina echoed, having run to our side of the verandah. "Now?"

From the ship's gunnels onto which I moved, I watched Ina look down the street. I was sure she was calculating whether she should go inside, change, and possibly miss seeing Eddie altogether or stay on the verandah and have him see her looking quite deranged. Ina appeared at that moment as she appeared most summer mornings. Her hair protruded from her scalp in every direction. Her skirt was at least two sizes too big and was constantly being hiked up. Her shirt was covered in a sweater that must have once been Grandpa's. She looked like the quintessential mad scientist.

The look always improved somewhat just before Father came home at noon. It would be completely remediated, however, a few hours later. At around four o'clock each afternoon, Ina would retreat into the house and undertake what Archie, Frances, and I referred to as the Dr. Jekyll and Miss Hyde transformation. Within fifteen minutes, she would re-emerge attired in a clean, properly fitting dress, her hair neatly brushed into a thick knot at the nape of her neck. The conversion ostensibly undertaken to meet Father's exacting end-of-day standards was, we all knew, actually completed on the off chance that Eddie would stop by our house at the conclusion of his daytime shift at Brown's Bottling Works.

That morning, as she deliberated whether to expedite her daily transformation, the decision was made for her. Archie's spyglass was not particularly effective. Eddie was only five houses from ours when his sighting was first announced. Yanking down the sheet that was the stern of our ship, she ran to her side of the verandah, picked up one of her pans of evaporating water, and doused its contents over on her thick hair before thrusting her head through the circle that was our ship's porthole. The white sheet fell over her shoulders, covering her arms, her legs, and her less than flattering attire. I glared at her in disbelief as she walked toward the wide verandah steps and feigned complete surprise at Eddie's arrival.

Ina's delight in Eddie's visits was, she proclaimed, due to his unstinting interest in her experiments, an interest she was sure she derived from his family's success in another scientific foray. She considered him to be a kindred spirit, and her faith in his scientific interest was not without basis. Where Ina frequently failed to find in our household an interested listener for her many hypotheses, methods, observations, and conclusions, in Eddie she always found an enthusiastic conversationalist.

Ina was not the only person who looked forward to Eddie's after-work visits. In view of the change in his long-term employment prospects, his father determined in the spring of 1911 that in addition to attending university in the fall, it would be beneficial for Eddie to gain the experience that could come from working in a business run by a non-family member. Brown's Bottling Works was the chosen employer, and for the whole of that summer, Eddie, a year out of high school, was responsible for overseeing the many high school students involved in the summertime bottling production. He supervised the younger boys as they measured and poured the requisite amounts of syrup and water into glass bottles bearing Brown's trademarked raised bunch of grapes. He directed the students as they capped and packed the bottles before loading crates of them onto wagons to be driven around town and to Erin, Orangeville, Streetsville, and more far-flung places.

In addition to their wages, at the end of each day each boy was able to take home one bottle of soda. For his greater responsibilities, Eddie was entitled to two. Arriving at our house with those bottles in hand, there was always a contest to see who could first command Eddie's attention, Ina with her thirst for the knowledge in his head or Archie, Frances, and me with our thirst for the bottles in his hands. The drinks had to be imbibed before Father came home, for Father, the dentist, could no more tolerate our consumption of soda pop than he could any commotion on our verandah.

On that August morning, Eddie quickly parted with the bottles of soda pop and complimented Ina on her practical new lab coat. He then tried to answer our many questions regarding his early arrival.

"I can't tell you why. I really have no idea. At eleven o'clock old Doc Brown came onto the factory floor and told all of the high school students that the day was done." Eddie applied the honorific we all did to the sage drink inventor, who was most assuredly not a doctor. "He told them to go home and come back tomorrow, if their parents allow it. He told them to take their bottle and he paid them a half-day of wages. Then he turned to me and said that since there were no high school boys to supervise, I didn't need to stay either. He handed me my two bottles and told me to come back tomorrow, if I am able."

"That can't be it," Archie replied. "There has to be more of an explanation. Are there not enough orders for the soda pop? Have the delivery horses gone lame? Has old Doc Brown run out of water? Why wouldn't the boys' parents permit them to return tomorrow?" Archie always hesitated when he referred to the parents of children these days. He lost his own father, the well-known lawyer, the year before, shortly after the big flood.

"No. Nothing like that. The orders, supplies, and wagons were all the same as usual," he replied. "And I have no idea why the parents would not send their children back there tomorrow. I expect most of the parents would like the boys to go back there this very afternoon."

"Is there anything else you aren't telling us?" Ina asked from above the porthole and ship stern wrapped around her. "Has this to do with

Doc Brown's secret recipes? Might he be developing a secret new formula this afternoon?"

"I don't think so," Eddie said with some resignation. "Doc Brown is pretty old now, at least in his fifties. I don't think he's inventing anything new these days. He needs good young chemists like you to do that sort of thing now." Eddie never lost an opportunity to extend a compliment to Ina. Having confirmed that Jim was not at home and having received an update from Ina on her barometric pressure experiments, Eddie continued his walk home, his hands relieved of their two-bottled burden.

Ina pulled the sheet over her head and returned it to us as she went inside to prepare for our meal. With a promise to rendezvous on the port side two hours later, we hailed our rivals across the street before Frances and Archie left for their respective homes.

The resumption of the scientific experiments and the Atlantic crossing of the *Rose* were not to be, however, for when Father joined Jim, Mother, Ina, and me at the dining room table at noon that day, he was in a particularly sour mood. In addition to his usual complaints, he was upset by a rumour to the effect that someone in the town had contracted scarlet fever. He did not know who it was, but he heard that the public health department was pulling yellow banners out of storage and preparing to place infected people and those with whom they had come into close contact into quarantine. Although there had not been a significant outbreak of scarlet fever in the province since the year I was born, the ailment struck someone in the vicinity every year. As a result, I was well aware of its symptoms, which generally emerged two days after the carrier spread the airborne infection to others.

At that time, quarantines were considered the best method to protect a population from contracting a number of virulent diseases. For the most part, the fact that someone in the town was in quarantine was not terribly alarming or life-altering to those who were not so restrained. The exception arose when the quarantine was imposed due to a suspected case of scarlet fever. The grievous nature of the virus, as it related to children, arose not from that particular infection but from the more dangerous secondary infection that sometimes followed: rheumatic fever. It was that fever which routinely left its young victims blind, deaf, or dead. As a result, when quarantine was established in the town for scarlet fever, my life changed in three distinct ways.

Firstly, I was required to avoid congregating indoors or in any other close confines with unrelated children. Thus, the posting of a yellow quarantine banner on the door of a local house ended many indoor activities for me, including attendance at school and church. The Northern Flats that surrounded the Etobicoke Creek behind the high school became the refuge of the young. So long as we did not swim in the Etobicoke when the waters were warm, low, and full of effluent or when the waters were high and swift—matters generally assured by the vast number of overseeing teenagers—the Flats were considered the safest place for children to congregate during a period of quarantine.

Secondly, cream became a large staple of my diet. Determined by many a wife's tale to have medicinal effects on those suffering from the scourge, mothers often plied their children prophylactically with the dairy product while a scarlet-fever-quarantine was in effect. During that time, I could expect to have it served to me three or more times a day in a variety of forms: the warm, thick fluid enlivened my porridge in the morning, the cool, whipped form was dolloped on my pudding or fruit at noon, and a frozen ball of it graced my dessert bowls after tea. With each meal my usual glass of milk was infused with an equal amount of the rich liquid. The novelty of the indulgence soon turned to one of drudgery. We were likely the only generation of children in the twentieth century who came to abhor most forms of cream.

Thirdly, in a manner not limited to quarantines of the scarlet fever variety, within hours of the state being declared, I could expect to become the sole occupant of my bedroom, for Ina would no sooner stay at home while any local quarantine was being observed than she would kiss the lips of a tuberculosis victim. On the one occasion that Father insisted she stay at home, she isolated herself in our room, refusing to leave for any reason. Such a situation would have been tolerable for the rest of us if it brought her even an iota of solace, but in fact it brought her none. The wailing that emerged from within the barricade of our room displayed to the rest of us the real distress she encountered in those times.

On this occasion in August 1911, as on all others, Father had barely reported the rumoured outbreak to us when Ina asked to be excused from the table. While such a concession was rarely granted before a meal was complete, we all knew that it would not be declined on a day like that. Within minutes, Ina re-emerged in the dining room with a small travel bag in her hands, a hat on her head, and a cloak over her arm. We knew the request that would come and the dispensation that would be granted. She departed immediately for the train station, promising to send a telegram to Father following her arrival at Aunt Lil's. She would send a similar communication to Grandpa, who was then visiting friends in Toronto, urging him to delay his return.

Perhaps because none of Father's vitriol could be aimed at the not-long-departed Ina, by the time he left our house to return to his office that afternoon, I bore the brunt of it all. The last thing Father commanded as he stormed out the door and stood on the verandah was that it be cleared of all of the clutter—Ina's as well as mine. "Jessie, you know I cannot long abide this disorder. Do something to improve yourself. Go for a long walk! It would better occupy your time."

Frances and Archie, who heard the bluster as they approached the house, joined me in dismantling our fine ship. Having heard Father's instructions and having some sympathy for our situation, Mother joined us on the verandah with a basket of apples, biscuits, and bread, and a suggestion that we proceed to the Flats.

We had not walked long toward the Flats when Frances speculated that the suggested destination was likely to be full of potentially infected children, all of whom would be drawn to us by the basket Mother had assembled. She suggested that our health and appetites would be better served walking to a place outside of Brampton and its contagion. Archie concurred and suggested the destination of Derry West, the home of his cousins. Frances's concerns regarding the distance to that locale were squelched by Archie, who was certain that we could walk the distance and back in an hour. My concerns regarding lack of parental consent were as easily dismissed by Archie's recitation of Father's last command to me that I take some exercise and, specifically, "go for a long walk."

Upon reaching the four corners in the town's centre, instead of turning right to walk to the Flats, we turned left to begin our walk to Derry Road. As we walked along Main Street, we gave no consideration to the fact that our route deprived our mothers of any notion of our true destination and resulted in us walking without adult accompaniment along the open parts of the Etobicoke parallel to Main Street, something Frances and I were forbidden to do. Wearing our normal play clothes and shoes and carrying a basket of food, we commenced the eight-mile trek with all of the confidence in our quick return that can be assembled in the minds of those truly ignorant.

We walked south, passing a number of the big mansions that dotted Main Street. Very much in the centre of the town, we considered how delightful it would be to live in a house with so many rooms.

"I could have a room to myself," I wistfully declared.

"You could have a wing to yourself," Archie added.

We walked south. We reached the outskirts of the downtown area, where the houses were fewer and farther between. Our gait was spry. Filled with a sense of adventure, Frances and I defied the warnings of our parents. With Archie by our side, we deliberately chose to walk next to the Etobicoke. Picking up sticks, we threw them into the creek on the one side of the road and then crossed to see them emerge on the other. On that day, the water was low and slow. We frequently had to wait for the re-emergence.

We walked south. On our left, we passed the Bull farm, named not for the type of cattle bred there (although certainly there was a bull or two among the herd of Jersey cows) but for the name of the family that owned it. Bartley Bull had been a conglomerator of residential, agricultural, and commercial interests in Toronto and Brampton in the last century.

"My father once told me that the Bull family will eventually sell this land, although not as a whole," Archie told us, hesitating at the reference to the father he missed so much. "One day, the family plans to divide it into hundreds and hundreds of lots, to build a house on each and then sell each lot and house separately. They just have to wait for the population to grow so there will be enough people to buy the homes."

I thought of Grandpa and the four houses he built on the farmland on the other side of the town fifty years earlier and all of the other houses that he had since built in the downtown area. The thought of hundreds being built on the one piece of property struck us as preposterous. Laughing at the notion, we each vowed to purchase one of those Bull houses when we were adults so that we could always be neighbours.

We walked south. We waved at the drivers of passing carriages and horses. We complimented each other on our fortitude in walking as far as we had without a single complaint and readied ourselves for the last leg of our journey, which we mistakenly considered was equal to the distance we had thus far covered. We had in fact travelled less than a quarter of the way to the settlement of Derry West.

We walked south. We became peckish. We stopped walking just beyond the road that separated Chinguacousy Township, in which we lived, from Toronto Township, next to it, at the trunk of a large maple tree lying just off the side of the road. We steadied ourselves on its spongy bark. We reached into the basket that Mother prepared and which we had each readily carried in turns. We devoured the biscuits as the large herd of the Neelands' big-eyed, fawn-coloured Jersey cows ate their cud beyond the fence behind us. We considered how wonderful it would be to have a glass of fresh milk anytime you wanted it and imagined it improving the taste of Mother's already delicious baking.

We walked south. We passed the Fallis farm with its large beech tree near a pond. The tree had boards banged into its trunk, forming a ladder to a wooden landing about fifteen feet above the ground. To the right of the landing dangled a rope, hung from a branch ten feet above. We imagined swinging from the rope before releasing ourselves into the pond's cool waters below.

We walked south. We passed grazers: more cows, woolly sheep, and horses. A big dog barked ferociously as we approached. None of us had a dog at home. We sought to outdo each other with our professed love and desire for the ownership of such a pet. We called various affectionate greetings to the canine. It eventually approached us but never left its property, even when we fed it Mother's bread.

At last, when the sun was clearly on the waning side of its daily traverse, we came to Derry Road. Turning west, we could see the village of Derry West, its two churches, one schoolhouse, the Temperance and Orange Halls, its post office, and the surrounding homes. Our oasis in sight, we quickened our pace as Archie told us what to expect of his cousins and their warm hospitality. He was sure we would all be offered a cold drink and fresh-baked cookies. His aunt, he told us, was one of the world's best bakers.

"There it is," Archie said. "Let's run the rest of the way. My cousins' house is among the first in the village. Jessie, just put down that empty basket. We can pick it up when we walk back." I readily obliged. My right hand was sore from carrying it. "And don't forget," he said, "we can run faster if we stretch out our arms and holler as we go." Assuming the entirely non-aerodynamic stance he had long advocated and wasting much-needed lung capacity, we followed him and made a fast, loud, and large introduction into this small, quiet village, the doors of which we realized, as soon as we came to the first, were covered in quarantine-warning yellow banners.

We walked north. Archie and Frances made me retrieve the empty basket. The sore on my hand was quickly developing into a blister. It was nothing compared with the sore feelings I felt at having to again carry the basket. I was sure that I had borne a disproportionate share of that burden.

We walked north, passing the bread-eating dog. Though we had nothing more to offer it and called for it not once, it ran to us, sniffing our legs and behinds and refusing to go home no matter how many times we pointed it in the direction of its master's farm.

We walked north. A blister was developing on one of my toes. We halted our trek for a few minutes. Archie and Frances leaned against a fence post, the dog sitting on the ground beside them. After extracting my right foot, I reached into the shoe, hoping to stretch the leather to provide a bit more space. Within seconds, my fingers inadvertently pushed through the seam between the lower sole and the upper leather.

We walked north. We passed the pond, the beech tree, and the rope. From this light, it was clear that the ladder-like steps on the tree trunk were a great distance from each other and started about four feet off the ground, the landing looked narrow and precarious, the rope threadbare and the pond muddy and algae-filled. We couldn't imagine swimming in it.

We walked north. We passed the Neelands' farm and their dang dairy cows. Who would want to drink more milk? Were we not already required to drink three glasses a day? Our stomachs grumbled at the thought. It was nearly teatime, and we were still a long way from home.

We walked north. We took little notice of the Etobicoke, though we passed over it a number of times on its winding course under the road. Archie could not see why Frances's parents and mine cared so much about how near to it we walked. "Really," he said, "even the worst swimmer could climb out of that water. It's slower than a turtle and only a few times deeper than my bathtub!"

We walked north. At last we entered the more populated area of Brampton. Our joy at soon being able to rest our sore feet was somewhat diminished by the knowledge that our backsides were not likely to fare so well and the meal we so greatly desired was likely to be deprived of us until morning. It was half past six. Our parents would be angry. They would come to know that we walked near the Etobicoke without any supervision; mine would see that I ruined a pair of shoes, and, if the black dog continued to follow us home, they would likely surmise that we wasted Mother's bread. In my home, these were all corporal offences.

We walked north. We turned on the one who had proposed the scheme. Frances and I were united in our suggestion that Archie pay more attention in geography and math class in the future. How could he have thought this to be a one-hour excursion? Not wanting to take all of the blame, he reminded us that it was Frances's idea to avoid the Flats and my father's command that I take a long walk. Our bickering came to an end when we approached Gage Park. As I vigorously tried to shoo away the black dog, Frances tugged at my sleeve and pointed to two of the nearest trees.

"Look," she said when my eyes did not immediately catch the object of hers. "Isn't that Millie and Sarah standing on the lower branches of those two trees?" I turned to where she directed me. "And who are those boys with them?" she asked excitedly, knowing as I then knew that teenagers in love climbed trees together.

Her eyes were better than mine. I couldn't make out any of them, but I immediately suggested that the males could be Jim and Eddie. I had known for over a year at that point that Millie was Jim's heart's desire. In all that time, I had never witnessed any reciprocation on her part, but for Jim's sake, I hoped that she was merely shy about her feelings.

"It won't be them," Frances declared confidently as we continued walking. "I hear that those girls are now sweet on Grenville Davis and Clarence Charters." Poor Jim, I thought.

We reached the big bridge at Wellington Street and crossed it, our heads down, the black dog still at our feet. Frances crossed the street again to be closer to her home. Archie ran ahead, seeking to eliminate by at least one minute the anxiety he suspected his mother was suffering, though such a concern had not previously occupied a moment of his time. His flash of energy was an incitement to the dog, which followed Archie the rest of the way.

I was alone then when I walked the final distance to my home. When I was half a block away, passing the registry office between the courthouse and the jail, I made out the shape of Mother standing at the bottom of our verandah's steps, her arms bent at the elbows, fists dug into her hips. It was not a welcoming stance. She looked cross. But then I took in her unusual garb. Absent was the ever-present apron. Her dress was fuller than what she ordinarily wore, and it was black. Mother never wore black. Black was reserved for widows. I realized then that it was not Mother standing at the base of the verandah. It was my Aunt Rose.

I recalled the time that Ina went missing on that windy rainy night four years earlier; how Grandpa and I stayed at home waiting for her to return while Mother and Father went into the storm to look for her. I assumed that Aunt Rose was playing the role of the then absent Grandpa in this lost sheep re-enactment and that Father and Mother were now out looking for me. I wondered how long they had been gone. Poor Mother. Poor Father. I had not intended to cause them any distress.

With my form in sight, Aunt Rose left the verandah's steps and began to walk toward me. Her steps were quicker than mine, and within seconds we met across the road from the Hudsons' house. Its front door was still reverberating from Frances's quick entrance.

"Aunt Rose," I said as we met, the concern in my voice now only for my parents. "Where are Mother and Father?"

"They are fine, dear," she replied, reassuringly. "They are at home. They have been there for a couple of hours now."

Relief washed over me. They had not spent the past hours in frantic search for me. My relief, though, was quickly replaced by curiosity. "Why were you at our house, Aunt Rose? Were you waiting for me?"

I looked in the direction of my home and noticed for the first time that all of the curtains on the main floor were drawn. That was odd for the hour, especially given that it was not a particularly hot day. I moved to the side of my aunt, whose back was to our house and whose torso was blocking my view to our front door. As I moved one way, so did she. As I moved the other way. Aunt Rose, like a shadow, moved that way as well. Looking up into her eyes, I saw an unfamiliar look. It took me a few seconds to place it. Pity. My aunt regarded me with unmistakable pity. Slowly backing up three, five, ten steps, I summoned all of my remaining strength before running around her and the remaining distance to my house, the yellow quarantine sign on the door growing larger and larger as I approached it.

Aunt Rose, who had followed at a slower pace, eventually caught up to my then frozen form pitched on the sidewalk in front of our house. I stared up at the vacant verandah that earlier that day had been festooned with activity; the heavily curtained windows that hid the front foyer; the garish yellow sign that proclaimed better than any words could: "Grave illness resides here."

She stood beside me, her one arm wrapped around me, staring at the house. "One of your father's afternoon patients left his office symptomatic. The public health department arrived almost immediately afterward," Aunt Rose explained.

I pictured Mother and Father in our house, fevers raging, joints aching, throats ravaged, and glands swollen. Their tongues would be bumpy and white, their chests, abdomens, and armpits covered in red tiny bumps, their fingertips peeling. Mother would be caring for Father; no one would be caring for Mother. We stood in silence until I spoke, quietly, barely more than a whisper.

"Can I go in there with them?" I thought of the number of times I wished for Dr. Heggie to be summoned to tend to my mother. Now I only wanted one person to do so—as young, feeble and useless as she might be. I needed to go to her.

Aunt Rose answered as I knew she would. With a firm squeeze of my shoulders, she instructed me to stay where I was. Walking onto the verandah, she pulled back the screen door and gave five quick wraps on the big glass-topped wooden door. Seeing something just beyond the glass, she turned and walked back to me. My parents knew I was with her. She took my hand in hers and led me back down the street to her house.

Although my aunt went to great lengths to soothe me that first night in her home, the tears that were the frequent companion of my childhood joined me while I lay in the big bed in the spare room.

The initial days of my parents' confinement were extremely difficult for me, but their ease was contributed to by various members of my family. Though my aunt urged me otherwise, I spent the first two days sitting across the road from my house, watching for any movement from behind the curtain-covered windows. On the morning of the second day, my cousin John presented me with a stool he had built in his basement workshop. While it had no upright piece on which to rest my back, it was a vast improvement from the low seat the sidewalk provided. It also served another purpose, which earned it the name the "kissing stool."

From my long observations, I soon noticed that Mother occasionally pulled back the curtains of the foyer window to look at the street beyond. Seeing me sitting on that street, through a variety of hand gestures we eventually worked out a system whereby once in the morning and once in the afternoon, I would carry my stool onto the verandah, set it below the foyer window, stand upon it and kiss her lips through the clear pane.

Our communications improved with the aid of Hannah, who brought me paper, ink, and tape. Following the exchange of affections between Mother and me, I would tape a page of big-lettered words to the window next to me, and Mother would tape a similar page to her side of the window. In this way I came to know that while she missed us all greatly, she and Father were both well and symptom-free.

My brother Jim saw me once a day, sharing my aunt's table each evening and receiving reports from me on our parents' health.

It was only as I moved back home when the quarantine was lifted that I realized how much Mother had also contributed to my comfort. As I unpacked my nightgown, toothbrush, tooth powder, my porcelain-faced cloth doll Susie, and my valise of clothes, I began to reflect on the logistics of the arrangements. "Mother," I asked as I approached her room, "how did all of these things get into Aunt Rose's house last week?"

"I delivered them to Aunt Rose, Jessie, just as a similar delivery was made to the McMurchys for Jim."

I thought about that for a moment. "Were you let out of the quarantine to make the deliveries?"

"Oh, I see. No. I made the deliveries before we went into quarantine. Father stayed at his office for three hours before coming home. A public health worker told me when he would be coming. That gave me time to make the arrangements." I thought about that further.

"But who were you exposed to that had been infected?"

"I wasn't exposed to anyone who had been infected, as it turned out. Your father, of course, had been exposed to an infected person."

I thought about that further. "Mother, did the public health nurse make you go into quarantine with Father?"

"No, Jessie, the public health department did not require me to go into quarantine. They required your father to go into quarantine. But I did not want your father to be alone in the quarantine, particularly if he became ill and required assistance."

My thoughts as I lay in bed that night were not of the Presbyterian Church or how Grandpa became self-made and others-destroyed or of that elusive phrase, the "Scottish Fiasco"; no, my thoughts were of love and its many forms. My father, who rarely displayed any kind of love, went into quarantine to provide the best protection possible for me, Ina, Jim, and other children. That was a powerful form of love.

My mother, who I loved and adored above all others, had deliberately put herself in a position that, taken to its extreme, indicated she would rather die with my father than live with me. That was a powerful and somewhat disturbing form of love.

The love of Jesse and Louisa Brady was born over a single dinner, lit in a single proposal and smouldered into a hot coal over three years while the two of them were separated by an ocean and without any communication between them. Their courtship did not involve the drawing of pictures or the climbing of trees. Was there any hope then for Jim and Millie? Was his heart destined to be broken, as Grandpa's was early on?

I had a lot to think about. As it turned out, I had plenty of time to do so. Within a week, our house was once again in quarantine. This time it involved all six of us, Grandpa included, as first Ina, then Jim, and then I developed the tell-tale strawberry-like white bumpy tongues and sandpapery red-skinned symptoms of scarlet fever. Fortunately, when those symptoms left us, they were not replaced by others more serious.

Chapter 13

THE MIGHTY ETOBICOKE

From my earliest days, there were two things I knew about running. Firstly, being able to run at a great speed and for a great length of time were valuable traits in a family like mine that prized athleticism over most other pursuits. Secondly, running was nearly always thrilling, unless one was running away from something, in which case it could be terrifying. What I did not appreciate until May 30, 1912, was that sometimes people run toward terrifying things. There was one other thing I learned about running on that fateful day: a mother running down a street in full flight is a certain cause for concern.

Though it ended otherwise, the day itself started quite normally. Frances and I, just nine years old, were in our third year at the two-room Queen Street Public School. As junior second-formers, we were at that most confident stage in our tutelage there, experienced enough in the ways of the little school to lord our wherewithal over the junior and senior first formers but not yet cowed by the insecurity that would come the following year as we prepared to progress our studies at the larger middle school.

Our routine had not changed much since we began attending the school. I continued to be frightened each time I approached the intersection of Queen and George Streets and the Kelly Iron Works Repair Shop on the southwest corner. Recognizing the need for protection, I endeavoured to ensure that I was never alone as I walked past that juncture four times a day. My dependence on Archie before he left the school for the middle school two years before Frances and me, and on Frances and other friends—or even on complete strangers, on those rare occasions when none of my friends were available—was always great.

Though Frances never complained, I am confident that she looked forward to the relief from the responsibility of that accompaniment almost as much as I did the need of it. The middle school we would attend fifteen months later and the high school we would attend thereafter were located on the east side of Main Street. Once enrolled in either of those institutions, it would not be necessary to pass the Kelly Iron Works Repair Shop on my way to my daily studies. I anticipated the carefree walk I would make to those schools, all by myself, if I so chose. I practically delighted in the thought of the mere cemetery I would pass on my way to the high school.

Frances and I were alone as we walked home from school that Tuesday afternoon at the end of May. Passing through the town centre, halfway along our route, we encountered, as usual, a number of friends and acquaintances. The first of which we took particular notice were Millie Dale and Sarah Lawson. The two twenty-year-olds were leaving Robinson & Stork's store, bags in hand. We had already crossed to the other side of the intersection, and so as the older girls stood outside the store, we were able to take in their full stance as well as the store behind them.

"They look just like the models in the window," Frances said in amazement. Aside from the absence of heads and appendages on the seamstress models, I had to agree. The live girls both wore canvas-like straight-lined skirts with coloured blouses. They wore nearly identical stockings, which were visible to a full three inches above the ankle. One was dressed in tan and blue, the other in grey and yellow. Both girls, having received business program diplomas in Toronto earlier that year, were employees of the Dale Estate. The sign in Robinson & Stork's window indicated that ready-to-wear skirts could be purchased for between $1.65 and $3.50 and blouses for up to $1.00. I wondered whether I would ever be able to afford premade apparel. To that point, my clothing acquisitions from that store had been in lengths of fabric and New Idea patterns.

"Nice to see those girls on the ground, though, isn't it?" Frances said, snickering slightly. "Remember when we saw them in the trees last summer?"

"I remember," I replied. "They were with Clarence Charters and Grenville Davis." My heart ached for Jim every time I thought of Millie in the branches with one of those boys.

"I heard that one of those girls and one of those boys don't climb trees together anymore."

My thoughts went hopefully to Jim. "Which girl?"

"I can't remember." For a gossip, Frances's skills needed to be honed.

"You do know the difference between them, don't you?" Many people confused the two girls, who looked so similar. Both had lovely figures contained within identical five-foot-four inch frames. Both had creamy white skin and a wide smile. Neither girl had freckles or moles. Both had big eyes and perfectly formed ears. As was typical for the day, they both had long hair, which they wore tied back with a ribbon. Aside from the colour of Millie's blonde hair and Sarah's brown hair, they were practically indistinguishable—when they were quiet. But once they started speaking, there was no difficulty identifying the elocutionist, for the lovely lilt that emitted from Millie's lips was contrasted by a dreadful high, scratchy din from Sarah's.

"Of course I know the difference," Frances replied matter-of-factly. "They go to my church." The Hudsons attended the Presbyterian Church, the church my family would not enter. "I just can't recall which of those girls I heard about."

"I don't know how you can listen to her voice," I said.

Frances replied, knowing that I was referring to Sarah. "You get used to it after a while. I don't even hear the scratching sound anymore. You should hear her sing. Mother says she is a lovely soprano." In actuality, I had not often heard Sarah. The complaint about her voice was one I regularly heard uttered by Ina, who, being eight years older than me, had more occasion to associate with Sarah.

We did not consider crossing the road and speaking with Millie and Sarah, who we were certain would barely take notice of us. Instead we turned our attention to Archie and two of the *Excelsior* ship-hands, Morley Burrows and Willie Core, who were walking toward us. With school packs slung over their shoulders and hand-made wooden boats in their hands, the three boys were on their way to launch their home-made versions of *Titanic II, Titanic III,* and *Titanic IV.* They vowed that their boats would achieve in stability, buoyancy, and engineering soundness what six weeks earlier their namesake had not. With no parental requirements to first attend to their studies and chores and no prohibition on playing near the Etobicoke Creek, the boys were on their way to the nearby park, where the creek ran next to Main Street. The big willow tree just north of the Wellington Street Bridge was, they told us, an ideal launch site.

We wished them a *bon voyage* and continued on our way. Play before homework and chores was not something permitted to Frances by her father, who was the principal of the local high school, or to me by my father, who was the chairman of the local high school board. At the corner of Chapel and Wellington Streets—only a block away from the launch site of the three *Titanics*—Frances turned right toward her house, and I crossed the street to mine.

Within an hour of my arrival home, my schoolwork and my mandatory thirty-minute piano practice complete, I was in search of *Oliver Twist,* the book I had borrowed from the library the week before. My father compelled me to undertake thirty minutes of reading a day, in addition to the homework dispensed by my teachers. The book was neither in my room nor the sitting room. I would not have left it in the kitchen, the dining room, or the parlour, places from which a stray object was sure to be confiscated by my father, who required all things to be left in their proper place.

Thinking that I might have had it with me the day before, when I spoke to Jim in his room, I returned upstairs. The orderliness of his room allowed me to quickly confirm that my book was not on his chest of drawers, his dressing table beside the door, or his tall secretary's desk behind it. Looking at the empty surface at the top of that desk, I was reminded of the furtive examinations in which I had formerly engaged, leafing through the drawings he stacked there, trying to ascertain the identity of the girl whose face he was drawing.

While Jim had been away at the university over the past year, I had been deprived of the opportunity to leaf through his drawings. I had no idea if his heart continued to be set on Millie. It was not something I would dream of asking him. There was one sure way to know.

I stopped and listened. The only sounds I heard were those emanating from the street. It was a nice day, and Jim's window was wide open. There was no one else upstairs in our house. Jim was still at work; Father, Mother, Ina, and Grandpa were downstairs. I pulled opened the door to Jim's closet, dragged over the sturdy desk chair, and climbed atop it, reaching for one of the large stacks of drawings stored on the cupboard's high shelf. There were hundreds of drawings there.

Jim's hand had been prodigious while he had been studying at the university. In my effort to see a drawing of a particular girl's face, I first had to review many less animate objects. He was obviously still fixated with automobiles, for there were dozens of them drawn in his firm hand. Most were in the style of the day: carriage-shaped, with big wheels. Some, though, were less conventional—elongated, lower, and narrower, with smaller wheels. I laughed at the look of them. Eventually, in the third stack of drawings, I came upon what I desired most to see: a fully drawn face of Millie Dale, slightly more detailed than the image I had seen the prior summer on the debating society's program. But it was the same face. I smiled and rose to return the stack of drawings to the shelf. It was as I was dragging the chair back to its position next to the desk that I heard the sound of running feet on the street below.

Through the screen of the window that overlooked Chapel Street, I watched Morley and Willie run up Wellington Street before turning the corner at Chapel and running past our house. I wondered where Archie was, but the sight of running boys was nothing to be alarmed about, and so I was perfectly sanguine as I went downstairs to the verandah in further search of my book. I hoped I had not left it outside the previous day. The dampness of the intervening night would surely have swollen its bindings, something the library would not look upon kindly.

The verandah was clutter-free at that time—just as Father liked it. It was too soon in the year for Ina to fashion another science lab, or me and my friends to establish a make-believe ship. It took me but a moment to confirm that *Oliver Twist* was not on the swinging chaise lounge, the seats of the large wooden chairs, the tops of the little tables between them, or on the floor below them. I considered whether I had put the book in my school bag that morning. Certainly it had not been in my bag when I arrived at school. It occurred to me that it might have fallen out of my bag on my way there. Other items had occasionally been lost that way.

I had no time to consider the matter, though, as the notion had barely occurred to me when I again heard running feet. This time they approached our house from the opposite direction. The sense of alarm that eluded me three minutes earlier suddenly claimed me in full force, not because of the exertion of the two boys, but because this time that exertion was mirrored by two women. Following closely behind the two boys, at a pace that could only be adrenalin-induced, ran Archie's mother, Elizabeth McKechnie, her black widow's weeds streaming behind her, her eyes wild with panic, her skin ashen. Behind them all, with an identical countenance, was her eldest daughter, Emily, then eighteen. Emily slowed down when she saw me.

"Jessie!" she screamed. "Get help! It's Archie. He fell in the creek!" *Fell in the creek*, I thought. *What's the panic?* Archie scoffed at those scared by the creek. He was ten years of age. He knew how to swim. His mother deemed him to be of sufficient maturity to walk and play by the creek. I stood there, fixated on those thoughts for what seemed like minutes but must only have been seconds, for when Emily yelled at me again, she was not much further along. "Jessie! Move! He's missing!"

Then I did move. I really moved. I ran into the sitting room, where Mother, Father, Grandpa, and Ina were gathered. Father threw down the day's edition of the *Mail & Empire* and removed his pipe from his mouth. With quick commands, he had us on our way. Mother was to summon our male neighbours. Ina was to run to the fire hall to have the alarm sounded and then go to the McKechnies' to wait with Archie's youngest sisters, one of whom, Katie, was her particular friend. Grandpa and I were to go to the Dale Estate and summon my brother Jim. Father was leaving for the Wellington Street Bridge. "And Jessie," he commanded as we were all about to set off, "once you have spoken to Jim, you are to come straight back here. You are not to leave this house until I say you may!"

With thoughts a-jumble, I took Grandpa's outstretched hand, and we began our journey to the Dale Estate, three-quarters of a mile away, my emotions too occupied, too contradictory, functioning on too many levels to speak. I wanted to be at the creek looking for Archie in the water. I wanted to find him sitting on a tree stump on its banks, wondering what all the fuss was about. I wanted Grandpa's calming hand around mine. I wanted to run ahead of Grandpa and leave him and his slow legs behind me. I wanted to run into our church, which we passed on our way, and pray. I wanted to get to Jim as fast as we could. I was relieved to hear the sounding bell of the fire hall, calling all able-bodied men to the station. I was annoyed by the clanging—it aggravated my already pounding head.

We were only halfway to the Dale Estate when, seeing figures ahead, my mind cleared and my nerves calmed. There, running toward us, were ten, twenty, thirty men. On hearing the fire alarm, Tommy Duggan, the manager of the Dale Estate, had released all of his available men. Leading the group were the youngest among the workers, with my brother Jim at the lead. The sight of him was an epiphany for me. With every cell of my body, I knew how this would end. Jim would find and save Archie. He stopped briefly to hear our account of the calamity while others ran by us, and then he shot off, quickly regaining his position at the head of the pack.

As Grandpa and I walked back toward our house, we could see people gathered at the Wellington Street Bridge, yards away from the willow tree where less than two hours before Archie, Morley, and Willie had launched their ships. Grandpa's firm tug on my arm as we arrived at Queen Street made it clear that we would not be going home via the bridge. Instead, we took the route I normally took to and from downtown—the one away from the exposed running creek. In front of the fire hall on Chapel Street, just behind the new Carnegie Library, we passed a number of volunteer firefighters. With a big map rolled out on a table in front of him, Mr. Harmsworth, who had succeeded my Uncle James as the fire chief, was directing the men to positions as far south as the township line.

With some rearrangement of the verandah furniture, Grandpa and I assumed a position in which we could see west along Wellington Street to the big bridge and north along Chapel Street to the fire hall. As late afternoon turned to evening, and then evening to night, we watched dozens of people move between those two epicentres. We watched and we waited. We heard the chimes of St. Paul's ring six o'clock. We heard the bells of Grace toll seven o'clock. We heard the arrival of the 7:15 train from Toronto. We saw men rushing home to pick up their wading boots. We saw women delivering sandwiches and coffee to the fire hall and the bridge. We did not see Ina. We did not see Jim. We did not see Mother. We did not see Father. We watched and we waited.

We heard rumours. We heard reports. We heard speculation. Archie was found! Archie was not found. Archie's blue shirt was seen! It was someone else's blue shirt that was seen. Archie had been pulled out of the creek by Mr. Bull, just beyond the southern portion of his farm. Mr. Bull was away from town and could not possibly have pulled Archie from the creek near his farm. None of it was reliable. One report was barely in circulation before a contradictory report was received. We watched and we waited.

While we frequently asked those passing by us for reports, Grandpa and I were otherwise quite silent. At one point, I heard Grandpa and our neighbour Mr. Trimble refer in a quiet, code-like way to the correlation between passing minutes and diminishing prospects. I could guess what they were referring to. I could guess what they were thinking. I did not ask for an explanation. I did not want to discuss it. I did not believe it. I watched and I waited.

At one point, when the traffic between the bridge and the fire hall dissipated and many minutes had passed since anyone had spoken to us, and even more time had passed since we had spoken to each other, Grandpa broke the silence. "Jessie," he said, "are you alright?"

"Yes, Grandpa," I replied calmly, "I'm fine."

"It's just that you seem strangely calm. Are you not very worried?" Grandpa ventured.

"I'm not very worried," I said. "I know that Archie is fine."

"I am relieved," he replied, "and a little curious. What may I ask is the source of your confidence? Is it your faith in the Lord?"

"No," I said, and then, fearing the blasphemy of that statement would render my confidence baseless, I quickly qualified it. "Not just that. It's also my faith in Jim."

"Jim? What are you thinking?"

"Jim saved William Whittaker." I was referring to the little boy who Jim and Eddie had pulled onto their *Folly* in the big spring flood two years earlier. "If Jim could save William Whittaker, I know he can save Archie."

"That is strong faith."

"Yes, I have a lot of faith in Jim," I said, steeling myself and then, to cover my bases, "and also in Jesus."

"Your faith in your brother is to be admired, but as he is just human, I wonder if we should say a little prayer." I took Grandpa's hands in mine and bowed my head. "Heavenly Father," he began.

But was my faith really that strong? It was tested a number of times, and I cannot say that it never wavered. The first test presented itself when Mr. Peaker, one of our neighbours, advised us of the need to expand the search parameters. It was nearly 7:45 p.m. when he hurried up the street. He told us that the search parties had not found Archie in the immediate vicinity. He was going to speak with Mr. Harmsworth about sending some parties further south—at least as far as Derry Road. From my walk the summer before, I knew how far away that was. It was a long way for a person to float.

My faith was tested again with the return of Mrs. McKechnie half an hour later. How could one's faith not be shaken at the sight of a clearly broken woman being led home in the arms of her nearly grown daughter and another woman—for it took all of the strength of Emily McKechnie and my mother to convey Mrs. McKechnie up Wellington Street to Chapel Street and then one block further to her home on Peel Avenue.

It was 8:15 p.m. She had been down at the creek for nearly three hours, looking for her son, waiting for news that someone—anyone—had found him; her only son, and for the two years since the death of her husband, the only man of the family. Not a word was uttered from our verandah as they passed us. Mother's eyes clearly communicated to us the need for absolute silence. The three women were only just around the corner on Peel Avenue when quieter, slower steps followed them. Aunt Rose and Mrs. Hudson, both carrying plates of food, deposited their children on our verandah and then walked the remaining distance to the McKechnies' home.

The silence in which Grandpa and I had mostly sat did not suit my cousins Hannah and John, or my friend Frances. After grousing about the fact that they, like me, were prohibited from participating in the search, they began to reminisce about some of their favourite experiences with Archie.

"Don't you remember," Hannah said, "that one time we were at Gage Park waiting for the band to begin, and the band members were so late that Archie started juggling to entertain the crowds? He was the funniest little guy." She moved her hands in the air, keeping aloft imaginary balls. They all joined in her laughter.

"And what about the time last month when we were playing baseball? He was the pitcher, and he walked every single player before they pulled him. Of course, he went on to score three home runs. He was the best player and the worst player of the same game!" recounted John, also provoking warm laughter among the three of them.

Sensing perhaps that it was not yet the time to laugh, Frances changed the subject and invoked a more sentimental memory. "Whenever I think of Archie, I am going to think of the card he gave me this past Valentine's Day. It was so special. It was a postcard with a picture of an orange on the front of it. It said 'Orange you glad we are friends?' It was special because I knew it was just for me. We were so close."

Their sweet and humorous reminiscences came to a halt following an angry outburst. "Oh! Be quiet all of you!" I heard someone yell. It was some time before I realized that the bellower of these words was me. The others on the porch seemed as startled as I was that I could so raise my voice, but having done so, I felt the need to speak further. "You know, Frances, it isn't that you and Archie were close. You *are* close. And Hannah, that may be the funniest thing you have seen Archie do, but it won't be the last. And John, that will not be the last baseball game you'll see Archie play. I won't have you talking like he's dead! I won't. He is *not* dead. He hasn't come home yet. But he will. He will come home!"

They were silent; ashamed, I thought.

"What makes you so sure, Jessie?" Frances asked sheepishly.

"I have faith." They all bowed their heads.

"I have faith in God. And I have faith in my brother Jim."

"In Jim?" Frances asked.

"He saved William Whittaker two years ago, didn't he?" I spat. They all nodded in agreement—all except John.

"What about the little dog?" he asked. William Whittaker's dog, whose fall into the swelling creek had led to the near loss of human life, was not as fortunate as his master.

Grandpa and I sat in silence for a long while after Frances and my cousins were retrieved by their mothers. By nine, the sun had set. The nearly full moon was barely perceptible through the night's heavy clouds. The light in the foyer behind us supplemented the illumination cast by the street lamps in front of us. Grandpa asked me if I was ready to go inside, but I was determined to wait for Jim, to see Archie returned to his mother.

The traffic between the fire hall and the bridge dwindled. With the loss of that traffic, so too went any reports on the state of the search. Finally, around 9:15 we were visited by two people who seemed knowledgeable. Jim's friends Millie and Sarah, having spent hours wading in the banks of the creek, felt they could do no more in the darkness but await the word of others. Wet and dirty, their new shoes and stockings ruined, they asked if they could sit with Grandpa and me and wait for Jim. Over the next half hour, the two girls told us everything they knew, their report being imparted in turns by Millie with her sweet angel's voice and Sarah with her high scratchy intonation.

In short, it was clear that the fate of the second, third, and fourth *Titanic*s was no different than the first, all sinking on their maiden voyage. The demise occurred within moments of their launch, so the boys sought other means of amusement, and after seeking out the appropriate implements, they commenced a game of spearing litter floating atop the creek with long alder sticks. The water was fairly clear and the targets of their efforts fairly sparse. Eventually, though, a book was seen floating down the creek, and Archie called it as his quarry. Slightly too far from the shore, he lost his balance as he reached to spike it and fell into the water just south of the willow. Within seconds, he was carried downstream, pulled under the surface by the strong current. He rose twice and was then submerged and seen no more. Rescue parties had waded into the creek, combing its edges and dredging its centre as they were able.

The Southern Flats—the flood plains area around the creek south of Wellington Street—had been searched, as had the other areas around the creek, in case he had escaped the torrents. I pictured him walking from the waterway, disoriented or having taken some solitary refuge, perhaps in a state of shock.

Some members of the rescue parties were by then well south of Derry Road. Jim was not among them. He was convinced that Archie was closer to home and was searching the wooden areas around the creek's in-town beds. Within minutes of relating that fact, Sarah's father was at the base of our verandah, requiring her to leave with him. Millie declined Mr. Lawson's offer to accompany her home, declaring her intention to wait for Jim, who, given the hour and the darkness, would likely be not much longer.

Shortly after they left, Grandpa went inside. He had not long retired when Father approached us, also wet and dirty. Father had just left the McKechnies' house, where Mother and Ina were planning to spend the night. Pre-empting any command that I go inside, I quickly announced my desire to stay with Millie and wait for Jim. Father muttered something to the effect of "nothing being right on this night" and left us alone on the verandah.

Assuming the role formerly occupied by Grandpa, Millie, a near stranger to me, sat quietly next to me, gently rocking the chaise lounge on which we sat. What conversation we initially had was with those few people passing by, slowly making their way home.

Mr. Peaker was the last person we spoke to for a long while. "Is that all that can be done tonight then?" Millie asked him.

"It's too dark to do more. We'll start again in the morning," he replied. I thought about Mr. Trimble and Grandpa's earlier conversation regarding the passage of time and diminishing prospects and then banished it from my mind. Jim wasn't home yet. As long as Jim was out there, I would not give up hope of him finding Archie. "We're sending word down the line.

The other men will be home soon. Jim will be back here before you know it, Miss Lawson." He walked on.

"Miss Lawson?" Millie said.

"Well, you do look a lot alike," I said in sympathetic explanation. "And with your hair all dirty and the lighting so poor, it's hard to tell it's not brown like Sarah's."

"I grant you that it may be hard to see me tonight, but surely the lack of light hasn't affected his hearing!"

Though the light was poor, I could not hide the shock I felt at hearing Millie making fun of the voice of her best friend.

"Don't be so shocked," she said, smiling and poking me in the ribcage. "She and I make jokes about her voice all the time."

"You do?" I had been taught never to make fun of a person's ailments. "She doesn't mind?"

"Mind? She has the best stories about her voice."

Perhaps it was because the hour was so late, or perhaps because I had been waiting for so long; perhaps because my mind just needed something else to think about, but for the first time since five that afternoon, I allowed myself to think about someone other than Archie.

"Like what? What does she say about her voice?"

"Well..." Millie said, thinking through a response. "Like how her parents first reacted to her voice."

"What did they do?" I asked, taking the bait.

"They were hoping she wouldn't be born with that voice, obviously," she began. "Sarah's mother told me once that when she was expecting Sarah, she hoped her child would inherit the prominent cowlick that marked her husband's line or the strawberry-on-the hip birthmark which marked hers. She and her husband knew that no child was ever perfectly formed, and so they hoped the imperfection that would mar their baby would be minor in nature. Unfortunately, Sarah was born a perfect-looking baby. To her parents' dismay, she inherited her father's flawless skin and her mother's fine, smooth hair."

"Did her parents know right away that she inherited the bad voice?" I asked.

"They suspected it. Her high-pitched cries foreshadowed what was to come, but it was not until little Sarah uttered her first 'mama' that her parents knew for certain that Sarah had inherited the Lawsons' signature vocal chords—an extremely high-pitched scratchy, somewhat irritating voice first uttered here in Brampton by her grandfather, the early pastor of the Queen Street Primitive Methodist Church." I knew about that holy man. A few years earlier, my Aunt Lil told me about the settlement in Brampton of my paternal grandparents. The evangelical Pastor Lawson, the nephew of William Lawson, one of the town's founders, was responsible for Selina, my grandmother, moving to it. His voice was the most conspicuous of his many odious and insightful characteristics.

"Sarah has a sense of humour about it. Get her going, and she will tell you that as a babe, strangers ran from her pram holding their ears after admiring her quiet form, uttering a little coochie-coo and then hearing her echoing reply."

"That sounds awful," I said, disgusted at such poor manners. I hoped that mine had always been better. "Did her parents ever try to fix her voice?" I asked, suddenly quite happy for the distraction I suspected Millie was intentionally providing.

"Her parents tried everything suggested to them. For a time, she drank six glasses of unpasteurized milk a day and one teaspoon of pure honey each morning. She gargled with a combination of salt, water and mashed garlic after each meal. She slept each night under an open window."

"Did it make any difference?"

"It did when she caught a cold and her voice became hoarse. Otherwise, it just led to her bones, teeth, and nails growing strong and people with sensitive olfactory faculties keeping their distance."

"Oh, that's terrible," I said. "I feel sorry for her."

"Well, don't feel too sorry for her. She actually has an amazing singing voice."

"She can sing?" I asked in surprise. Frances had told me the same thing, but I found it hard to believe.

"She sure can. The girl who has a voice like nails on a chalkboard when she speaks has the voice of an angel when she sings. She is the lead soprano in our church choir and often performs solos."

"It's too bad for her that she can't sing all the time."

"I guess so, but in truth, once you get used to her voice, you don't really notice how different it is."

Eventually, my eyelids became heavy. Despite my efforts, they fell shut for longer and longer periods.

"Do you want to go into bed, Jessie?" Millie asked softly at one point.

"No," I said emphatically, straightening my back. "I am staying here until Jim comes back."

"Why don't you at least lie down, then? You can stretch your legs out on the lounge and put your head on my lap. My skirt is dry now." Grandpa had come out earlier with quilts for the two of us. I did as she suggested, and after she covered me, she asked me a question.

"Jessie, are you scared?"

"No. I'm not scared. I know Archie will be fine." A few minutes passed, and then I broke the silence with a confession. "Earlier tonight, I was mad. I wasn't very nice. And I think I was a little jealous."

"What happened?"

"Earlier tonight, when my cousins Hannah and John and my friend Frances were here, they started speaking about Archie as though he was … gone; as though he wasn't coming back. That made me mad. And then Frances described a Valentine's Day card that she got from Archie earlier this year, she said it was especially for her. She made it sound like she was the only one he sent such a card to."

"And you were mad because he didn't send you a card like that?"

"No. I was mad because she made it sound like that—like she was special. But she wasn't. He sent me one too. Hers was a card with an orange saying, 'Orange you glad we are friends?'"

"That is sweet. Did yours say the same thing?"

"No. Mine was a picture of a pear. It said, 'We'd make a good pear.'"

"I see. It was more special, wasn't it?"

"I think so. But it doesn't matter, because that was just this year's card. Next year's may be even more special."

After a long period of silence, she asked me again if I wanted to continue to wait outside for Jim. "You aren't worried about Jim, are you?"

"No! I am not worried about Jim. I know that Jim is fine, and when he comes home, Archie will be too." She stroked my curly hair and gently rocked the swing.

"You have a lot of faith in your brother, don't you?"

"I do. He's a good man." I'd heard others use that expression to describe Jim.

"Yes," she said quietly. "He's a very good man."

It was some time later that I heard footsteps on the stairs leading up to and then crossing the verandah. A few minutes passed; a silent exchange? Then Jim picked me up and carried me up to my bed.

* * *

Three days later, I stood with Jim and Millie under the big willow beside the creek across from St. Paul's Methodist Church. It was two in the afternoon. Main Street was quiet. Nearly all of the town's adults and many of the town's children were in the pews of the large church. In my hand I held a yellow rose, a pear sprig, and a stick of balsam, all tied together with a yellow ribbon. Millie and I had made it that morning. Slowly, I walked to the creek's edge with Jim and Millie an arm's length behind me. Crouching down, I gently placed the nosegay in the water, as close as I could to its edge, before slowly releasing it. It floated before me, clinging at first to the shoreline, hesitant, it seemed, to move away from the shallow bottom. There it bobbed for a few moments, catching itself on a small outcrop of mud and grass as the water behind pushed to dislodge it.

Eventually, the south-flowing water lapped over it, freeing it from its mooring and forcing it into the open stream. I kept up with it at first, rising from my crouching position as it overcame the outcrop, walking slowly as it made its way to the centre of the creek, walking fast as it got its bearings and then running, slowly at first as it became a part of the stream and travelled to and then under the bridge, and faster still as it embraced the current traversing the east side of Main Street before winding its way behind the large Main Street houses until finally, with it well out of sight, I ran as fast as I possibly could, arms raised over my head and hollering as loudly as my lungs would allow: "A-R-C-H-I-E."

Chapter 14

HAGGERTIEA

The discovery by Mr. Peaker of Archie's lifeless body on the morning of May 31, 1912 confirmed the immediate loss of one of my two dearest friends and began the gradual loss of that status by the other, although the discovery of the first in the outcroppings of the creek behind Mr. Thauburn's large Main Street home, equidistant from the McKechnies' Peel Avenue home and the Wellington Street Bridge, could not be compared in devastation, certainty, or finality to the loss of the other.

No seismic argument, no cataclysmic misunderstanding, no authoritative command from our parents for disassociation separated Frances and me. The fabric of our friendship was not so much torn as it was frayed; over time the solid cloth began to evidence moth-like holes. Our friendship always remained true; it just ceased to be as abiding. I never said a poor word about Frances or harboured an ill thought. I have no reason to believe she behaved otherwise toward me.

Between us, though, a cleaver had been wedged. Heavy, hard, and hot, it was forged of six sentences uttered by a desperate nine-year-old who until that time had not known that faith in one's brother was an insufficient lifeline. Over and over my mind replayed my admonition that fateful night to my friend and cousins: "I won't have you talking like he's dead! I won't. He is *not* dead. He hasn't come home yet. But he will. He will come home!" As Frances and I could never entirely get over our loss of Archie, we never entirely recovered from our short exchange on my family's veranda that terrible night. Though Frances was too good to ever say "I told you so," she was clearly no more able to put behind her the wrongness of my intuition than I was able to put behind me the rightness of hers.

It would take some time for that cleaver to be fully lodged. We passed a long summer waiting for school to resume; waiting for a return to a regime in which we weren't expected to play and weren't expected to be gay. Without Archie, there were no forbidden walks along the Etobicoke; no surreptitious auditings of the stories of the jail's governor; there were no ship buildings or seafarings, all activities Frances and I formerly undertook with him. Not even the annual month-long visit of my Turner cousins from Winnipeg brought me any pleasure that summer. Though Mother and Grandpa worried about my disposition over those warm, sunny months, Father dismissed it. It would pass, he said, and in the meantime, he urged physical activity, or if I could not find my way to run or throw a ball, he urged reading. In the end, he delighted in the number of books I borrowed from the Carnegie Library, an activity I deemed ideal for my solitary mood.

At last September arrived, bringing an end to the long, miserable summer. My pleasure in my return to school and its full-day routine was dampened by only two things. Firstly, I had an elevated sense of unease regarding the four times a day I would be required to pass the Kelly Iron Works Repair Shop. After three years of being my near constant escort as I walked by that one block area, I sensed a continuing waning in Frances's patience regarding my fear of Scary Scott. I had never in all the years she coddled me told her the heinous things Scary Scott's brother perpetrated on that young girl in the upper floors of the nearby Alderlea. I had not told her why I with my long, brown, curly hair (in contrast to her shorter red hair) was singled out for his grunts and wild gesticulations. I came to realize that if I was not ready to walk to and from school when Frances was ready, I might find myself walking alone. I sensed she would no longer wait for me.

Secondly, Father advised me the week before school began that there was to be a change in my teacher. Miss Wilson, who taught our class through junior and senior first form and junior second form, was returning to the first form room. A new teacher, Miss Neelands, was assuming responsibility for the junior and senior second formers. I had looked forward to my final year at the little school, being confident in all of its ways, reserving my anxiety for thoughts about the school I would enter the following year. I had not expected to have to learn new ways in my final year in the little school.

* * *

Miss Neelands began the first day of the new school year by asking each student to stand at the front of the room and announce to one and all his or her name, favourite subject, and favourite hobby. Having been schooled together for two or three years, we knew that the only people enlightened by the exercise were Miss Neelands and two new students at the back of the room. The two new students were the last to be called upon, and they were called together. The odd-looking siblings stood on display in a manner not dissimilar to livestock at public auction. No words were necessary to convey the fact that neither this boy nor this girl hailed from Peel County.

Jane, the first to be introduced, was nearly the same height as our teacher. She was clearly the tallest girl in our class. Her straight brown hair hung in a most non-Brampton sort of way, unadorned from the crown of her head almost to the end of her long back, accentuating her thin, long face and nose. Her mouth was wide, but her lips were narrow. Her brown eyes were large and possibly too far spaced. Her forehead and eyebrows I could not describe, so covered were they in her long bangs.

Mother called girls like this "unrisen bread"—girls who would round out in time and become real beauties. Looking at Jane then, all skin, bones, and hair, I didn't know from where she would obtain the necessary yeast. Her lank appearance was accentuated by her unusual dress: pale lavender wool hanging straight from her shoulders to just above her knees, broken only by silver buttons that formed a line from her collar to her hips and three wide pleats that fell from where the buttons stopped. The light, solid colour of the fabric, the absence of any gathering and the just below the knee hem length emphasized her foreign origins.

Her brother Douglas, a year and a half younger, had the same build, although he was fully four inches shorter than his sister. The same features of his face, with his cropped brown hair, gave him a handsome look for which he did not have to wait. His clothes, like his sister's, were of a fashion atypical for the school.

Miss Neelands extolled their many interests and accomplishments. Jane was a voracious reader who loved to skate, swim, and sew. (I cringed at the last word.) Douglas was an avid golfer, lawn bowler, and pianist. As Miss Neelands spoke, they both looked at the far wall rather than at any of us. I sensed that they had made such appearances before, a matter confirmed when Miss Neelands announced that they had lived in many places in their short lives, Toronto being the last of them. Given the number of schools they had attended, it was determined that they would both start in our classroom, although in time Jane, who was older than Douglas, might skip ahead.

As Miss Neelands described more of their background and I stared at the objects of her discourse, I was struck by a premonition. This girl Jane and I would become the closest of friends. My home would be hers, and hers mine. We would attend university together. We would stand up for each other when we each wed. We would be godmothers to each other's children and spend our twilight years together, two otherwise lonely widows. Her brother Douglas would be like a brother to me.

My premonition ended with a round of applause, my hands joining the cacophony, for a reason I did not know. My mind had been so far away. Though I was confident at that moment that Jane and I would one day be the best of friends, I sensed that relationship was yet some time away. For the time being, therefore—for possibly up to a year—I would treat the new students as did all others in my class: as people to be observed from a careful distance.

Father and Mother were excited to hear that the Thompson children were registered in my class. The arrival of the Thompsons in Brampton was heralded by its business leaders who looked to John Thompson—a successful foundry operator—as a means to re-establish the prominence once held by the town in the manufacture of iron works.

"I don't understand what is so special about that family," I made the mistake of muttering that night at tea. Rather than being admonished for speaking at the table when not asked to speak, I was made to listen to a lecture on the importance of iron works to the history of the town and to learn "what was so special" about the Thompsons.

* * *

Among the titanic founders of Brampton, one must include John Haggert with John Elliott, William Lawson, Edward Dale, and William Buffy (though some would not like to include the latter). Haggert was a Scotsman who settled in the area in the late 1840s. Over the next four decades, Haggert made an indelible impression in Brampton civics, where in 1874 he was elected as its first mayor; sports, for which he is credited with having brought to the area curling and lawn bowling; and, most significantly, industry. As an industrialist, he was responsible for founding a production plant that provided gas lighting through the Brampton business area and a number of houses. He also operated a five-acre lumber yard. But his largest contribution by far was his operation of an iron foundry business.

Of course, no nineteenth century village could function without one or more foundries, so the mere existence of such an enterprise in a village like Brampton was not particularly noteworthy. What made the Haggert foundry noteworthy was its size, its product line, the quality of its goods, the volume and range of its sales, and its tenure. A continental leader, Haggert's iron works, in its various corporate forms, was for many years the largest employer and most profitable business in the town.

The business that started in 1849, powered literally by ten men and a single black horse, grew to a steam-generated four-storey plant employing over 140 men. Producing some of the finest machinery in the province, its steam engines, boilers, harvesters, self-rakes, reapers, mowers, sowers, feed mills, and stoves won prizes at exhibitions in Toronto, Philadelphia, and Sydney.

Unfortunately, the financial success of the behemoth business over the first four decades of its existence could not be sustained. The reason lay in part with the economic, industrial, and agricultural conditions of the late 1880s and in part with a particularly poor business decision made by the foundry's president. While no one could accuse John Haggert of being short-sighted, he could rightly be accused of not being far-sighted enough. Haggert, initially with his two brothers, William and James, revolutionized farming in Canada and around the world. With foresight, ingenuity, and skill they created and mass-produced "Bell's Chic," a heavy reaper that allowed farmers, using only three horses, the ability to reap up to five acres of field a day.

When an American inventor named Royce proposed a lighter-weight reaper with wheels much smaller than those of Bell's Chic, which would require fewer horses to operate and which would till even greater acreage per day, many people laughed. John Haggert did not laugh. Royce came to Brampton with his plans and lived with the Haggert family as the foundry employees worked to create the prototype. The employees were given a day off of work when the prototype was finally produced. They were given another day off when the prototype was taken to a field, and, contrary to the expectations of many, was found to function as promised.

But there the celebrations of the Haggert foundry ended. John Haggert shook the hand of Royce and sent him on his way. For whatever reason, Haggert, who had made so many wise decisions concerning the future of agriculture and industry, made one particularly poor one. Royce, rebuffed by Haggert and armed with evidence that his lightweight reaper could be built and could perform to specifications, went to see another farm machinery manufacturer. It was a less prominent operation than that of Brampton's Haggert Iron Works, but Royce thought the operation had potential, and what's more, its owners were interested in his product. The Massey Brothers of Newcastle, Ontario, were delighted with the opportunity. It would be a century before the Masseys would look back.

It would have been difficult for the Haggert company to withstand John Haggert's bad decision had it been made in the 1870s. Being made in the next decade, it was impossible. While the enterprise had incorporated and been recapitalized in 1880—including with the funds and business credentials brought by Kenneth Gilchrest, Matthew Elliott, Gilchrest's brother-in-law, and other prominent Bramptonians who joined its board— by the late 1880s the company was facing many other challenges.

The effect of the two rail lines running through Brampton, which had previously granted the Haggert foundry such advantageous shipping conditions, was beginning to be neutralized as rail lines proliferated throughout the country. Similarly, the flourishing number of newspapers and the pages of advertising within them allowed farmers and other purchasers of iron goods to see the many other providers of stoves and farming implements—and their prices. The world-renowned Haggert foundry was losing its monopoly.

The opening of the Canadian West and a recession in the late 1880s created an exodus of farmers from Ontario to the western prairies. As they went, so too did the demand for Haggert goods. The development of the international wheat industry was the final straw. By 1891, the Haggert foundry was in liquidation, and the family's fortune and the fortunes of many of its investors and suppliers were all lost.

The closure of the Haggert foundry left gaping holes, and not just in the pocket books, balance sheets, and bank accounts of Bramptonians. It also left a gaping hole in the real estate of the four corners centre-town area. The town council worked assiduously to fill the half-block vacancy created by the closure. Initially thinking that another foundry owner could make a success where Haggert had ceased to, the town encouraged the JM Ross Company to move its operations to the vacated premises.

The enterprise, which manufactured engines and threshers, faced many of the same challenges as its predecessor. Before long, the company succumbed to the "encouragement" offered by the town of St. Catharines and moved its operations there. Brampton was no stranger to such inducements. At the time the JM Ross Company was relocating, the town was reeling from the failure of a third foundry in the town—this one operated by Young Bothers, to whom it had loaned $30,000 a year before the Haggert demise. The town began to reconsider its commitment to the iron industry.

By the time Jane and Douglas Thompson joined my second-form class, a good twenty years had passed since the Haggert, Ross, and Young debacles. The Pease Company, with which their father was associated, came to Brampton with a promise to build modern household furnaces, to employ dozens of men, to build housing for those men, and to ship the manufactured wares across the country.

The owners were not interested in occupying the space formerly occupied by the Haggert or Ross works. That large amount of space would assure their demise. In any event, the premises were not available, being by that time the home of Best Knit, a manufacturer of sweater coats, the Brampton Box Factory, and the Brampton Dairy Company. The new foundry instead planned to take up premises near the junction of the two Brampton railway lines.

The town, which had been iron-shy for twenty years, was once again willing to embrace the industry. Council proposed, and the residents by vote agreed, to extend a twenty-year, $43,000 interest-free loan to assist the Pease Company in the development of its plant.

The town's confidence in the Pease Company was based on two factors. First, and most notably, the owner of the foundry was no fly-by-night operation. The Pease Company was part of a worldwide conglomerate that produced boilers, furnaces, and locomotives that utilized coal. Originally named for Sir Joseph Whitwell Pease, the business supplemented his extensive stone and mineral quarries in Britain and beyond. The furnaces produced in the Brampton plant would be marketed and sold through offices across the country, supported as was necessary from the Canadian head office in Toronto.

Secondly, and in no small measure, the town was confident in the management of the new foundry. John Thompson was like a returning son—or more accurately, a retuning son-in-law. Thompson had successfully operated foundries all over North America, including in Ohio, the place from which he hailed, and Toronto, near the place from which his wife hailed. Following in the footsteps of his father, John Thompson spent his youthful summers and autumns at state agricultural fairs and the intervening winters and springs reading industrial journals. He knew the Haggert Manufacturing Company from his undertakings in all seasons. His marriage in the mid-1890s to a woman from Brampton who longed to be united with her parents and siblings seemed fatalistic to Thompson.

John Thompson's domicile in the United States came to an end in 1910, when his successful operations there were purchased by the Pease Company. With a covenant not to compete with Pease, John Thompson had three options: retire and live off his significant investments, pursue another line of business, or work for the very business that purchased his. Just middle-aged, he considered himself too young to retire and too old to learn a new business. With no excuse not to accede to his wife's request to be nearer her family, Thompson took an executive position with Pease, initially in Toronto and shortly afterward in Brampton as head of the new operations there. Though he had some doubts about the readiness of Canadians to purchase furnaces for residential installation, the fact that the Brampton foundry would also manufacture furnaces for commercial use gave him the confidence to proceed.

* * *

"So I hope, Jessie, you will be particularly solicitous to the two Thompson children. The presence of the Thompsons and the Pease Foundry in Brampton will be very good for the town's business prospects."

"I will, Father," I replied dutifully, thinking that perhaps I would not wait a full year to make overtures of friendship to Jane and Douglas Thompson. An observation period of half that time might suffice.

Mother, it seemed, was almost as excited as Father was about the arrival of the Thompsons. But her pleasure was derived not from any improved economic prospects for the town, and not because of the society that would be provided by Mrs. Thompson, who had been removed from Brampton for so long Mother was not sure she would know her, Mother's enthusiasm sprang instead from the location at which the Thompsons would reside.

"And living not just anywhere," Mother said at the end of Father's dissertation. She turned her attention to Grandpa, "But living, Grandpa, in your Haggertlea!" Grandpa's hand was on the table, and she patted it as she said the words. I was startled by the suggestion and her tenderness with respect to it. What did she mean calling it Grandpa's Haggertlea? He had never lived in the big mansion house that overlooked the old

Haggert foundry. Perhaps he built it, I thought. This was a revelation to me, if so—a further chapter in Grandpa's all-too-secret career path. A path Mother never discussed with me.

Mother patted Grandpa's hand for only a second. In the moment she realized my regard for the gesture, she lifted her hand from Grandpa's and placed it across her mouth. I sensed she regretted what she had said.

Grandpa flushed slightly. "It isn't really my Haggertlea," he said bashfully.

"You're right," Mother agreed, apparently trying to end the conversation.

"You made it what it once was," Father chimed in, proudly. "And it made you what you—"

A loud crash stopped Father in mid-sentence. We all jumped a little before turning to the source of the clatter.

"Oh, clumsy me!" Mother said, leaning over to pick up broken china. The lid to the soup terrine had somehow leapt from the table in front of her to the bare floor behind her. "It looks like a clean break," she said as she began to pick up the pieces just beyond the carpeted area underneath the table and chairs. "We'll get that fixed in no time. Jessie," she said, "will you please help me clear the table?"

I stared at her without moving. I had never seen my mother drop anything from the table. No one would describe my mother, with her piano and organ-proficient fingers, as clumsy.

"Now, Jessie," Mother said adamantly, "the apple pie is ready to be served, and I don't want it getting too cold."

I burned my tongue on the pie when it was served shortly afterward. I ate it far too quickly, thinking subconsciously that though I was incapable of setting the course of the dinner conversation (a matter strictly in the purview of my father), I might somehow, by the speed at which my fork moved from plate to mouth, set the pace. I was desperate to be away from the table, though for once not to avoid a particular conversation but rather to commence one. Father had mentioned that the Haggerts immigrated to Canada from Scotland. Did the construction of Haggertlea involve some sort of fiasco? Though I learned many things at our dining room table, matters pertaining to Grandpa's career path were not among them. I was determined to learn the answer.

Fortunately, it was a Tuesday night. If it had been a Thursday night in the fall, winter, or spring, Grandpa would have been off to his weekly choir practice at our church, with Mother and Father. If it had been a Thursday night in the summer, he would have been on his way to Gage Park for the weekly performance of the Citizens Band. A Monday or Friday might take him to throw some bowls on the lawns of Rosalea Park or some stones at the curling club. Every second Wednesday of the month was reserved for meetings of his Golden Star IOOF Lodge, and every fourth, meetings of the Odd Fellows.

But on the remaining nights, the only thing that regularly called to Grandpa was the comfortable chair in his room and the solace to be found with a good book behind a closed door. As I walked up the stairs half an hour later to knock on his door, I resolved to discuss the narrow question of Grandpa's involvement with Haggertlea. In five years, with very little to show for my efforts, I had at least learned that nothing was to be gained by using the phrase "self-made" with Grandpa. As for the terms "others-destroyed" and "Scottish Fiasco," he was not even aware of my knowledge of them.

"Come in, Jessie," he bade almost before I knocked at the door. I shut it once inside. He was sitting in his big dark blue chair in the corner of his room, a book in hand. I moved to sit on the side of his bed, where I could face him.

"How did you know it was me?"

"I had a feeling you might be dropping by this evening."

I marvelled at his perceptiveness. "What did you think I might want to talk to you about?" I asked slowly.

"Ah. You are taking a different tack this time. Well, I can do that too. This time. I think you want to know about Haggertlea."

I nodded, silently congratulating myself on my alternative approach. I let Grandpa continue to lead. "I think you want to know why your mother referred to it as 'my Haggertlea.'" I nodded again.

"Well, there are no secrets when it comes to Haggertlea," he continued, confirming in saying so that other matters were indeed secret. "Do you remember where we left off?" It had been five years, but I recalled every detail of Grandpa's early years in Brampton. I had been waiting since then to hear the rest of his story. I settled in on his comfortable bed.

"You had just returned from England with Grandma Brady. A man named Judge did a terrible job building one of the four houses you were working on, and so you and Grandma moved into it so that you could fix it before selling it. Your best worker, Cowan, teamed up with someone else to build houses in a row and on speculation, just as you and the Duke did. But you weren't upset, because your work had received the attention of other people in Brampton who wanted you to build houses for them.

"They weren't necessarily the types of homes you wanted to build, but they were an improvement on the one-and-a-half-storey roughcast homes you and Nelson had built, and you knew that one day people would want you to build houses with towers, turrets, and verandahs out of brick and stone. And you hoped that one day those projects would put you in a position to build churches and other public buildings in Brampton."

"You have a good memory."

"I do have the song," I said in reply.

It was easy to remember most of those details because I grew up surrounded by them. By the time I was able to walk the streets of Brampton, it was filled with houses, churches, and public buildings built by my grandfather. Years earlier, I set them to song. Singing it always made Grandpa happy, although he seldom needed cheering. He had a pleasant disposition. He modestly responded to each stanza I sang before adding a detail or two, often quite praiseful of his work!

Coming to a two-storey red-bricked house with three bay windows, one on the second floor projecting over the front door to form a porch, I sang:

This is the house that Grandpa built
Grandpa built, Grandpa built
This is the house that Grandpa built
All on a Monday morning.

"Well, I didn't build it all in one day," he'd say. "But I rather like the outcome, particularly the decorative buff quoining on the corners and the keyhole window below the upper peak of the roof."

Walking along, I'd point out another house, this one with bay windows on a number of walls and a high dormer lifting out of the roof.

This is the house that Grandpa built
Grandpa built, Grandpa built
This is the house that Grandpa built
All on a Tuesday morning.

"Well, I didn't build it all myself," he'd say. "But yes, I was the general contractor. It was one of my earlier projects. To do it again, I'd add significantly more detail."

Not waiting for him to finish, we'd turn the corner, and I'd point to another house, this one with a large verandah and three dormers jutting out of the curved roof.

This is the house that Grandpa built
Grandpa built, Grandpa built
This is the house that Grandpa built
All on a Wednesday morning.

"I did, and I must say it is a darling house, but roughcast! I could not convince the owners to build in brick. It was built too early in my career. Probably won't be standing in another ten years."

Pointing to a house with a severely pointed tower and many rooflines, I began again, singing aloud all he did on a Thursday morning. The song went on, stopping, of course, on a Saturday. Grandpa would never think of working on a Sunday. If the walk went on longer, the song began again at Monday. As there was no shortage of buildings that Grandpa built, the song could last through months of Mondays if the walk was long enough.

"Yes, you do have that song." He chuckled. "I wonder if you can think of any trends that emerged from that song and my responses to it."

There was only one that I could think of, and it had to do with timing. When Grandpa arrived in Brampton, most of the buildings were roughcast—covered in a plaster-like substance. Grandpa longed to build in brick and stone as he had in England with his father. Even after he built the four-house subdivision, many of his works were roughcast, and most of them lacked the architectural detail and the asymmetry of his later houses.

"That's right," he said when I put it to him, "and that is what changed with the building of Haggertlea. When it came to the construction of houses, Haggertlea changed it all for me. It allowed me to move from roughcast to brick and stone; to build large houses with verandahs, turrets, and towers. The turning point was not designing and building the first little subdivision in 1859, although I thought it would be. It was not even designing and building the New Wesleyan Methodist Church in 1867, although I thought it would be too. The event that changed the course of my future construction work, the course of the town's residential architecture, was the building of Haggertlea.

"January 26, 1868 was a joyous day for me. It was on that day that the New Wesleyan Methodist Church—Grace—our church—was dedicated. Every pew in each of the three dedication services was filled. Your grandmother and I attended each service, taking in the many compliments bestowed. Reverend Egerton Ryerson, the pioneer preacher and public education proponent, came from Toronto to give the sermon at the first service. He was so impressed with our new church that he told me he would refer other commissions to me. Over the years, he did, but as they were outside of Brampton, I never pursued them. I had no desire to build in any other community. But what's more, I didn't need to. By the time Ryerson's first referral came to me just after the dedication services, I was already in discussions with John Haggert.

"Haggert was proud of Brampton and its many fine businesses and homes. He knew that people from around the county had begun to admire the town's few mansion-like homes. Alderlea, the grand Italianate Villa mansion down the street from the Haggert property, was the talk of the county. George Wright's Gothic Revival 'Castle' had had that distinction for more than a decade. As a Brampton booster, John Haggert wanted to add another feather to the cap of that reputation.

"As you heard at the table, Haggert was an ambitious man. In addition to being a leader in business, he aspired to be a leader in politics—to become Brampton's first mayor. In this way he would join the ranks of Wright, who had been the county's provincial member of the legislature, and Gilchrist, who was then a warden of Peel County but had far greater aspirations. Haggert wanted a house, like Wright's and Gilchrist's, appropriate for a man with the responsibilities of public office.

"Finally, and maybe most importantly, his business was a success, and I think it's fair to say he wanted people to know it. Gilchrist had made his money operating a general store and a quarry and acting as postmaster. Wright operated a mill. In Haggert's view, those were traditional industries. Their owners built beautiful homes in a traditional style. Haggert's success was derived from a modern foundry; a foundry that was revolutionizing farming and other industries. He wanted a grand, estate-like house built in a more modern style.

"He hired an architect, a contractor, and me as the mason. We began to work together to design a house that met his objectives. Together we chose the second empire style, which became popular when Napoleon III engaged George E. Haussmann to redesign Paris. With its flat mansard roves with tiles that extended down over the face of the attic floor, projecting dormers, bay windows, and intricate details, the style contained many design elements I longed to build—but not all of them. I convinced Haggert and his team to add a few less conventional elements.

"Disregarding the symmetry normally associated with the style, we made the focal point of the house an off-centre tower. The tower, which increased the height of the house by over a third, was square in shape and soared above a large door, which allowed access to the home's gardens. The front of the house, like Alderlea's to the south, faced Main Street below, with terraced lawns leading down in this case, first to George Street and then Main Street beyond. The mansion was accessed by those in carriages from Elizabeth Street at its back.

"To the right of the tower, we constructed in the mansard roof an arched dormer. An identical protruding dormer at the back of the house presented an interesting architectural feature outside the house and two unique rooms inside.

"On the far side of the lot, but at an equal set back to the house, we built a two-storey carriage house—with exactly the same mansard roof and dormers as the main house. Oh my," Grandpa laughed, "that carriage house was bigger than most Brampton houses of the time. It really was excessive. But John Haggert, a foundry owner, had a lot of iron carriages! And he had the horses to pull them.

"The house, once complete in 1870, had nearly ten thousand square feet and included twenty rooms, including a suite of rooms in the attic for servants. The flat mansard roof vastly increased and improved the living quarters for the staff residing there.

"Finally, we connected the two buildings at the front with a curved-top glass conservatory entered from the main house. In the end, Haggertlea had all of the features I longed to see in a Brampton home—except for one. Try as I did, I could not convince Haggert to include a verandah! However, I realized that the Haggerts were not likely to be among those who spent their leisure hours sipping tea with their neighbours. It is fair to say that no house on their street—or anywhere in the town—was its equal."

"I didn't even know about a conservatory," I said. The terraced grounds of Haggertlea continued to be visible from George Street below, but the glass conservatory Grandpa described was no longer in existence.

"Yes, the house has seen better days. The carriage house was abandoned years ago. Only a portion of the main house is still in use. Maybe Mr. Thompson will restore some of it to its former grandeur. Although I am not sure how he will fill it with only two children!"

Grandpa yawned loudly and made it clear that our little visit was complete. "But that's not the end of your story," I cried.

"It is the end of my story as it relates to Haggertlea," he replied.

"Did building it make you a self-made man?" I asked.

He chuckled. "Haggertlea was one of my most important commissions. I was well on my way to becoming self-made." We were up to 1870. I knew there were other important buildings to be constructed. I knew a fall would follow. I just didn't know when or how.

Chapter 15

CHRISTMAS WITH JANE

B y late autumn, Frances and I were somewhat chummy with Jane and Douglas Thompson. It was not until December, though, that the two of us were invited to their home, a delay resulting not from any lack of hospitality on the Thompsons' part, but rather from the time necessitated in restoring their home to a state appropriate to receive guests. Indeed, I suspect that our mothers were somewhat envious that such an invitation, when it was finally issued, was first proffered to their daughters, but it was clear on seeing the house that Mrs. Thompson did not yet consider it to be suitable for her peers.

The interest and excitement of the women in the community for the restoration of the Thompsons' house was almost equal to the interest and excitement of the men in the community concerning the resurgence of an iron business. By the time Haggertlea was purchased by the Thompsons, many parts of it were in disrepair. Though John Thompson proposed to restore all of Haggertlea, he had no intention of restoring it to a single-family home. Focussing initially on the tower and the portion of the house north of it, he tore out many of the inner plaster walls and reconstructed a beautiful twelve-room home, still commodious enough for his family of four. Once complete, he planned to restore and then lease out the remainder of the once-great house.

Frances and I first entered Haggertlea the Saturday before Christmas. From the Elizabeth Street entrance, we were admitted to a two-storey rotunda. We starred in awe at its circular shape, the door frames evenly spaced around its walls, the wrought iron balustrade that encircled the walkway around its second floor, the doors that opened into its upper rooms, the black-and-white marble flooring, and the white marble staircase that hugged the walls as it rose. It was, as it turned out, the only portion of the house we saw that day, for we had only just entered it when we were caught up in Jane's arms and bidden to keep on our outdoor clothes.

"No. Don't give me your coats and boots!" she said, jumping on her toes and clapping her hands, her loose long brown hair bouncing up and down. "You're going to need them. We're going with my father to cut down our tree."

I had never seen anyone so excited about terminating the life of a living thing. I wondered which tree was to suffer that fate. Haggertlea had many large maple and elm trees on its grounds.

"Which tree?" I inquired. "Is it on the side lawn?" As I asked the question, Douglas emerged from one of the upper rooms, leaned over the second floor railing, and holding a string tied to a stone, allowed it to fall gently to the ground floor.

"No! No! It's not on our property at all!" Jane replied. "We have no excess evergreens here. We're going to Mr. Van den Bark's. He has all kinds of trees for removal. We're going to buy one of those for our Christmas tree," she explained. "Then we'll come back here for hot chocolate."

Comprehension washed over me. Jane Thompson, who was just becoming my friend, was about to be the first of that distinction to have within her house a Christmas tree. I was not unfamiliar with the concept. We had such trees in our schools and in our churches. The Turners displayed one in the window of their large Church Street-facing dining room every Christmas when they lived in Brampton. Before my Uncle James passed away, the Darlings placed one in the tower of their parlour.

But this was not a tradition that my immediate family observed, and in that I was in good company with my closest friends. The Hudsons never installed a Christmas tree. Archie's family once had a tradition of acquiring such trees but ceased the practice when his father passed away. Mrs. McKechnie said it was not a custom to be maintained without a man in the house. She told Archie they could resume it when he turned sixteen. It made me sad to think that the McKechnie women would never again partake in a custom they clearly enjoyed.

Mr. Thompson and Douglas joined us in the rotunda. "What do you think, Douglas?" Mr. Thompson asked. "Eighteen feet in height?" They looked up at the two-storey space overhead and the vast space around them. The black-and-white harlequin floor on which they stood was devoid of much other than the occasional chair against the circular wall and the chest at the base of the circular staircase.

"Maybe a little taller, Father," Douglas replied. "Let me measure the string one more time against the yard stick."

I turned to Jane and Frances and whispered, "Are you going to plant the tree in your front entranceway?"

"Well, we aren't going to plant it, of course," giggled Jane. "But yes we are going to put it here—in a bucket. We will tie the top part of its trunk to the balcony to make it secure. I know it's a bit strange to put a Christmas tree in a foyer rather than in a parlour, but Mother and Father think that this room is so grand, it could accommodate a really large tree. Then everyone will be able to see it as they arrive. And the carollers will be able to see it as they sing outside our house. Don't you agree?" Fortunately, I was saved by Frances from having to confess my ignorance on the subject. But the relief I momentarily felt at her interjection was quickly overtaken by the greater consternation caused by its content.

"We just got our tree last week," Frances said. I stared incredulously at her. She had a tree in her house too? I had not been in her house in the past week, so I could not vouch otherwise, but I had been in the Hudson house over many Christmas seasons. I was sure I had never seen a tree inside it.

"It's the only good thing that comes of my grandfather's decision to spend Christmas with my uncle in Port Credit. This year we don't have to worry about his allergy to trees.

"We had great fun last weekend stringing popcorn and cranberries: five popcorns, two cranberries, five popcorns, two cranberries. Then we wrapped the strings around and around the tree. We all thought it looked delightful, particularly from a distance. But Mittens thought it looked delightful up close as well. Even more, he thought it tasted delightful. On Tuesday night while we were all asleep, he left the foot of my bed, made his way to the tree, and began to nibble at the popcorn. I suppose he was fine on the lower branches, but when it got too high for him, he either jumped to a branch or climbed the trunk. Whatever he did, he brought the whole tree crashing to the ground in the middle of the night.

"We all rushed down to see what the commotion was. Mother and Father cleaned up what they could at the time and left the rest for the morning. Mittens was shut in my room with the door closed until we removed the last of the edibles from the tree. I must say it looked quite bereft and forlorn after that. But Mother said 'no more food on the tree or no more Mittens.' We have to keep Mittens."

"Of course you have to keep Mittens! Cats live for a very long time. Christmas trees last a week or two at the most," Jane said, imparting yet more knowledge about Christmas trees than I had thus known. "We don't string popcorn for that very reason. We put painted pine cones and little wooden ornaments on ours. But you should see our tree once we put all of our presents underneath it! Our grandparents and all our aunts and uncles and cousins will bring or send theirs. By the time we are ready to open presents, they fill around the base of the tree past where the tips of the lowest boughs extend and another three or four feet beyond. On Christmas Day, we pull the presents out from under the tree one by one and open them. It takes us all afternoon!"

I noticed that this revelation momentarily even stopped Frances from continuing the dialogue. Surely few families in our town were so well off as to have enough gifts to take them the entire afternoon to open.

"We aren't going to put our presents there," Frances said, stopping to take her hankie from her coat pocket and dabbing at her nose, obviously trying to think of an explanation "...because..." She dabbed her nose again, still in thought. "The branches of our tree are so ... low." Then the explanation came to her. "And our presents are so big, they would n-e-v-e-r fit under our tree." She shoved her hankie back in her pocket and, clearly as eager to change the subject as I was, went on, "Should we get ready to go?"

I thought of our Christmas gifts and what I suspected were the Hudsons'. Ours could easily have fit under a tree, if we had one. They could easily have fit under a quarter of the tree. But in our family, we kept our gifts hidden in our rooms until it was time to exchange the one gift we bought or made for each of the immediate members of our family.

We walked to the restored carriage house at the side of Haggertlea. Two horses were harnessed to the large cutter. Climbing onto the backward-facing seats, we waited for Douglas and Mr. Thompson. Within minutes they joined us, first placing at the back a small sleigh, a number of ropes, and an axe. Mr. Thompson took the reins of the horses and we left Haggertlea, moving swiftly along the less traversed side streets, laden with the snowfall of the previous day.

Within thirty minutes we were at the Van den Bark tree farm far west of our two-room school house and the populated area of the town. In the spring and summer, those in the vicinity who required a mature tree to be transplanted to their gardens or lawns arrived at Mr. Van den Bark's property with ropes, spades, lengths of burlap, and some form of conveyance to remove a selected tree and replant it on their own property. Mr. Van den Bark made no guarantee as to the success of the endeavour, and as often as not, the same customers returned the next year to repeat the exercise. Of both these transplant successes and failures, I often heard adults alternatively singing the praises of and cursing the business of Mr. Van den Bark.

But I had not formerly known of this wintertime enterprise. It had never previously occurred to me to ask from where our churches or our schools had obtained their Christmas trees. As I surveyed the numerous horses, cutters, and sleds on his property at that moment, it was clear that this was the source.

Mr. Thompson suggested that Jane, Douglas, Frances and I select the tree to be felled. Once Jane's red scarf was tied to one of its branches, he would join us with the axe and sled. The four of us walked only a few steps when Jane, seeing a big white pine, wrapped her red scarf around one of its branches and declared the tree to be "the one"—the tree made for the rotunda. I marvelled that the exercise could be completed so quickly. We would be back at the Thompsons' drinking hot chocolate in no time. My thinking was premature, however, for Jane had only just made her declaration when Frances made a similar one.

Seeing the slightly taller white pine to which Frances beckoned us, Jane agreed that the tree selected by Frances was "the one"—the tree made for their rotunda. The scarf was removed from the branch of the former and tied to a branch of the latter. All was settled, the anticipated smell of hot chocolate returned to my senses and Jane's father sent for, until I called out in respect of a spruce tree a further ten feet along. On being joined by Jane and Frances and my tree inspected, a similar declaration was made, and the scarf was moved once more. Over the remainder of the afternoon, we selected at least two dozen trees, each more perfect than the one before, each more truly made for the Thompsons' rotunda than the last selected.

Eventually, Mr. Thompson settled the matter for us, declaring that he could not possibly fathom a tree more perfect for his rotunda than the one we found near the beginning of our excursion. He chopped it down, tied it with ropes, and with Douglas's help dragged it to the front of the lot, where it was paid for and affixed to the cutter.

By the time we returned to Haggertlea, it was dark. To my surprise, Father, who had been at our church rehearsing for the next night's cantata, was at Haggertlea waiting to escort me home. Although he ostensibly wanted to ensure that I would not be late for tea, since my promptness for meals had always been my own responsibility, I suspected he was instead curious to see the state of the renovated mansion. He was disappointed in that respect, as neither he nor I was invited inside on our return. We had arrived back at Haggertlea too late to enjoy the promised hot chocolate.

Father and I left the Thompsons without seeing the tree my friends and I had so carefully selected lifted off the sled, lodged in its bucket in the rotunda and tied to the second floor balcony. Nor was I invited to return to Haggertlea at any other time that season to see it decorated and overflowing with presents. But in the years that followed, I saw many trees as perfectly made for the Thompsons' rotunda as was that white pine selected the Saturday before Christmas in 1912.

I could barely contain my excitement as Father and I walked home that evening. Not even the prospect of walking along George Street directly toward the Kelly Iron Works Repair Shop—a route Frances and I had assiduously avoided in our unescorted walk to Haggertlea that afternoon—dampened my enthusiasm. The temperature was rising. Big flakes of wet snow were falling heavily. I skipped ahead of Father down the hill on Nelson Street and then walked slowly backward so that I could see his face as I described the lengths Mr. Thompson and Douglas had taken to measure the rotunda for the tree. Once Father caught up to me, I skipped ahead, then turned and walked slowly backward again as I described the process by which we selected the tree.

"You know, Father," I ventured after completing that account, "I think Mr. Van den Bark may be right for failing to clear his land of trees." I frequently heard Father complain of the blight the stand of trees was to the cleared neighbouring properties. But as I looked at the activity on Mr. Van den Bark's land that day, I concluded that he might be smarter than others gave him credit. "Instead of paying someone to clear his land, Mr. Van den Bark is being paid to have others clear it." Any approbation that might be accorded me from what I thought was an astute observation was quickly denied. Apparently, cutting down trees at their base and leaving the stumps in the ground, as happened for these wintertime cuttings, did not constitute the clearing of land.

Only as we approached the Kelly Iron Works Repair Shop did my enthusiasm wane. I slowed and moved beside Father, barely matching his step. We walked in silence, the squelch of our feet in the accumulating wet snow the only sound around us. George Street was dark. The lights that lined Main Street were too far away to illuminate the area in which we walked. I looked to see if Scary Scott was sitting in his usual place on the stoop but in the dark could not make out his presence. It was not the time of day during which he ordinarily occupied his stoop—given the insufficiency of young passersby to view—but I did not underestimate his uncanny ability to know when I was in the vicinity.

While I did not know whether the stoop was occupied early that Saturday evening, it appeared that the repair shop itself was. The greatest light in the area was that which emanated from the glass window atop the door that opened onto the stoop. As we walked toward it, the light from the window lost some of its illumination. Assuming that someone was walking toward the door from within the shop, I moved closer to Father.

Moments later, an elongated luminescent rectangle appeared at the back of the stoop. A tall, thin man stepped out of the open door. Before he had a chance to cross the threshold, however, a short, stocky man sprang from the corner of the stoop and forced his way in, knocking back the exiting person. The door was slammed behind him. I was not able to make out the face of either person, but in the dark, even from behind, I knew the bounder to be Scary Scott.

Though I was prepared for the worst when it came to Scary Scott and the Kelly Iron Works Repair Shop, the incident shook me. Three and a half years of accumulated anxiety that I would be the victim of such speed and force manifested itself in a loud long scream into my father's back as I wrapped my arms around his stomach. From his rigid frame, I suspected that Father was struck by the incident as well, but recovering before me—or perhaps because of me—he immediately admonished me.

"You cannot really be scared of an imbecilic cripple, can you?" he said as he peeled my arms from around him. "How could he possibly harm you? You would be well served to think beyond your own petty fears." Father was right. How could Scary Scott hurt me when I was with my father? But as I realized my position of relative safety, I began to think of the man who had unsuccessfully exited the Kelly shop. "F-father," I stuttered as I sought to regain my composure, "should we go see if that man is alright?"

"What man?"

"The man who tried to leave the repair shop. Maybe he is being held there against his will." I thought of the girl with the brown curly hair held in the sewing room of Alderlea all that time and how grateful she would have been if a passerby had attempted to help her escape.

"You mean Mr. Kelly?"

"Was that Mr. Kelly?" I asked in reply. I realized I did not know what Mr. Kelly looked like, and in the darkness I didn't think I would have been able to make out his features, even if I did. Only from the silhouette of his hat and the absence of any billowing skirts had I been able to discern the person to be a man rather than a woman.

"It must have been. Who else do you think that lunatic would lunge at? Mr. Kelly has handled him for years without our help. He won't need any help now. Or if he does, he'll finally understand that the boy needs to be put away."

I wasn't sure that the man pushed back from the door frame was Mr. Kelly, but I was relieved to leave the area and said not another word as I followed Father around the corner and up Queen Street.

By the time we approached the Wellington Street Bridge, I had collected myself. My mind returned to the day's earlier discussion. "Father," I finally asked, "can we purchase a Christmas tree for our house this year? It seems a lot of people in Brampton do that." There wasn't enough distance remaining on our walk for Father to provide a lengthy response, but he only needed a few footsteps to give his reply.

"I don't know what Mr. Thompson told you about Brampton Christmases, but I'd remind you that he has only just arrived in this town. While he may know a lot about foundries, he is not likely qualified to tell you how most people here decorate their homes for Christmas! I don't know about what happens in other places, but here, a tree like that once cut down and put up in a house is a fire hazard. Look what happened to poor Mrs. Taylor's home last week!"

I knew about Mrs. Taylor's home, of course, and the fire that destroyed it. On the sound of the fire hall alarm, Father and Jim rose from their beds to join the volunteer firefighters in their unsuccessful quest to save the Mill Street house. I had not known that the cause of the fire was a Christmas tree. Obviously, though, I wouldn't wish such a conflagration on our family or on anyone's family.

Father remained outside, shovelling the new fallen snow from the sidewalk around our house and the steps to our veranda. Entering through the back door, I removed my boots and brought them and my snow-covered coat to rest beside the kitchen stove. Mother was there with an apron wrapped loosely around her, baking some biscuits for our tea. With little enthusiasm, I told her about my activities with the Thompsons and Frances.

"That sounds like a wonderful experience, Jessie. You must have had a great deal of fun. So why are you glum?"

"Because I am worried, Mother!" I said, speaking through tears.

"Whatever are you worried about, child?" she asked, producing an ever-ready handkerchief from her apron pocket. She was used to my tears.

"I am worried that the Thompsons' Christmas tree is going to catch on fire and burn down Haggertlea and everything and everyone that is in it!" I wailed. I was so absorbed by thoughts of Jane and Haggertlea I didn't even express the concern for the Hudsons down the street.

"Well, surely Mr. Thompson won't let that happen, Jessie. Mr. Thompson isn't ignorant enough to put candles on his tree, of that I am sure."

"Candles?" I sputtered. "No. No one said anything about putting candles on the tree. They are going to put painted pine cones and wooden painted ornaments on it." Then it dawned on me. "Is it only the candles that make the trees catch fire?"

"Generally, yes. Or because the tree is placed too near the fireplace." I felt quite confident that Mr. Thompson would not allow any candles to be put on their perfect tree. Given that it was to be positioned in the middle of the rotunda, the tree would also be far away from any open flames.

My concern for my friend's safety adequately addressed, I then turned to the next cause of my ill humour. Father's explanation as to the absence of a tree in our house was clearly not sufficient. "Mother, why has our family never had a Christmas tree?"

"It's not that we have never had a Christmas tree—" she said, but before she could go further, Father walked into the kitchen also through the back door. His coat and hat, like mine, were covered in snow.

"Now, Jessie," he said, clearly annoyed, having heard the beginning of Mother's reply, "don't be bothering your mother with that same line of questioning. I told you on the way home that Christmas trees are fire hazards, and that is why we will not have one in this house! I trust your mother told you the same thing." Glaring at Mother, he continued, "Settle yourself with the tomfoolery decorations your mother has everywhere in this house, and there will be no more talk of a Christmas tree!"

Mother and I both looked away from him. I knew there would be no more to be learned on the subject from Mother. But clearly there was more to be learned. I looked up. "Is Jim at home?" I asked.

"No. He went out to the Dales' house for the afternoon." He spent a lot of his spare time at the Dale home now that he and Millie were tree-climbers, as Frances called them. "He'll be back soon. Ina's upstairs, if you would like to say hello to her." Saying hello to Ina was never anything I particularly liked to do, but in this case I eagerly sought her out.

Ina was in the hallway looking into the full-length mirror affixed to the outside of the linen closet door, just beyond Mother and Father's room. It was the only full-length mirror in our house. This was where Ina, an amateur actress, always practiced her theatrical lines. The little alcove gave a semblance of privacy, and the mirror gave her a good opportunity to see what the audience would see.

She stood there in a dark brown long-sleeved dress, nearly completely covered by a length of gold fabric, cinched at the waist. The fabric had been donated to the church by one of Brampton's local upholsterers. The gold brocade had been rendered useless for its original purpose as a result of an oil stain that ran down its centre. Fortunately, once gathered up around Ina, the oil mark was barely visible. On her head, Ina fashioned a laurel crown made of wire with some leaf-shaped cardboard cutouts.

"Go, I bid you, into the night. Follow that star to Bethlehem, and when you arrive seize the baby that they call Majesty. Seize him and bring him to me so that I may be done with him," Ina ordered the imaginary wise men just beyond herself in the mirror.

"What do you want?" she said, seeing me approach her in the mirror. "Make it quick. I have to get back to this. I only received the script three days ago, and the play is to be performed in the cantata tomorrow night."

I acceded to her request and asked her directly whether there had ever been a Christmas tree in the house when they were younger.

"Every year," she said without hesitation, "Father used to purchase the trees from Mr. Van den Bark. He would deliver a tree to our back door when we lived on Peel Avenue. Father and Grandpa—or Father and Jim, once Jim was old enough—would put it on the back porch until the snow fell off. Then they would wrap it in a sheet and drag it into the sitting room. They would put it in a little can and tie it with ropes to the windowsills. I'd get a little ladder and place an angel on the top of it. Then we'd all hang gingerbread from its branches." Her voice became soft and trancelike as she described it. She sounded ... I struggled for the word ... happy.

"Gingerbread?" I asked.

"Oh yes. Gingerbread in all kinds of shapes. Bells, candles, wreaths, little men, even dogs. Mother would bake them and then sew thread into each of them so we could hang them from the ends of the branches. One per branch—at least that was the way it started. By the time Christmas arrived, we were lucky if there was one cookie remaining for every third branch. Mother's gingerbread is so delicious." She smiled as she recalled it, her eyes looking far into the distance. It sounded wonderful.

"When did we stop having a Christmas tree? Do you remember?"

"Of course I remember," she snapped. The spell was broken. She was back to her usual caustic self. "I remember it as clear as can be. Like many good things, that tradition stopped when you were born!"

I hung my head in silence. "Oh, don't worry about it," she said. "I've gotten over it." With that she turned to the mirror and began again. "Wise men, give me your wisdom. What does that star portend?"

Leaving her, I returned to the first-floor sitting room and pulled a chair in front of the fireplace. Deeply engaged in thoughts of Christmas trees, I was surprised to feel a quick tug on one of my curls. Jim was home. I noticed that his pant legs were very wet.

"You had better change your slacks or get them dry here at the fire before Father sees you like that," I scolded before seeing him walk as he crossed the room to retrieve a chair. "Why are you limping?" I asked, my tone softened. "Did you slip and fall on the way home?"

"Yes. I had a little fall. I am sure I can dry my pants here. But what about you, Little One? You don't seem too happy for a young girl less than a week before Christmas. Father Christmas is still packing his bag of toys for good, happy children. Don't you want to be one of them?"

"I do, but I don't think I am a good child. I make bad things happen to this family. Because of me, our family can't properly celebrate Christmas." Slowly I told him about my afternoon; about the excitement of cutting down the Thompsons' tree; and then about how Father refused to let us have a tree and how Ina told me that our family had always had a Christmas tree until I was born.

Jim shook his head. "That Ina. She wasn't wearing some actor's robes at the time she told you that, was she?"

"Yes, she was!" I said, not appreciating either the rhetorical or sarcastic nature of his question. "She told me this just now. I interrupted her rehearsing her lines as King Herod for tomorrow night's play."

"That wasn't the kind of acting I was thinking of, but I suppose in that role she was even less likely to display any Christian kindness. Jessie, it is true that when Ina and I were younger we always had a Christmas tree, and I must say, it was something we looked forward to every year. While the tradition changed shortly after you were born, it changed not because you were born but because we had just moved. Father took on an incredible financial burden in having this house built for us. That burden manifested itself in many ways but one way—which seemed quite appropriate—was his insistence that we cut back on unnecessary expenses.

"I think Father always viewed the purchase of a Christmas tree that would stay in our house for less than a fortnight to be a frivolous expense—even though the branches would make good kindling and the trunk good fire logs in the year to come. But you know he is a proud man. He would never have it said that we did not have a Christmas tree because he could not afford the expense. So instead, he has maintained that our abstinence from the custom has to do with the fire risk. And given that initially the concern appeared to arise after we moved into this beautiful new house, perhaps it was somewhat true. In fact, knowing how honest Father is, I would have to say that it was a genuine concern of his, but I expect, Jessie, that was not the only concern. No one would want us to lose this house—either from a fire or from a bankruptcy.

"As for whether we can properly celebrate the season without a Christmas tree," he went on, "look around you. There are symbols of Christmas everywhere in the decorations Mother puts up year after year. Look at the star hanging over the mirror in the dining room. That symbolizes the star that led the shepherds and wise men to Jesus. Look at the candy canes, filling that huge glass bowl on the sideboard." He rose and limped to the dining room. He picked a candy cane out of the bowl and then brought it to me. Holding it first with the round part up, he asked, "What does this look like to you?"

"A cane to help an old man walk? Maybe you could use one of those!" I suggested.

He chuckled. "I will manage without it. It is a cane of sorts, but that's not what it symbolizes. Look at that shepherd boy in the crèche on the table in the corner. What is he holding?"

"A crook," I replied. "It's a shepherds' crook?"

"Exactly. The crook that shepherds used to bring the lambs away from danger and closer to them; the crook that God uses to lead us away from the darkness and to the light. And if we turn it upside down?" It took me a few seconds but then I saw it. "The letter 'J' for 'Jesus.'"

"But you know it isn't really the symbols that count. It is what is inside you at this time of year that counts. The symbols just remind us of what we are celebrating. And that's something I know you will remember with or without them, and certainly with or without a Christmas tree."

He was right, of course. I had always enjoyed the Christmas season and what it meant to us. I hadn't needed a Christmas tree to feel that way. Jim knew he had succeeded in cheering me. He tugged one of my ringlets and hobbled upstairs to change for tea, forsaking the drying properties of the fire.

Chapter 16

THE JOHNSTONS

"One in, one out," was one of Father's most oft repeated phrases. Though I knew the expression typified his approach to accumulation, it was only after hearing Jim's explanation of our Christmas traditions and the circumstances in which our family was placed after moving into our large home that I realized the predilection came from necessity rather than from desire. Because we could not afford to amass a great number of personal effects, Father sought to make a virtue of their absence.

We had a generously sized house that was adequately furnished and equipped. We each had one Sunday outfit and three everyday outfits, suitable for the season in which they were worn. New items came into our house as replacements for those that were outgrown or outworn—certainly not for the mere purpose of meeting fashion dictates. This wasn't to say, however, that we didn't occasionally cause our formerly loved items to be prematurely worn out.

Father applied the phrase "one in, one out" not only to goods but also to causes and pursuits. One could have only so many causes if one was to accord each with the devotion required to meet its purpose. (Five, it seemed, was an acceptable number, judging by Father's pursuits at any time.) Although it was never expressly said, I expected that the saying applied as well to people, certainly to close friends. It was the application of this principle that contributed to the calamitous spring of 1913, although the seeds of it were sown much earlier in the form of a house fire, the drowning of a young boy, and a hankering for new shoes.

My father was a dentist, the chairman of the high school board, the chairman of the local water commission, the leader of our church choir and a landlord. Rarely a day passed that we did not hear about the trials and tribulations of each of them.

His role as a landlord related to the Queen Street building, which my father inherited from his father Jas. The largest part of the building—the commodious street level space—was highly desirable real estate. Located in the downtown four corners area, it was never vacant, and the long-term retail tenants required little of Father's time or attention. The same could not be said, however, of the small second-floor "front apartment." Comprised of only two rooms, its short-term, often unreliable tenants shared with Father and his patients the street level door, the long dark staircase accessed from it, and the second-floor water closet. The front apartment produced a meagre and somewhat irregular flow of income, which barely compensated for the time and trouble Father incurred in renting it.

Father maintained a list of qualities he sought in a front apartment tenant. The list grew with each departing occupant and generally took the form of an opposite trait to that person's predominant characteristics. Father would describe his ideal tenant as one who was neat and tidy and would, therefore, take good care of the supplied furnishings and fixtures; one who was gainfully employed and would pay the rent when due; one who was churchgoing and who would respect the sanctity of the Sabbath—because one should; one who spoke comprehensible English in order to understand Father's many dictates; one who cooked "English" (or bland) food, in order to prevent the seepage of strong odours into the waiting and other rooms of his dental practice; one without children, in order to avoid the chaos that could ensue if they were not well mannered (this was not always revealed in a first impression); and, above all, one who was male. In addition, the tenant might be somewhat handy and thus able to attend to the occasional repair required in any domicile.

Alas, being easily able to describe the ideal tenant did not make it easy to obtain one. I recall only two tenants who appeared to meet this complete description. Eventually, Father found faults even in them. As a result, the list of required qualities for a tenant of the front apartment continued to expand, while the supply of eligible candidates to occupy it continued to diminish.

Although Father was attentive to his list when considering prospective tenants, there were times when circumstances required him to partially disregard it. Such was the case following the 1912 December conflagration of old widow Taylor's Mill Street home. The fire left Mrs. Taylor without her mother's petit-point covered chairs and her grandfather's family bible. It also left Mrs. Taylor and four others homeless. Mrs. Taylor and her caregiver niece soon found a home in that of Mrs. Taylor's nearby sister. Mr. MacIntosh, an apprentice butcher, moved to Orangeville, some twenty-five miles north of Brampton. But two of the tenants, a widow named Aggie Johnston and her daughter Enid, fared not so well in relocating. Being the first among their family to settle in the New World and having only done so six weeks earlier, they had no relations to take them in. Various members of our church took them in for short periods of time, but a more permanent solution was required.

It was Mother who, six weeks after the fire, prevailed upon Father to offer the Johnstons the tenancy of the front apartment. Mrs. Johnston's obvious deficiencies in being a woman and the mother of a minor child aside, Mother touted her gainful employment, the fact that she could read and write, her likely preference for bland food (she was of British stock), and her obvious devotion to God (she attended our church). While Mother made no attempt to vouch for her tidiness, she speculated that given Mrs. Johnston's occupation, she was likely clean. Against his better judgement, Father agreed to the arrangement, in part at least because the apartment had been vacant for nearly two months, and no other acceptable tenant had recently presented himself.

At about this time, the town of Brampton was developing a certain reputation for the production of fine shoes. It was not always thus. Brampton's initial foray into the industry was disappointing, to say the least. Following the liquidation of the Haggert operations in the large downtown "Iron Block," and the subsequent closure and relocation of the J.M. Ross iron works from those premises and of the Young Brothers from their premises at the nexus of the two rail lines, the Brampton town council resolved to refocus its energies. The councillors were excited by the interest of not one but two prospective shoe manufacturers who were considering operating in those premises. The suggestion by some that Brampton should promote the new shoe manufacturing concerns as the natural successors to the early nineteenth century endeavours of William Buffy, the alcohol-dispensing retailer and shoe seller, was not well received. Brampton was still too Methodist to celebrate that early first settler. In any event, the promotion of any such connection would have been short-lived. The two businesses barely began their operations in the old Haggert block when Wes Williams, the owner of the Canada Shoe Company, moved his plant to Milton, and the owner of the Elkman Shoe Company closed down his business.

Though the old Haggert premises were once again vacant, the hopes of those who saw a future for the town in the manufacture of shoes were not similarly hollow. For while Wes Williams was moving his shoe company out of Brampton, a certain George Williams was moving his in. On the condition that the Williams Shoe Company repay the $30,000 loan advanced by the town to the Young Brothers, it was granted the foundry premises at the junction of the two railways. The repayment terms were not conventional. Instead of paying principal and interest to the town, the Williams Shoe Company agreed to employ men. At twenty-five dollars per man, per year, the Williams Shoe Company, which in 1912 employed nearly 150 men, was well on the way to retiring its debt. It was to this industry that Mrs. Johnston was drawn on arriving in Canada, for while these factories focused on the hiring of men to make the shoes, they were perfectly welcoming of women to polish them.

In early February 1913 the Johnstons moved into the front apartment. Enid Johnston was well known to me. In addition to being a regular parishioner at our church, Enid was a member of my senior second form class. On her enrollment in the school late in November, Miss Neelands urged our entire class to make the red-headed girl feel welcome. Though I knew it would be a proper Christian thing to do, I was by that point just beginning to make Jane Thompson feel welcome. Thinking that I had done my fair share in that department, I felt relieved of taking on any responsibilities towards Enid. Seeing how Enid interacted with others not so similarly relieved, I was ever grateful for the earlier urgings of Father toward Jane.

I had clearly befriended the right newcomer. Jane was quickly proving to be a kind, fun, and interesting friend. Enid, whose physical appearance could not have been less like Jane's, also had a contrary disposition. A short, stocky girl, Enid did everything too hard. In the schoolyard, she threw a ball at the catcher rather than to the catcher. While "it" in a game of tag, Enid pushed rather than tapped those she caught. She was incapable of talking quietly, let alone whispering. She loved to postulate about matters in a way bound to create rumours. "Look at how thin Ed Hale is," she would say in her strong Cockney accent, loud enough for everyone around her to hear. "Maybe his mother is a bad cook." Worst of all, she stole things. Items she admired in our classroom were soon absent. We all learned to keep the few valuables we brought to school on our persons.

By March, a month after the Johnstons settled into the front apartment, I concluded that Father found them to be suitable tenants, notwithstanding that they were females and one was a minor, for in Father's daily litany of complaints, I rarely heard anything untoward about them. In fact, at times they commanded not only Father's respect as tenants but his compassion as less fortunate citizens. His attention in that regard was specifically directed at Enid, who, he had noticed in her many comings and goings from his building, was somewhat friendless. What, Father asked me, had I done to make the poor girl feel welcome at our school? He could see that Jane was beginning to share the position in my heart and social calendar formerly occupied by Frances and Archie. Given the circumstances, he suggested I had room for another friend—one who could take the place of Archie; someone more adventurous than Jane and Frances; someone more athletic.

His initial entreaties were somewhat innocuous, but by early April, when they failed to have any discernable effect, Father became more forceful. He strongly urged me to invite Enid to swing a baseball bat. When I demurred, Mother joined in the appeal. At school, two days later, Enid announced to me that it had all been arranged. I was to meet her the coming Saturday at Rosalea Park at ten o'clock in the morning. As she owned neither a bat nor a ball, she expected me to bring both. I left the park at noon that Saturday, equipment in hand, bruises on my arms and legs where her fastballs struck me and with a conviction never to repeat the exercise.

My parents' resolution was otherwise. My dislike of the girl and my stated desire to spend no time with her made them determined to teach me valuable lessons about charity and the need to do willingly things one did not want to do at all. The next week I learned that Father had arranged another gathering for Enid and me, this one in the front apartment. In response to my question to Mother as to what we were to do at that time, I was presented with five large, tangled skeins of yarn. To facilitate the knitting that the church women were doing to clothe the poor in the House of Refuge, Enid and I were to untangle and wind into balls all of the yarn. It would, in Mother's estimation, take no more than three or four hours.

Setting out on my knitting-ball expedition, I thought there could be nothing worse than spending an entire afternoon with Enid. I learned on that afternoon that there was one thing even less pleasant than being with Enid; that was being with Enid and her mother. Aggie Johnston was an odd-looking woman with a square face, accentuated entirely by her short ginger hair, which she wore pulled straight back from her forehead. Her cheekbones were prominent but low. Their placement in the middle of her cheeks near her rather large nose and lips gave her an unusual appearance, which was reinforced by the peculiar manner in which she spoke.

In short, every sentence emanating from her large lips was punctuated by a laugh. No sentence was too mundane, too sad, too moronic, or too sophisticated to be uttered without ending in a slight giggle, a chortle, a snort, or a full guffaw. I was in a constant state of doubt when speaking with Mrs. Johnston. Her snicker following our exchange of greetings sent my hand to my head to confirm that my hat was not on backward. Every conversation with her was filled with both relief, once I confirmed she was not laughing at me, and disappointment, when I realized there really was nothing funny in what was being said.

I returned home that Saturday afternoon with ten large well-wound balls of wool and three scratches on my left hand from where Enid's fingers and her uncut nails had too vigorously retrieved from mine bounds of tangled wool. This, however, was not the account of Father, who used the time I spent in the front apartment attending to paperwork in his office behind it. Declaring the afternoon to be a shining success, he announced that he and I would spend each of the next six Saturday afternoons in a similar manner.

Mother concurred in the plan, excited not only by the good lessons she and Father were teaching me, but I think as well by the notion that Father would willingly choose to spend more time making his dental practice profitable. Mother was indifferent to my private pleas, my weekly accounts of cuts, and bruised skin and feelings. To her, this was simply evidence of the lessons Enid had yet to learn in becoming a good friend. Once she had more "practice" she would be gentler.

There was one week, though, when Mother did express some concern relating to my weekly assignation. Each week, it was my responsibility to conceive of the manner in which Enid and I would entertain ourselves. If I could not devise the means, Mother and Father would suggest some chore that could be undertaken for the benefit of the church. Not wanting to polish brass as we had the prior week, one Saturday in early May I packed up the porcelain animal figurines that Grandpa had given me over successive birthdays and Christmases. Replicas of the Canadian wild, the two-inch-high ornaments lived a docile life on top of my dressing table. Only occasionally did they venture farther afield, going as far Haggertlea once and to Frances's home twice. Having survived those outings, Mother proposed that I take them with me to the front apartment. She rebuffed my concern that the fragile pieces would either be broken by Enid's rough hands or stolen by her slippery fingers. When I still balked, Mother offered to again retrieve the church's brass. Reluctantly, that Saturday I placed the twelve animals in their red felt wrappers, packed them in a box, and carried them with me to the front apartment.

Enid was curious to see the twelve figurines and urged me to place them on the table as quickly as I could. In response to my declared need for a clean, flat surface, she took her broad right arm and swept the little table at which the Johnstons ate clear of the accumulated paper, wrappings, and bits of food.

"Freddy Fox," I said, naming each animal pulled from its felt wrapper. "Peter Porcupine." His needles were thin, and though they were not pointed enough to inflict harm, they were delicate enough to be harmed by us. One by one, they all emerged. Samuel Squirrel. Douglas Deer. Bartholomew Bear. Charlie Chipmunk. Matilda Moose. Paul Partridge. Randolph Raccoon. Finnegan Frog. Tommy Trout. Warren Wolf. Despite her initial enthusiasm, Enid was dissatisfied with each animal. The names I had chosen did not suit their wildness; their faces were too tame; their colours not precisely as she thought they should be.

Of the entire twelve, there was only one she thought equal to its reputation—though it required a different name—Warren Wolf. Enid announced she would rename him Waldorf Wolf and remove him from the other eleven, who were a softening influence on him. Assuming that this was part of the game in which we were engaged, I initially played along, moving the handsome animal, his head raised above his sturdy neck in a long howl, to the other side of the table. But shortly afterward, I wondered whether Enid proposed to keep my small wolf. The answer came to me at 3:55, as I began to rewrap the animals in preparation for my departure promptly at four o'clock.

"Wait," she said as I reached across the table. "You aren't taking Waldorf. He's mine now."

"He is not yours!" I declared. "My grandfather gave him to me. I did not give him to you." I reached for him, and being quicker than Enid, was the first to put my hands around his porcelain skin. Enid's hands, having missed the porcelain, instead grabbed skin and bones, which she released only at the sound of a sharp crack. Opening my hand, I was dismayed to see the severed head of Warren Wolf surrounded by a quickly growing stain of red blood.

* * *

"Come here, child," Mother said when I arrived home fifteen minutes later. Warren Wolf's felt wrapping was balled up in my hand. Father had not noticed it when he picked me up from the front apartment. He had only walked with me a short distance before meeting Mr. Peaker on the street. As the two had town business to discuss, I was urged to go home without him. Mother pulled my hand under the tap.

"Why didn't you properly clean and bandage this?" Mother asked with slight irritation in her voice. She felt the use of a dusty wrapper a poor means to ensure hygenic coagulation. I explained that when the wolf's neck was broken in my hand, I could see neither soap nor a clean piece of linen.

"Why didn't you ask Mrs. Johnston for them, then? Did the cat have your tongue?"

"No," I replied, concentrating on my hand. "Mrs. Johnston wasn't there."

"She wasn't there?"

"No. She goes out sometime after I arrive." That was a blessing to my mind. "Sometimes she returns just before four. But today she didn't."

It was 1913. No one judged a person critically for leaving two ten-year-olds at home alone. Mother didn't ask where Mrs. Johnston went after I arrived. This was just as well. I didn't think she would believe me if I told her.

Chapter 17
MOTHER AND HER SHOES

L ike every member of our family, my mother did not have an abundance of clothes. Just as her personality did not tend to draw attention to herself, her wardrobe did not either. She was partial to form-fitting, dark-coloured bodices with high necklines and long sleeves. In the summer, when it was warmer, she varied the length of her sleeves, exposing a quarter of each arm. Whether any buttons, beads, or little bows appeared on the bodice of her dress or any pleating or gathering appeared around its midriff, a family member would be hard pressed to know. When Mother was at home with her family, her dress was nearly always covered by an apron. Only when sitting at the dining room table would the apron be removed.

Though the fashion of the day dictated the display of a little of a lady's ankle, Mother would have nothing of it. Throughout my childhood, her long, floor-length hemline never varied. It is peculiar, therefore, that Mother's one fashion fascination was the item she so rarely exposed: her shoes. Of course, most of us have at least one fashion obsession. For some it is hair bows. (My friend Jane had at least a dozen.) For others it is ornamental jewellery. (My Aunt Rose was rarely seen without a large brooch pinned at her throat.) For men it could be an assortment of ties. (My Uncle William had in excess of seven!)

At a time when an average Brampton woman possessed possibly three pairs of footwear—a comfortable, lace-tied, thick-soled shoe for working in the house, a sturdy above-the-ankle boot for outdoor wear, a dress slipper for evenings and parties—my mother had ten pairs of shoes.

If asked, she would sincerely declare it gluttony to possess so many, but as she came into her extended collection through circumstances that did not require a significant outlay of funds, she considered their possession to be a pardonable sin.

To her standard three pairs, two were added over a similar number of years by a local cobbler who gave them to Father in lieu of cash to settle his dental bills. They were not particularly nice, and neither pair fit properly, but relegated to garden and other outdoor activities, they found a home in her collection. A delicate pair was left at our house after an evening soiree. Try as she did, Mother was never able to find the feet to which they belonged. A seventh pair was left at the house by Aunt Lil. Faded green but quite stylish, Aunt Lil replaced them in the few days it took Mother to notify her by mail where she had left them. Father carried the final two pairs into the house one night after work, a pair in each hand and his pockets turned out. He reported that the front apartment tenants had skipped town before paying their rent, leaving behind the shoes and other sundries. I lay in bed that night picturing the departed tenants skipping down the street in the dead of night, barefoot.

From that point on, Mother considered it acceptable in God's eyes to replace a pair of shoes within her ten-pair stable, so long as the replacement was acquired with money that was not needed for some necessity, and so long as the pair being replaced was worn out. The problem was that Mother took such good care of her shoes, they rarely achieved that tired state. Though we were generally prohibited from storing things under our beds, Mother's shoes were stored in one neat long row under hers. There, she advised, they would not be trodden on by others, exposed to unnecessary sun, or found to take up too much room in a closet.

No pair of shoes made it to this unique storage location without first being specially tended. Outdoor shoes were properly dried and then brushed to remove the dust of our dirt roads, the pollen of our spring growth, and the salt of our winter walkways. Laced shoes were properly untied before being removed, and the laces, once the foot was extracted, were tucked inside the shoe under its tongue. Wet shoes were first dried near a fire. Once a week, Mother would select three pairs to be polished by Father, though never more than three. She wouldn't think to expose all ten pairs to anyone, not even Father, though he knew full well how many pairs she possessed.

Father was surprisingly obliging about the shoe polishing. I conjectured that his easy acquiescence to this chore was related to his profession; attending to it allowed him to practice his trade of polishing on objects bigger than teeth. It likely helped Mother that Father too had a certain fetish for shoes—in his case, not in number but in style. Father liked nothing more than a pair of white leather shoes, which he wore regardless of the season or the colour of his pant or sock. Unless they were patent leather (and they often were), white leather shoes required a good deal of polish.

Mother's routine rarely varied. The shoes were always lightly walked on, delicately tended, and carefully stored until a day once a year or sometimes once every eighteen months when she would notice a desirable pair of shoes in the window of one of the local stores. Consciously or unconsciously, one pair of her cherished shoes would suddenly become neglected. An indoor pair of shoes might be worn outside on a rainy or muddy day. A pair of boots reserved for snow and ice might be exposed to too much salt and then left to dry too close to the fire. Punch might accidentally spill from a glass and stain a pair of evening slippers.

Knowing the care Mother applied to her shoes, the sight of any such injury would send the rest of her family scurrying to the rescue of the prized article, expecting as usual to be warmly rewarded for the thoughtful attention. Many a time Mother would take the precious shoe from our hands, look the rescuer in the eye, and utter her profound thanks. "Oh my goodness, Jim," she might say. "Whatever was I thinking leaving the shoes there in front of the fire for so long? And you, so many things on your mind—your examinations, your work at the Dale Estate, but still you thought of me and my old shoes. Shall I make you your favourite dessert tonight?'"

But at other times, when a pair had been singled out for unusual wear and tear, our attention was not rewarded but was instead met with irritation. "Oh!" she might say, taking a pair of suede ankle boots from my hands as I entered the back door. "You say they were left outside the back door in a snow pile? I don't know how that could have happened. Well, place them there by the fire to dry, won't you. Not there, child. They are soaking wet. Put them right up to the grate. Now, go upstairs. Surely you have homework to do."

Once Mother began to cruelly treat a pair of shoes, we knew the path she was on, and thenceforth we became silent co-conspirators in the shoes' demise, each hoping it would occur before the coveted replacements in the store's window were sold to another.

Father was Mother's chief supplier of new shoes, the occasion generally being a birthday or Christmas. Very rarely, he bought them for her for no reason at all, particularly if a long period had passed since she last acquired a new pair, or if she had been staring for a very long time at a pair displayed in a store window. Sometimes, if money were not then available, Father would ask the proprietor to put the coveted pair aside so that he could purchase them over time. He would never think of buying them on credit. The first time Father arranged for a pair to be put aside, Mother became quite sullen. Naturally, she thought someone else had purchased them. Although Father pretended to be irritated by her "gluttony," he, like the rest of us, enjoyed seeing elation replace disappointment when the desired pair of shoes was given to her sometime later.

One early June day in 1913, Jane and I came across Mother standing outside of Robinson & Stork's, staring into the front picture window. The object of her attention, I was certain, was a pair of shoes. Seeing the opportunity for a good joke, I signalled to Jane that we should quietly approach her. I had it in mind to tell her that Father had been able to mend the brown high-tops she had been neglecting for the past two weeks. I dated the commencement of that treatment to the date on which the two-toned, graceful heeled high-top shoes in front of her arrived in the Robinson & Stork's window. But as we approached her, I could see that her gaze was actually fixed beyond the items in the front window. Following her line of sight, I noticed Father midway back in the store, examining a bright red-and-gold shawl.

"Mother!" I exclaimed, causing her to jump. "Are you peeping on Father's birthday shopping?" Her birthday was less than a week away.

"Certainly not!" she said defensively. "At least I hadn't intended to. I was only thinking that I needed a new pair of shoes. I thought I might select a pair, in case your father wished to give them to me for my birthday." She looked back inside the store.

"I do hope your father is not going to waste his money, though, on a new shawl. My existing shawls are perfectly functional, and I wouldn't feel comfortable wearing something as flamboyant as the one he has in his hands." The red and gold colours were quite visible through the glass, even from that distance. I agreed the shawl was not in keeping with Mother's very modest wardrobe.

"It's just Mr. Cooper, Mother. You always say he won't let you leave the store without trying to sell you something more than what you went in for. Let's go home before you ruin any surprise Father may have for you." I knew that Father intended to purchase the new shoes for her that day.

"Very well. I don't want to hurt his feelings. But Jessie, if he does ask your opinion, please do let him know that the two-tone shoes alone will suffice. I am afraid that with those extra hours he has been working Saturday afternoons, he may feel he has the luxury of buying me something I do not really need. I can think of many better uses of a few extra dollars than the purchase of a new shawl." I agreed to convey that message if asked, but I had no illusions that I would be. Father rarely sought my opinion.

Days later, we all had the pleasure of seeing Mother's delight as she received from Father the two-toned graceful heeled high-top shoes she desired. Only I knew the additional pleasure she had in not having to feign a similar feeling over the receipt of a brightly coloured shawl.

The month proceeded apace, and I found myself in the happy position of once again looking forward to summer. After the forlorn season I'd endured the year before, I particularly relished the thought of the arrival of my Turner cousins, summer picnics, swimming, tennis and croquet matches, and outdoor concerts. That summer I knew I would also have the pleasure of introducing Jane to most of those pursuits. Combining all of this with my graduation from the little Queen Street Public School and the end of my four daily walks past the Kelly Iron Works Repair Shop, I didn't even mind the prospect of continuing to spend two or three hours every Saturday afternoon with Enid.

The end of the month coincided with a Sunday night concert at our church. That concert, like most concerts and cantatas there, was arranged by my father. Aunt Lil's account years earlier to me about the role my grandparents Jas and Selina Stephens played in the music ministry of the Primitive Methodist Church—he the leader of the choir, she the organist—was easily comprehended by me. My parents shared the same roles at Grace Methodist Church. Music brought my parents together, and it bound them through their married lives, whether in their weekly choir practices and church services (Father singing and Mother playing), the regular Sunday night concerts and cantatas (Father organizing, hosting, and sometimes singing; Mother sometimes playing), or the occasional Gilbert and Sullivan performances (Father performing and Mother playing as he rehearsed).

Neither of my parents was particularly sentimental, but I did hear Mother on a number of occasions tell the story of their meeting in 1890, just after Father returned from the Philadelphia Dental College, where he completed his postgraduate work. Though Brampton was then a small town and both were from established Brampton families, the two had not previously met. There were a few reasons for this. Firstly, though my paternal grandfather Jas Stephens and my maternal grandfather Jesse Brady were acquainted, their relationship was of a business nature only. The Stephenses and the Bradys did not socialize.

Secondly, though both families were Methodist, they did not practice the same Methodism. Ever since Jas and Selina Stephens moved into Brampton to assume the positions of choirmaster and organist, the Stephenses had practiced Primitive Methodism. Jesse and Louisa Brady, on the other hand, were committed Wesleyan Methodists, Grandpa singing in that church's choir. The 1884 merger of the four Canadian branches of Methodism (only three of which were present in Brampton) resulted in a few practical changes for Brampton Methodists. The Queen Street West church of the Episcopalian Methodists was sold to the Anglicans. The Anglicans renamed it Christ Anglican Church, added a chancel, installed a bell, and otherwise renovated it to make it acceptable for their worship. The Wesleyan Methodist Church was renamed the Grace Methodist Church. The Primitive Methodists, still worshiping above the meat market on Queen Street, were redesignated the Queen Street Methodists, a name they would hold for a further year, until they moved into their new church to be called St. Paul's Methodist Church.

But there the changes ended. Though the Wesleyan Methodists and the Primitive Methodists were part of the same Methodist Church, they did not worship together; they did not mingle; they did not share pastoral staff. The Grace Methodists, who prided themselves on including the town's most distinguished Methodists among their congregation, rather looked down upon the former Primitive Methodists. The St. Paul's Methodists, who prided themselves on their louder devotion and their larger congregation, rather looked down on the former Wesleyan Methodists. The notion of actually merging the two congregations into a single church, as the Church of Scotland and the Free Church Presbyterians within Brampton had done in 1879, was summarily dismissed. The Primitive Methodist Stephenses and the Wesleyan Methodist Bradys did not socialize.

Finally, my parents had not been in the same classes at school. That was because my mother was, shockingly, two years older than my father. In addition, Father had been absent from Brampton for the better part of four years obtaining his dental qualifications. Mary Brady and Jethro Stephens did not socialize.

The two finally met in Mr. Treadgold's piano shop early in the summer of 1890. They were both there ordering sheet music, Father for the choir of St. Paul's Methodist Church, which he had rejoined on his return from Philadelphia two months earlier, Mother for the choir of Grace Methodist Church, for which she had been playing the organ for years. Jethro Stephens, then twenty-five years of age, was engrossed in a conversation with Mr. Treadgold, informing the longstanding piano retailer of current American musical trends. Eventually, Mary Brady, then twenty-seven years of age, her order for a new hymn already placed, interrupted them.

"Excuse me. I've overheard your conversation. You are just back from America. You must know how to spell Mississippi. Could you please spell it for me?" Jethro obliged and then asked her if she planned to go there. "Not at all," she said. "It is the name of a popular song. I'm hoping Mr. Treadgold will be able to order the music for me. It's from the United States."

From that conversation a romance began that culminated in a marriage fifteen months later. Jethro brought his musical talents to the church of his wife, leaving many to wonder why more families could not do more to merge the two Brampton Methodist churches.

* * *

A mass of people was assembled outside Grace Methodist Church when we arrived that late June Sunday night. This was a common occurrence before Sunday night concerts and cantatas, since the productions generally required time for platforms and stages to be set up or for visiting performers to rehearse. As most cantatas and concerts were organized by Father, and as Mother frequently accompanied the performers on the organ or the piano, the two of them were usually among those inside preparing to receive those outside. Jim, Ina, and I would find ourselves waiting outside, often without even the company of Grandpa, who was a devoted member of the church choir. On that particular night, one of the travelling performers was the accompanying organist. Thus, Mother found herself on the outside of the church waiting with her children.

Unless it was quite cold or raining, the assembled did not particularly mind the time spent waiting outdoors. The delays gave the congregation an opportunity to fraternize that they could not do sitting quietly in the sanctuary. Jim and Ina separated from Mother and me almost as soon as we arrived, seeking instead the company of their friends. I would have left Mother's side in search of the Thompsons had I not seen the look of horror on her face as I turned to ask if I could go.

"Mother," I asked, "are you not well?"

"I don't know," she said slowly. Her face was flushed. She began to remove her brown shawl. "Jessie, you mentioned some time ago that

Mrs. Johnston is often absent when you visit Enid on Saturday afternoons. Where does Mrs. Johnston go when you are there?"

"I don't know, Mother."

"Does she not give you any explanation?"

I was incapable of lying to my mother, even though I knew my response would earn me a reprimand. "She does."

"If she tells you, then why did you say you don't know where she goes?"

"Well … I…" I had to be careful. We were raised to strictly respect our elders. "I don't really … believe her."

"You believe Mrs. Johnston is telling you a falsehood?" Mother was indignant.

I rushed to defend myself. "I know it isn't right to accuse her of being untruthful," I said in front of the big church doors and under the massive church spire.

Mother sighed deeply. We were near the railing of the church steps. She put a hand out to steady herself. "Ordinarily that would not be right, but for now, please just tell me what she tells you."

"She tells me, Mother, that she is in Father's dental office," Mother's face fell, "helping him clean his office and instruments and organizing his compounds." I knew all of those terms, because before I started visiting our building once a week to play with Enid, I would often visit it to attend to those very things myself.

Mother looked at me in consternation. "And why do you think that may not be the case?"

"She isn't a good housekeeper, Mother! The front apartment is always messy and dirty. I don't think she could be cleaning Father's office. I think she must go somewhere else when I am there! She only knows how to clean shoes."

"Thank you, child," she said slowly. "I'm afraid I am feeling a little under the weather. Why don't you find the Thompsons and let Ina and Jim know, if you could, that I will see them at home later."

"Mother, would you like me to go with you?" I always liked someone to be with me when I felt ill. I thought Mother might like some company at this time.

"No. Thank you, child. Not this time. You stay here and enjoy the cantata. I'll be fine."

I climbed the steps leading to the church doors. Over the heads of those gathered, I watched Mother leave and the Thompsons arrive. Walking to join them, I passed Enid wearing an old big brown sweater and her Mother wrapped in a bright new red-and-gold shawl.

* * *

Loud applause greeted the singers, musicians, and my father, the choir leader, at the end of the concert. The ninety-minute performance by the visiting altos, sopranos, mezzo-sopranos, tenors, and basses was deemed by most adults to be the perfect length and by most children to be about eighty minutes too long. For my part, I would not have minded the length had I not been worried throughout about my mother's health. The last ovation was barely given when I said my good evenings to the Thompsons and started to walk home. I had not gone far when I felt a familiar tug on one of my locks.

"Little One," Jim said, "where is Mother? I was looking for her in the church and couldn't see her." I told him how she had taken ill just after we reached the church.

"Did she? I feel terrible. I didn't notice anything. Why didn't you go home with her? Was the concert that tempting to you?" He laughed a little as he asked.

"I offered to go home with her, Jim. I did. But she said I shouldn't."

"Alright. Let's get home as fast as we can. Maybe it was something she ate. She certainly won't want to be under the weather when the Turners arrive tomorrow."

Silence and an empty first floor greeted our return home. Walking upstairs, we could see the door to Mother and Father's room shut tight. Jim knocked on it lightly. There was no answer. He tried the handle. The door was locked. Neither of us knew the door had a lock. Jim called for Mother, once; twice; three times.

Mother finally replied, though in a voice I barely recognized. "Yes, Jim. I can hear you. I am fine but I would prefer to be alone now. Is Jessie with you?"

"Yes, Mother," I replied. "I'm here." I was quite worried ... and then hopeful. "Would you like me to get Dr. Heggie?"

"No, child. That will not be necessary. Please just let me be, and when your father and Ina get home, please ask them to do so as well." Grandpa was not at home and would not be coming home that night, having decided to spend some time with friends in Toronto, as he often did to make room for the Turners.

Jim tugged on my arm and led me back downstairs and into the sitting room. We were far out of reach of Mother's ears. "Jessie," he said, "what happened after Ina and I left you and Mother at the church tonight? Tell me everything." It was an account I gave repeatedly that night and the next day and the next. I spared no detail in the retelling, except the part about Mrs. Johnston's poor housekeeping and my doubts about her whereabouts while I was visiting Enid. It wasn't very Christian of me to think that she might not be doing exactly what she said she was doing. She might be a perfectly good cleaner of other people's tables, chairs, and instruments, even if she did not appear to be in possession of such talents within her own living quarters.

It was not enough information, though. It was not enough information for Jim. It was not enough information for Ina. It was not enough information for Aunt Rose or even insightful Aunt Charlotte when she arrived. Somehow, though, it seemed to be enough information for Father, for when I gave him the account, he asked no further questions.

Mother stayed in that bedroom for five days. During that time she let no one enter and would provide no explanation for her seclusion. She left the room to use the bathroom and to receive the meals we put outside the door. Father slept in Grandpa's room. The Turners, on their arrival, decided that until Mother was "better," all four should stay with Aunt Rose. We tried to coax her out, Ina with a promise to attend to her every need, Jim with a promise not to ask her any questions and Father with some incomprehensible apology. My futile attempt to entice her out of her room involved slipping sheet music under her door. Playing the piano had always soothed her spirits in the past.

Eventually, it was Aunt Charlotte who succeeded. One day while Father was at work, Aunt Charlotte exercised her authority as the eldest of the Stephens daughters. A command and control voice was applied to the door, accompanied as always by terms of endearment. There was a statement of duty and responsibility; a declaration that the time for feeling sorry for oneself had now run out; a request that she open the door immediately and let her in; and a threat to call the locksmith if she did not. Four hours later, she and Mother emerged. The only child home at that time, I was given a long hug and issued an apology and a covenant. Mother promised me that she would never again seclude herself from me. As she and Aunt Charlotte walked down the street to see Aunt Rose, I looked out the window for a rainbow.

The three ladies returned to our house just before five o'clock and took up three of the four seats on the carpeted area of our parlour. Uncle William delivered Father to the ladies, who asked Father to take a seat on the fourth chair positioned on the carpet. Uncle William was excused. Seeing this gathering in the making from my window, I assumed a hidden position at the top of the stairs, glad that the conversation was occurring in the parlour rather than the sitting room, from which I would not have heard a word. The conversation below only barely began when Aunt Rose said in a louder-than-usual voice. "Jessie, if you are not now in your room reading a book, you should be." A terrified look crossed my face. What was I to do? To get up and move would, through the inevitable creaking of the floor, confirm that I was preparing to eavesdrop. To stay the course seemed wiser, particularly because Aunt Rose, I noted, merely told me what I should be doing, not what I must do.

Then they began, Aunt Charlotte taking the lead with Aunt Rose her sure second. Mother and Father said almost nothing, but at times I thought I heard both of them sobbing. What Father had done, they said, would affect us all. As such, the rectification of it was the business of all of us: Aunt Rose, Mother, and the children, each of whom would have to live in this town for a number of years to come. The shame attached to Aunt Charlotte, Uncle William, and the boys was not as great, of course, given their distant residence. Father was without any delay to: evict the tenants of the front apartment; offer those tenants a reasonable sum to relocate to another town, at least a day's distance away; accompany

Mother on walks throughout Brampton at least once a day and attend whatever society events at which they might be lucky enough to continue to be received. Finally, Father was to perform whatever other act of contrition Mother required of him in order to tolerate his continued presence in her life.

With that, the meeting ended. As Aunt Rose and Aunt Charlotte rose to leave, I tiptoed back into my room. Lying on my bed, I considered what I heard. Father had hurt Mother in some way that required her forgiveness. At that time, I did not know why. Our family was shamed in some way. I didn't know how. It involved Mrs. Johnston, and I suspected it had to do with more than her bad housekeeping. The Johnstons were to move, and at Father's expense. I didn't know where, but I, for one, was glad to say good riddance.

Chapter 18

INA'S JOURNEY

The months that followed were difficult for all of us, but among us children, for Ina they were the worst. Her trial arose not from the doors from which we were shunned, for contrary to Aunt Charlotte's prediction, the lashes hurled toward our family were never aimed at the three of us. We found ourselves as welcome in the homes of the McMurchys, the Dales, the McKechnies, the Hudsons, and the Thompsons after the affair as we were before.

It arose in part from the change in Father's financial circumstances, which were felt almost immediately after the revelation, for although Mrs. Johnston left town quickly, she did not leave quietly. In the space of a week, Father lost the rental income from the front apartment and much dental income from the back. The censure that Aunt Charlotte predicted was levelled immediately and precisely. With Mother still at his side, the enforcers of morality (namely the women of the town) chose the target of their wrath: Father's dental practice. One by one, they moved their dental business to Drs. French and Peaker. Gone with the revenues derived from treating the women were the revenues derived from treating their children and at least half of their husbands.

Cost-cutting, which had always been a part of our lives, came in earnest. The "drought," as we referred to this period of time, required us to delay the incurrence of expenditures that had already been delayed many times; forced us to avoid even the little waste our family previously generated; to call upon the dregs of the preserves and other canned goods that Mother had hoped we would never have to consume; and to utilize those funds saved for a "rainy day"—an ironic term, given the name we coined for the downturn in Father's business.

We were helped by the subtle generosity of a number of people. Aunt Rose went through a particularly forgetful period in her housekeeping, regularly purchasing too much from the butcher and the grocer. She begged Mother to take the excess for fear it would otherwise go to waste. The few patients that continued to see Father were especially prompt in their payment and extraordinarily committed to payment with cash. The church ladies begged Mother to allow her kitchen to be used to prepare sandwiches for funeral teas. An extra loaf or two of sandwiches were often forgotten behind as they moved the results of their efforts to the site of the mourners. Grandpa took longer trips to Toronto, leaving one less mouth to feed.

It was Ina, though, who made the biggest sacrifice. As a result of the drought, Father could simply not support both Jim and Ina at university at the same time. Without the means to pay her tuition and board, Ina deferred her university admission and took a job as a local telephone operator. But this change in her circumstances; this alteration that required her to defer the scientific study she had long hoped to pursue; this modification that required her to assume a full-time job employing not a whit of her scientific inclinations; this sad turn of events was not the road to her state of depression. In fact, it was barely a way station en route.

By August 1913, Ina was fully ensconced in a valley of despair. She arrived there by a path that was long and wide; her journey to had been so gradual that she only realized her destination on her arrival. Indeed, the journey began on a plain. She walked along its even course for years as she—then a young girl—encountered her brother's best friend Eddie in the town, at church, or at other highly populated events.

Her pace toward the valley increased as Eddie and Jim celebrated their eighteenth birthdays and she her fifteenth—a conflux of the ages at which the occasional presence of an unrelated minor in our home could be tolerated by Father and the attentions of a boy could be desired by Ina. With each private conversation she and Eddie shared on our verandah, him with his extra bottle of soda pop, her surrounded by her scientific laboratory—the speed of her journey accelerated.

Ina surged ahead on that path as she and her maturing friends were included in the activities of Jim and his friends. As she and Eddie organized a social outing for their two groups of friends in the summer of 1912, she was oblivious to the path's gradual descent.

It must be said that the relationship between Jim and Millie that began to form in June 1912, in the shadow of Archie's death, was never welcomed or regarded with particular warmth by Ina. As the rest of our family basked in the glow of their young love, Ina scoffed at its every manifestation. Though it was never spoken of with Ina, Mother and I assumed that Ina's antipathy toward the relationship sprang from two fears: the first that Jim's time with Millie would necessarily correlate with a corresponding reduction in the time he spent with Eddie, and second that Jim's time with Millie would similarly correlate, albeit to a lesser extent, with an increase in the time he spent with Millie's friend Sarah, a girl Ina considered odious in the extreme.

If these were her fears, I can say they were somewhat justified. In fact, Millie's presence in Jim's life did not lead to a material lessening of the presence of Eddie. Although Jim would occasionally spend a part of an evening or a Saturday afternoon with Millie and members of her family or ours, most of the time Jim was with Millie, the two young lovers were also with Eddie and Sarah.

I confess to not always being sensitive to Ina's insecurities and jealousies regarding Eddie and Sarah, or perhaps I should confess to being perfectly sensitive to them but inflaming them nonetheless. One night in July 1912, two months after Archie drowned, Ina and I were lying in our bed, trying to sleep. Too hot to get comfortable, I was reflecting on the concert we attended that night at Gage Park. I did not want to attend. I did not want to do anything gay. But Father had insisted. I sat glumly on a picnic blanket with Mother, Mrs. Hudson, and Frances while Jim, Millie, Eddie, and Sarah sat on a similar blanket under one of the big alders. Jim and his friends found considerably more frivolity in the strains of the Citizens Band than did Frances and I.

Ina was on her back, looking at the ceiling, when I broached my question. "Ina, do you think Eddie is sweet on Sarah?"

Bolting upright, Ina declared that to be the most preposterous thing she had ever heard. "Aside from the fact that Sarah has not the sense to dote on a boy of Eddie's calibre," she declared, "I cannot imagine Eddie ever abiding a voice like that in a companion. Anyway, Sarah has a beau in Milton who I understand is her second cousin on the Lawson side.

"No," she stated firmly as she lay back on the mattress, "I have spent enough time with Eddie McMurchy to know that he is not sweet on Sarah Lawson. He is simply too good a friend of Jim's to come between Millie and her friend."

Ina's dismissal of the suggestion was so decisive that I chided myself for ever entertaining it. Indeed, the activities of Ina and Eddie over the next couple of weeks seemed to prove the point. One day, when Eddie was on our verandah waiting for Jim to come home, Eddie and Ina took a break from their discussion of changing wind and precipitation patterns and began to plan a cycling excursion.

Together they mapped out the journey for a "hundred-acre ride." Under Ina's strong organizational direction, they determined that the ride would begin at our house; that it would be held two Saturdays hence; and that there would be twenty cyclists, ten of her choosing and ten of Eddie's. My entreaties to join them were quickly rebuffed by Ina, who predictably told me that a sixteen-mile ride was not something that could be undertaken by a young child. Three weeks later, with Ina and Eddie in the lead, the peloton—which, of course included Jim, Millie, and Sarah—began its long ride. It was the last social event engaged in by Jim and Eddie before they returned to Toronto for the second year of their university studies.

My suspicions about Eddie's feelings towards Sarah began to re-emerge, though, toward the end of that year. After Frances and I assisted Jane in the selection of her family's first Brampton Christmas tree, our family was invited to Millie's parents' home for a pre-Yuletide celebration. A number of families we knew were in attendance, including the McMurchys and the Lawsons.

Never missing an opportunity to display any type of flower, the Dale home was festooned with red roses and poinsettias. Fastened to the doorframe leading into their parlour was mistletoe. On seeing the sprig,

Eddie proclaimed that he would stand under it until all of the young ladies entered the parlour. In that manner he secured kisses from a good many of the single women at the party, including Millie, Jane, me, Ina, and Sarah. The kisses were all playful, but I noticed that the one bestowed on Ina brought a particular glow to her cheeks, and the one bestowed on Sarah lingered slightly longer.

Hardly realizing the depths of my sadistic nature, while lying in bed that December night, I again broached the subject of Eddie's feelings for Sarah. The question posed five months earlier was met with the same accusation of audacity, the same denial of any reality, the same declaration about Sarah's voice—but significantly, no similar reference to the second cousin from Milton. Indeed, it had been some time since anyone in Brampton had referred to that liaison.

The next summer, as our family cowered in the disgrace of the Johnston affair, Ina and Eddie organized the second annual "hundred-acre ride," fully anticipating an encore of the previous year's successful outing. As they arranged the route (a different hundred acres), the meeting place (our house again), and the invitation list (the same as the year before), Frances and I formulated how we would participate. The gist of our scheme was to wait until the cyclists gathered at our house, assert loudly the false pretense of our afternoon activity, and then join the peloton at its tail. Ina and Eddie, as the leaders, would not notice us until we were too far along on the route to be sent home. With this in mind, we assumed our expected positions on our verandah, looking suitably dejected while Ina and Eddie's excited friends gathered before us, their bicycles lying on the grass waiting for the last two participants to arrive.

Neither Frances nor I noticed Millie climb onto the verandah. Putting an arm around each of us and drawing us even closer together, she whispered in our ears. "Girls, I was just in the back of the house and noticed two small bicycles there at the ready." My cheeks turned red as she continued. "You wouldn't be planning on taking a long ride, would you?" As we stood there dumbfounded, equally unable to lie about or confess our intentions, she continued in her whispering voice. As she did, there came riding up the street toward us a remarkable sight.

Greeted by the applause of nearly every other cyclist, were the last two members of the official party, perched together on a single bicycle. The boy pedalled up the hill to our house with a clearly elated girl behind him, her hands not holding on to the seat below her, as was the customary position of a casual passenger, but instead wrapped around his chest, her head not well behind him, looking forward from around his torso, but rather next to his, her chin resting on his shoulder. Eddie and Sarah had arrived.

That was the second blow in this, Ina's *annus horribilis*, and of the two events, Eddie's was the worst, because it struck her as a betrayal of a romantic attachment that for many years she believed he fomented. The fall of 1913 and much of the following winter were particularly difficult for Ina as she forwent her higher education and worked as a telephone operator, dealing alternatively with anger at both Eddie and our father and, as significantly, with self-pity. It was not until the spring of 1914 that she returned to something of a normal state and living with her became at least tolerable.

The improvement was fostered principally by two things: the balm of time that had mended her broken heart and the distraction offered in the organization of her high school graduation dance. But it was aided by a third: the continued development of Brampton's shoe manufacturing industry.

* * *

Though the seeds of Brampton were sown with Methodist stock that eschewed both the partaking of alcohol and participation in dancing, over the nine decades that had passed since William Buffy first established his alcohol-dispensing retail business in Brampton, the town's feelings toward various diversions had altered. In the case of alcohol, it had altered many times. The devil's temptations that the evangelic leaders Lawson and Elliott had driven out of the village in the 1830s had slowly re-infiltrated. By 1874 there were fifteen licensed taverns and shops within Brampton's boundaries.

In response, temperance movements like the one in which my mother was involved were formed to eradicate through moral suasion and, if necessary, statute, not just the public houses in which alcohol was sold but also its private consumption everywhere. Banding with the Methodists, other church groups, and ostensibly nonpartisan groups like the Alliance Party, they supported a "Banish the Bar" statute. The Act would allow citizens to vote to make illegal in their own county an activity that was otherwise merely immoral. By 1913, a year before the good men of Peel County would vote to become officially dry, Brampton had been without licensed shops or taverns for a number of years.

But while many a group existed with the goal of rooting out the evils of alcoholic consumption, no similar fervour was attached to the once similarly denounced pastime of dancing. Although some churches continued to frown upon the activity, by the early twentieth century it was so well accepted as a leisure activity in our town that it formed the high point of social interactions among our young adults, including serving as the focus of the high school graduation celebrations.

The dance of the graduating class of Brampton High was generally held in the home of the student with the largest parlour and the most willing parents, or, in some years, the home of a similarly qualified extended family member. In this respect, Ina's class was fortunate to have a castle within the extended family of one of its students. Castles are known to have particularly large parlours.

The soaring brick structure located on a large lot across from the Grand Trunk Railway station was referred to as the Castle by its owner as well as by all other Bramptonians. True, it had no dungeons. It had no moat. Its rooms numbered fewer than a hundred. Its outdoor walls were of brick, not stone, its indoor walls covered in paper and paint, not tapestry and frescoes. It was built in the 1853, not 1583. But built in the high gothic revival style and designed by the internationally renowned architect William Hay, it had many other castle-like features, including a multiplicity of wings (at least two), a tall, pointed tower, a belvedere, and four high-peaked roofs.

The Castle exuded the wealth and influence of its initial owner, George Wright, a local businessman and politician, who before 1855 served at various times as a municipal councillor and reeve and as the federal Member of Parliament for the county. Although the palatial aspect of the Castle was diminished over time (it lost its back wing, the side tower, and the belvedere in a fire in 1902), it would be the better part of a century before it lost its natural lustre.

For most of Ina's graduating year, she and the other members of the graduation dance organizing committee worked to make the fete the most memorable graduating class dance held to date. They threw themselves into the arrangements for the theme, the decorations, the band, and the supper. They were well on their way to meeting their objective when disaster struck. Two nights before the scheduled celebration, an illness of an indeterminate nature settled on the godmother of Edith Wilson, the matron of the Castle.

Though doctors came to the bedside of the matron, a diagnosis could not be conclusively provided. The illness, which was manifested in a headache, nausea, fatigue, and a rash, could have been caused by any number of things: a case of influenza, which annually struck the community; a latent case of the measles, although there had been no recent outbreaks in Peel; rheumatic fever, possibly caught from a travelling salesman she passed as she exited and he entered her husband's place of business; or a host of other contagious diseases. There was no question of the dance being held at the Castle, or in Edith, who had been in close contact with her potentially contagious godmother, attending. The class unanimously chose to postpone the dance until Edith's godmother was restored to good health.

Unfortunately, it took nearly ten months for that restoration to occur, and when it did it was no longer possible for Edith to offer the Castle as the location for her class's graduating dance. The very cure for her godmother's condition was the payment of her husband's creditors, something that could only be accomplished by the sale of his business or the sale of the Castle.

Edith's godparents were none other than Mr. and Mrs. George L. Williams, he the owner of the Williams Shoe Company, the manufacturing concern that had been operating successfully in Brampton since the last decade of the previous century. It was clear to all that the efforts the Williams Shoe Company had taken to establish its reputation for quality shoe products had paid off, as had Brampton's efforts to promote itself as a community able to provide the skilled manpower necessary to create that success. In the same year that the Williams Shoe Company was preparing to retire its $30,000 debt to the town, a man named J.W. Hewetson was looking for a place to establish his children's shoe manufacturing company. Hewetson could think of no better place than Brampton, the town where Williams had so successfully established his shoe company and trained so many men.

The town prepared to welcome the new manufacturing concern with open arms and an open wallet, with the people voting to provide $20,000 of financing to the new venture, repayable with interest over twenty years. While Williams was openly supportive of Hewetson and his company joining the ranks of the Brampton shoe manufacturers, he recognized Hewetson for what he was, a smart, hard-working gentleman and a competitor, although initially a competitor in only one line of Williams' products: children's shoes.

Accordingly, Williams also prepared to welcome the new concern, in his case by upgrading and modernizing his plant and borrowing heavily to do so. While the amounts borrowed would have been gradually paid off in time, the load was too much for Mrs. Williams, whose body bore the stress of the indebtedness poorly. For $9,000, Williams sold the Castle to Eliza Hewetson, the wife of J.W. Hewetson, his new competitor.

The transaction was considered a great success by many: the Williamses, who with the sale had been able to settle their debts; the 150 Williams Shoe Company workers who continued to be gainfully employed by their esteemed proprietor; the Hewetsons, who, though newcomers to Brampton, acquired the landmark residential property; and the town council, which was confident it would soon see two thriving shoe manufacturers within the town's limits. Unfortunately, the transaction, which spurred in so many the urge to dance, left those young graduates who never needed an excuse to dance without a location to do so.

Lamenting the position in which the committee found itself, Ina (still its chairwoman) and Edith struggled to decide what to do. "Should we just go back to the school gymnasium?" Edith asked as she, Ina, Jane, and I stood outside our church one April evening, waiting for the doors to open for a Sunday night cantata.

"We can't do that," Ina groused, "particularly now. We've been away from the school for ten months. It would be humiliating to go back there for the graduation dance. I can't believe how unlucky we've been!"

But the class was not quite as unlucky as Ina thought, for among those who overheard the conversation was Jane's mother. Quite familiar with the plight of the class, she left her spot near the four of us and went in search of her husband. Minutes later, the Thompsons offered the Brampton High School class of 1913 the use of Haggertlea for their belated celebratory dance.

* * *

As the much-anticipated night finally approached, the only matter left to cause Ina any consternation was the fact that Jane's mother, who had graciously opened the doors of her home to Ina's class, also opened those doors to Frances and me. "You had better not participate in any of the activities. I won't have you ruining my graduation dance!" Ina hollered when she learned of the invitation. Pettiness prevented me from providing her with the assurances she sought; namely, the fact that our invitation had been confined to keeping company with Jane on that night, out of the way of the festivities of the graduates.

Thus, on the second Saturday night of May, 1914, from the second-floor balcony, Jane, Frances, and I had a full view of thirty members of the 1913 Brampton High School Class and ten of their guests as they entered the Haggertlea rotunda. As though viewing a performance at our local Giffen Theatre, we watched the girls arrive, beautiful in gowns of tulle and chiffon and pretty, delicate shoes, their hair arranged in stylish rolls, curls, and sweeps. The boys were almost unrecognizable in their black pants and jackets, their crisp white shirts and ties accentuating their freshly shaved faces and their recently shorn hair. Many of them had grown taller and broader in the year that had passed. The prevalence of corsages and boutonnières made it clear that the Dale dump pile had been well foraged that day.

Once all the guests were in attendance, Jane, Frances, and I changed positions on the balcony in order to gain a better view of the dancing in the salon, accessed from the rotunda through a set of doors across from the base of the round staircase. Unfortunately, the balcony did not fully extend over that portion of the rotunda. A pinched triangular area where the banister met the wall above the circular stairwell provided us with our best vantage point, though even then we were limited to seeing the dancers as they passed by the doorway to the rotunda.

Squeezed into the narrow area, we looked down, waiting to see the waltzing couples. We heard the music emanating from horns, strings, and piano keys. We imagined the boys leading the couples, the girls with their left hands on their partners' shoulders, the boys with their right hands on their partners' waists, the raised hands of the couples clasped together, just as we had been taught in school. The music played. We waited. No dancers could be seen.

We changed positions, lying down on our stomachs, our heads facing the salon and our legs bent upward at the knees. The band continued to play. We waited. We pushed our faces as far as we could against the balcony's spindles. No dancers came into sight.

Another tune began. Finally, we sensed movement. A girl's hemline swirled within our view. Moments later, we saw a man's black trouser leg and matching black shoe. We squirmed backward a bit to give ourselves a slightly wider spectrum. Eventually, we saw an entire woman, and then an entire man. Finally, more and more dancers could be seen.

Within an hour, we were able to sit cross-legged in our pinched triangle, watching couple after couple dance below us. As they came into sight, we whispered the names of the ever-changing couples. Over time, we noted that some of the boys had paid more attention in their dancing classes than others.

"And he is so handsome!" Frances said, speaking of the most superior of the dancers. He was a tall, good-looking boy with black hair and green eyes. As we stood on the balcony stretching our legs, we took imaginary turns dancing with the handsome, talented Michael Lynch.

After the supper that was served to the graduates in the dining room and to Jane, Frances, and me in the kitchen, we returned to our position in the triangle of the balcony. As the band resumed its play, we detected a new phenomenon among the dancers. While the dancing before the supper had conformed entirely to the etiquette we were taught in school, with each boy seeking a different partner for each dance, after supper a certain amount of pairing transpired. It was no great surprise to see Katie McKechnie frequently dancing with Rolly Flemming or Jessie Groat regularly dancing with Jimmie Bovaird. The affections of these two couples were well known and of no particular interest to us. Our eyes were on the tall, handsome, sure-footed Michael Lynch as we each guessed the name of the girl on which he might focus his remaining attentions.

I proposed Constance Hunter, the girl we agreed was the most able female dancer. "They could win dancing contests with their combined skills," I ventured.

Jane proposed Violette Landsdell, who wore the most beautiful dress. "They would be so perfectly matched."

Frances proposed Pearl Ferguson. "She is the prettiest. They would have beautiful children together."

Jane and I looked quizzically at her. "I thought we were choosing dancing partners," I said.

While we were all prepared to concede our proposed girl to one chosen by the others of us, none of us was prepared for the subject of Michael Lynch's eventual pairing.

"There is Michael dancing with Constance," I said. "They move together like the mercury in my father's office. They should enter a dance contest."

"There is Michael dancing with Violette," Jane said. "They make such a pretty pair. They should be shown in a magazine." Jane regularly read magazines.

"There is Michael dancing with Pearl," Frances said. "Someone should take a picture of the two of them. They could show it to their children later in life."

"And there is Michael dancing with ... Ina," Frances said.

"She looks quite pretty when she smiles like that," Jane noted. Ina had gone out of her way to prepare for the evening. The blue dress Mother made set off her eyes of the same colour. Her brown hair was rolled around the back of her head, complimenting her round face and soft features. Uncharacteristically, not a hair was out of place, no button undone.

"There is Michael dancing again with Constance," I said a few minutes later, feeling confident that my conjecture would be correct.

"You wait," Jane countered. "The next one will be Violet."

"Or Pearl," said Frances.

But Michael's next partner was not Constance or Violet or Pearl. Rather, it was once again Ina. Though Michael continued to dance with Constance, Violet, Pearl, and every other girl in attendance that night, after the supper hour every other dance was reserved for Ina. With each dance they shared, she seemed to grow taller. With each waltz in which he led her, she melted more into his steps. With each time he pulled her close, she smiled wider, her handsome face matching his in radiance.

"Maybe they should be in the dance contest," I grudgingly offered.

"Or in the magazine," Jane suggested.

"Or have babies," Frances said, to revolted looks from Jane and me.

"Did you know that Michael Lynch was sweet on Ina?" Jane asked as Frances and I were gathering our things to leave. Mrs. Thompson had come to collect us while Mr. Thompson readied their automobile. It was after one in the morning.

"I didn't know," I said. "I am not even sure Ina knew."

"Nor should you know," Mrs. Thompson interjected. "And that is the way it must stay. What you saw while looking on at the dance is none of your concern. You girls are free to talk about how lovely the girls looked and how handsome the boys looked. You can speak of the good music and the delicious food. If I hear any other reports of this dance generated by any of the three of you—you will not be welcome to witness another. Do you understand me?" We all indicated that we did.

Chapter 19

THE DROUGHT

It would be difficult to say that Father's practice ever thrived. With two or three dentists in a town as small as ours in a time before oral hygiene was commonplace, none of the dental practices were likely to be wildly successful. Nonetheless, prior to the revelation of Father's indiscretion, his practice did moderately well. If he did not have enough patients on a day to occupy his every business hour, this suited him well enough. On most days he saw a sufficient number of patients to earn a reasonable living while leaving him with the time he much desired to attend to his voluntary pursuits.

Following the revelation of Father's indiscretion, his patient load was reduced to one or two people a day. Members of our own family, people from the country who somehow missed the whispered pronouncement of Father's debasement, and men who were or at one time were themselves in similarly compromised positions or for other reasons refused to follow the moral dictates of their wives formed the stalwarts of Father's dwindling patient list.

Though Father had less reason to be in his offices, the decline in his business resulted in him spending more time there. Before the onset of the drought, he would, without compunction, tell a full waiting room at three thirty in the afternoon that he had a meeting to attend and was accordingly finished seeing patients for the day. He would urge his prospective patients to return the next day, and most of them did. But during the drought, he knew he could not afford to turn away a single person. Nor could he fail to be available to receive and treat a person, regardless of how early or how late the prospective patient arrived to see him.

Similarly, though Father required less assistance in his lab than ever before, during the drought I found myself spending greater amounts of time there. As an indication of how few people attended his offices at that time, Father actually enjoyed my presence.

He was fastidious about the need to keep all of his working instruments and areas clean and to keep the amalgams and other elements of his practice organized. But sometimes over the course of the week a shortage of time led to a failure to meet that standard. On those occasions, once I was old enough to read, I was allowed to assist in bringing order to his lab. From the age of eight, the only time in my childhood that I did not make at least a twice-monthly appearance to attend to these matters was the four-month period in which Mrs. Johnston was ostensibly doing so. On her eviction from the front apartment, my services were sought once again.

I revelled in being in Father's lab room, from which the clean chemical smell of the offices emanated. It was in this room that all of Father's powders, unguents, solutions, and contrivances were stored and prepared for application. In a dark oak chest five feet tall, with over two dozen variously sized drawers, space was provided for every tool and compound used in his practice. When there were no chemicals to sort or beakers to clean, I happily sat on the wooden floor, leafing through the six-volume set of the *Canadian Dental Encyclopedia*, various dental journals, or supply catalogues stored on shelves next to the big cabinet.

In the end, the drought lasted about fifteen months. Father's practice never completely returned to its former state, but by September 1914 it was as near the profitability of its former days as it would ever become. Not all patients returned to him, but a good many did, and the growing ranks of the town's new residents contributed to a large swell of new patients.

The seeds of the resurrection of Father's practice were actually planted much earlier and in a most unexpected manner. One late afternoon in September 1913, three months after Mrs. Johnston left town, I was in the lab dusting Father's vials and beakers when the bell above the waiting room door announced the admittance of a heavy-footed man. I expected him to take a seat in that room before being brought by Father into the treatment room. But the heavy-sounding feet did not rest in the waiting room, and they did not enter the treatment room.

"Good day, young man," I heard a familiar voice say as he entered Father's office. "Business is slow, I see."

"Not any slower than expected," Father replied in an amazingly matter-of-fact way. "How are you, Handle? I suppose you didn't drop by to obtain dental services."

"No. No. I don't need those," the man said somewhat light-heartedly. "The wife insists I take that business now to Peaker."

"She's a woman of fine character and judgment," Father replied with only a hint of sarcasm. "So how can I help you?"

My mind drifted back to the conversation I had overheard six years earlier, the day Uncle William announced that he was resigning as mayor and relocating to Winnipeg. I thought of the advice provided by Mr. Handle regarding whether Father should seek that position in my uncle's stead.

I should have moved to shut the door to Father's office so that their conversation could not be heard by any patients who might enter the waiting room or by me in the lab room, kitty corner to them. But there were no patients, and at that late hour of the afternoon there were not likely to be any. As for me, I was, in truth, as curious and inclined to eavesdrop at the age of ten as I had been at the age of four. I quietly picked up another beaker and slowly moved my cloth over it.

"I've come to speak with you about the high school board and the water commission. There's a sense among some of the ladies of the town that there should be a change in leadership the next time the elections for those offices come up."

"Now hold on," Father said, incredulous. "Why should they wish to remove me from my positions there? I get no compensation from them. It is something that I give to the community. Those women aim to harm me—how do they accomplish that by removing me from those positions?"

"Well, young man, I think they realize that you get a certain amount of, shall we say, satisfaction from holding those positions, and while no one disputes that you are a fine leader of both boards, the ladies are not in a mood to see you being satisfied at the moment."

"And the men? The actual electors? Are they going to stand for this? We are in the midst of some significant projects in both organizations. Are the male electors going to allow their wives to dictate who should complete those projects? How can you allow them to do that, Handle? You, who understand perfectly well what this community needs and what I have to offer? How can you come here asking me to resign?" Father was quite agitated at this point.

"Now it's your turn to hold on," Handle replied, trying to calm Father. "I didn't say that I supported it. I didn't come here to ask you to resign. Not at all. I agree the town needs you in those positions, but it will take a lot to get the men to stand up to their wives on this point. The women have already identified two potential candidates to unseat you. You're going to have to do something special to ensure that those two men will reject the implorations of their wives."

"Something special?" Father asked, calmer but still somewhat indignant.

"Something special," Handle repeated. "Something to lift you in the eyes of all of the men in this community—and maybe in the eyes of some of the women too. A way to redeem yourself."

Father laughed. It was not a friendly laugh. "Really, Handle. What could I possibly do to turn this around? Is there an orphanage of babies with rotted teeth I could extract? Perhaps a subdivision of houses I could single-handedly construct to assuage the town's housing crises? Maybe I could dig the necessary culverts to divert the Etobicoke to meet the town's long desire?"

"Well, you could try to do those things, but I am not sure any would be enough. No, young man, you are a pariah at this time. If you want to maintain those positions—and if I may say, if you want to earn a living to support your family—you're going to have to do more than treat orphans, build houses, and divert that creek."

"You obviously have something in mind that I cannot fathom, Handle. What is it? Make it plain."

"It's lacrosse, young man."

"Lacrosse?" Father asked, clearly not comprehending the suggestion.

"Lacrosse," Mr. Handle affirmed.

Father's request for clarification did not relate to the meaning of the word "lacrosse." It was a word well known to everyone in our town; surely to everyone in the country. Officially Canada's national sport, the game had been created by America's indigenous peoples centuries earlier. A hard ball and long wooden sticks capped with a leather net formed the necessary equipment as each team of twelve attempted to throw the ball from those sticks through the opposing team's goal net. It was a fast-moving, high-contact game requiring excellent running, throwing, and catching abilities.

The game was first played in Brampton in 1871 under the tutelage of a teacher named George M. Lee. Assembling the first team, he named it the Excelsiors after the Longfellow poem of that name, intending to evoke images of loft and height. Since then the game had been played by generation after generation of Brampton men, with the very best forming the town's official teams. One of my favourite pictures of Father dates back to the early 1890s. In it he is standing alone, lacrosse stick in his left hand, the net resting on the ground. His hair is cropped, his chest covered by a grey, skin-tight, scooped-neck long-sleeved shirt worn above tight-fitting pants that end just below the knee. His feet are shod in elf-like white leather pointed and curled up at the toes.

It was the official uniform of the Brampton Excelsiors in 1890, 1893, and 1894, the first years that the team claimed the Ontario championship. After years of competition, with the title thrice in hand, Father retired from active play but not from the game. For years afterward he served in a volunteer capacity, first on the executive of the provincial association and later on the national body. Even twenty years later, Father was conceded to be the most knowledgeable and well-connected lacrosse fan in Brampton. That was saying a lot in a town where children learned about lacrosse almost at the same time they learned how to spell.

Growing up, all of my friends knew without question the score of the last Excelsior game and which team ours beat in the process. While our family and most of our neighbours received the Toronto *Mail & Empire* and the *Toronto Telegram* newspapers year round, during lacrosse season none of us could do without the Brampton *Conservator* and its midweek reporting of Saturday's game. It was always a front-page story, and the local paper set out in minute detail every goal and play of "the boys" under headlines like *Another Big Victory for the Excelsiors* and *Young Torontos are Vanquished* and *Weston went Down 11 to 3*.

In 1912, both the junior and senior Excelsior teams won the Ontario championships, neither of them losing a single game in the season. In the fall of 1913 they were well on their way to achieving the same distinction. It was no wonder that the senior team was invited to take on the western holders of the national Mann Cup in a tournament scheduled to be played in Vancouver the next year.

"Lacrosse?" Father's laugh this time was not nearly so derisive. "How in the deuce could that help me? I'm too old to play again, and what would the Excelsiors need with me? Both of our teams are winning every game they play."

"They are winning every game they play in Ontario," Mr. Handle clarified.

"Yes, and the senior team will win next year against the Vancouver Athletics. I am confident of that."

"They'll win if they get there," Mr. Handle clarified again.

"Get there? Of course they'll get there. They've been raising money for it now for over a year." Father was very familiar with their fundraising efforts. In addition to his general interest in the matter, Jim was a part of the team destined to head west.

"Yes, they have," Mr. Handle confirmed, "for over a year. As a result of their great efforts, and with just nine months to go, they have raised enough money to get the team from Brampton to Winnipeg."

"To Winnipeg?" Father queried.

"One way," Mr. Handle replied.

"How can that be? They have the gate money from their games, the boys have been washing horse carriages and automobiles, they have been seeking pledges, they have organized dances—"

"Yes. A lot of work. But that's small potatoes. The gate money barely covers the salary of Carmichael. He was a big expense when we brought him into Brampton to coach our boys. Worth every cent, but it doesn't leave much to pay for train fare for twenty people travelling over five thousand miles, not to mention their food and lodging for a month."

"So what do you expect me to do? You see how vacant the waiting room is. I am clearly in no position to make a financial contribution."

"No. The team doesn't need your money. It needs your commitment."

"My commitment?" Father asked. "I've been an Excelsior fan since the day I could hold a stick. How much more of a commitment do you need from me?"

"We need your time. And it looks to me like you've got a fair bit of that. The financial position of the club is going to be announced at the meeting next week. Mackie's term is up. He doesn't want to run for re-election. You need to take up the position as president and raise the money to get this team to Vancouver—and back—next summer."

"Really, Handle, how could I get elected to that position? You said yourself, I am a pariah. No one will vote for me right now."

"Well, it's true that few women would vote for you right now, but at least for the foreseeable future the fairer sex is without the franchise to do so—either generally or within the association of the Lacrosse Club. Furthermore, as long as your candidacy is not announced before the annual meeting, no member of the club will have been told by his wife not to vote for you while there. As for the men, they know what you are: a sinner. We're all sinners. Show a little humility. Give them something they want: a plan for how to make this trip a reality. Run not for your aggrandisement but rather as your penance, and they will elect you. Get things well in motion by this December, and they will again respect you. Your seats on the Water Commission and the High School Board will be safe. Succeed by next summer, and your practice will be restored."

Silence filled the air. "Can I think about it?" Father eventually asked.

"Think all you want. The meeting is in a week's time. Think of a good plan." I heard a chair pushed back and heavy feet walking across the vacant the waiting room toward the exit.

"Oh, and young man," Mr. Handle said, "I wouldn't include any bake sales in that fundraising plan of yours. It's going to take a while for the ladies to agree to contribute inventory to a cause with which you are associated—even this good cause."

We barely saw Father over the next nine months as he worked to make the dream of the Excelsiors a reality. Engaging all of the local merchants in the fundraising process, Father gave window signs to each merchant that agreed to sponsor the team through the provision of cash or other contributions in-kind. Collection cans were placed on the counter of every willing retailer, and woe betide any retailer who said he was not willing.

In May of 1914, Father organized a concert. With a little convincing, Mr. Giffen, the local theatre owner, agreed to donate the use of his premises. Ten local artists and one visiting Torontonian comprised the list of soloists, accompanists, tenors, and readers, who entertained the full house for twenty-five cents a head.

He renegotiated the concession arrangements, increasing the percentage earned by the team from every bag of popcorn, hot sausage, and soda pop sold during a local game. He encouraged Jim's friends Millie and Sarah to recruit two dozen "tag-girls" to sell tags while the team played in Brampton. Since no true fan wanted to be seen without the game's particular tag, everyone in the uncovered bleachers paid the recommended price of ten cents per tag, and everyone in the more expensive covered seats paid more.

The result of Father's efforts was plain for all to see on Wednesday June 17, 1914 as a crowd of more than one hundred people assembled at the Grand Trunk Railway station to send off "the boys." The Citizens Band played and the crowd cheered as the team climbed on to the temporary platform. The mayor called out the name of each team member. Though he tried to be even in his enthusiasm, the mayor couldn't help but inject some extra emphasis as he called the name of Walt Mara, his son. Similarly, though we tried to applaud each member equally, those in the Stephens area could not help but cheer more lustily when the mayor called out Jim's name and announced his recent return from the United States, where he played for University of Toronto's lacrosse team.

Eventually, Father brought the applause and music to an end. He then urged the boys to assume the necessary gentlemanly conduct and irreproachable behaviour while away from home, both on the field and off, in order to duly reflect the morals and principals of the town they were so proudly to represent. It was a measure of the restoration of the town's opinion of Father that such sentiments could be both sincerely made and sincerely received. With a final wish for great success on the Vancouver field, he released the team to their family members for final adieus moments before the train reached the platform.

Jim extended happy farewell embraces to everyone in our family and to his friends, Eddie, Millie, and the now ever-present Sarah before boarding the train with his teammates. As the band resumed its anthems and the children skipped and ran down the platform, the team members extended their torsos out the open windows of the train, their waving hands, exultant faces, and shouts of joy echoed in five times the measure by their friends and family on the platform. Looking around at the enthusiastic throng, I could see not a single stoic face, but of those nearest me, there were three whose cheers ended just slightly too soon. The first was Millie. This would mark the longest period of time she had been apart from Jim since he became her beau two years earlier. Even while Jim was away at university, he often came home on the weekend for a day or two. This trip would separate them for a month.

The second was Eddie, whose enthusiasm for the departure of his chum was not quite in keeping with the scale on which he did all other things. Like all Brampton boys, he was a lacrosse player. He was a good player, but he was not quite good enough. The look on his face was wistful.

Frances, who was standing with me, noticed Eddie's look too. "Is he jealous that Jim's on that train instead of him?" she asked quietly.

"I don't think so," I replied slowly. "I think he's sad that Jim's on that train and he isn't too." This was, it occurred to me, the first major life experience the two friends had not undertaken together. Jim and Eddie shared every youthful classroom, friend, club, and sport. Together they abandoned their weekend and summertime play for responsible part-time and summer jobs. They attended the same university, where they lived in the same boarding house. To this point in their lives, only one thing truly differentiated them: their abilities on the lacrosse field. I could see how much Eddie wanted to experience the Mann Cup championship with his closest companion.

Looking back toward the departing train, I suddenly noticed Father. The year before, he had betrayed not just Mother but our entire family, our social standing, and everything he had instilled in us about honesty, respect, and honour. He jeopardized his livelihood and consequently ours. He lied to me and used me. He humiliated Mother. Had this been the only circumstance that led Mother to feel inadequate, blameworthy, and unloved, I am not sure I would ever have gotten over my anger toward him. The episode with Mrs. Johnston being just a more vivid and public display of the conduct toward Mother I had so often witnessed, my feelings toward him passed from anger to ambivalence with some speed. However, that day, seeing all he had accomplished for the boys, for the town, and indirectly for his family, I couldn't help but feel true affection for him. Like Eddie, he too wanted to be on that train.

The last major decision Father made before the Excelsiors travelled west was the appointment of a team manager, the person who would make all of the physical arrangements for the team while away. It was a decision he deferred making until the very last moment. Had the drought persisted through to May of 1914, Father would have assumed the position of team manager himself—his dental practice could not have been more harmed by a one-month absence. But by early May, rain was sprinkling over his practice. The drought was ending. His success with the team meant that he could not join it on this, its most highly prized journey. Tom Thauburn was appointed as manager, a post he served well.

The clap of Tom Mara's hand on Father's back broke his trance. "Capital speech, Doc," the mayor said. "And what a crowd. I counted a good hundred people. Let's hope that at least half that many greet the boys on their return."

Chapter 20
THE MANN CUP

Grandpa bought a map of Canada, which we pinned to the wall in the kitchen. Every day, as we broke our fast, we marked the course of the train carrying the Excelsiors to the west coast. The journey to Vancouver was direct. Coach Carmichael wanted the boys to have an entire week in Vancouver before the first game was played so that they could become fully acclimatized to the western air and grounds.

While the boys practiced on the western turf and toured the western sites, the club president and the friends and family of the team members were not idle. Father arranged for flyers to be distributed and posted. Advertisements were placed. Entertainment and communications methods were organized. The first game in the west to be played on Saturday, July 4, was expected to be nothing short of a spectacle. Back in Brampton, Father hoped a large crowd would gather to be entertained in extravagant fashion while they awaited telegraph reports sent by Mr. Thauburn at each quarter's end.

There was no question about where the fans would congregate. Jennings Rosalea Park, a sports park nestled between the backs of the buildings that lined two of the downtown streets, was donated to the town by Richard Jennings, another grower of roses, other flowers, and vegetables. Though his generosity was not forgotten, the use of his name in all but official documents relating to the athletic facilities soon was. In common parlance, the park was simply "Rosalea."

From its covered grandstand and its uncovered bleachers, fans watched the junior and senior Excelsiors lacrosse teams, the Brampton Brownies hockey team, the Excelsiors rugby team, and Brampton's local baseball team as they took on competitors from near and far. On its grounds, men and women of all ages threw bowls and played tennis and cricket. On its banked track they ran and cycled. Before the curling club was more permanently established, it was also one of the homes of that club. Teams prepared for their play and regaled each other with tales of their athletic prowess in the two-storey clubhouse, replete with lockers and cold showers.

Father was not disappointed by the crowd that gathered that Saturday afternoon at Rosalea. Nearly a thousand Excelsior fans lined the seats of the covered grandstand and the uncovered bleachers or stood in the wings, watching the entertainment Father arranged while we waited for the results of the game being played 2,800 miles to the west.

Sitting on the uncovered bleachers during the first quarter, Jane, Frances, and I eagerly purchased the day's oversized ten-cent tags offered by one of Millie and Sarah's tag girls. We barely paid any attention to the Citizens Band marching in the field as we postulated with our friends on various Excelsior matters, having no doubt that our team would be victorious. The first question of import was the identity of the likely lead scorer. Jane, who had a pencil in her bag, agreed to be the recorder of the predictions, using the space on the back of her large tag for the purpose. The boys in our group were equally divided in predicting that George Sproule and Grenville ("Dutch," as they called him) Davis would be the lead scorer.

Frances demurred, discounting Davis, who she said was too interested in girls to be that good on the field. Her proof for that was the time three years earlier when we saw him and fellow teammate Clarence Charters in the Gage Park trees with Millie and Sarah, the day we walked home from Derry Road. The boys entirely dismissed that line of reasoning. "It was a long time ago," I said in support of their position. "If you don't think a boy can be a success on the field and also have a sweetheart, then I think there may only be about two Excelsiors able to score goals!"

As for the score, most of those around me predicted a three-point spread between the two teams, but as the discussion ensued, Jane's brother Douglas Thompson and Morley Burrows thought the number too low.

"The spread will be four points," one said.

"No. Five points," the other said.

"No, six points," said the first. They became louder and more emphatic with each increasing number. Eventually, when they sounded like auctioneers, we told them to stop. But we all recognized that the point spread was important. In this tournament of two games, the winner was the team that scored the most cumulative points.

Twenty minutes or so into our revelry-like predictions, we saw Father walk onto the field. The band stopped playing and the crowd hushed. "Does he look like he has good news?" Jane asked. It was hard to tell when Father was happy, even when quite near him. There, with so much distance between us, I was even less sure. Shrugging, I gave him my full attention.

Father lifted his bullhorn to his mouth and began. "Ladies and gentlemen, boys and girls, I have the results of the first quarter of the Vancouver game." He turned toward Michael Lynch, an employee of the CPR telegram service. As Father thanked Michael for his speedy delivery of the report, I could not help but remember how he swept Ina off her feet as they danced in the Thompsons' salon the month before.

Frances leaned over the laps of three of our friends to whisper to me her lack of surprise that someone who could dance so well could use those same feet to quickly deliver a telegram. She began to ask me whether my parents yet knew of the dalliance between Michael and Ina when to my relief the three people over which she lay urged her to sit up and be quiet. "We want to hear the score," they cried.

Father opened the envelope and placed the bullhorn back at his lips. "Mr. Thauburn has advised us that the number of spectators in attendance in Vancouver to view our boys is a record-breaking two thousand people." Great applause greeted that announcement. "Those spectators have as yet to see the prowess of our team. But they will! I have no doubt, they will!" With that introduction, Father announced that the score at the end of the first quarter was one for the Vancouver Athletics and zero for the Brampton Excelsiors.

News of that sort might put a damper on the enthusiasm of some fans—but those would not be the fans of the Brampton Excelsiors, a team that had played two consecutive seasons without losing a game; a team with unparalleled speed, strength, and precision. The Brampton fans were in no way daunted by the Athletics' early lead. They rationalized that this was in fact exactly what Coach Carmichael would have intended.

"Let the cup holders think our team will be easy to beat. They'll lower their guard. They will become careless and be trounced," Douglas pontificated.

As Father left the field, the Citizens Band began a merry tune, and all assembled broke into song. They were only stopped in their boisterous merriment by the next bit of entertainment, an acrobatic routine by a group from Norval. The crowd ooh-ed and ahh-ed at the displays of almost inhuman contortions and death-defying tricks atop wires that were installed earlier in the day. So confident were the fans in the abilities of our boys out in Vancouver that they barely gave them a thought until Father returned to the field forty minutes later with his bullhorn.

The good news was that Bill Stevens of the Excelsiors had scored a goal in the second quarter. The bad news was that the Athletics scored two. At halftime, the score, therefore, stood at three for the Athletics and one for the Excelsiors. Father reminded the crowd that the team had plenty of time to turn the game around, although the little pep talk seemed hardly required, because for the most part the fans were still undaunted. "Bring out the juniors!" they cried. A short thirty-minute game was to be played by the junior Excelsior team against the junior St. Simon Athletics of Toronto, a team that generously agreed to serve as the Brampton juniors' whipping boys while we all awaited the results of the national championship.

While the crowd was undaunted initially by the single-goal lead and later by the two-goal lead of the cup holders, that attitude was not shared by all of the fans. Certainly it was not shared by me. On hearing that our team was behind, I became anxious and distracted. I barely saw the acrobatic girl from Norval lying on the field on her stomach with her legs extended backward up and over her head; I hardly noticed the boy walking across the tightrope while blindfolded. As for the mini-game that was being prepared, I knew I could not possibly sit through it.

Jane, sensing my state, suggested a walk, to which I readily agreed. Frances was at this point absorbed in a conversation with two of our other classmates. Stepping over dozens of knees, Jane and I eventually reached the steps leading to the ground. We walked behind the uncovered bleachers and the covered grandstand and then in front of the refreshment stands, the bandstand, and the clubhouse before exiting the field.

"Thanks," I said when we were finally on the street. "I'm sorry I'm so distracted. I can't seem to have fun while I'm so anxious. I know that this is just a sport, but in my family, this is very serious."

"Oh, I can understand that," Jane said. "People in my family take foundry work seriously. There seems to be no way to joke about that in our house. When my father gets too anxious about work, he goes for a walk. Says it clears his head. That's why I thought it might clear yours too."

We walked in silence for a few minutes toward Church Street until we came face-to-face with the massive Presbyterian Church.

"There it is," she said. "The forbidden sanctuary."

Jane was by that point in our friendship well aware of the church and the fact that no one in our family was allowed to enter it.

"But you don't know why?"

"No. I don't know why."

"Well, what do you know about this church?" she asked as she started walking on the grass toward it.

"Hardly anything," I replied, keeping a good distance behind her. "I know my grandpa was responsible for the plastering on the inside and the stonework on the outside." Then I remembered one other thing. I had learned this fact with Archie while we surreptitiously listened to the governor's story. "I know that the stone was donated to the church by Mr. Gilchrist, the man who once owned Alderlea."

"Let's see what else we can find out," she urged, walking toward the church.

"I can't go in it, Jane!" I exclaimed, thinking that was her intention.

"No! No! We don't need to go in. There's a lot we can find out from the outside." She continued walking across the lawn to the southwest corner of the edifice. "Look. Here is the cornerstone. It was laid in 1880.

So we know that your grandpa worked on it then. You should write that down." She handed me the pencil she used to record the predictions about the game. I turned over the large Excelsiors tag I was wearing and wrote on the back of it: *1880 Presbyterian.*

"The stonework is lovely," she said.

"He loves working with stone, although he doesn't get the opportunity to do so all that often. One of his favourite roles as a stonemason is selecting the stone at the quarry. It is delivered to him by a combination of train and wagon in really huge blocks. Then he has to 'dress it,' which means he cuts it into the right shape and size, and unless it is intended to be smooth, he has to chisel the outside to look uniformly bumpy. It's called rustication. I always call those bumps 'dimples.'

"Then he has to organize which piece will go where on the wall. He has to make it look like the placement is random, but it really takes lots of work to make it look that way. At the end he has to lay the stones and apply just the right colour of mortar in between them." We both stood back and looked at the variegated two-coloured stones that made up the exterior of the Presbyterian church, some a dark pinky-brown colour and others a lighter sand colour.

"The walls are so big and thick," Jane observed. "You don't see too many buildings here like this. In other cities we've lived in, there is much more use of stone. I think buildings made of stone look more permanent. People here seems to favour wood, roughcast, and brick exteriors. Father says it is because Brampton has fewer people of great wealth, and those that have it choose not to be ostentatious about it. Still, it would be nice to see a few more stone buildings."

I suddenly became very defensive of my town. "You know, Jane, many people from neighbouring towns drive through our town just to admire its fine homes, and the town is considering passing a by-law requiring all new houses be built of brick, stone, or cement, so I don't think you will see too many more wood or roughcast homes."

"Oh, I know that there are a lot of lovely houses here. But I'm speaking of institutional buildings: churches, town halls, government buildings. There aren't many in Brampton made of stone."

I disagreed, and because we needed to fill in time and to walk to ease my anxiety, we set out on a little tour to prove our respective points. We began walking along Church Street toward Main, passing as we did the house that had been lived in by the Turners and my Stephens grandparents before them. We were soon at our church, a Gothic revival-style house of worship constructed around a fifty-foot-high, twelve-by-twelve-foot bell tower. It had three double-hung pointed arched doors below and to each side of the tower. The sign chiselled into the stone above the central door read "Grace Methodist Church, 1867 to 1887," showing not the days of use (for it was obviously still actively in use in 1914) but rather the two dates of consecration.

"It was first constructed by Grandpa in 1867 and was then renovated by him in 1887." We stood back and looked at it: two-toned brick, red with yellow trim. It included not a block of stone.

"Add that to your notes, Jessie." Dutifully I wrote down: *1867 Grace—Brick*. I then added the word 'stone' to the description previously made regarding the Presbyterian Church.

As we continued our purposeful walk south on Main Street, we suddenly saw Michael Lynch bolt out the door of the CPR offices, a telegram in his hand. "The news, Michael," I called to him. "What is the news?"

"I can't tell you, Jessie," he said pausing for just a moment. "You know I am bound not to disclose the contents of a telegram to anyone but the addressee." I barely heard the last words as he ran quickly away from us.

"It must be the end of the third quarter. Shall we go back?" Jane asked.

"Let's not just yet," I said. "We will know soon by the sound of the crowd whether things are more settled."

But my prediction on this matter was not quite right. By the time we arrived at Queen Street, the crowd had indeed roared, but it was not so great a roar as to definitively indicate that the Excelsiors were in the lead. "Let's keep going," I said. "We have only a few more buildings to look at, and there is still a full quarter to go in the game."

At Queen Street we turned and walked to the second building east of Main, the three-storey Dominion Building, which housed the post office.

We crossed to the far side of the street to admire Grandpa's masonry work. The mostly rusticated brown stone was accentuated by ribbons of smooth stone. Bands of carved stone balls set inside larger bands of smooth stone wrapped around the building below each level of windows. The arched shape of the windows and doorframes were accented by fan-like stone work above them. There was an engraved coat of arms below the newly constructed clock tower.

"Now this is a sturdy building," Jane said, obviously impressed. "I've never seen anything quite like this before." Somehow, when uttered by Jane, the observation did not sound preposterous, though it came from a thirteen-year-old. The roman numerals in the coat of arms indicated it was constructed in 1889. I turned my tag over and wrote: *1889 Dominion Bldg–Stone.*

We carried on along Main Street before venturing a short distance up John Street. The one-and-a-half-storey Roman Catholic St. Mary's Church was just four years of age, although from the date chiselled into its cornerstone, we could see that construction had commenced a year earlier. Made of red brick, it replaced an old Presbyterian "kirk" that had been renovated in 1879 to suit Catholic worship. Grandpa had not worked on either the original Presbyterian church or the Catholic church that replaced it. I lifted my tag and added another row to the chart on the back: *1909 St. Mary's–Brick.*

Tracing our steps back to Main Street, we stopped in front of St. Paul's, cranking our necks way back to take in the full measure of its 124-foot-high tower. This church, the biggest in the town, was designed to hold a thousand people. All of the stone was rusticated, and it was the same pink-brown colour as the Dominion Building, except for a lighter off-white coloured stone, which trimmed the windows and the rooflines and occasionally decorated other points on the walls. Similar in style to the Presbyterian Church, the large square bell tower was also positioned to one side of the building. The twin sets of double doors were accessed from two wings straddling a wide, centred flight of stairs well above the running creek in front of it. Based on the sign to the right of the door in the bell tower, I added the following words to my list: *1885 St. Paul's–Stone.*

Just as we were approaching the Baptist church beside St. Paul's, we were approached by Mrs. Cooper, who lived on Main Street south of Wellington. She rushed toward us wearing an Excelsiors tag that fluttered to her side.

"Hello, girls. You are a long way from the game. What are you doing here?" she asked curtly.

"We needed to stretch our legs a bit," Jane replied, saving me from any explanation. "Are you coming from the park now?"

"I am. I have to get home to get tea ready for my family. Mr. Cooper does not want to be left waiting for food once the game is done."

"Could you tell us the score, please?" I asked. "We weren't there for the reading of the results of the third quarter."

"Not there. You, Jessie Stephens? Your brother on the team? Your father the president? I can't imagine what could take you away from it for that long. I am of a mind not to even tell you the score. No, in fact, I won't tell you. Now, you two girls should get back to the game, where you belong." She continued walking hurriedly down the street.

We did not stop long at the Baptist church, given the admonition of Mrs. Cooper. Its cladding was entirely of brick. I updated my list based on the cornerstone: *1876 Baptist–Brick.*

"We should get back," I said, beginning to feel guilty for having been gone so long and not even knowing the score in the game.

"Let's just walk up Wellington Street and look at the jail," she said as we passed the back part of the Main Street-facing courthouse and then the registry office beside it. "I can't understand why the courthouse only has stone at the base, with the rest clad in brick. But your grandfather did nice work on both buildings—especially the stonework on the jail. My father says they are both a credit to the town."

"Actually, my grandfather didn't work on either building," I corrected.

"Really? Why ever not?"

"He told me that his price was too high."

"You get what you pay for, that's what my father says," Jane was quick to reply. "What year was that?" We found the corner stone for each building, and I recorded: *1866 Courthouse–Brick* with rusticated stone base and *1866 Jail–Stone*. Then, not wanting to confuse those built by Grandpa and those not, I annotated all other entries to indicate that matter.

"Jessie, between building these huge churches, the Dominion Building, and all of the houses in Brampton, your grandfather must be very well off."

"He isn't, though," I replied. "He definitely is not well off."

We turned on to Chapel, walking toward Queen Street. We stopped outside of the Old Fire Hall, the main floor of which was originally used as a market hall. Until the turn of the century, a long room on the second floor had served as the council room for meetings of the village and then town council. The building, which had a forty-foot fire hose tower, was constructed of red brick.

"When was it built?" Jane asked. As we searched for a dated cornerstone, a loud cheer erupted from Rosalea. I jotted the last note on my tag and handed the pencil back to Jane.

"Do you think that is a cheer for the Rag-Time Band? Or do you think they have the results of the fourth quarter?" I asked. Father would be furious if I was not at the park when the final results were announced. "It's too bad we couldn't cut through the mill, isn't it?" We were only a block away from Rosalea as the crow flies, but we were physically separated from it by the large woollen mills facing onto Queen Street, a recently added warehouse behind it, and the meandering Etobicoke next to them. To get to Rosalea, we needed to walk—or run—a further five blocks.

"It's too soon for the results of the fourth quarter," Jane said. "And the Rag-Time Band—well, they aren't that good. Something else must be going on."

We walked quickly, thinking that we would soon be back at the park, but by the time we reached Main Street, we realized our destination was elsewhere. Streaming down Main Street towards us were the Excelsiors fans. Too impatient to wait the three minutes it would take Michael Lynch to run from the telegraph office on Main Street to Rosalea, the crowd was marching to Main Street to be nearer the source of the telegrams. Straggling behind them, rather than leading the parade of fans, was the Rag-Time Band.

As the crowd encircled us, we learned that Dutch Davis scored in the third quarter, leaving the Excelsiors one point down at the end of that quarter with a score of three to two. But during the fourth quarter, the reporting protocol changed. Mr. Thauburn indicated he would have a telegram sent after each goal was scored. The loud roar Jane and I heard while on Chapel Street was in acknowledgement of the fourth-quarter goal of George Sproule, who tied the game at three to three.

The fans' trek was rewarded. Just as last stragglers arrived in front of Thauburn's store, Michael Lynch emerged, telegram in hand. Within seconds, Father was at his side, silently reading the communication. The crowd became quiet, and Father, having raised his bullhorn, announced to thunderous applause that Dutch Davis had scored again, putting the Excelsiors in the lead with a score of four to three. This was Davis's second goal of the game, joining one each by Sproule and Stevens. The Rag-Time band struck up a tune as the fans around them clapped and danced in the streets. At Queen Street at the south and Nelson at the north, horses, carriages, and cars were diverted or just plain abandoned as people from all directions joined the throng.

Ten minutes and four Rag-Time songs later, Michael Lynch again emerged from the telegraph office. Although he was duty-bound not to disclose the content of the communiqué, the look on his face as he passed it to Father said as much as Father's words that followed. With five minutes remaining in play, the game was again tied with a score of four to four. The crowd was awash in silence until Mayor Mara joined Father. Gently taking the bullhorn, he lifted it to his mouth and shouted his testimony. On many occasions, he had seen the boys score a goal in the last five minutes of a game. The band evidenced its concurrence, and with only slightly less abandon, the clapping and dancing resumed.

One tune was all that could be played. Three minutes later Michael Lynch once more emerged onto the street. This time he lost all restraint. "He scored again!" he shouted. "Davis scored again! Five to four, with one minute and fifty-one seconds left on the clock!" The crowd cheered lustily and then held its breath. People gazed at their pocket time pieces. When two minutes passed and no further telegrams were received, the crowd let out a sigh of relief. When five minutes passed and no further telegrams were received, the crowd became hopeful. When seven minutes passed and Michael Lynch walked out of the telegraph office, his eyes cast downward as he and Father exchanged a solemn look, the crowd realized that … there is a little actor in each of us! Father and Michael clasped their hands around the telegram, and with no need for the bullhorn, they yelled, "They won! The boys won!" Davis's goal with one minute and fifty-one seconds remaining was the last to be scored.

Suddenly we were all in each other's arms. Friends, family, strangers alike, no one escaped the embrace of a dozen or more people that day. As I was clasped by Jane, and then our neighbour Mr. Trimble, Old Dr. French, Millie, the jail's governor and his two children, and Colin Heggie, all of whom were in my immediate vicinity, I noticed Ina running through the crowd before Michael caught her up in his arms and spun her around and around.

It was a long time before the crowd thinned and the road reopened. Grandpa eventually led me home. With the difference in time zones between Vancouver and Brampton, the game was over three hours later than it would ordinarily have been for us. We walked along Main Street to the Wellington Street Bridge, our hands held. I was allowed now to walk this stretch of the road without adult accompaniment. I didn't really need my hand held. But I never declined an outstretched hand from Grandpa. As we reached the top of the bridge, the wind caught my tag and spun it around until it finally came to rest Excelsior side down.

"What is the writing you have on your tag, Jessie? It looks like a list."

I looked down at it:

Year	Bldg	Clad	Mason
1880	Presbyterian	Stone	Grandpa
1867	Grace	Brick	Grandpa
1909	St. Mary's	Brick	Not Grandpa
1885	St. Paul's	Stone	Grandpa
1876	Baptist	Brick	Not Grandpa
1889	Dominion Bldg	Stone	Grandpa
1866	Courthouse	Brick above a stone base	Not Grandpa
1866	Jail	Stone	Not Grandpa
??	Fire Hall	Brick	??

"It is a list," I confirmed. I chose to read him part of it only: "1867, 1880, 1885, and 1889. Do you know what happened in each of those years?"

"I believe I do," he said, giving my hand a squeeze. "I believe I do."

Chapter 21
THE HOMECOMING

Travelling to Brampton at the beginning of July 1914, Aunt Charlotte must have wondered how she would find the inhabitants of the Stephens household. Having left us in such disrepair the previous summer and being entirely unaware of the counsel provided by Roger Handle, she must have taken great pride in the advice she bestowed.

By the time the Turners arrived in Brampton, such rain was falling on Father's practice, one would hardly have known there had ever been a drought. Mother could by that point easily walk through the town, attend visitations, and entertain society members unmolested by looks of pity or feelings of shame. Jim was happy in his relationship with Millie and was at the height of his lacrosse career both at the university and with the Excelsiors. I was free of the duplicitous felicitations of Enid and at peace with my memories of Archie. Ina had emerged from a valley of despair Aunt Charlotte had not even contemplated, and though most of our family was at a loss to explain it, she had recently begun to take pleasure in working in Brampton at the local switch.

It was not just our family that was thriving. The Turners arrived to see the local economy in a boom. The Pease Foundry, operated under the direction of Jane's father; the Dale Estate; the two shoe manufacturers; and many other local industries were all in high production, employing between them hundreds of men and women, many of whom had relocated to Brampton for the express purpose of finding gainful employment. The addition of so many to the local population created increased demand for every manner of consumer goods, including housing. In a single week, forty-eight lots were sold in one subdivision.

Drilled well water was flowing into Brampton at the rate of five million gallons a day, thanks in part to the efforts of Father and the water commission. So many people in Brampton were then able to afford motorcars that a local branch of the Ontario Motor League Association had been formed.

Adding to these milestones was the success of the Excelsiors, the Ontario Lacrosse Association championship two-time titleholders, and their victory in the first game played with the reigning Canadian champions in Vancouver. The entire town waited to re-experience the euphoria. It was a feeling that should have been experienced three days after the first game, but in a surprise move, the Vancouver cup holders chose to postpone the second game of the match from the immediately following Wednesday until the next Saturday.

Unfortunately, the euphoric sensation was not to be repeated. Rosalea was filled with even more fans than the week before when we received the disappointing results of the second game. The Vancouver Athletics, we eventually learned, used the week between the first and second games to relocate within the city's boundaries three ringers—key goal scorers who had previously moved out of the city and hence out of the population of eligible amateur players. Our boys lost the second game six to two, giving the Athletics a total of eleven goals in the match to the Excelsiors' seven.

The Excelsiors were not the only challengers for the cup that year. The Calgary Chinooks also lost to the fortified Vancouver Athletics, but their total goals exceeded those of the Excelsiors. Later in the fall, when the trustees of the Mann Cup eventually ruled on the composition of the Vancouver team, they stripped the Athletics of their title and ordered the delivery of the solid gold cup to the Chinooks.

But that was all for the future. The day after the second game, Father placed a notice in the *Conservator*, urging the citizenry to extend a genuine welcome home to the boys "who have given us their best." Over the next eight days, as the boys travelled east, stopping along the route for exhibition games in Kamloops, Calgary, Medicine Hat, Regina, and Winnipeg, a large homecoming celebration was being planned.

Storefronts were decorated with white flags, bunting, and signs. A parade route was established ending at Gage Park. Motor cars decorated with Dale flowers were organized by the new motor league, ensuring that each team member and his parents would be escorted by automobile from the CPR station to a point just outside the park, in order that the boys would both lead the parade and then be seen by every one of its participants as they filed into the park for the culminating reception.

Not being part of the vehicular escort and having no special role in the official greeting party, I assumed a position on our verandah with Aunt Charlotte and Grandpa. Aunt Lil, who had made her annual trip to Brampton earlier that day, was also with us. We cheered as each team member passed, Aunt Lil's enthusiasm not diminished by the fact that each was in a dreaded automobile. We clapped to the drums of the Citizens Bank, the Salvation Army Band, the Fife and Drum Band, the Scouts Bugle Band, and Rag-Time Band. We applauded at the clubs interspersed between the automobiles, the dignitaries, and the bands, calling out the names of the marchers we knew, which between the four of us on our verandah was a good many.

"Yoo-hoo!" Aunt Charlotte called to Mr. Peaker as he marched by under the Old Countrymen's Club banner.

"Halloo, Jimmy!" Aunt Lil shouted at Mr. Potts, an old school friend and a leader of the marching Boy Scouts.

"Hurrah!" Grandpa called out to Mr. Williams, who marched under the flag of the Christ Church Athletic Club.

"Hi there, Michael!" I called out to Michael Lynch, who bore the flag of the St. Mary's Athletic Club. He turned his beautiful green eyes toward me and waved back.

"Hurray!" I cheered when the Junior Excelsiors passed us. I knew too many to individually cheer them on.

As the last member of the official parade party marched down the streets, the throngs who viewed them joined the procession. Our house was one of the last on the route, so we were among the last to join the procession. "It's a good thing we sent Ina to the park earlier with our picnic blankets," Aunt Lil said as she picked up her carpetbag and walked toward the verandah's steps. All of the adults had suggested she leave the bag behind in the house, but in her usual unpredictable way, she would not part with it. "It won't bother anyone," she insisted as she lugged it along beside her.

When at 7:45 p.m., an hour and a half after the boys arrived at the train station, the team members, the bands, the dignitaries, and the other marchers gathered in Gage Park, a crowd of one thousand people was assembled, ten times the size of the send-off crowd. The Citizens Band took central position, accompanied by Mayor Mara, Frances's father, W. J. Hudson, who had taught all the boys at one time or another, Sam Charters, our Member of Provincial Parliament, and Father. The band began to play, and Fire Chief Harmsworth, a noted tenor, sang out from the dignitaries' platform made for the occasion:

Home again, home again from a foreign shore;

And oh! It fills my soul with joy, to meet my friends once more.

From the base of the platform, the boys replied in tune, as they had rehearsed:

O you old Brampton,

You're the best old town we know;

O you old Brampton,

Where the eastern flowers grow.

Where the girls are the fairest,

And the boys are the squarest;

O you old Brampton,

You're the best old town we know.

To thunderous applause, the team was then welcomed onto the platform made for the occasion. Many speeches followed, but there were three that I particularly recall. The mayor said that all of Brampton was proud of the boys and satisfied that they had done their best and brought credit to the town. Coach Carmichael declared that in his seventeen years as a professional coach in all parts of Canada, he had never been with a cleaner-living bunch of boys. Not a single one even smoked—an observation that the crowd warmly endorsed, though a number of men in the official party, including my father, hung their heads slightly at the last accolade.

Finally, Father read a poem written for the team by Jocko Vinson, the coach of the Vancouver Athletics—presumably before the allegations of cheating were lobbed his way. Father said that the themes of the poem exemplified the fine sportsmanship for which the town, and the Excelsiors not the least, were known and should be proud:

The Brampton boys are leaving us for their homes and
*   sweethearts too;*
But have shown to Old Vancouver what their little band could do.
They have proved themselves just gentlemen and were pretty
*   hard to beat;*
And to watch them at their running, why, it surely was a treat.
They were game and showed their mettle, and proved that they
*   were fast;*
And they raced the old Vancouver team until the very last.
We've had challenge teams come from the East, and also from
*   the West;*
But the most good-natured team of all, the Bramptons were
*   the best.*
We've done our best to welcome you, just as we all should do:
For we're all true British subjects of the old Red, White, and Blue.
And I wish you all a safe return, and no matter where you be,
Always remember Jocko, who belongs to the good old VAC.

After loud applause, the formalities were complete and the crowd was invited to greet the Eastern victors while indulging in ten large cakes provided by the Queen Street Bakery and set up at tables throughout the park.

No invitation was required on my part. I could hardly wait to greet my dear brother, who I had not seen in a month, and to then consume a piece of my favourite cake. But before I had even risen from my cross-legged position on the ground, I realized I would have to take my turn. A long line of people who had been standing rather than sitting through the ceremony had already gathered at the base of the platform where the team members were assembled. Other lines were forming too, some near the dignitaries and many near the cake stands. People scattered in every direction, torn between being among the first to clasp the hand of a returning hero and among the first to obtain a piece of cake.

I began walking, deliberating which line to join first, when Mother caught my arm. "Jessie, where are you going?" Leaving me no time to explain, she went on. "I thought you could stay here and watch your aunt's bag until someone else comes back. You can't get to Jim just yet anyway, and I need to have a word with Mrs. Peaker about tomorrow's meeting of the WTU." Mother had already seen Jim at the train station, and she didn't particularly like cake. She could get on with her ordinary tasks.

I must have looked deflated, for although her suggestion was most certainly a command, she went on, "You don't mind, do you? I won't be long." Still not replying, she added, "And I will bring you a piece of cake when I come back." I gave my assent. I could tell it would be a while before I saw Jim. At least I would get my cake.

* * *

I fold two of the picnic blankets and stack them next to Aunt Lil's big bag. Sitting on the slightly higher platform, I can better view my friends and family beyond. I can see Frances, Jane, Willy Core, Morley Burrows, and Collin Heggie lined up for cake at a table near the bandstand. They don't seem to notice my absence.

Jim is still near the platform with the other team members. Each has a separate line of people formed to greet him. The line for Jim is full of his friends and their family members. He is speaking to each one of them in turn. I think it is going to take a long time for those at the end to speak with him when I realize it is going to take even longer. Running toward the head of the line, completely out of order, is a girl with shoulder-length blonde hair. Turning away from Mr. Mara, Jim runs toward her. As he catches Millie in his arms, Eddie and Sarah run up behind her. Eventually Jim puts Millie down, and she joins him as he continues to greet those waiting patiently.

I look for Ina, who is at that time breaking away from her friends—well, away from all of her friends but one. She clasps Michael's hand briefly and leads him towards Jim, again ignoring those who have waited patiently in line and the rules of civility with which she has been instilled. For a moment she turns back to look at Michael, the look familiar; the smiles on both of their faces blissful. In the next moment, Ina's arms are wrapped around the shoulders of her brother. She introduces Jim and Millie to Michael, and the three of them recount for Jim the role Michael played in the telegram process. Their faces are all alight. Looking at them, I am reminded of the many years I prayed for a loving sister. I suddenly realize I have two, and neither came to me in Dr. Heggie's big black bag.

It is heartening to see the line of those waiting to greet Father. It is almost as long as that for Jim. Like Millie, Mother has assumed a position next to Father, having finished her discussion with Mrs. Peaker and clearly having forgotten about me and my cake. I don't mind. It is nice to see Father receive the approbation he so deserves. It is even nicer to see my parents standing together. As he pulls her tenderly toward him, the two assume an intimate posture I have rarely seen and certainly have not seen in the past year.

I look around for the rest of my family. Aunt Charlotte, now only a Brampton resident one month a year, is, like many of the society ladies, assisting Aunt Rose as she cuts and serves cake. She's at the table that includes within its line my cousins John, Hannah, Roy, and Bill. The three younger cousins are listening raptly to Roy, who seems to be telling them a joke.

Uncle William is in deep discussions with his brother and the mayor. Uncle William's brother aspires to be mayor himself someday. I suspect they are strategizing over future local elections. As I lean against Aunt Lil's big bag, I note that she is nowhere to be seen.

Sitting in the shadows of Alderlea, in the park that was once its lawn, I am reminded too of those not with us. There is Uncle James who, strangely, I think of more often in death than I did in his life. This is not just because of the armour his unspoken presence gave me as I walked to school. For those days of walking past the Kelly Iron Works Repair Shop are now done. My walks to and from school now take me in the opposite direction of those of my former years.

Then there is Archie, who succumbed to that creek he likened to a bathtub only a hundred yards from where I sit. He would have been mad as all get out if he'd been here today. Yes, mad. He'd be mad that the team did not win; mad they'd been cheated of their victory; and mad that I'd been made to sit here while everyone else got their cake. But his sour mood would have been short-lived. He was never mad long. He'd soon be planning a rematch of the tournament on our turf, in Brampton, where everyone is honest. And if he were here, he would bring me a piece of cake.

I can see Grandpa leaning over a peony bush on the far side of the park. I can tell he likes it. His nose is buried deep within its flower. I hope he won't inhale a bee. He's probably considering whether such a bush would be compatible with our rose bushes. Or maybe that's not what he is considering. I realize how little I still knew about this man who has lived with me nearly my entire life, who is my chief confidante and whose name I share. I realize how much a mystery he is to me. It's been seven years, and I still do not know why our family is not allowed in the Presbyterian Church; I do not know what the Scottish Fiasco is. I do not know how Grandpa became others-destroyed. But as I look again at everyone around me, at how happy everyone seems to be, I wonder whether it really matters.

Maybe the past doesn't matter. Maybe the only thing that matters is the future.

Maybe the only thing that matters is the cake which I am beginning to feel I will never receive.

About to reconcile myself to that sad fact, I look the other way. Coming toward me from that direction are Jane and Frances, each holding an extra piece of cake.

It's July 1914. The future looks bright indeed.

A PREVIEW OF BOOK TWO,
THE BELEAGUERED

How fleeting is contentment? How transitory peace? How ephemeral joy? When these states leave us, must they take with them our innocence? In my case, in the case of my family, and in the case of my community, it seemed they must. They would be lost by prejudice; they would be lost by ignorance; they would be lost by fear; and they would be lost by patriotism. But that summer—my twelfth—I did not yet know it. It was July 1914. I had never been happier. My future, I thought, had never been so bright.

You might think this a rather grandiose statement to be uttered by an eleven-year-old—a mere child. But I had in the days and years before been beset by many disquieting trials, most of which were finally, contentedly resolved. That day sitting on a park lawn, I marvelled at the joy I felt within myself and around me.

* * *

At 9:30 p.m. the music ended. The bandleader bid us a good evening, and the crowd, which remained large, began to disperse. The cake from my aunt's bakery had long been devoured, the tables from which they were served long since removed. My friends who had sat with me for the past hour rose to depart with their family members. Mine returned to me. Aunt Lil, whose overnight bag I had been required to watch for a few minutes an hour and a quarter earlier, expressed surprised delight that it was where she had left it.

* * *

In the short walk to our house, my family's party was reduced by half. Jim and Millie left us almost immediately. He promised to return home directly after taking Millie to hers. Aunt Rose, her two children, and Roy and Bill peeled off as we walked passed her home on the way to ours. Though Aunt Lil was to spend the night at Aunt Rose's house, she declared herself not yet ready for that pleasure and continued to our house, across the street and three doors beyond.

Our verandah was equipped as an outdoor parlour with wicker chairs, tables, stools, and a swinging chaise lounge. All were put to good use that evening. The day had been hot and the house, so long closed up and empty, was stuffy. Mother and Aunt Charlotte joined the rest of us on the verandah after opening the bedroom windows. "The house will be cooled down in no time," Mother said as she and Aunt Charlotte claimed the last two chairs.

Although the verandah was the location of many lively conversations, it did not appear that it would be so that evening. The excitement of the day had deprived us of much of our remaining energy. Ina and Grandpa sat on the chaise lounge, Ina's long leg causing it to swing gently back and forth. Grandpa's eyes were beginning to close. Eventually he emitted a short snort. Awakening, he stood abruptly, wished us a good night, and went inside.

Aunt Lil and Aunt Charlotte sat in two wicker chairs, staring into the starlit sky beyond the verandah's roof. Father and Uncle William stood leaning against the railing, each with pipe in hand. I was perched on a small stool next to Aunt Lil, who sat comfortably in a large chair.

Eventually, Aunt Lil, who, surprisingly, had hardly made a controversial statement all day, broke the silence by beginning a conversation, high on the outlandish scale. "Ina," she said, "I am a little vexed with you."

"With me, Aunt Lil? What did I do?" Ina was clearly surprised by any suggestion that she would annoy her favourite aunt.

"Surely, dear sister," Aunt Charlotte interjected, directing her statement toward Aunt Lil, "this is not something to be discussed at this time." She furrowed her eyebrows and nodded slightly, identifying me and the gentlemen on the verandah as those who should not be present for such a conversation.

"I don't know what you mean, Charlotte," Aunt Lil replied. "I am certainly qualified to determine whether it is the appropriate time to speak about a matter with my niece." Although the conversation may have begun as one between Aunt Lil and Ina, by this point everyone on the verandah was following it.

"As you say, sister," Aunt Charlotte conceded. "Sometimes discretion is the better part of valour, but I share your vexation, so do go on."

"I have upset both of you?" Ina cried. "But how?"

Aunt Charlotte deferred to her elder sister.

"Dear Ina, it became very evident to me down at the park that you have a secret you have been keeping from me. I'm hurt that you did not confide in me earlier."

"Confide in you?" Aunt Charlotte again interjected. "You are vexed because Ina kept a secret from you? Surely, Lillian, you are more vexed by the subject of the secret than by the fact that it was kept."

"The subject of it? Not at all," Aunt Lil replied.

Father and Uncle William looked at each other in complete ignorance. "What the deuce are you talking about?" Father asked irritably. "I'm concerned if Ina has caused either of you offence, but for the life of me I have no idea what secret she has kept from you."

"You have no idea, Jethro?" Aunt Charlotte asked. Father replied in the negative.

"You should know, Jethro, that Ina has a beau, and he is entirely unsuitable," Aunt Charlotte said in an upbraiding tone.

Mother rose from her chair, and after vacillating over who most required her support—Father or Ina—joined Ina on the chaise. I could tell that Mother was not completely surprised by Aunt Charlotte's accusation. Uncle William turned to Father. "At times like this, I am most relieved to have only sons. I think I will take my pipe and go for a walk. Join me, Doc, if you like. It sounds like the ladies have this well in hand." Father hesitated only momentarily before following Uncle William down the verandah stairs. Ina shrank into Mother's arms.

"Charlotte, why do you say that he is unsuitable?" Aunt Lil asked. "He appears to be a nice boy. He comes from an old Brampton family." In those days, an 'old Brampton family' was a proxy for a 'good Brampton family.' This was not to say that newcomers could not also be good Bramptonians— they just had to work harder to prove their mettle. "Things like that don't matter to me," Aunt Lil continued, "but I know they matter to you."

"Yes," Aunt Charlotte replied. "They matter a great deal, but…"

"His family is an old Brampton family. His great uncle, John Lynch, was one of Brampton's first settlers." In her history teacher sort of way, Aunt Lil laid out the key facts. John Lynch settled in Brampton 1819. He was a great promoter of the area, prodigiously writing advice to early settlers as to what to plant, where to live, and what to build in order to make their life in the colonies a success. Together with his brother-in-law John Scott, in 1839 he established a brewery and an ashery. Within fifteen years he left that business and became a real estate broker and land conveyance, coming to own great tracts of Brampton land. He advocated for the incorporation of the village and became its first reeve. He was an active justice of the peace for twenty-five years and was instrumental in bringing the railway to Brampton.

"None of that matters to me, of course," Aunt Lil concluded. "What matters is that he is kind to Ina, which he seems to be. I noticed from the team shirt he wore that he is an athlete, another attribute I know this family values."

"I am glad you noticed his shirt," Aunt Charlotte replied in a scandalized tone. "Did you notice the name of his team?"

"I did indeed. The 'St. Mary's Athletics,' it said."

"Exactly," Aunt Charlotte pronounced. Even in the dim light, I could see that Ina and Mother understood the significance of that statement.

"That young man is a papist, obviously. And a relation of John Lynch. Heavens. The Lynches aren't just any Catholics. They are the preeminent Catholics of Brampton." Then demonstrating that she too was once a teacher, she continued. "Was it not John Lynch who in the mid-1860s donated the land on Centre Street for the construction of Brampton's first Catholic church—Guardian Angels—and its Catholic cemetery?"

I recalled the account described by the governor that day years earlier to a group of teenagers on the lawn of the jail. The father of the vile boy was Catholic. Mr. Gilchrist allowed him time to work on the reconstruction of a new Catholic place of worship after the Guardian Angels Church was burned to the ground in 1878. The devastation of the fire was complete in part because the rope in the bell tower of the fire station was off its runner when the fire was first reported.

"But so what if he is Catholic, Charlotte?" Aunt Lil queried. "Why should that matter? You are all Christians. I have never understood your commitment—or our brother's commitment—to this divide." I looked over at Ina. Her face was buried in her hands, resting on Mother's shoulder. I liked Michael Lynch, and I did not care that he was a papist. I also liked the new Ina—the Ina with Michael as a beau. She was much nicer to be with. She was almost kind to me. I did not relish a return of the old Ina— the Ina without Michael. So I ventured into the discussion, recalling other facts I learned from the governor those many years ago.

"I agree with Aunt Lil," I said. A minor could go very wrong in our family in disputing the position of an elder, but one generally had a hope of avoiding censure when the view was supported by at least one adult in the conversation. "There are other good Catholics in Brampton, and some of them are even of old families. And if Ina and Michael marry, then he will become Methodist." In Brampton, it was the custom that the husband joined the wife's church after they wed. Astonishment greeted my declaration. Even Ina raised her head and uncovered her face to hear my oration. Believing I needed to educate my sister, mother and aunts, I went on.

"Look at Mr. Gilchrist," I offered, slightly louder, more confidently, remembering so much of what the governor had said. "He was born and raised a Catholic. He became a Primitive Methodist later in his life, and look at all of the good things he did for Brampton. He was a town councillor and a Member of the Legislative Assembly and a businessman who employed many people. And he donated the concert hall to the town."

They continued to stare at me. I thought more examples were needed, so I continued. "And even though he was not Baptist, he donated the land down the street to that congregation for the construction of their church." The fact that he also donated the land for the Primitive Methodist Church did not seem particularly noteworthy, given that he was of that congregation. So I did not mention it.

They continued to look bewildered, and so I offered my last salvo. "And even though he was born Catholic, he donated the stone that was used for the construction of the Presbyterian Church."

At that Mother stood up. Mother was a model of tolerance. Many people told me that she was the sweetest person they knew. She certainly was the sweetest person I knew. Although she was sometimes stern with me, she was never cross. I knew that she did not share the prejudiced views of Aunt Charlotte and Father. As she walked slowly toward me, I rose to receive the embrace I was sure would accompany a compliment on my brave and principled stand.

But Mother stopped her approach too far away to take me in her arms, and her eyes, when cast upon me, were anything but proud.

She lifted her right hand and slapped me hard across the face. It was the first time anyone had ever struck me. My eyes filled with tears. My hand rose to touch my smarting cheek. "My dear," she said in a cold voice I barely recognized, "wherever would you get those notions? Don't let me or your grandfather ever hear you speak that way about that man again!" She turned and went inside, the screen door slamming behind her.

Ina stopped seeing Michael Lynch. When Aunt Lil returned to Toronto the next day, Ina went with her. It was a long time before I again uttered the name of Kenneth Gilchrist. But Mother's admonition never left me. "Don't let me *or your grandfather* ever hear you speak that way about that man again!" Had Mother just given me a piece in the puzzle that was the mystery of my grandfather? I did not know, but I was once again determined to find out.

AUTHOR'S NOTE

This is a book of fiction inspired by stories relayed to me by my cousin Jessie Current over countless holiday dinners commencing when I was a child, coffee shop conversations I enjoyed as a student, and visits we had later in life in her various senior and nursing homes. The stories are supplemented with the historical facts and strung together by imagination bound only by the realm of the plausible.

Without parsing the entire book to denote which passage falls into which category, let me indicate a few matters that are absolute fact and absolute fiction. Eddie McMurchy, Sarah Lawson, and Michael Lynch are all fictitious characters stated to be nieces and nephews of the town's prominent citizens.

The character of Jane Thompson is inspired by Laeta McKinnon, Jessie's closest lifetime friend; Frances Hudson, by Frances Fenton Carroll, another dear life-long friend. Millie Dale is inspired by Jim's true and special friend, Allie Beatty, who was a relation by marriage to the Dale family. All of the McKechnies, Colin Heggie, and the many other friends of Jesse, Jim, and Ina mentioned in the book were their true and dear friends, but the interactions portrayed within the book are generally of my imagination. In reality, both Laeta McKinnon (Thompson) and Frances Fenton Carroll (Hudson) were slightly older than Jessie. Frances's father, W.J. Fenton (Hudson), was the long-time, highly regarded principal of the Brampton High School.

Laeta McKinnon's father, John McKinnon (Thompson), was a senior executive with the Pease Factory. Among other things, the factory did produce furnaces. He and his family lived in a large Brampton house, but it was not Haggertlea, which continued to be occupied by members of the Haggert family until 1944.

The aunts, uncles, grandparents, and cousins of Jessie are all inspired by her real-life family members: her aunts Rose Roberts Golding (Darling), Lillian Roberts (Stephens), and Charlotte Roberts Milner (Turner); uncles James Golding (Darling) and William Milner (Turner); grandparents Louisa and Jesse Perry (Brady) and James and Selina Roberts (Stephens); and cousins Jim and Hannah Golding (John and Hannah Darling) and Roy and Bill Milner (Turner).

Jesse Perry (Brady) was a prominent Brampton contractor and mason. His works include the Brampton churches now known as Grace United Church, St. Andrew's Presbyterian Church, St. Paul's United Church, and the Dominion Building. His union with Louisa was sealed with the eight-word letter described, but it is not known where he or she was when it was sent. To my knowledge, his brother was not her former fiancé. Jessie was not allowed to enter the Presbyterian Church. However, the characters and stories involving Nelson, the Duke, Judge, and the building of the first subdivision are all fictitious.

Jessie's brother (Jim Roberts) played with the Brampton Excelsiors when they sought the Mann Cup in Vancouver in 1914.

William Golding (Darling; the Duke) was in life a gentleman farmer and bakery owner. He came to Canada and lived his life generally as portrayed in the book. Three of his great-great-great grandchildren were born in Brampton.

James Golding (Darling) was the second and eighteenth mayor of Brampton. The elected and appointed offices Darling is said to have held in the book were held by James Golding. The only material deviation relates to the time of his last term of office and death, both of which occurred in 1909 rather than 1910 as portrayed in the book.

Kenneth Gilchrist is inspired by the real life Kenneth Chisholm, a dominant force in the town's early years. All of the staff and family members of Gilchrist referred to in the governor's story are fictitious. As with Darling, the elected and appointed offices Gilchrist is said to have held in the book were held by Gilchrist. He did build and reside in Alderlea.

As for the death of Archie, sadly, it occurred generally as described.

The governor of the jail did entertain the town's teenagers with horror-light fictions. Jessie was scared of a boy whom she passed on the way to school each day.

In at least one particular respect, the story does no justice to Jessie's family. For simplicity, Frances Mary Perry Roberts, Jessie's mother (Mary Brady Stephens), is portrayed in the book as the only child of Jesse Perry (Brady). In fact, she was one of four children who survived infancy. Her siblings included Samuel, who as an adult resided in Toronto, and two sisters Ada Louise, who came to be Mrs. Morton Blain, of Cleveland, Ohio, and Minnie Esther, who came to be Mrs. McPherson, of Colorado. Jessie's uncle, Samuel Perry, and his family were as central in Jessie's early years as those of her paternal aunts.

If Jessie were alive and able to read this book today, she would say that my treatment of her father was a little too harsh and that my treatment of Jessie herself was a great deal too good. As for the generous treatment of her brother, who she adored she would say, I believe, that it was just right.

People have asked me whether Jessie knew I was writing this book. She did. She knew it was a book about Brampton in its early years and that it would feature her family. I confess I never told her—for fear that her modesty would order me to do otherwise—that she would be made the central character. In the early years of the several I spent on this endeavour, a red-covered journal and a mechanical pencil accompanied me on my weekly visits to her nursing home. She was more lucid then and readily able to elaborate on stories previously and frequently told.

As time went on, the incidents she was able to recall became fewer and fewer. Eventually, she could not recall any incidents that occurred after 1930; then she could not recall those that occurred after 1920; then those that occurred after 1915. When she began to confuse me with her Aunt Rose (my great grandmother), I realized that the exercise that formerly gave us much pleasure was too great an effort for her. I stopped bringing the red-covered journal into her room, but whenever a new nugget was spontaneously divulged during our visits, I would rush to the car to record it.

Although Jessie and I stopped working on "the book" together, she never forgot that it was a project of mine. In 2008, a few years after I began my efforts, I bought for her a new book written a year earlier about Brampton's Flowertown past. Authored by Dale O'Hara, a descendent of the Dale family featured so prominently in these pages, *Acres of Glass* presents the history of the Dale Estate and its great accomplishments. Jessie's regular visitors passed many pleasant hours reading and rereading aloud to her its increasingly familiar passages about her home town. Every such reading on my part was followed with compliments—not on my oration but on my writing. "My dear, you did a wonderful job on that book!" Apologies to Dale O'Hara for the credit regularly bestowed on me, always declined and uniformly redirected.

Jessie died in Mississauga, in Peel County, just south of Brampton, on February 15, 2011. She was 108 years old. She never forgot the lessons of frugality she learned as a child in Brampton. She lived modestly her entire life, saving and conservatively investing. Among her legacies was a $1,000,000 gift to the University of Toronto. The endowment, which the university has named for Jim, Ina, and Jessie Roberts, will support indefinitely the academic pursuit of science by four undergraduate and two graduate students a year. Wherever possible, those undergraduate students will hail from Peel County.

ABOUT LYNNE GOLDING

Lynne Golding was born and raised in Brampton, Ontario. She obtained a bachelor's degree in History and Political Science from Victoria College at the University of Toronto before studying law at Queen's University in Kingston, Ontario. She is a senior partner at the international law firm Fasken Martineau DuMoulin LLP, where she leads their health law practice group. Lynne currently lives in Brampton. She is married and has three grown children. Lynne is a winner of the Ontario Book Publishers Organization 2018 What's Your Story Short Prose and Poetry Competition. This is her first novel. Visit her website at lynnegoldingauthor.com.

BOOK CLUB GUIDE

1. At the end of the book, the author says that Jessie would consider the treatment of her father within it as a little too harsh and the characterization of herself as far too good. How flawed is his character? When was he at his best? His worst? Is it likely that Jessie was as good as she is portrayed? What of Ina? Is she a sympathetic character or not?

2. Based on the book, how important was religion to life in the community and to Jessie's family?

3. Was the town's treatment of Jessie's father following the disclosure of his infidelity appropriate?

4. Jessie overheard a number of conversations not intended for the ears of the young. Which were the most important to the development of the story line?

5. Jessie's grandfather believed that verandahs would lead to the formation of communities among neighbours. Did they serve that purpose then? Do they serve that purpose now?

6. Jessie was miffed that her mother voluntarily went into quarantine with her father. Were the actions of her mother justified?

7. Is prohibition a necessary condition for a good life? Why was it thought to be so?

8. Based on the book, how important were sports to life in the community in the early 20th century? How important are they to communities now?

9. The children of the early 20th century were given a great deal of independence. How does that compare with the amount of independence given to children of the early 21st century? Which approach is better?

10. In addition to the foregoing, how different was family life in the first decades of the 20th century from family life in the first decades of the 21st century?

11. The book features a small town that has since become a city of over 500,000 people. The book refers to other small towns of the time, many of which are now villages, at best. What factors existed in the early years that led the town to become a city?

12. As a matter of speculation (the answers are not in the book), what led to Aunt Lil to live a life so different from her siblings? Why could Jessie not enter the Presbyterian Church? Was the governor's account true? Who was the man who unsuccessfully exited the Kelly Iron Works Repair Shop as Jessie and her father walked home from Haggertlea the Saturday before Christmas 1912?

WRITE FOR US

We love discovering new voices and welcome submissions. Please read the following carefully before preparing your work for submission to us. Our publishing house does accept unsolicited manuscripts but we want to receive a proposal first, and if interested we will solicit the manuscript.

We are looking for solid writing—present an idea with originality and we will be very interested in reading your work.

As you can appreciate, we give each proposal careful consideration so it can take up to six weeks for us to respond, depending on the amount of proposals we have received. If it takes longer to hear back, your proposal could still be under consideration and may simply have been given to a second editor for their opinion. We can't publish all books sent to us but each book is given consideration based on its individual merits along with a set of criteria we use when considering proposals for publication.

Thank you for reading *The Innocent*

If you enjoyed *The Innocent*, check out more literary fiction from Blue Moon Publishers!

Primrose Street by Marina L. Reed

To Love a Stranger by Kris Faatz